CHERISH HARD

A HARD PLAY NOVEL

NALINI SINGH

eISBN: 978-1-942356-61-5

ISBN: 978-1-942356-62-2

Cover image by: Jenn LeBlanc/Illustrated Romance

Cover design by: Croco Designs

"That First Kiss" © Copyright Nikita Gill / Quoted with Permission

OTHER BOOKS BY NALINI SINGH

The Rock Kiss series

Rock Addiction

Rock Courtship: A Novella

Rock Hard

Rock Redemption

Rock Wedding

The Psy/Changeling series

Slave to Sensation

Visions of Heat

Caressed by Ice

Mine to Possess

Hostage to Pleasure

Branded by Fire

Blaze of Memory

Bonds of Justice

Play of Passion

Kiss of Snow

Tangle of Need

Heart of Obsidian

Shield of Winter

Shards of Hope

Allegiance of Honor

Silver Silence

The Guild Hunter series

Angels' Blood

Archangel's Kiss

Archangel's Consort

Archangel's Blade

Archangel's Storm

Archangel's Legion

Archangel's Shadows

Archangel's Enigma

Archangel's Heart

Archangel's Viper

For detailed descriptions of these books, as well as additional titles, visit Nalini's website: www.nalinisingh.com

CHERISH HARD

She walks in beauty, like the night
Of cloudless climes and starry skies;
And all that's best of dark and bright...
From "She Walks in Beauty" ~ Lord Byron

PROLOGUE

S AILOR WASN'T SURE WHAT THE hell he was doing at a college party. He was technically still in high school. Okay, not technically. *Actually*. Not only that, but he was a high school kid with buzz-cut hair and a huge black eye. The only things going in his favor were that he'd had his growth spurt at fifteen and seemed as if he belonged at a college party.

"He looks like he just got out of prison."

Sailor put on his most charming smile and turned to the sneering blonde who'd whispered the words to her friend—while knowing he'd overhear. Girls generally liked Sailor when he didn't look like a prison brawler, and he liked them back.

"Rugby," he said, pointing to his eye. "An accident with house paint that wouldn't come out." He pointed at his hair, which his older brother Gabriel had buzzed off for him earlier that day while their two younger brothers laughed hysterically. "I won't be making that mistake again."

The two girls didn't look like they believed him, but

hey, he'd been polite like his dad had brought him up to be. Since Sailor had never been drawn to girls who got all snooty and looked at him *that* way—down their noses, as if he were crap scraped off the bottoms of their shoes—it was no skin off his back what they thought.

"You know, some girls go for cons fresh out of the slammer." The comment came from one of his rugby friends, the same one who'd gotten him an invite to this party for which he was definitely underage, even if he didn't look it, his tall body muscled as a result of the game they both loved.

Punching Kane in the gut for that grinning comment, Sailor carried on through the crowd inside the gigantic metal-sided warehouse that a twenty-one-year-old named Cody had rented for this party. They were charging a ten-dollar cover to pay the rental fee for the warehouse and for the sound system that was blasting booming rock music through the cavernous space.

Sailor figured he'd wasted ten bucks. He was tired from a full day at school followed by his part-time job, and he needed to rest. The only reason he'd come out was because his parents were worried that between school and the part-time jobs he kept picking up despite their telling him to take it easy, he was working too hard, with only a few games of rugby to break up the routine.

When he'd unthinkingly mentioned this party, his mother's eyes had lit up. She hadn't even blinked when he'd added it was a college party and that alcohol would be a given.

"I trust you, Sailor," she'd said, her clear gray eyes holding utter faith. "Go, have fun. Kiss a pretty girl. Get into a little trouble."

And Sailor hadn't been able to bear breaking her heart.

So he'd stay an hour, buy himself a Coke from the bar since he had no plans to get shitfaced, then go home and crash like he'd intended—and hopefully sleep till ten in the morning. Even though tomorrow was Saturday, he hadn't booked any lawn-mowing jobs because Gabriel had a huge game coming up that night and Sailor knew his brother would want him around during the buildup.

Gabe didn't get nervous, not usually. But this was a seriously *major* deal. There were rumors he was being scouted for the national team, that if he played as he'd been playing for the past six months—like a fucking lightning storm—the next time he stepped out onto the rugby field, it'd be for his country.

Sailor was freaking out on behalf of his brother, knowing Gabe was on the verge of achieving his biggest dream.

Sailor loved the game too, but he had different goals.

After finally managing to make it through the crowd to get his Coke, he'd just rejoined his teammates when he realized the group was still standing near the blonde with the beautiful face and the ugly insides. And she was being catty about someone else.

"Ugh, can you believe Cody's dating *that*?"

"I know, right," her flunky said.

"Not for long though." The blonde's tone was smug. "I heard he's going to dump her soon."

Sailor was facing the right direction to see who Queen Mean Girl was skewering this time. He wanted to laugh. No wonder she was being bitchy. The girl with the moonlight skin, flaming red hair, and curves that made Sailor's entire body go hot outshone her without even trying. If he'd been the guy lucky enough to have caught the redhead's attention, he'd stick close to her too.

The redhead smiled.

Sailor's stomach grew tight. "Who's that?" he asked Kane, the other teenager having entered college this past year. He and Kane had met at the school's rugby training camp a couple of years back, the age gap between them meaningless when compared to the bond forged by their joy in the game.

"Who?" Kane asked.

"The girl with Cody." Sailor knew Cody because the older boy played rugby too; they'd met a few times when Sailor had joined in a social game outside school, but they weren't best buds or anything.

"The redhead? Girlfriend I think." A nudge with one heavily muscled shoulder. "Out of your league, Sail. She's a college girl."

Sailor had a strict "no poaching" policy when it came to his friends' girlfriends—because what the fuck kind of friend didn't understand loyalty? But even from the few times he'd met Cody, he knew the other guy was a bit of an ass. So maybe Sailor would ask Kane to tell him the instant the redhead realized Cody's ass-ish nature and kicked him to the curb.

Then maybe Sailor would see if he could get invited to a few more college parties, parties she'd also be attending. Kane would get him in. It might be that the redhead liked blue eyes. Possibly even enough to ignore the fact he was younger than her and still in high school. Of course, those blue eyes were currently bloodshot, with one circled by black-and-blue bruising.

He was scowling at himself when the redhead looked at him a little shyly. Her glance scuttled away just as fast. She probably thought he was a criminal too. His mother and father would be so proud. His brothers, on the other hand, would crack up like maniacs when he told them this story.

Cody stopped not far from them before turning to face the redhead. Sailor was annoyed that Cody's big head was blocking his view, but then the other kid moved. Whatever he was saying to the redhead had her going pale. Sailor saw her lips form the words "What? No, you—"

He couldn't make out the rest.

Cody's voice rose just as there was a break in the music. "Jeez! Do I have to spell it out? I realized last night that I can't sleep with a tub of lard like you, not even for a chance at your mother's corporation!"

Sailor was moving toward the two even before Cody stopped speaking, but he was too late. Eyes glittering wet and face so stark that it was as if Cody had stolen the life out of her, the redhead took a shaken step backward, and then she ran through the silent crowd, her stunning hair flying behind her.

The music boomed again. People began to dance.

Forgetting manners and good behavior, Sailor kept on shoving through the crowd with brute force, imagining the dancers as opponents on the field. It worked. He went through the warehouse door seconds after the redhead had left it clanging.

Stepping out into the silent and barely lit street—the warehouse was located in an industrial area—he saw her running into the night. "Hey!" he called out, feeling like he was letting moonlight stream through his palms. "Wait! You shouldn't be alone in the dark!"

She turned, looked at him—and ran even faster.

A taxi turned the corner at that instant.

Flagging it down with a desperate hand, she jumped in, the taxi made a U-turn, and then she was gone.

The next day, an ecstatic Kane got the news that he'd been picked up to play for a team in Japan, and Sailor lost his sole line of information on his redhead. He went through endless photos from the party on social media, but she'd been there such a short time that no one had caught her or tagged her in any of their images. Cody had erased her from his profile. And no way would Sailor ask that asshole anything about her; she deserved better than to have her name come from Cody's lips.

It was as if Sailor had dreamed her up.

His mysterious redhead with the moonlight skin.

Seven Years Later...

The way you feel when you kiss him
for the first time.
Like fire within your bones.
From "That First Kiss" ~ Nikita Gill

1

THE GARDENER WITH THE THIGH TATTOO

HER OVARIES WERE MELTING. OR *exploding.* *Or something.*

Ísalind Magdalena Rain-Stefánsdóttir, known to everyone but her father as Ísa Rain, told herself to step away from the window. *Right* now. Before the object of her fascination saw her and she turned as red as her hair. But her feet refused to move. Like a junkie, she had to have just a little more. Her teeth sank into her lower lip, her fingers curving over the edge of the window ledge.

He wasn't human.

That was the only explanation.

No one was that perfect. Like soda-commercial perfect. Her toes had curled at first sight of him, but she'd managed to resist temptation for an hour. Then she'd peeked out because she couldn't help herself, and what was he doing but taking off his T-shirt! That was just wrong. It didn't matter if he was getting hot and sweaty doing all that manual labor fixing up the school's gardens; it simply wasn't fair to the female sex for him to take off his T-shirt and reveal all that rippling, golden muscle.

If that wasn't bad enough, he was wearing khaki work shorts, and they were short enough to reveal the edges of a tattoo that circled the upper part of his thigh. Ísa wanted to run outside and order him to put on some damn clothes. How was she supposed to keep her head down and concentrate on her lesson plans when he was out there exuding male pheromones like they were going out of style?

"Ms. Rain, what's so interesting?"

Jumping at the sound of the principal's voice, Ísa turned—and tried not to look too guilty. Thank God she'd finally conquered the blushing that had tormented her through her teenage years. Sometimes Ísa thought she'd spent ages thirteen to seventeen alternating between carrot orange and tomato red.

Her mother had *not* been impressed.

"How," Jacqueline had asked, "do you expect to negotiate multimillion-dollar deals if you can't maintain a poker face?"

Never mind that Ísa had never wanted to wheel and deal in the boardroom. Her desires were softer, yet far more subversive. They involved poets and novelists and a world of imagined wonders that CEO and financial powerhouse Jacqueline Rain simply could not see. At times Ísa was sorry that her mother had no ability to experience the magic that colored Ísa's world.

The rest of the time when she was around her mother, she usually had to fight the urge to go homicidal.

"Nothing," she said brightly to the principal. "Just taking a break."

After fixing the long chain around her neck, the older woman walked over to the window. "Nice view."

Ísa felt her cheeks go hot red in flagrant disregard of

all her commands and thoughts to the contrary. Mumbling something incoherent, she went to stand by her desk where she shuffled paper around just to give her hands something to do. She should be mortified—and she was—but she was also disappointed at losing that "nice view."

Principal Cafferty laughed. "Admiring a fine hunk of a man is hardly a crime, Ms. Rain. If I were twenty years younger, I'd do more than get an eyeful." A wink that made Ísa burst out in laughter herself.

"Maybe we should give him detention for having abs-of-distraction," Ísa suggested after catching her breath.

"Ah, but then he might feel compelled to put his T-shirt back on. And that would be a crime against womanhood." Expression solemn but for the dancing light in her eyes, Principal Cafferty walked over to lean her hip against the opposite side of Ísa's desk. "I just came to see how you were. You're still okay with spending your summer teaching the evening class?"

"Of course." It was only a single ninety-minute class per week, which, when you threw in the preparation involved as well as the student work she'd be reviewing, worked out to about five hours overall. "Adult students who want to study poetry will be a nice change from fifteen-year-olds who think English class is the third circle of hell."

Violet Cafferty grinned. "I had a little pushback when I hired you, young as you are in comparison to the other staff, but the students have excelled since your arrival. You'll have to tell me how you do it."

"Music," Ísa replied, finding her feet again as they settled on her favorite subject. "Good music, good lyrics—that's poetry too. Once I make them see that, they're willing to come along with me for Shakespeare and modern lit."

"I'm glad you're with us, Ísa." The principal, a bone-thin woman of forty-something with a penchant for tailored pants paired with brightly colored shirts, straightened from her leaning position. Today's choice of shirt was a vivid red that would've made Ísa look like a stoplight but was sophisticated and elegant on Violet Cafferty.

"If you need anything," the other woman continued, "or if you have questions about student enrollments, there'll be a skeleton staff in the office for forty-five minutes on the days you'll be teaching—they're to arrive twenty minutes prior to the beginning of the class so you can clear up any outstanding issues."

After getting Ísa's nod, Principal Cafferty said, "There'll be two other adult classes going on at the same time as yours. Diana Eastin and Jason Jeng will also both be present at the school on those evenings."

Ísa already had all that information but listened regardless. She knew Violet Cafferty was going over it again because Ísa had just completed her first year at this school —and it didn't help that Ísa still looked ridiculously young. Her appearance occasionally made people forget she wasn't a new teacher straight out of training.

Maybe the principal was just being extra cautious because this was Ísa's first time teaching a night class. Her previous school had only offered sports and craft classes at night. Ísa and her best friend had taken one on fencing and had nearly succeeded in stabbing each other to death three times in a single lesson.

It was a good thing the swords had been tipped by rubber safety caps.

"We'll be fine," she said once Violet Cafferty paused.

"Have fun on your vacation and don't worry about us." Ísa had long ago overcome the crippling shyness that had hamstrung her as a teenager plucked from a tiny village school in one country and thrown into a massive high school in another.

Not surprisingly, her accent, red hair, and weight had quickly made her a target. A hint of the accent remained even after all these years, she still had the red hair, and she'd never be as thin as Principal Cafferty even if she ate nothing but celery for a month, but she'd quickly learned strength as a survival strategy.

Then there was her mother. With the Dragon, it was either fight or die.

"Rarotonga looks beautiful," she now said to the woman who'd put Ísa's career on the fast track by hiring her to teach at one of *the* most prestigious public schools in the country. "Is your friend from New York already on her way there?"

Violet Cafferty nodded. "She's champing at the bit to ring in the new year in a bikini rather than buried under a foot of snow." A beaming smile. "Sun, surf, and bottomless margaritas, here we come!"

The principal left the room soon afterward, telling Ísa she'd be available in her office for thirty more minutes before she was officially on summer break. Tempted as Ísa was to return straight to the window and her own personal gardening porn show, she kept her head down and finished up her lesson plans; having never before taught adults, she was building in a lot of room for discussion and for following avenues her students wanted to explore.

It took her just over an hour.

She couldn't help glancing out the window when she

was tidying up, but the gorgeous, sweaty gardener with ink-black hair, no shirt, and a sexy tattoo around his thickly muscled thigh was gone. "Drat."

Disappointed, she packed everything into the pink satchel with white flowers that she'd bought with her first paycheck. Some people said pink clashed with red hair, but Ísa didn't care. The bag was pretty and it made her happy.

As her little sister Catie had once said, "Life's too short to waste on boring accessories."

After doing a final check to make sure she had everything and that the room was set up for her first adult class next week, she was about to walk out into the otherwise empty hallway when her phone rang.

It came up with no name, just a local number.

Guessing it was a welcome call from a store whose loyalty program she'd recently signed up to because of how much she loved their fifties-style dresses, Ísa answered with a cheery "Hello."

"Ísa?"

Astonishment froze her in place. That voice...

2

ÍSA'S PATH TO RUIN AKA THE INCIDENT WITH THE HOT GARDENER

"**I**T'S CODY," HE SAID. "CODY Schumer?" A nervous laugh from the man she'd once thought she'd marry and live with happily ever after behind a white picket fence, complete with a dog.

A chocolate Labrador, to be precise.

Thankfully Ísa had long ago ceased to feel even a glimmer of the attraction that had drawn her to Cody "Slimeball" Schumer when she'd been a twenty-one-year-old with a few stubborn stars in her eyes and a hunger to be loved that was so deep it was a hole in her psyche. Being brutally dumped at a college party while at least fifty other people watched had cured her of any illusions she might've had about the man.

But she'd flat-out refused to allow the experience to rip the final stars from her eyes. Ísa still believed in love and in happily ever after and in white picket fences and in chocolate-colored Labradors with goofy grins. She also believed that slimeballs never changed their slimy stripes.

It was morbid curiosity more than anything else that made her continue the conversation. What possible reason would Slimeball Schumer have to call her? Hadn't he gotten the message when she and Nayna gleefully egged and toilet-papered his pride-and-joy ride one dark night after the dumping?

They'd used pink toilet paper with princesses on it.

It was the most illegal thing she and her best friend had done in their entire lives—and it had been *glorious*. Especially because Cody had been utterly impotent, unable to prove his accusations. He'd huffed and puffed and gotten exactly nowhere while Ísa and Nayna maintained angelic expressions and shined their halos.

"Cody," she said with a probably evil smile, her back pressed to the cold of the classroom wall and her eyes facing the window through which she'd ogled the hot gardener. "It's been a long time." Time she'd spent burying the memory of this ass and the night he'd humiliated her.

"Yeah," Cody said with a warmth she'd once assumed was real. "I guess you wiped my number from your phone, huh?"

Ísa blinked, shook her head. Slimeballs were clearly deficient in the brain-cell department. Had he honestly expected her not to go nuclear on him after what he'd said and done?

"No job's worth prostituting myself!" he'd said mockingly in the moments before that final, humiliating "tub of lard" comment. "You should've bought me a Ferrari, fatty. Then maybe I could've forced myself to do it."

What a prize.

Not.

None of that even factored in the worst thing: the day after dumping her in the nastiest way possible, Cody had hooked up with the stunning blonde who'd made it her mission to torment Ísa through their high school years. "Was there anything in particular you wanted, Cody?" Like a kick in the butt?

Her curt and businesslike tone seemed to startle him for a second.

When he finally spoke, he said, "Suzanne and I wanted to tell you before the news hits the world. I know we still have some of the same friends."

That much was true. Though most of those people were shared acquaintances rather than true friends. The latter wouldn't touch Cody with a ten-foot pole.

"Suzanne and I are pregnant!"

"I didn't realize you had a uterus," Ísa said, even as the meaning of his words filtered down to create a big fat lump of coal in her stomach.

"Huh?" A chuckle. "Oh, you're being funny. You always were funny."

Biting back further snarky remarks—*Had he been this vacuous when they'd dated? Had she been that desperate?*—Ísa said, "I hope the baby is healthy and that the pregnancy goes well." It wasn't the poor child's fault it would have Slimeball Schumer and Suzanne for parents.

That you couldn't choose your parents was a truth Ísa knew far too well.

"Thanks," Cody said cheerfully. "We're getting married too. I just... Anyway, Suzanne really wanted you to know."

"I hope you two have the life you deserve." She hung up before he could say anything further.

Then she just stood there, staring at the wall around the windows across from her. That wall had been painted by the art students who'd had her classroom before the school turned it into an English class—the art class had been moved to a location with much better light. Colorful and bright in its interpretative splashes of pigment, the wall suited an English class.

Ísa could point to it—and did—to demonstrate how any piece of art, including poetry and novels, could be seen in many different ways depending on the eye of the beholder. At this instant, she saw it only as a smudge of color, Cody's words reverberating inside her. Her cheeks flushed, her heart raced, and her knees, they threatened to shake.

Snark, it appeared, could only protect you for so long.

Even reminding herself that Suzanne was clearly clinging desperately to her past Queen Bitch status had zero impact.

"I don't love him, not even a little bit," she said, and it was true.

The hopeful, innocent thing she'd felt for Cody had died a final death that horrible night when he'd ripped her to pieces and laughed at her pain. She'd given him her battered, bruised heart and he'd kicked it.

Ísa wasn't stupid enough to hold a torch for a man capable of such casual cruelty.

But marriage and children and a stable home base—not only for herself but for her much younger sister, Catie, and brother, Harlow—that had always been her dream. It was why she was putting herself through the hell of online dating with the precision of a business merger to end all business mergers.

With her students on vacation since the end of the previous week and Ísa having no real obligation to come into school until her night classes began, her diary currently looked like that of a hyperactive serial dater, one who was heavily overcaffeinated at this point.

MONDAY MORNING: Coffee with Manuel. Dark haired, dark eyed. Likes novels and poetry. Fingers crossed!

Postmortem: Did like books and poetry. Also liked the waitress, with whom he made a date while I was sitting in front of him. Then asked me if I was "open to exploring my sexuality without boundaries."

MONDAY AFTERNOON: Coffee with Beau. Five foot nine. Blond. Mechanic. Comes across non-douchey in online conversation.

Postmortem: Non-douchiness was a front.

MONDAY NIGHT· Coffee with Carl. Sweet guy who likes gaming. That's okay—if he's the one, I can read while he games.

Postmortem: His current game was so hot he couldn't step away from the computer to come meet me. Didn't message me until I'd been waiting for twenty minutes. Can never go back to that café.

TUESDAY MORNING: Coffee with Henry. Five foot seven. Brown hair. Lawyer. Seems very practical and sensible and sweet.

Postmortem: Thank God I only ever agree to meet for coffee on the first date. The man spent the entire date on the phone, talking business. If he can't even commit to a half-hour coffee date, I don't think he'd be able to commit to a wife and child.

TUESDAY EVENING: Coffee with Tana. Six foot one. Some kind of finance job. Doesn't say much online, but some people aren't good at online conversation. Doesn't seem like a serial killer.

Postmortem: No chemistry. He gave me his business card in case I want to invest in the future.

WEDNESDAY MORNING: Coffee with Wyatt. Thirty-three. Has a name like a cowboy. Wants to work on a farm.

Postmortem: Wyatt forgot to add forty years to his age when setting up his profile. Also forgot to state his photo was from a few decades back. Not ageist but would really like my future husband to have his own teeth.

WEDNESDAY AFTERNOON: Coffee with Gareith with an *i* in there. Okay, parents gave him the name so can't judge him on it. Manager at grocery store. Seems very normal. I am afraid.

Postmortem: He changed his name to Gareith Atlas Bonemaker on his eighteenth birthday and thinks the Great Bonemaker has PLANS for him to LEAD a REVOLUTION.

WEDNESDAY NIGHT: Midweek sanity check with Nayna. Some best friend. Snorted wine out of her nose after hearing of Wyatt + Gareith situation. Then forced me to make more dates.

THURSDAY MORNING: Tea with Ken. No more coffee. Brown hair. Will wear rose in lapel so I recognize him. That's kind of cute.

Postmortem: Am in shock. He was good-looking, articulate, and polite. Of course we had zero chemistry. Maybe I need to have my hormones checked.

THURSDAY AFTERNOON: Tea with Stuart. Rocking a bald look. Sexy. Likes dogs.

Postmortem: Wore dog collar. Wanted me to walk him and call him Woofy. Am sure he will find right woman one day.

IT WAS ONLY Friday of her first full week of dating, and Ísa was already exhausted. Which was why she hadn't made any further dates. But she would. Because sitting around and waiting for the right man to come along was a recipe for ending up without the life she'd always wanted.

Marriage by thirty. A child by thirty-two. All of it drenched in love.

That was Ísa's timeline, and she was sticking to it. She had two years to make the first part of it happen. But while—after a lifetime of learning not to depend on anyone—she was still scrambling to find a man she trusted to stick around, Slimeball Schumer was about to have all those things with the girl who'd tortured Ísa for years.

It just seemed so deeply unfair.

Ísa barely restrained the urge to kick the nearest piece of furniture. Maybe, she thought hopefully, fate would throw her a bone and have it rain on Cody and Suzanne's wedding day. Complete with hail. And flying toads. And a truck that sprayed mud on the bride's conceited face.

The vengeful visual kept her company as she closed the door to her classroom. Her phone rang again right then, the sound echoing through the empty hallway. Wanting to bang her head against the wall as she recognized that ominous ringtone, Ísa briefly considered just getting on a plane and flying back to Iceland. She'd been happy there, spoke the language, and neither one of her parents currently used it as their home base.

Perfect. Except that she'd be abandoning Catie and Harlow to the Dragon. And that was the one thing Ísa would never do. Whatever road she took in life, she was bringing her siblings along with her.

The phone kept ringing.

Jacqueline Rain, CEO of Crafty Corners and various other enterprises, didn't know the meaning of giving up.

"Hello, Mother."

"Ísa, I wanted to make sure you remembered the board meeting today."

Ísa did bang her forehead against the wall at that. "I have no reason to attend the board meeting."

"You're a thirty percent shareholder."

Only because you forced the shares on me on my twenty-first birthday. "I'm sure you can represent my interests."

"I have no time for this, Ísa. Make sure you're present." Jacqueline hung up.

Gritting her teeth, Ísa thought fiercely of the meditation technique she'd learned at the Buddhist retreat Nayna had booked them into last year. Ísa's best friend hadn't realized the retreat was being held at a silent monastery until they'd arrived and been shown the rules.

They'd lasted four hours. Enough to learn the basics.

But it turned out you couldn't mutter angrily under your breath about dragons and swords and still find your Zen.

The worst of it was that Jacqueline wasn't simply being abrasive and aggravating. No, Ísa's mother knew *exactly* what she was doing, knew she had Ísa over a barrel because of Harlow and Catie.

As if the thought had conjured her sister out of thin air, her phone beeped with an incoming message: *Aren't you seeing the Dragon today? Wear your fireproof armor.*

Smiling despite herself, she messaged Catie. She didn't know how her sister did it; despite not living in the same city as Ísa or Jacqueline, she was always up to date with the news and gossip. Part of it was Catie's close bond with Harlow, but equally important was Catie's ability to make friends wherever she went—including at Jacqueline's company.

Message sent, Ísa shoved her phone into her satchel and strode down the hallway; her footfalls echoed in the eerily empty space... and the niggling seed of righteous fury bloomed into full flower once more. Not just because of Jacqueline's blatant manipulation but at the memory of Cody and Suzanne's happiness.

As a bullied teen, Ísa had comforted herself with the thought of Suzanne becoming a sad, lonely woman with no friends—and no hair. Teenage Ísa had thought the latter the worst possible punishment for a girl who had the habit of flinging her waist-length blond locks around like she was in a shampoo commercial.

Fuming for her poor teenage self, she made sure to set the alarm system and lock up. Principal Cafferty had made it clear Ísa would be the last person in this building after the principal herself left just after five. Everyone else was already well into their summer vacation—even the other night-class teachers would only come in for their hours of teaching; the sole reason Ísa was here was because she hadn't been able to work on her lesson plans at home.

Her upstairs neighbor was having repairs done to her bathroom that required banging and hammering.

Not all of it involved nails and wood.

Hopefully the repairs would be finished by now. There was only so much ecstatic orgasmic screaming that a single woman in online-dating purgatory could stand without being driven to violence.

She spotted the tan-colored gardening truck the instant she came down the front steps of the school's imposing redbrick main building and turned left to head toward her car. The hot gardener had parked it right next to her zippy blue compact. The front of the truck had four doors with tinted windows while the large bed was piled with shovels and other manly tools as well as a huge sack of clippings.

His light brown T-shirt was hanging over the top of the tailgate.

Which meant he was still walking around topless somewhere around here.

"Get in your car, Ísa," she muttered to herself, well aware what would happen if she came face-to-face with that delicious hunk of manhood. Because while she might've conquered her shyness, she knew her limits.

Confronted by a bare-chested man who made her ovaries explode, she'd turn bright pink, lose her ability to form speech, and end of story. "Oh—"

She would've bounced off that sculpted chest if he hadn't grabbed her by the hips.

"Hey, sorry," he said with a startled smile that lit up the dazzling blue of his eyes. "I didn't see you."

"No, um, my fault." It looked as if he'd crouched down to check one of his tires or something else but had risen to his feet right when she swung around to get into her car. And God, his skin was so hot and smooth and he was so tall and his shoulders were so broad and her mouth was drying up. The stuttering would begin at any moment.

The same stuttering Suzanne had mocked relentlessly when they were fourteen. Until Ísa had gone silent around everyone except the few friends she trusted. And now that horrible, ugly-hearted girl was getting married, having a baby, getting a happily-ever-after. Added to which, Ísa's mother was jerking her on a string like she was a marionette, and her last "date" had asked her to call him Woofy and reward him with doggy biscuits.

The blue of the gardener's eyes flickered with a hot flame.

And she thought... I *know* him. But before she could follow that faint thread, all the fury and hurt and frustration and sheer aggravation in Ísa ignited into an incandescent inferno.

She went mad.

Grabbing the hot gardener's beautiful face in her hands, she said, "I want to kiss you."

A wicked grin. "Go on ahead."

And Ísa pressed her lips to his.

3

ALWAYS KEEP A CLEAN BACK SEAT

WHOA.

The seriously cute redhead with skin like moonlight and curves that wouldn't quit who reminded Sailor of... *someone* hadn't been joking with that breathless statement. She was kissing him. She wasn't very good at it. But who the fuck cared when she tasted so damn good? And felt so good? And smelled so good?

And also didn't seem to care that he had to smell of grass and dirt and sweat.

Moving his hand from the lush curve of her hip and up her spine to grip the back of her head, he angled her just right, and then he feasted. She moaned in her throat, a husky purr of a thing that had his cock coming to hard attention. Sailor immediately decided he wanted to hear that sound again, would learn what made her utter it.

Shifting on his heel, he pressed her up against the door of his truck. Her body was sweet and lush, her breasts soft mounds he wanted to bite and caress and see naked. First things first however: he licked his tongue over hers.

She turned her head.

Sailor groaned inside but pulled back, his chest heaving. "You want to go?" He didn't normally pounce on women two seconds after meeting them, but in his defense, she was the one who'd done the initial pouncing.

Sailor liked to think of himself as a good guy—but he was still a *guy*. And she was the most erotically gorgeous woman he'd ever held in his arms. It wasn't as if he was going to turn her down when she made the offer.

Big gray-green eyes held his, the pupils dilated. "Do you have a girlfriend, wife—"

"No." Sailor wanted to put his hands all over her, wanted to trail his lips across her skin until it flushed a delicious pink. "I'm married to my business. She's also my very demanding mistress. Doesn't tolerate other women for long periods."

The redhead looked toward the redbrick of the school building. "It's light. Someone will see."

Breath catching in his throat, Sailor said, "Back seat of my truck?" He hadn't made out in a car since he was seventeen. However, for this sexy redhead who kissed like an innocent but had a body made for sin, he was game.

"What?" Her eyes went huge. "*No.*"

He kissed her again, her kiss-swollen lips too tempting to resist and her taste making him want to lick his tongue into other, more secret places. Only when he had her gasping for breath, her nails digging into his chest, did he say, "Windows are tinted, windscreen looks out toward the empty grounds. No one will see."

Her chest heaved up and down even as the confusion and shock in her eyes tugged at his memories.

Then she said, "Okay."

Hot damn!

Sailor pushed off her. "Let me just move some stuff

from the back seat to the bed of the truck." He didn't want to give the redhead time to change her mind, but he hadn't exactly been expecting a back seat make-out session. He had parts for a sprinkler system stacked back there.

He was halfway through his task and moving as quickly as possible when he heard the slam of a car door. Two seconds after that, the blue compact next to his truck backed out with a screech. The car raced down the drive the next second, taking his former partner-in-kissing with it.

Sailor stood there, not sure just what had happened. His head was ringing, his cock was painfully hard, and he had the feeling he'd just been used and discarded by the cute redhead with the equally cute accent and curves made for his hands to plunder.

His brain went click.

Firelight hair. Moonlight skin. Gray-green eyes.

He'd thought she was cute seven years ago too, when Cody had brought her along to that party in the warehouse. Sailor had only had a short while to admire her before Cody turned into the asshole of the year and dumped her in front of the entire party. Sailor couldn't remember the other male's exact words, but he vividly remembered the pain and shock in the redhead's eyes.

That night she'd disappeared without a trace into the night.

As she'd now disappeared down the drive.

Hands on his hips, Sailor narrowed his eyes at the long length of that drive. "I'm not sixteen anymore, Ms. Redhead. And I know where you work." His lips curved into a deeply satisfied smile.

This wasn't over yet. Not by a long shot.

4

IN WHICH DEVIL ÍSA MAKES
HER DEBUT

"OH MY GOD! OH MY God!" Ísa couldn't believe what she'd done—and what she'd *almost done.*

She'd made out in the parking lot of her *school.* A stately and prestigious school known for its high standards and pristine reputation. Teachers attached to it did not go around accosting innocent gardeners and agreeing to crawl into the back seat of their trucks!

If anyone had seen her...

"Breathe, breathe, breathe," she told herself. "It was only a kiss." A hotly sexual kiss that had made her nerve endings sizzle and her thighs clench together in delicious, greedy want.

Clearly there was nothing wrong with her hormones.

If not for that piercing instant of blinding sense when she'd realized she was about to put her entire career in jeopardy because of a combination of Slimeball Schumer, Suzanne, Jacqueline, and a hot gardener whose *name she didn't even know,* she'd be in the back seat of his truck right now.

Probably with her panties off and her mouth fused to the gardener's.

Her thighs twinged, her core feeling hot and swollen. Ready.

Devil Ísa sulked. And whispered, *Go back. Get into that back seat.*

"Stop it," she told herself, horrified. "That was a moment of madness, never to be repeated." Ísalind Magdalena Rain-Stefánsdóttir did not accost random hot men on *school grounds*. While it was still light out!

And she definitely did not dig her nails into his sculptured chest and have thoughts that involved licking him up like her favorite ice cream.

"Argh!"

No way could she turn up to the board meeting in the state she was in. She had to calm down. Maybe have a few stiff drinks—and her head examined. Followed by a cold shower—because her body was not getting with the program. It wanted more of the hot gardener's hard body, more of his ravenous kisses, more of his appreciative hands roaming all over her.

No man had ever touched her that way, as if she were a porn fantasy come to life.

Turn around and go back, Devil Ísa whispered again, her horns shiny and red. *Live a little. Or a lot. I'm easy. Be easy. I'm sure he'd forgive you for running away if you turned up and began to unzip your dress, all slow and sexy.*

"Shut up," Ísa muttered to that lunatic part of her psyche.

Devil Ísa shrugged and crossed her legs. *At least then you'd have a wild and fun story to tell your grandchildren. Unlike the current scintillating tale of your life. A huge yawn.*

It's like you're a ninety-year-old trapped in a twenty-eight-year-old's body. Boooooooooring.

Ísa's eye caught on the street name she was about to pass. She made the decision without even thinking about it, turning left instead of going right. Heading down the main strip used by countless commuters through the day, she reached the busy section of boutique restaurants and trendy cafés where traffic was clogged up from dawn to midnight.

Who were these people who always had time to sit around sipping lattes?

Devil Ísa had the answer. *People who have a life of their own. Hurlow's seventeen. Catie's thirteen. Not long before they don't need you. What're you going to do then, grandma?*

"I have a plan!"

Woof, woof.

Ísa wondered if this was what it felt like to go insane. Having an argument with yourself was surely not a sign of sanity. But she'd heard more than one author talking about the voices in their head, so at least she wasn't the only one. *It's a creative thing,* she told herself. *It means my poems don't totally suck.*

Sure, granny.

The light changed.

Changed back before her car made it to the top of the queue.

The fruit and vegetable shop on the corner was doing a brisk business, and across from it, a number of people sat at the outdoor tables of a café that had been there forever. Usually when she came this way and had to stop at the red light, Ísa liked to people watch, especially when the all-sides crosswalk signal came on and people streamed left and right and diagonally across the intersection.

It felt as if a microcosm of Auckland passed through Mount Eden on any given day while the mountain itself rose behind them like a silent guardian.

Today wasn't a normal day.

Skin about to split from the force of the emotions inside her, she had to sit through another light change before she could slip through to the other side of the intersection. Less than ten seconds down the road and she was out of the Mount Eden gridlock and heading toward the upper end of the long road.

Her destination, however, lay well before the end—in a quiet section sandwiched between the café district she'd just passed and the bigger businesses close to the city proper. She was nearly there when she lucked into a parking spot on the street.

Getting out, she barely remembered to lock the car before she looked both ways, then ran across the street to the white villa that functioned as the offices of Hillier & Co. Chartered Accountants.

Nayna's green MINI Cooper was the only car in the staff parking lot.

Dammit, she was an idiot. She could've parked next to her best friend's car—but well, she wasn't exactly thinking straight, was she?

Not with the gardener's scent still in her lungs and Devil Ísa along for commentary.

Telling herself to breathe, just breathe, she ran up the villa steps and turned the knob on the front door. When it swung open, she wanted to slap the person who'd forgotten to lock it. The firm had a policy that if only one person was to be at the office after closing time, the second-to-last person had to lock up behind themselves for safety.

Îsa did that before walking quickly down the thickly carpeted hallway. It wasn't as if this well-heeled area was a hotbed of crime, but the villa *was* on a main street with countless people passing it day and night. No use taking chances, especially with a lone woman within.

As she'd expected after spotting only Nayna's car in the parking lot, the front offices were empty, as was the receptionist desk usually occupied by the two admin staffers shared between the four accountants in Hillier & Co.

Going all the way to the back of the villa—and passing the firm's little kitchen and social area along the way—she turned left into Nayna's office. As the most junior member of the firm, Nayna had had no choice in her office space, but the back room got plenty of light, and Nayna actually preferred it to the larger offices up front.

Her best friend looked up with a start from behind a pile of papers, her face a lovely oval and her relentlessly straight black hair pulled back into a sensible bun, her skin tone dark mahogany.

Taking off the little glasses she wore for reading, Nayna pressed a long-fingered hand to her heart. "Îsa! You gave me a fright!"

A huge smile followed, the other woman getting up from behind her desk to reveal the black skirt she wore with a silky blue shell. The matching black jacket was hanging on the back of her chair. "You've got great timing though. I'm starving—missed lunch and just ordered a giant pizza. We can—"

Pausing mid-monologue, Nayna took a good look up and down Îsa's motionless body... then did it again. "You look like you've been doing the wild thing in a messy bed with a hot, hot man."

Ísa knew her friend was joking, but she groaned and collapsed into the small leather sofa on this side of the office. It was where Nayna met with clients, preferring the less formal approach. "You won't believe what I did." She hid her face in her hands.

"*No.*" Work forgotten and eyes huge, Nayna kicked off her low-heeled pumps and sat down on the sofa beside Ísa. "Start from the beginning. And I mean *the beginning.*"

A tinkling sound rang through the room just as Ísa parted her lips to confess her sins.

Nayna glanced at her watch. "Oh, that'll be the pizza. Don't move."

As her friend ran barefoot out of the office, Ísa pressed her head against the back of the sofa and tried the meditation technique again. Devil Ísa was having none of that, insisting on tormenting her with the remembered feel of the gardener's silky hot flesh, the raw scent of his body, the voracious delight in his kiss, in his touch.

Her toes curled.

"Good thing you came along," Nayna said as she entered the room, pizza box and two cold bottles of water in hand. "Or I swear I'd have inhaled this entire pizza by myself. Here." She gave Ísa one of the bottles. "Grabbed this from the fridge. You look like you could do with some cooling down."

After placing the pizza box on the small table in front of the sofa while Ísa guzzled some water, Nayna found a couple of paper napkins in her secret drawer of candy bars and foil-wrapped chocolates—hidden under piles of the most boring tax forms she could find.

Napkins down beside the pizza, Ísa's best friend and partner in crime sat again, her legs folded under her. "Okay." Dark eyes locked with Ísa's. "Confess already!"

Ísa scrunched up the fabric of her dress's full skirt with her free hand, released it, her palm sweaty. "There was no sex," she said straight out. "Nothing even close."

"Then why do you look like you were busted by the cops with your bra off and a smokin' man between your thighs? Obviously it was one who knew what he was doing to get you into that state."

"This isn't funny." Ísa's glare had no effect on her friend.

"Spill!"

"You know I went in to school to work on my night-class lessons?"

Nayna, who by now had a generous bite of pizza in her mouth, nodded; she'd had a firsthand hearing of the upstairs neighbor's vigorous hammering habits when she'd dropped by for lunch one day last week, on her way back from an external meeting.

"Well," Ísa began, "there was this dangerously hot gardener outside."

Nayna squeaked. "Oh please, Ísa," she said after quickly swallowing her bite of pizza, "please, please, please, please, *please* tell me that you made out with him at least."

Ísa stared miserably at her friend. "I *attacked* him like a wild animal."

A blink. Two. At last Nayna whispered, "Really?" When Ísa just nodded dumbly, her best friend gave a shout, then, slice still in hand, rose and did a little dance, complete with a booty shake and a one-woman stadium wave. "My hero!"

Ísa scrubbed at her face with her hands. "No," she said, "no, no, no. What if someone saw? I'm a teacher, Nayna.

Not only did I throw myself at him, I did it on school grounds."

Sitting back down on the sofa, Nayna stuffed the rest of the slice into her mouth and managed to swallow it before saying, "School's out for the summer right? Was anyone else there when you left?"

Ísa shook her head.

"In that case, I think we can chalk this one up to experience and, well, an attack of gardener hotness. Consider it compensation for all those teenage years when neither one of us got any action at school."

Ísa laughed, the sound coming out this side of hysterical. "I need ice." She pressed the cold water bottle to one cheek, then the other.

It had no discernible effect.

"Lots and lots of ice," she added. "I can't stop thinking about his eyes." Such a distinctive lightning blue, a color her mind kept insisting she'd seen before—but Ísa wouldn't have forgotten eyes that striking. Or a man that primal. "In fact, I think I'll go home and have an ice bath."

"I don't care how mortified you are right now"— Nayna's grin cracked her face—"you'll look back on it one day and cheer your badass self."

Huffing out a breath and seriously doubting her friend's prediction, Ísa said, "Enough about my bout of temporary insanity. How's the suitor situation?" Ísa was still struggling to accept that her savvy and highly educated friend was happy to go along with her family's desire for a traditional arranged marriage, but if Nayna was at peace with it, then Ísa would support her all the way.

"All my eager 'suitors' so far," Nayna said in a tone as dry as the desert, "are more interested in me being a newly minted chartered accountant than anything else. Most of them are accountants too—they want to acquire a future business partner via marriage." She made a face. "It's all very dynasty building. Your mother would approve."

The words "your mother" had Ísa glancing at her watch with a scowl. "Damn it," she muttered. "I have to go home and have a shower to wash off my stress-sweat... and the dirt from his body that transferred to me." She'd just noticed the specks on the deep aquamarine of her dress.

Devil Ísa whispered, *Since you're dirty anyway, how about you track him down and crawl into the back seat of his truck?*

"Don't forget the party on Saturday!" Nayna called out after her as she reached the front door. "Wear your shortest dress! You might get lucky and spot another hot gardener!"

5

BANGING AND HAMMERING
(UNFORTUNATELY NOT OF THE ECSTATIC KIND)

S AILOR BANGED IN A NAIL with unnecessary force.

Beside him, his brother raised an eyebrow, Gabriel's gray eyes a reflection of their mother's. "What's that poor plank done to you?"

Nail pounded in—so hard it wasn't going to dare come out ever again—Sailor stepped back to look at his and Gabriel's handiwork. He'd come to his parents' place straight after the fiasco at the school, he and Gabe having agreed to drop by this evening to have dinner with their parents and younger brothers—and fix this part of the fence. It had suddenly fallen down after a piece rotted way without anyone noticing.

"How old is this fence?"

"How long have Mom and Dad been married? Take that and subtract two years."

Sailor's mind spun back to the day they'd moved into this villa. The paint had been peeling and chipped back then, the yard an overgrown mess. But it had been a place Alison and Joseph Esera could afford. They'd all done plenty of grunt work to whip it into shape—and its value now was enough to cause a heart attack in a healthy man.

This area was one of the hottest on the Auckland property market.

But to Sailor, this home was memory and warmth and love and safety. "We got lucky with Dad, didn't we?" He only ever used that word to refer to Joseph Esera, never when he was speaking about the man who'd fathered two children, then abandoned them and his wife without a backward look.

His brother glanced up from where he'd crouched down to collect the bent nails they'd put on the ground while they finished up, his shoulders broad and his body built for the hard physicality of rugby. "Yeah," he said simply, his eyes holding memories shared only by him and Sailor and their mother.

Their younger brothers, Jake and Danny, had never—and would never—experience the icy fear of being thrown out of their home, their clothes thrust into trash bags. Sailor was the youngest of their original family, remembered the least, but he didn't have to remember all the details to remember the emotions.

The bone-numbing fear and raw confusion.

His five-year-old hand clenched tight around Gabe's as their mother battled to make sure the people evicting them wouldn't confiscate her boys' things.

Sailor was so fucking glad that Jake and Danny would never be in the same position. Nor would their mother. Unlike the man who was biologically Sailor and Gabriel's father, Joseph Esera would cut off his own arm before turning his back on his family.

"We also got lucky with Mom," Gabe pointed out as he rose to his feet, the bent nails in hand. "She never once gave up. Even after that bastard stole all the money she'd worked so hard to save. Even after he forced her to go to welfare when that was her worst fucking nightmare."

Gabriel's anger was a brutal wall. It had always been that way. He'd been the older son, the one who understood the most, the one who'd grown up too fast in the wake of their father's abandonment. The one who remembered each and every detail of the nightmare.

And the one who'd protected Sailor from the worst of the impact.

"I got lucky with both of you," Sailor said quietly.

Gabriel's gray eyes held open affection as he punched Sailor in the shoulder. "We did it together, shrimp."

Sailor had often wished he had the same eyes as his brother. Because then he'd have their mother's eyes. Instead, he'd been born with the eyes of the asshole who'd fathered him. But that asshole had no place in this yard full of memories of love.

Shoving Brian Bishop aside with long practice, Sailor packed up his tools. "You ever had a woman just decide you're not for her and run away? *Actually* run away."

Gabriel made a valiant effort at looking solemn. "You must've stunk real bad."

"Fuck you," Sailor said without heat, though he was wondering if it had been that after all. His redhead had seemed to like him, dirt and sweat and all, zero hesitation in her touch or her kiss, but maybe she'd changed her mind after he'd made the mistake of breaking skin contact.

Idiot.

"Who was she?" Gabriel asked after he'd gotten rid of the bent nails.

"Trouble."

His brother chuckled. "You taking Ms. Trouble to that big party on Saturday?"

"Did you not hear that she *ran away*?" Sailor had intended to let down his hair at the party being thrown by a friend of a friend, but now he'd probably spend the whole night brooding over his redhead.

"Gabe! Sail! Dad asked if you want a beer." Their youngest brother ran over with two cold bottles in hand.

At fourteen, the baby of their family was still more cheerful child than moody teenager—which was a good thing, because Danny hadn't yet got his growth spurt and was one of the shortest in his class, boys and girls included. That he was also one of the most popular was courtesy of not only his speed on the rugby field but also that same sunny personality.

Ruffling his brother's hair, the texture a little rougher than Sailor's own but the color the same inky black, Sailor took one bottle while Gabe took the other. "Thanks, Danny." He bumped fists with his brother.

Danny then exchanged an extremely complicated set of handshakes with Gabriel. At age twelve, he'd spent an entire weekend teaching Sailor, Gabriel, and Jake that handshake. As his youngest brother talked his eldest one into passing around a rugby ball, Sailor stood with his back to the repaired fence and got a start on his brooding. If he caught up with his cute redhead a third time around, no way was he letting her slip away again.

A rugby ball plowed into his stomach.

Catching it reflexively without dropping his beer, he narrowed his eyes at a grinning Gabriel. "Dude, you're the captain of the national team." The most decorated and internationally recognized player in the squad. "Show a little dignity."

"Hey!" Jake's dark-haired head popped out from the upstairs room he'd shared with Danny until Sailor moved out several years back. "Are you guys playing without me?" Scowling, he pulled his head back in, and Sailor knew he was running down the stairs to join them.

Putting his beer down by the fence, not far from where Gabe had left his, he spun the ball in a spiral to Danny. His little brother caught it, then did a run straight at Gabe as if intending to go through his muscled bulk. Instead, he found himself picked up and swung upside down.

Rather than giving up the ball, Danny reached out his arm and plonked it on the ground behind Gabe, then did a victory dance while still upside down. Sailor grinned. If everything went according to plan, he'd have even less free time in the coming months. He'd miss these nights just hanging out with his family, but he had dreams that haunted him and demons that howled.

He had to quiet those demons, had to become a man like the one who'd raised him. A man who provided for those who were his own instead of taking and taking and taking until there was nothing left. A man who built something. A man who was *nothing* like the one who'd sired Gabriel and Sailor.

A man with ambitions like that, he had no time for distractions.

Especially not distractions in the form of cute redheads who kissed and ran.

6

STUBBLE BURN IS HARD TO HIDE FROM
THE DRAGON

Í SA TURNED THE SHOWER TO ice-cold after racing home from Nayna's office, yelped after getting in; that had done nothing to quiet her libido or her racing heart, though it *had* successfully frozen her blood. Turning up the heat, she washed off the scent of sin and temptation and blue, blue eyes and lips that devoured her own. Afterward, she rubbed herself down with clinical precision in an effort to hide all evidence of her shower.

If her mother commented on it regardless, Ísa would tell Jacqueline that she'd been exercising. The best thing was, it wasn't even a lie—she and the gardener had surely burned a few red-hot calories. And Jacqueline would be happy to hear of Ísa's sudden enthusiasm for after-work sessions. She'd never understood how she'd birthed a child who was so much more into curling up with a cup of tea and falling into poetry than in going for a "head-clearing" run.

The one thing Jacqueline had never done was disparage Ísa for her size. "Curves can be useful," she'd said more than once. "But you need strength and endurance to back it up."

Ísa had taken the advice, but in ways she found interesting. Running, Jacqueline's choice of exercise, didn't qualify. Team sports would've been good if she'd had the coordination. Since she didn't, she focused on things like aerobics classes where she and Nayna could hide out at the back, far from the sleek gym bunnies who could twist themselves into pretzels without breaking a sweat.

The regular back-line students often sent each other into hysterics. Last session, Nayna had ended up facing the opposite direction from the rest of the class. The session before that, Ísa had almost smacked another back-liner in the face with her outflung hand.

Too bad this evening wouldn't be filled with laughter and camaraderie.

After pulling on a simple gray dress with a fitted bodice and full skirt, the outfit topped off with a thin but businesslike black belt, she twisted her hair up into a bun, then reached for her makeup.

With skin as pale as hers, powder was a moot point unless she wanted to imitate a Kabuki dancer. Ísa tended to stick with mascara and a touch of eyeshadow, maybe a slick of gloss on her lips. Anything more and she felt as if she resembled a clown. Like that orange-haired one associated with burgers and nuggets and fries.

Suzanne had enjoyed pointing out the resemblance.

"Ronald. Hey Ronald, how's it going, Ronald?"

And now the poster girl for mean girls of high school was getting married and having a baby.

Realizing she'd forgotten to tell Nayna that infuriating piece of news, she quickly messaged her friend as she ran down to the car. She was on the road when a ping told her

Nayna had replied, but she didn't look at the message until she'd pulled into the parking lot of her mother's base of operations in the glossy downtown district.

Her parking spot was an assigned one.

And it boasted a shiny gold-on-black sign: Ísalind Rain, Vice President.

Argh! That hadn't been there the last time.

Getting out, she checked Nayna's message:

Life sucks. But don't worry—I'm Hindu; I believe in reincarnation and karma. She'll come back as a lice-infested cockroach in her next life, with Slimeball Schumer as a rat. A one-eyed rat. Finally their exteriors will match their interiors.

Meanwhile, you and I will return as supermodel brain surgeons and seduce every smoking-hot gardener in sight.

Ísa GRINNED as she made her way through the front doors of Crafty Corners HQ and into a color-filled lobby that was a cheerful assault on the senses. Waving at the sole receptionist currently on duty at the main welcome desk, she ran up the steps rather than using the elevator.

The upstairs reception area was another pop of color, the sofas a mix of fresh orange, lime green, and sunburst yellow, the walls warm and creamy. Her mother's junior assistant sat not at a traditional desk but behind a seat-height counter on which crafting and work supplies were stacked in neat groupings.

The slender brunette was currently involved in putting together an intricate jewelry box.

"How many of those have you made now, Ginny?"

"Oh, thank God it's you, Ísa." Ginny stopped pretending to be an industrious crafter and slumped back in her wheelchair. "I swear to God, if I have to glue one more set of tiny windows onto one more set of tiny doors, I'm going to start gluing the stupid doors to people's heads."

Ísa nodded in heartfelt sympathy. She'd worked several summers in the business and never again wanted to craft anything. *Ever.* But Crafty Corners thrived partially because people wanted to buy into the Craft Is Family motto. Any employee at their desk who might come into contact with the public was to always be involved in a craft project or to have a half-completed project within easy view. As if they were so in love with the company's creations that they couldn't stop themselves.

Poor Ginny had drawn the short straw here—the senior assistant, Annalisa, got to sit behind another door and had a much more sane working environment. Though, to be fair, Annalisa had done her time in the crafting salt mines for three years before she was promoted out of the front line.

The whole concept sounded idiotic, but Ísa had seen it work over and over again. Investors, reporters, all types of normally sensible people laughed and fell for the illusion, many even stopping long enough to help glue or paint a piece. Which was why the company Jacqueline Rain had created as a broke student was now a multimillion-dollar operation that exported worldwide and had *seventeen* thriving stores in New Zealand.

New Zealand wasn't that big a country. Still less than five million people at last count. And yet... seventeen

Crafty Corners stores. All flourishing. All with waiting lists for their highly reviewed "Crafting and Cookies" nights—at which the newest and hottest crafting secrets were revealed.

Then there were the twenty-eight stores in neighboring Australia.

Ísa didn't know how her mother did it.

"Is Jacqueline in her office?" she asked Ginny.

The other woman pointed toward the boardroom down the hallway. "Already in there."

Taking a deep, calming breath, Ísa squared her shoulders and prepared to face the Dragon, but she still wasn't prepared for the impact her mother had on her when she opened the door. With dark auburn hair that she wore in a chignon and pale skin that she'd passed on to Ísa—though where Ísa was ghost pale, Jacqueline had a rich cream tone to her skin that made you want to stroke it—Jacqueline Rain was one of the most beautiful people Ísa had ever met.

Add in willowy height and flawless bone structure, and Jacqueline would be stunning even at eighty.

"Ísa." Jacqueline raised her cheek.

Dutifully giving her mother a peck, Ísa took the seat next to her around the polished wood of the conference table. "What's with the vice president tag on the parking spot?"

"I thought you'd like to taste the future you could have." Jacqueline took off her Tiffany-blue cat's-eye reading glasses. "I fail to see why you prefer dealing with snotty teenagers all day when you could be working in one of the top businesses in the country."

"I don't want to do crafts all day, Mother."

"Ísa, you know that's just window dressing with the frontline staff. Stop being deliberately obtuse."

Unfortunately, her mother was right; the family-friendly, crafty atmosphere was just for public consumption. Behind the scenes, Crafty Corners was a cutthroat business. And Jacqueline was the head cutter of throats.

"Why am I here?" she said. "You know I always vote with you." It wasn't that Ísa didn't have her own views, but Jacqueline was brilliant. She knew exactly what she was doing, and voting against her out of spite wasn't an act of which Ísa was capable. "Also, you have the controlling share. So why do we have to go through the song and dance?"

"Because the other shareholders like to know what's happening with their money," Jacqueline said. "Since those shares make you a millionaire, I'd think you'd pay a little more attention."

Ísa wanted to bang her head against the table; at this rate, she should just get a helmet and be done with it. The only reason she hadn't tried to sell back her shares—because of course, contractually, she couldn't sell them to anyone else without first giving Jacqueline the option—was that the instant Ísa defected from the company, Jacqueline would cut her off.

Ísa had zero fucks to give on that score. But if she couldn't get to Jacqueline, or if Jacqueline stopped taking her arguments into account, then she couldn't speak for Catie and Harlow. And neither her half sister nor her stepbrother would stand a chance without Ísa working on their behalf. Oh, Jacqueline wouldn't cut off the money Catie, in particular, needed, but... the two would get forgotten.

Ísa knew how much that hurt.

She would not permit Jacqueline to do that to another child.

That didn't mean she was ready to sit back and be rolled over by the Jacqueline Rain train. "You know I'm not suitable to be your heir," she said. "I have no business experience except for the summers I worked for you."

"You're downplaying your abilities." Leaning back in her chair, Jacqueline pinned Ísa to the spot with the striking green of her gaze. "You absorb everything and you understand all of it."

Bad luck for Ísa, but Jacqueline was, once again, right.

It was like Ísa had absorbed the information in the womb while her mother was wheeling and dealing and cut-throating.

Trying futilely not to grit her teeth, she picked up the agenda for this meeting. She was halfway through it when her mother said, "What have you done to yourself?" Her well-manicured fingernails brushed the side of Ísa's neck. "If I didn't know better, I'd think that was stubble burn."

Ísa's fingers jerked up to her throat without her conscious volition.

How could she have missed that?

Because you don't make a habit of jumping hot, half-naked gardeners, that's why, Devil Ísa answered. *Pity.*

Thank God eagle-eyed Jacqueline had already returned to her work, dismissing the possibility that Ísa would turn up to a board meeting with stubble burn on her neck. Not that Ísa could blame her mother on that point.

Hard as it was to admit, Cody had done a number on her self-confidence. He'd been the first boy she'd ever trusted not just with her heart but with her body, and he'd made her feel horrible about it. She'd risen from the humiliation on a wave of fury and fierce determination, but it had still taken her two years to step back into the dating pool.

She'd met a couple of nice men, but no one who'd shaken her world.

Still, as Manuel, Beau, Carl, et al. could testify, Ísa was no longer a dating shrinking violet. The online-dating maneuver might succeed in driving her mad, but no one would ever be able to accuse her of not trying hard enough. And it'd all be worth it if she found him, found the one man for whom she'd be more important than meetings or negotiations or "time-critical" emails.

The one man for whom she'd be a priority.

Ísa had never been that for anyone.

I'm married to my business. She's also my very demanding mistress. Doesn't tolerate other women for long periods.

She sighed inwardly. It looked like she couldn't even jump the right hot gardener. No, she had to accost one who was devoted to his business—it was like she had radar tuned to the kind of people who'd ignore adult Ísa as her parents had ignored child Ísa. Just as well she'd never see him again. The way her body had ignited for him, she didn't trust herself anywhere near his vicinity.

Not when he was unsuitable, blue-eyed trouble.

Her toes curled inside her heels. Her lower body clenched. And her breasts, they seemed to swell inside the cups of her bra.

And Devil Ísa whispered, *Nothing says you have to marry him, you idiot. Don't you want to look back and have some wicked stories with which to scandalize your grandchildren?*

7

SAILOR THE MERCILESS

S AILOR WENT TO BED ON Friday night with a lush redhead on his mind. Was it any wonder that his body refused to settle down?

Groaning, he fisted the hard length of his cock and stroked. And thought about punishing his redhead for the torment. He wasn't into pain or whips and chains, so maybe he'd tie her up and tease her until she begged for mercy.

He wouldn't have mercy, he decided.

He'd lick and suck and keep her on the edge while he feasted. And he'd tell her how he'd thought about her as he stroked his own body. How he'd fantasized about sinking into her in a single deep thrust and feeling her so tight and wet around him. How he'd imagined stripping her bare so he could fondle her breasts and scrape his unshaven jaw over the delicate perfection of her skin.

His body shuddered; his back arched.

Crashing back down, the release easing his sexual tension but doing nothing to take his redhead off his mind,

Sailor said, "Definitely no mercy." His chest heaved up and down. "When I catch up with you, spitfire, it's going to be all about revenge."

Sweet, slow, erotic revenge.

Wickedness is underrated.

~ *Nayna Sharma*

8

MISBEHAVING DEVIL WOMEN

ATURDAY NIGHT ARRIVED FAR TOO quickly.

Ísa had spent Friday night dreaming of tangled limbs in the back seat of a certain truck; memories of the dream, of a blue-eyed man with a sinful smile, had even infiltrated her waking hours to leave her breathless. Tonight she decided she'd exorcise his ghost. Tonight she was going to have *fun*, dammit, and not be the granny her subconscious kept accusing her of being.

The worst thing was that Devil Ísa was right.

It felt as if she'd been the adult in her family since she was fifteen. Oh, Jacqueline could run a multimillion-dollar business empire and negotiate stellar deals, but when it came to holding their scattered family together, it was Ísa who did the heavy lifting. She'd realized on the day of Catie's birth that if she didn't step up to the plate, no one else would. Certainly not Jacqueline's fourth husband, the man who'd fathered Catie.

Ísa's father, Stefán, obviously had no reason to look out for his ex-wife's daughter with another man. Not that he'd much looked out for his own either.

Her phone beeped.

When she picked it up, it was to see her father's handsome face flashing on the screen as if she'd summoned him out of thin air just by thinking of him. "Hi, Dad."

"Your mother told me you're finally taking more interest in her company," he said in Icelandic, as if they'd just spoken yesterday instead of four months ago. "Good. Once you get some experience there, you can move into a vice presidential position in my fleet."

Ísa rubbed at her forehead. This, *this* was why her parents' marriage hadn't worked out. They admired each other enormously and remained close friends to this day, but they simply could not stop playing the game of one-upmanship when it came to business.

Even when it involved their daughter.

Switching to the same language Stefán had used, the language that still colored her English, she said, "How's"—*oh God, what was the name of her father's current wife?*—"er, Jenetta," she finished, hoping he'd blame the pause on the international phone connection.

"Oh, Jenetta and I parted ways two months ago, sweetheart. She was lovely, but a touch vacuous in the brain-cell department."

Ísa winced on behalf of the departed Jenetta. "So you're single?"

"Not for long! I was able to get an expedited divorce—I won't bore you with the details of how. The wedding's going to be in New Zealand. You know I like you to be part of the bridal party."

Any other person might've been confused. Any other person was not Ísa and hadn't grown up with Stefán. "What's the name of your fiancée?"

"Elizabeth Anne Victoria. Such an English name. Her

parents are viscounts or something." A verbal shrug that only a man who was one of the wealthiest in Europe could make—a man who'd already married and divorced a princess and two prima ballerinas. "I'll send you the wedding invitation, but here's the date."

Ísa dutifully noted it down.

Stefán hung up soon afterward as he'd received a call from a corporate partner on the other line. As she put down her phone, Ísa realized she had no idea of her father's current physical location. She'd also forgotten to subtly nudge him for more information about Elizabeth Anne Victoria—specifically, the new fiancée's age. Morbid curiosity had her googling for a woman with that name who was the child of a viscount.

Two results came up.

One was an eighty-year-old married matriarch.

The other a twenty-one-year-old lissome beauty whose Instagram feed was full of images of her in various bikinis with captions that were either "motivational" sayings about working hard and achieving the dream or giggly reports about her latest vacation to some sun-drenched island so exclusive you needed a private yacht to get to it.

According to her bio, she wanted to be the first woman to fly into space. Her goal was to be "an inspirational role model to younger women!" It seemed to have escaped Elizabeth Anne Victoria's notice that a number of women had already beaten her to the stars. And that, to achieve her goal, she might need to study something other than the "meaning of life through a cocktail glass."

"Lots of brain cells there, Dad," Ísa muttered, wondering if the ink would even have a chance to dry on the marriage certificate before Stefán got bored. For a smart man, he'd never made a sensible choice in marriage partners, Jacqueline included. He either chose barracudas like Ísa's mother or, lately, women who simply couldn't keep up with the brain that had taken a fleet of failing cruise ships and turned it into a global empire.

Putting down her phone, Ísa stared in the mirror again. Her father was about to cross the last line—he was going to marry a woman younger than his daughter. That was it. Ísa had *had* it. "I don't care what I have to do tonight," she vowed, "but I am not coming home without misbehaving at least once!" No more playing it safe. Not tonight.

Devil Ísa cheered.

Decision made, Ísa threw open her wardrobe. It was filled with full-skirted day dresses, well-cut shirts, and skirts that flattered her body but weren't too tight to wear to work. Clearly she couldn't wear any of those things to a party where she intended to commit at least one sin, maybe two. She wanted to look dangerous and sexy and delicious, not like a prim and proper high school teacher.

"No turning back, Ísa." Sucking in a breath, she pushed aside all the other clothes in the wardrobe to reach into the very back. Her fingers brushed the hard edge of sequins. Stomach tight and fluttery, she pulled out the hanger holding the dress.

She didn't know what Catie had been thinking, buying this for Ísa's birthday a couple of years ago. Her sister had talked Harlow into going along with the choice—the two of them had pooled their money to be able to afford it.

The dress was a vivid royal blue and sequined from top to bottom.

That sounded impressive until you took the length of the dress into account: the thing had no straps and the one time Ísa had worn it—for her at-home birthday dinner with Catie and Harlow—it had only come to halfway down her thighs. Bending over hadn't been an option, not unless she wanted to reveal the color of her panties to anyone behind her.

Resolve teetering, she almost shoved the dress back in. A woman with breasts her size was not meant to wear a strapless dress. But if she didn't wear this, it would have to be a T-shirt and jeans.

Real sexy. Real wild. Real breaking the rules.

Annoyed with herself, she stripped down—bra included—and wiggled into the dress. It had a zip down the side that made it easier. It was only when she began to tug up the zip that she remembered the dress's tight fit. It had made her feel like a fat sausage until Catie pointed out that the tight fit was on purpose so that her boobs wouldn't fall out.

"And it's *meant* to show off your curves," her sister had said with a sigh. "I wish I had some curves to show off, but since I don't, I'm going to make sure you don't hide yours."

According to both her siblings, she'd looked "hot, hot, hot" in the dress.

Dress on, she walked to the mirror again, then dared take a peek. The dress fit like she'd been painted into it, sliding down her back in a smooth curve before shaping itself over her rear. It was much the same in the front except that the smooth line was broken by clever ruching across the stomach that made it appear as if she didn't have a belly at all.

Up top, her breasts were impressively encased and pressed together just enough to create some admittedly sexy cleavage. Ísa took a second look... and smiled. She owed her little sister an apology, because the dress? It was perfect for the woman she wanted to be tonight.

Devil Ísa was now in charge.

Taking down her hair, she went to pick up her hair straightener—only to realize her wildly tumbled locks looked insanely sensual, as if she'd just gotten out of bed… or the back seat of the gardener's truck.

Blushing red-hot, she waved her hands in front of her face while still grinning; okay, yes, she'd run away before really doing anything, but at least she'd done *something*. And if she ever ran into him again, she wasn't going to run away. No, she'd take him up on his invitation to enter the back seat, should the offer still be open.

Her core threatened to melt.

"Focus, Ísa," she ordered herself. "Stop thinking about the gardener. I'm sure there are plenty more fish in the sinful sea. And you're going fishing."

She picked up her makeup and got to work.

Finished after a careful twenty minutes, she stepped back—and found a stranger looking out at her. A stranger in a smoking-hot dress with a tumble of red hair around her shoulders and lips so lush and plump they looked bitable.

Yes, her hips were wider than was fashionable, and she definitely had more curves than she should, but tonight Ísa was going to forget about should. Tonight she was going to celebrate who she was and let out the vixen within. Maybe if she did enough vixening, she'd forget the man with the blue, blue eyes who'd touched her as if he wanted to devour her in small bites.

Those eyes…

She frowned, still unable to shake the feeling that she'd seen them before, though that was impossible. She'd have remembered that gorgeous face, those sexy lips, that incredible build. No, she'd never met her gardener before that steamy kiss that haunted her dreams.

NAYNA WHISTLED WHEN SHE SAW Ísa. "Talk about sex on legs!" she said from the driver's seat while Ísa got into the passenger seat. She'd come downstairs to wait for Nayna, determined not to chicken out and change.

"Wow," Ísa said of her friend's own dress. "It looks like you wrapped a black bandage around yourself and said you were done. It's holy-crap fantastic."

The dress had thin straps, but otherwise it was similar to Ísa's in that it hit Nayna midway down the thighs. The bandage look was made all the sexier because it didn't cover every single part of Nayna's body. A little gap by her ribs, a hint by the curve of her hip, a strip along her lower back; the exposed sections were tiny, but that was why they looked so damn tempting.

Some of those exposed areas, however, were located in—

Ísa's eyes widened. "Are you naked under that?"

A distinctly naughty smile from her best friend. "Shh." Giggling at Ísa's scandalized gasp, she said, "I had to hide this from my mother. I put it in a box marked Tax Documents and left my stilettos in the car. Then, tonight, I walked out in a giant coat and sensible shoes."

Ísa couldn't understand Nayna's decision to live at home, just as she couldn't understand her friend's agreement to an arranged marriage, but it was what Nayna wanted. "I approve of your cunning ways."

"Did you see how it glitters when the light hits it?"

"You look like a goddess of the night."

Nayna cut herself off mid-laugh. "Damn." She pointed

to where she'd hooked up her phone to act as their GPS. "Can you fix that?" For some reason the screen had gone blank.

"What's the address?" When Nayna told her, Ísa didn't bother to reset the phone. "I know the way. My mother used to take me to parties around there."

Social events that had actually been more like business mixers.

Jacqueline training Ísa to be her successor. A mini-dragon. No matter if Ísa had no desire to breathe fire and cut throats.

"You met our host through work, right?" she said to Nayna about twenty minutes later as her friend brought the car to a halt partway down the long drive already clogged with a number of vehicles.

"It's a couple actually." Nayna turned off her engine. "The kind of power couple who end up in the social pages. This is their annual pre-Christmas-slash-anniversary party."

"Oh, I didn't bring a gift."

Reaching into the back, Nayna held up a beautifully wrapped package. "Already taken care of. It's a his-and-hers spa package from that fancy place we took Catie to when she turned thirteen."

Once out in the balmy night air, they took care navigating the drive, neither one of them used to walking in such spindly high heels. Ísa also had to fight the urge to keep tugging at her dress. It wasn't going to get any longer no matter how hard she tugged.

"Devil women," she said to Nayna, hooking her arm through her friend's. "That's what we are tonight."

Nayna nodded, something haunted in her eyes. "Wild,

wild devil women," she said. "Definitely not good girls who do what their families want."

Ísa wanted desperately to follow up on what she'd caught in Nayna's expression, in her voice, but there was also a desperation in her friend that said Nayna needed to have a good time. Tonight was not the time to talk about her choices and whether she truly could live with them.

"I dare you to kiss a random guy tonight," she said instead of digging into Nayna's heart and fears. "A gorgeous, ripped guy you'd never normally approach." Her friend was confident in her work, but she was Ísa's best friend for a reason—neither one of them was exactly the femme fatale type.

"Dare accepted," Nayna said firmly. "Since we'll never again see each other, who cares if he thinks I'm a crazy woman?"

Ísa decided she'd have to keep an eye on her friend tonight. There was an edge to Nayna she'd never before felt. Or... maybe she *wouldn't* keep an eye on her. Nayna already lived life by too many rules. Tonight was about breaking them. "Just tell me if you're going to go off with someone so I don't worry."

"You do the same." Nayna took a deep breath as they reached the open front door. "Let's go do bad-girl things."

They entered to find the party already in full swing. To their right was a massive living area that flowed out onto a huge deck that, in turn, led into the glowing blue waters of a pool that already boasted several swimmers. The cathedral ceiling soared high above, a huge crystal chandelier glittering light across every surface.

Music filled the space, not so loud as to halt conversation, but more than loud enough for those who wanted to dance—as a champagne-flute-waving group was doing in one corner, that section decorated with disco ball lights that turned it into a mini dance floor filled with beautiful bodies.

Walking gingerly into the area where yet more beautiful people laughed and mingled, Ísa had a sudden attack of nerves. What the hell was she doing here? She didn't look anything like these skinny creatures with their lustrously tumbling hair and skin tanned to golden perfection. If she tried to tan, she'd turn into a crispy critter.

"Nayna!" A stunning brunette walked toward Nayna with her arms wide open.

Going into them, Nayna hugged the other woman before passing on the gift package. "This is my friend Ísa."

"I hope you two brought swimsuits," the brunette said after a hug of welcome. "Though"—a wink—"from the look of it, not everyone is bothering with suits."

The brunette was tugged away by another woman a second later while a grinning Ísa looked at Nayna in a silent question. Not saying a word, the two of them began to head toward the pool.

And the back of Ísa's neck prickled with a sudden, visceral awareness.

Of hot, blue-eyed trouble.

9

VOODOO GAMES

ÍSA TURNED AROUND WITH A pounding heart... to see only the glossily beautiful people she'd already spotted, including a couple of men who were trying to catch her eye. Ignoring them, she kept on looking for the cause of her prickling awareness.

Nothing. No sign of her hot gardener.

Disappointment was a leaden rock in her stomach.

"Oh my God." Nayna's awed whisper snagged her attention. "Is he even real?"

Following the other woman's gaze, Ísa saw that it was locked on the heavily muscled form of a tall male with bronzed skin and rough scruff around his jaw, his black hair tumbled.

He was dressed in a classic white T-shirt that hugged his pecs and biceps, teamed with a pair of jeans that were well-worn and comfortable rather than being too tight—no showing off the goods like some of the men around here. Of course, that just made women all the more curious about what lay underneath.

Confidence pulsed off him in waves.

Ísa could *definitely* see the attraction, even if her own female hormones were still sulking at being denied another taste of a certain gardener.

"Go for it," she whispered to Nayna. "That's your kiss target right there."

When her friend just stared at her, Ísa said, "Wild women, remember?"

"Not humiliated women though." Bland words that didn't manage to hide Nayna's disappointment. "Have you seen the woman he's talking to?"

Ísa glanced over just in time to see the gorgeous stranger's eyes skim across the crowd and land on Nayna. Her best friend wasn't looking, more interested in making sure her dress was covering her butt, but that dark-eyed glance didn't skim away from Nayna as it had everyone else. Not until the busty raven-haired beauty in front of him put a hand on his forearm and literally tugged for attention.

Ísa smiled. "If he's not taken by that woman, and my instincts say he's not," she whispered to her friend, "then I think you've got a good shot. He was just staring at you."

Nayna was unimpressed. "Probably wondering what a nerd like me is doing in this den of freakily good-looking people." Grabbing Ísa's arm before Ísa could reply, she continued moving forward. "Come on, let's at least go see some skinny-dipping."

Sadly, when they reached the pool it was to realize that their hopes of wild debauchery were premature. The swimmers all appeared to be in swimsuits. "We'll be the skinny-dippers," Nayna announced. "After the lights are off and everyone's gone home."

Ísa's shoulders shook. "Deal."

Her own smile wide, Nayna turned to grab a drink

from the tray of a passing waiter, her sleek black hair shining with reddish glints under the outdoor lights. "You want one?" At Ísa's nod, she passed across the first flute and was reaching for a second one when her hand collided with a big male one. "Oh, I'm so sorr—"

Ísa watched her friend freeze as she came face-to-face with the man at whom she'd been staring earlier. The scruffy-jawed hunk smiled and said, "Here." He handed over a flute of champagne. "I'm Raj."

When Nayna shot Ísa a frantic look, Ísa gave her "wild devil women" messages with her eyes before deliberately melting back into the crowd. She didn't go far, wanting to be there if Nayna needed her. It wasn't as if she had anything else to do—unlike Nayna, she wasn't interested in breaking the rules with a single man at the party.

None of them had the right blue eyes. Or the right sinful smile.

She was going backward as she moved away from Nayna and the scrumptious Raj, so it was hardly surprising that she bumped into someone. Something cold and wet splashed against her bare upper shoulder.

Shivering, she turned to apologize since it had been her fault. "I'm sorry, I wasn—"

Blue, blue eyes looked into her own.

SAILOR HAD ONLY TURNED UP to this party because he'd promised Raj the company. His friend wasn't a big party person—like Sailor, Raj was more interested in putting his spare time into his business than in frittering it away with random strangers. However, the couple hosting this party were clients who'd turned into good friends, and they'd really wanted Raj to attend.

Sailor had come along so that Raj wouldn't have to talk to too many idiots—his friend had less patience with said idiots than Sailor—but Raj had been swarmed by women the instant Sailor stepped away to grab a beer from the bar on the other side of the room. Sailor himself hadn't escaped unscathed. Apparently, word had gotten around that Raj was in construction and Sailor a landscape gardener.

All these filthy-rich women apparently found that a turn-on.

Sailor barely stopped himself from growling at them like the feral beast they considered him. He wasn't about to become some woman's rough-sex fantasy, especially not when his own fantasies were going sadly unfulfilled. He'd have a few things to say to his cute redhead when he saw her again. She'd done some voodoo on him—he was comparing every woman he met to her. And all the other women were coming up short.

Their hair wasn't bright enough.

Their curves weren't dangerous enough.

Their lips not kissable.

It took a little fancy footwork, but he finally managed to disengage himself from the heiress who was trying to put the moves on him by complimenting him on his "delicious" biceps—why did that make him feel like a piece of meat when, if his redhead had said the same, he'd be strutting around like a peacock?

Probably because there'd been no calculation in those gray-green eyes when she'd pounced on him. Just want. Open, naked, unsophisticated want. His cock threatened to harden under the memories as he began to make his way back through the crowd. He'd just turned slightly to check if a red-haired woman he'd spotted out of the corner of his eye was *his* redhead when someone ran smack-bang into the front of his body.

It was instinct to catch her around the waist so she wouldn't fall.

His first thought was that she had a gorgeous ass, his second that her hair was exactly the same color as his redhead's. And his third, that maybe, just maybe, he'd found a woman who might banish his redhead's voodoo spell.

"I'm sorry," she was saying as she turned, "I wasn—"

Sailor's breath rushed out of him. He saw her eyes flare, read the tension in her body, and tightened his hold around her waist just in case she was thinking about running away again. Heart thundering at having captured his elusive prey, he leaned down to murmur in her ear, "I got beer on your shoulder. Let me clean that up."

He didn't give her a chance to respond before he leaned down to lick up the drops of beer that had hit her shoulder and collarbone, her breasts pushing into his chest and the soft puffs of her breath hitting his neck. He knew he shouldn't be doing this, but his redhead wasn't trying to pull away. Her breath had gone fast and shallow while her skin was soft and creamy under his mouth.

When he raised his head, he saw that her pupils were dilated, much as they'd been after their kiss. "My name," he said, "is Sailor. And I brought my truck."

Her throat moved as she swallowed... and one of her hands, it came to rest on his chest. After downing the champagne in her flute in one shot, she said, "I can't leave my friend." She looked back over her shoulder even as Sailor's brain scrambled to unravel the meaning of her words.

Then he got it, and every cell in his body roared to readiness.

She was going to come with him.

Forcing his thoughts into some sort of order, his body wrenching at the reins, he followed her gaze. "The woman in the dress that looks like it's made of bandages?" It was hot, but nothing compared to his redhead's painted-on gift of a dress.

Or to her come-to-bed tumble of hair and soft, lush lips.

When she nodded, he said, "Your friend will be fine. Raj is probably the safest man in this room."

Her eyes focused once more on Sailor. "Not you?"

"Oh, when it concerns you, spitfire," Sailor murmured, "I'm about as safe as a volcano." After putting her empty flute and his mostly full beer on the tray of a waiter heading back to the kitchen, he used his free hand to caress the luscious cream of her skin, stroking his way over her shoulder and down her arm. "Tell me your name."

A sudden, determined glint in her eye. "I don't want to have a name tonight."

Fire sizzled in his veins. "Are you looking to be bad tonight?" He'd get her name out of her, but he was more than willing to play a sexy game with her in the meantime.

When she nodded, he crushed her tighter to his body so she couldn't mistake just how much he wanted her. "Any particular kind of bad?" He'd take anything that involved him devouring her.

"I was considering skinny-dipping."

The ravenous thing inside him baring its teeth, Sailor released her only to link the fingers of his left hand with her right. "I think the pool is a little public don't you?" No way in hell was he sharing her centerfold-ready body with anyone else; she was *his* redhead, and Sailor decided he had a distinctly selfish streak. "This property has access to a private beach."

Their hosts hadn't announced that, no doubt because they didn't want beer bottles and champagne flutes ending up on the pristine sand, but Raj knew because he'd worked on building this property. He'd given Sailor a short outdoor tour before they'd entered the party. "I dare you."

She held his gaze, sparks in her expression. "I have to tell my friend. For all I know, you're a serial killer in your spare time."

Calmer now because she wasn't going to run away— not that she'd get far before he caught her, Sailor released her fingers. "Do you want to take a photo to send her?" he asked, resisting the temptation to bite down on her lower lip as he stroked his hand up under the temptingly high hem of her dress. "Just in case I do away with you?"

"Hmm, good idea. It's always the ones who don't look like serial killers." With that pert comment, she reached into her small and glittery black purse and took out a phone.

The message was on its way seconds later, a reply received not long afterward.

"Done?" When she nodded and put away her phone, he used this thumb to stroke her inner wrist and got a little shiver in response.

His body reacted as if primed. "You want to hang out at this party any longer, or are we going skinny-dipping?"

10

PUBLIC NAKEDNESS WITH A CERTAIN GARDENER (BLAME THE MOONLIGHT)

Í SA WONDERED WHAT THE HELL she was doing.

Being a devil woman, she reminded herself. Having fun for a change. Not being a grandma at twenty-eight years of age.

Still, she couldn't stop second-guessing herself as Sailor led her out of the house through a side entrance that opened out into a small, manicured garden. "I'll have to take off my heels," she whispered when she saw the pebbled path snaking through the garden.

"Want a piggyback ride?" A playful grin. "I promise not to molest your thighs."

Goose bumps broke out over Ísa's skin, her nipples tight. Reckless as she was feeling tonight, she might just have taken him up on his offer if she hadn't been worried her damn dress would split in two. "Maybe when we're naked," she said instead, Devil Ísa in full flower.

Groaning, he doubled over as if she'd punched him.

Her lips twitching despite the melting sexual heat liquefying her bones, she leaned down to slip off her heels.

The man named Sailor waited, his hand firm around hers, until she was done. Taking the heels from her, he carried them in his other hand as Ísa padded beside him on the grass that lay on this side of the pebbled path. The path ended at a weathered wooden gate, which, when opened, put them at the top of a narrow walkway that led down onto a beach Ísa couldn't yet see but could hear.

Her heart crashed in time with the waves as they made their way down to the beach while the mansion behind them pulsed with light and music. But she didn't turn and run away, she didn't stop and talk herself out of it, she didn't attempt to be a sensible adult. She followed a gorgeous, blue-eyed man down a dirt pathway to an effectively private beach.

The sand that had been tracked onto the path was gritty under her feet, the air coming off the sea cool but not cold.

"The water's going to be icy, isn't it?" she whispered to his broad back.

"Don't worry, spitfire. I'll keep you warm," was the deep-voiced response. "Stop here." Jumping down to the beach, he reached up to grab her by the waist, swinging her down as if she were a featherweight.

Something fluffy and mushy came to life inside Ísa. "Here?"

Shaking his head, he said, "Raj told me there's like a little cove area—not a proper cove, but caused by— There."

Ísa saw it at once. A huge tree had fallen into the water at some point and smashed up against some rocks where it appeared to be stuck. Between the jutting rocks on either side and the fallen trunk was a naturally created pool. The water within it was pretty calm, and it looked as if they could get to it by clambering over some rocks that didn't appear too sharp or slippery.

Of course, she'd be walking over those rocks naked.

Ísa looked up at the moon. Imagined it shining on the stark white of her body. Gulped. "Will you close your eyes while I go in the water?" Even Devil Ísa wasn't up for blinding him with her glow-in-the-dark form.

A glance back. "What're you going to bribe me with?"

Ísa scowled. "Not pushing you into the water right now." It was a toothless threat given his muscles and her lack of them.

Rubbing his jaw, he said, "Three tongue kisses. That's my price, and I'm not budging."

Ísa wanted to pounce on him all over again. "Two," she countered.

"Nuh-uh. Three. Or I'm keeping both eyes wide open." Leaning in, he pressed his nose to hers. "I really want to keep my eyes wide open."

And Ísa really wanted to kiss him and run her hands all over that sculpted chest. "Three," she whispered.

A wild grin. "Damn. I knew I should have asked for five."

Laughing because he made her want to do things like that, made her feel young and carefree rather than a woman who was old before her time, she leaned in and kissed him soft and sweet. "No tongue till you keep your promise."

"You're a tough negotiator, spitfire." Tugging her forward, he led her to a higher part of the beach. "We should be able to leave our stuff here."

It was an area on the sand made distinctive by a particular gathering of rocks. It'd be easy to find in the dark afterward... though the closer she got to skinny-dipping, the more it didn't feel dark at all. That moon was freaking big. And Sailor was already putting her heels on the sand and tugging off his T-shirt.

Dropping it on the sand, he reached down to pull off his shoes.

When he saw that she wasn't moving, he stopped. "You change your mind?"

He looked like she'd just told him she was taking away his puppy. So adorably disappointed that Ísa wanted to jump on him and kiss him stupid for making her feel more wanted than she'd ever before felt in her entire life. "No," she said, and put her purse on his T-shirt. "Just nervous. And I don't have much to take off."

"You're really mean," he said, his tone solemn. "Putting thoughts like that into my poor male brain." Undoing his belt after putting his socks into his shoes and setting them aside, he pulled off his jeans and threw them onto the growing pile of clothes.

Black boxer briefs didn't really hide much—especially not the hard ridge of his sizable erection.

Breath catching, Ísa had to force herself to turn away and not stare. "I won't look," she promised.

He laughed. "I don't mind. I like my sexy redhead looking at me."

Sexy redhead.

Ísa's stomach clenched. Oh, she liked being thought of that way. As a sexy redhead. The kind of woman who might be a femme fatale if it struck her fancy. The kind of woman who was about to go skinny-dipping with a relative stranger with demon-blue eyes.

Glancing quickly over her shoulder because she had no self-control, she saw that he was facing the water... and

that he'd stripped off his briefs while she hadn't been looking. God. She was about to go skinny-dipping with a man
straight out of a female wet dream. Complete with that
incredible tattoo around his left thigh and another one
high up on his right shoulder.

"Hurry up, spitfire, or I'll come help you."

Biting down hard on her lower lip because she wanted
nothing more, Ísa quickly unzipped her dress before she
could lose her nerve. It took a ridiculously short time to
wriggle out of it. That done, she almost tore off her
panties. "Okay, let's go," she said to Sailor after shifting so
that she was directly behind him.

Reaching back, he threatened to squeeze her butt. "No
hands," she said with a laugh, pushing those playful
hands away... but not too hard. Excitement skittered
across her skin. "Go, before I lose my nerve."

He laughed as if that was the funniest thing ever. "Spitfire, yesterday you accosted an innocent stranger in a
parking lot, and tonight you've decided to go skinny-
dipping with a party full of people only minutes away.
You have nerves of steel."

A sexy redhead with nerves of steel.

She was starting to really, really like Sailor. Not just his
body. Him.

But he was moving now, and she did everything in her
power to keep up. No way did she want to get left behind
buck naked while he was safely covered by the
night-dark water.

"Be careful on the rocks." Sailor reached back a hand.
"Here, grab my hand. I won't look."

Trusting him because he'd kept his word so far, Ísa
took his hand and he got her safely to the point where they

could slip into the water. He went first and swam a little way in the other direction.

Ísa dipped in a toe. "It's freezing!" she whispered loudly.

Obviously untroubled by the temperature, Sailor ran his hands through his hair. "My self-control is coming to an end. I'm about to turn around."

Gritting her teeth, Ísa sat down on the rock... then slipped in all at once. "Oh God! My insides are freezing!"

He laughed that big warm laugh that made her want to smile and swam back to her. She didn't resist when he pulled her against his body. He was hot and beautiful and it was dark and cold and they were in the sea.

Naked.

Something steely hot poked her stomach. "Is that your phone?" she asked, pressing closer instead of jerking away. "I hope it's in a waterproof case."

"Ha-ha, very funny." Sweeping his hands down her back, he cupped her backside as if that was a perfectly normal thing to do. His palms were callused, his skin rough. And the sound he made deep in his chest was one of raw male pleasure.

Ísa ignited just as she had at the school.

And then he kissed her.

There was tongue. Lots and lots of it. Wrapping her arms and legs around him, Ísa let the sea and Sailor hold her afloat as they kissed under a moonlit sky, the world cocooning them in darkness. His arms were so strong, his body so powerful that she felt petite for the first time in her life.

"I love your lips," she murmured.

He wove his hand into her hair in answer, the bottom

ends wet because she'd forgotten to find a way to put it up. "You have one hell of a mouth yourself, spitfire."

More kissing, more stroking, more of his body rubbing against hers.

Her bones were all but molten lava when she heard a shriek.

Startled into breaking the kiss, she looked toward the path heading down from the house. Two frozen seconds later, a woman came flying down. A man followed. Both tore off their clothes to dive into the waves.

Three more people followed, all ending up in the water.

"Damn." Sailor sounded like he was grinding his teeth. "Our spot's probably going to get invaded as soon as one of them figures out it's here."

Ísa held on tight to him. "I'm not up for a group skinny-dipping session." Being cuddled up to Sailor was a different thing to being cuddled up with strangers.

A soft kiss to her neck. "Follow me. They're too involved in their playing to notice us."

Ísa watched unashamedly as he hauled himself up, his biceps flexing with strength. Water sluiced off his flanks once he was on the rock, the thigh with the tattoo closest to her. "Here, spitfire."

Blushing like anything, Ísa nonetheless had no intention of staying in the water by herself. But when she crouched next to him after he hauled her up, she saw he'd kept his eyes closed. Her heart doing silly somersaults inside her chest, she leaned in and kissed him, then turned his face in the direction of the beach. "Let's go."

He led her quickly to the sand, their movements apparently going undetected by the partygoers playing in the water. Only once they got to the beach did Ísa realize she hadn't thought about how she'd be soaking wet after a skinny-dip.

"Here." Sailor threw his T-shirt over his shoulder. "Towel."

Yeah, he was pretty wonderful. And she wanted to see him again, find out if the fragile, hopeful thing she could feel growing between them had any chance in the light of day. Would he say yes if she asked him to continue the night? If she asked him out on a proper date?

Drying herself with efficient moves while nerves knotted her up all over again, she pulled on her panties and the dress—but the zipper got stuck. "Sailor. Help."

"I like my name on your lips, my red-haired woman of mystery." He kissed the curve of her waist as he hunkered down to tug the zipper free of the little piece of fabric on which it had caught. "I want to bite your skin. It marks so pretty."

"I might let you," Ísa said, her toes digging into the sand. "But we need to go on a date first." She was starting to feel things for him, dangerous things that had nothing to do with the primal attraction between them. "Want to go get late-night ice cream?" She didn't want this magical, moonlit night to end.

"I've got a better idea—how about a cookie bar?" Blue eyes seared into her as he rose to his feet after finishing the zipping up. "You can tell me your name while I ply you with chocolate chip cookies."

"Yes," she whispered, undone by the romance of it all.

"Now?"

"I have to drive home with my friend." No way would she abandon Nayna in an unfamiliar part of town. "Give me your number. I'll call you once I'm home and we can figure things out."

Cupping her face in his hands after inputting his number into her phone, he kissed her breathless. "I'll be waiting."

After arriving at the top of the walkway, Ísa texted Nayna. *Where are you?*

In the car, hiding.

Eyes flying up into her hairline, Ísa turned to a bare-chested Sailor—he'd thrown his dirty T-shirt over one shoulder with the ease of a man who had no problem being half-naked.

"I'm leaving now." Ísa's palms tingled with the urge to touch. "I'll call you in about thirty minutes. Maybe a bit longer." She had to find out what had gone wrong, why Nayna was hiding.

Another kiss, this one as sensual as the bribes he'd demanded. "Cookies with my sexy redhead." The masculine scent of him wrapped around her, his kiss flavored with the salt of the sea. "I can't wait."

Bubbles of light in Ísa's bloodstream, happiness a giddy dancer in her heart.

As she turned to run quickly to the car along the dark-ened edge of the property, her heels in one hand, her clutch in the other, Sailor shoved his feet into his shoes, which he'd carried up. "Hey!" he called out. "Wait! You shouldn't be alone in the dark!"

Ísa turned... and the present collided with the past.

Hey! Wait! You shouldn't be alone in the dark!

No. No.

Ísa stared at him. At those blue, blue eyes. At that black hair. It had been shaved that night, all the way down into a buzz cut. His body had been thinner and less developed, and he'd had one hell of a black eye. But it was him. That voice. That face. No wonder she'd kept thinking she knew him. She did.

From the most humiliating night of her life.

The night she'd spent seven years trying to erase from her memory banks.

Her stomach lurched.

11

NEVER TRUST A MAN WHO OFFERS YOU COOKIES

ALL BUT THROWING HERSELF INTO the passenger seat of the car, Ísa said, "Drive!"

Nayna quickly slid up from her slumped-down position in the driver's seat and, without a question, started the engine.

Sailor was standing on the grass across which Ísa had just run, watching the entire process with a frown she could see from here. What if he decided to come over? Ísa's heart pounded as Nayna pulled out and zoomed them down the drive. Her friend had turned the vehicle around at some point during her hiding and now they just had to go straight.

Until they were outside the gate and on the road.

"Oh thank God," they both said in unison.

Ísa looked at Nayna.

Nayna looked at her before returning her attention to the road. "You first."

"No, you," Ísa replied, needing time to unscramble the thoughts in her head. "Why were you hiding?" Worry and anger had her spine going steely. "Did that Raj guy do something?"

Nayna huffed out a breath, another. Hands tight on the steering wheel, she said, "It was fine at first. We were talking, flirting. Then... um..."

"I can see your smudged lipstick." She decided not to mention the marks on her friend's neck. Nibble marks.

The kind of marks Ísa might've had if the other skinny-dippers hadn't interrupted her and Sailor.

Nayna groaned. "I'm going to have to come up to your apartment to fix it before I head home. My dad will wait up until I get in."

"You need to move out."

"I will, when I get married." Nayna's voice was glum.

"You don't sound happy about it."

"Why do you keep going to board meetings?"

"Low blow," Ísa muttered, scowling at the best friend who knew her far too well. "So you and Raj snuck out and kissed?" That, at least, was an encouraging sign.

"We made out like hormone crazed teenagers," Nayna admitted, her skin flushing. "In a shadowy corner of the garden. He had his hands on parts of me that no one else has ever touched."

This was sounding *extremely* promising. But Nayna's expression was less than ecstatic. "What went wrong?" Ísa asked, worried. "Did he get rough? Wanted to go further than you were ready for?"

"No, no. Nothing like that." Nayna swallowed hard. "He started *talking*."

"What?"

"I'm going to have an arranged marriage, Ísa. I've agreed to that with my family. My father's set up meetings with prospective grooms." She pulled over to park on a quiet part of the street, the ocean crashing to shore on their right and large old trees arching their gnarled branches over the car from the left. "I have a voice, but I only get to choose from the men they've already vetted."

Despite her difficulty in accepting Nayna's decision, Ísa knew why her friend had made it, knew that Nayna was trying to mend her family's broken heart by shattering her own. Hurting for her closest friend, she said, "Raj talking changed that?"

"I just wanted to have this one crazy night, to be the woman I dream about being when I'm lying awake at midnight, a woman who doesn't care anything about the world and does exactly as she wants," Nayna said softly. "Raj fit the fantasy. Hard-bodied hot guy who wanted to do dirty things to me. Then he began talking, and he was saying things that made him sound smart."

Ísa just listened.

"I didn't want to know him." Nayna was almost crying. "I didn't want to find out that he's not just a good-looking hunk. I didn't want to know that he likes rock-climbing and that he was thinking about going to an exhibition on Egyptian art. He invited me." Her voice shook. "And I..."

"What, Nayna?" Ísa reached out to close her hand over her friend's. "What happened?"

"I told him to be quiet. That I wanted his body and nothing else."

Ísa's mouth fell open. "You said that?" It came out a squeak. "Really?"

Nayna threw her hands over her face as she nodded. "I had my hands on his naked chest at the time. His hand was... Let's just say he didn't take it well," she whispered through her fingers. "He turned to ice so fast it was like I was in Antarctica."

Finally dropping her hands, she banged her head against the back of the driver's seat. "When he turned around to swear at the night, I slipped off my shoes and ran away."

"Did he come after you?"

"I don't know." Biting down on her lower lip, Nayna folded her arms across her middle, as if hugging in the tearing confusion of her emotions. "The music was pretty loud by then, even out in the garden, so he probably didn't even know I was gone until he turned back around."

Ísa blew out a long breath. "Do you want to go back?" she asked, even though that was the last thing she wanted. For Nayna, she'd face even that nightmare. "Try to explain?"

"How can I possibly explain being that much of a bitch?" Her voice trembled. "Hi, Raj, I just wanted to use your body, then forget all about you, because sometime in the next twelve months, I'm planning to marry a man I don't love and probably won't even really desire."

She shook her head so hard that it sent the silky strands of her hair flying to stick to her cheeks. "Somehow I don't think that would go over well." A shuddering exhale. "Please tell me you had a better time." Pleading eyes. "I need at least one of us to have had a successful night of debauchery."

"Technically," Ísa said, "you did get in the debauchery before it all turned to custard. Was his chest nice?"

Nayna laughed wetly. "Oh my *God*, Ísa. I didn't know it could be so much fun to just..." She wiggled her fingers as if digging them into a man's pecs. "And the way he smelled... I wanted to bury my nose in his throat while I rubbed myself all over him."

Ísa nodded. "I did rub myself all over Sailor. Naked."

Nayna actually eeped before pausing to look carefully at Ísa's face. "That's not a happy-sexy-times face," she said, her tone morose. "Was he an ass?"

Shaking her head, Ísa confessed the truth. "He was wonderful. I knew he was a mistake, but I couldn't help myself from starting to fall." It was her turn to become agitated, her hands flying to thrust through her hair without her conscious volition.

"So what happened?" Nayna frowned. "I saw him with you before you two left the party. He was eating you up with his eyes."

"He was there that night... with the Slimeball." Ísa felt her stomach lurch as the horrible memory roared to the forefront of her mind all over again.

Nayna's eyes widened. "One of Cody's friends?"

"I guess so," Ísa muttered, hands fisting. "It was Cody's party after all." Nayna hadn't been able to come that night, her parents far stricter than Ísa's had ever been; often, as a teen, Ísa had wished for parents who actually cared about her whereabouts.

"Are you bothered because he saw what happened that night?"

"My ritual humiliation?" Face hot, Ísa told herself it was over, in the past. "No, why would I be bothered that a man I want to be naked with saw someone call me a tub of lard?" Her skin felt like fire.

"Your gardener *clearly* doesn't share that opinion from the way he looks at you." Nayna poked her in the shoulder. "Why are you acting crazy?"

"I'm not."

"Yes, you are." Her friend pinned her to the spot with her eyes. "Yes, it sucks that he had bad taste in friends at college, but remember that one day in high school when you thought Suzanne might be a nice person? We all make mistakes."

"I was new!" Ísa cried. "I had no idea she was hiding horns and a tail under her blinding smile and shiny hair."

"Whatever." Nayna waved off that moment of shame. "Back to your hot gardener. What's the deal? Why are you so discombobulated?"

Flushing, Ísa swallowed hard... and admitted the truth. Because yes, she *was* acting crazy and it wasn't only because Sailor had witnessed the most horrible moment in her life—though that didn't help. "I like him *so* much, Nayna. And if he was friends with Cody..." Her eyes grew hot. "You *know* the kind of guys Cody called friends." Ísa had never been comfortable with his crowd, and they'd been total assholes to her around campus after Cody dumped her.

"Did your gardener—"

Ísa shook her head. "I never saw him again after that party, but... if those were the people he hung out with back then, how can I trust my instincts about him now? How can I trust him not to turn on me? For all I know, he *still* hangs out with Cody and Suzanne."

Nayna released a shaky breath. "Okay, yeah, that I get. But you've had a chance to see this guy a couple of times now. Does he seem anything like the Slimeball?"

"That's just the thing. Cody showed no slimeball characteristics when we began dating." Ísa had believed the words he spoke, believed *in* him. "It makes me sick to think I might be repeating history. I just can't, Nayna." Not even for a blue-eyed man who asked her out on cookie dates and took her skinny-dipping.

Later that night, she opened her laptop and began to skim through the photos on Cody's social media profile.

His privacy settings were ridiculous—she could see pretty much all the images he'd posted. She ignored all the images of Suzanne, her search focused on only one person.

And then she found it: Sailor's face.

It was in a photo of a bunch of guys wearing rugby gear so muddy it was hard to tell what their uniform colors might be. Sailor had been snapped talking to an equally muddy Cody.

Fingers shaking, Ísa sat back and just stared. She'd hoped she was wrong and Nayna was right, that Sailor's friendship with Cody had been a college thing that had fizzled out when he figured out his friend was a monumental ass. But this shot was from the last rugby season.

Her hot gardener was still friends with the Slimeball.

SAILOR HAD A TERRIBLE NIGHT'S sleep. He'd been home from the party before eleven—and he hadn't even had to ditch Raj. His friend had been in a hell of a mood, with no desire whatsoever to interact with any other humans.

The other man wasn't a big talker, but Sailor figured it had something to do with the pretty woman in the bandage dress. The depth of Raj's reaction might've intrigued him on another day since his friend wasn't known for his temper, but last night Sailor had been distracted by the promise of seeing Ísa again, probably within the hour.

He hadn't worried too much about how she'd literally run across the grass and away from him, figuring her rush had something to do with the message she'd received from her friend. Some female emergency. After all, he hadn't done anything dastardly in the seconds before she'd run—

he'd literally just asked her to wait so he could walk her to the car.

Like a gentleman. And so he could sneak a final, scorching kiss.

After dropping Raj off at his place, anticipation a knot in Sailor's gut, he'd waited. And waited. And waited. And finally realized that there wasn't going to be any cookie-bar date. He'd been stood up.

The redhead had gotten away from him a third time.

And he still didn't know her name.

Aggravated, he'd gone online and ordered a pair of fur-lined handcuffs. The next time he saw his curvy little conwoman, he was going to lock her to some immovable object—namely himself—until he figured out why she kept leaving him in her dust.

Unsurprisingly, he'd dreamed of the cute, lying redhead all night long, woken up with a cock so hard it was painful. He wondered if his perfidious redhead realized he hadn't finished his job at the school. One of these days he was going to run into her again. And when he did, he was going to bring out those handcuffs. Then, when she was stuck and unable to run, he'd tell her what he thought of cute redheads who promised a man a night of sweet heaven and delivered a night of frustrated aggravation.

Snarling at the memory of how soft she'd been under his hands, how lusciously responsive, he tried to convince himself it was a good thing she'd stood him up. Sailor had a plan for his life, and a cute, sexy redhead didn't figure into it, not when his dreams depended on obsessive focus on a single overriding goal.

Neither his brain nor his body were convinced by the argument.

Rising in a black mood, he showered, then got himself

ready for work. Just because it was Sunday didn't mean he didn't have things to do—he wanted to put in a few hours on a small project he was fitting between bigger ones. And today was a good day for it; he had no other commitments —definitely no kissable redhead in his bed as he'd hoped for last night—and the weather was holding beautifully.

Once at the site, he put his back into it, worked like a demon, and was done by seven that night—an entire weekend ahead of schedule. Gabriel had invited him over for dinner with a couple of other rugby buddies, but Sailor told his brother he couldn't make it.

He needed time to brood.

Which he did until he fell exhausted into bed.

Waking the next morning with his mood not appreciably better, he showered and shaved with care before dressing in the single business suit he owned. He'd bought it a couple of years back, taking Gabe's advice and getting one good suit rather than three cheap ones; it was his go-to outfit for meeting with his loan manager at the bank. And today, for what might be his first major corporate client.

He paired the dark gray suit with a blue shirt that "made the most of his eyes," according to his mom, who'd given him the shirt on his last birthday. He made sure his hair was neatly combed and his dress shoes polished. For a second, as he looked in the mirror, he could almost touch it, the goal that drove him, the need to prove himself a gnawing on his bones that wouldn't stop until he'd done it.

Until he'd shown the world that he wasn't anything like the man whose face he bore.

"Keep going, Sailor," he told his reflection. "No excuses. No distractions."

Especially not a redhead who'd already haunted him for seven years.

Grabbing some coffee with a scowl, he thought about the handcuffs as he ate four pieces of toast before heading out for his eight thirty meeting in the city. Most days, he'd already have done at least an hour's work by now, but he hadn't wanted to risk being late to this meeting—or being anything but sharply dressed. He'd done his research, knew that the CEO he intended to approach was always crisply dressed, the people she worked with the same.

That appearance counted for a lot was going to be part of Sailor's pitch.

Speaking of which, his beat-up gardening truck, the bed full of bags of soil, looked utterly out of place in among the glossy BMWs and Mercedes in the parking lot of the building in Auckland's central business district. He could—and would—do nothing about that. Sailor was a landscape gardener and proud to be one, and this company was looking for a man just like him.

They just didn't know it yet.

"Balls to the wall, man," he told himself, then picked up his large presentation folder and walked through the front door of the Crafty Corners HQ.

12

DECAPITATED TEDDY BEARS AND A SKEPTICAL DRAGON

SAILOR MIGHT'VE BEEN TAKEN ABACK by the sight of the two receptionists stitching together a fluffy brown teddy bear if he hadn't already read up on the company. As it was, he smiled and said, "I have a meeting with Jacqueline Rain in ten minutes."

"Mr. Bishop?" At Sailor's nod, the Polynesian receptionist—dressed in gray pants and a pale pink shirt, complete with cheerful Crafty Corners cufflinks—put down the bear's decapitated head and rose to his feet. "Please follow me. Jacqueline told us to bring you right up."

Surprised by the courtesy, though perhaps he shouldn't have been given Jacqueline Rain's reputation in the industry, Sailor did as the receptionist had asked. Behind him, the other receptionist—a tanned blonde in a sky-blue dress —began pushing stuffing into the unlucky bear's head with sharp, stabbing motions of her shiny red nails.

Crafting was clearly a far more bloodthirsty hobby than he'd ever imagined.

Two steps later, he came to the realization that Jacqueline was probably calling him up early so she could get rid of him before her day began in earnest. It had taken a lot of fast-talking on Sailor's part to convince her to see him in the first place—and that was after he'd talked his way past two gatekeepers to be put through to her.

Sailor had no intention of letting all his hard work go to waste.

The receptionist led him to the left and up a curving flight of stairs to the mezzanine level. "This way," he said with a smile as he took Sailor through to a smaller but just as colorful reception area where a brunette woman in a sleek black wheelchair sat working on what looked to be a jewelry box in the shape of a love heart.

Looking up, she smiled, and it was bright enough to compete with the sparkles on her craft project. "You must be Mr. Bishop." She wheeled herself out from behind the counter. "I'll take it from here, James. Thank you."

The receptionist stepped back. "See you later, Ginny. That jewelry box is coming along great."

Sailor had to fight not to burst out laughing; he wondered how many jewelry boxes and other craft items these poor people had to make during the course of a working week. And where did it all go?

"If you'll come with me, Mr. Bishop." Ginny's words were accompanied by a subtly appraising look from a set of deep brown eyes.

Sailor kept his expression strictly neutral. Not only was he obsessed with a curvy bit of trouble who'd played him for a fool, he needed his head fully in the game this morning. The meeting with Jacqueline Rain could turbocharge his entire business plan, and Sailor had no intention of fucking it up.

Shoulders squared and the heat of battle in his blood,

he followed Ginny to her boss's office. It involved going a quarter of the way across a huge open space dotted with seating arrangements around tables set up with crafting sets, and what looked to be casual meeting areas bordered by potted plants.

Reaching a set of glass doors smoked just enough to blur what lay beyond, Ginny flashed her employee card over the scanner. When the doors slid open on a quiet swoosh, it was to reveal a craftless corporate setup that looked like it might be the domain of an executive assistant.

No candy pink or lime green here—the carpet was an elegant gray and the walls a soothing off-white. The color came from the large expressionist painting on one wall that burst with pigment without being overwhelming. The only pieces of furniture were a large glass desk decorated with a live white orchid in excellent shape and the designer ergonomic chair behind it.

No one sat at the desk, but the computer was humming and a mug of coffee stood beside it, as if the assistant had stepped away for a moment to do another task. Annalisa Rhymes, that was her name. He'd spoken to her when he called for Jacqueline.

And now here he was: the moment of truth.

Balls to the wall.

Knocking on the partially open door beyond the executive assistant's desk, Ginny poked her head inside. "Ms. Rain, Mr. Bishop is here."

She must've gotten a nod from within because a second later, she pushed the door all the way open. "Please go in."

"Thank you." Entering—and very conscious of Ginny leaving the door open in a not-so-subtle sign that his time with Jacqueline was limited—Sailor found himself approaching a heavy oak desk behind which sat an impressive woman with hair of darkest auburn. He'd seen her photo, but in person she reminded him forcefully of his cute, lying redhead; it wasn't just the color of her hair but the structure of her face along with an indefinable sense of presence.

He'd half expected her to stay seated, a little power play, but Jacqueline Rain was classier than that. She rose and held out a slim but in no way fragile hand. "Mr. Bishop."

Extending his own hand while wrenching his mind off the pleasurable memories that couldn't be permitted to derail this chance, he said, "Thank you for agreeing to see me. I'm aware you're busy, so I'll keep this quick."

Jacqueline raised a perfectly curved eyebrow and, retaking her seat, waved him into the chair across from her, the sprawl of aged and very expensive wood between them. "I'm listening."

It looked as if his attempt to deflect her brush-off was working, but he knew he had to hold her interest. Jacqueline Rain hadn't survived this long in business by being a slow decision-maker. He had three minutes at most before she cut him off. He had to make those minutes count.

As he'd made the most of his time in the water with a certain naked redhead.

Opening his presentation folder with a firm mental slap directed at his misbehaving brain, Sailor nonetheless didn't immediately set out the visuals he'd created using crappy old software on an equally crappy laptop. It still worked, and if he got this job, he could afford an upgrade.

"I know Crafty Corners is launching a new business," he began. "Fresh, organic, fully handmade fast food, with a customizable menu."

It had seemed like a strange concept when he'd first spotted a report about it in the business pages, but the more he'd read up on it, the more he'd realized that it was a genius move once you factored in the demographics of the areas in which the fast-food restaurants were to be based.

"That's hardly a secret," Jacqueline said with a well-known coolness. "And, quite frankly, Mr. Bishop, I fail to see what it has to do with a landscaping company. Your initial pitch intrigued me enough to agree to a meeting, but on further reflection, I see no point in expanding our landscape budget on the project."

Sailor didn't back down or flinch.

"As I walked in here," he said, "I saw a number of your employees working on craft projects. Clearly that's designed to hammer home your Craft Is Family motto."

Jacqueline leaned back in the black leather of her executive chair. "Go on."

"But," he said, "look at the sites you've chosen for your initial three Fast Organic outlets." He laid out the images in front of her, images he'd printed off the web. "Here's the parking lot out front." He pointed it out on the first site, then tapped the same on the others.

Jacqueline's eyes cooled further. "I'm quite sure I can recognize a parking lot."

"So will your customers." Sailor had been raised by a strong woman, knew how to stand his ground. "But these particular customers are going to be paying ten dollars for a wheatgrass shot. And thirty dollars for a tofu burger on organic rye baked that morning."

He didn't let it throw him when Jacqueline picked up her phone and began to scan through it; he knew he was talking sense, and he also knew that if she wanted him gone, she'd have told him the meeting was over.

"There's a high chance at least a quarter will be driving eco-cars that require charging stations," he said. "These are people who will analyze the site's entire look to see if it fits with their worldview *and* if they want to be caught dining there or carrying a take-out bag from it. They also have the money to stay or go."

Putting aside the phone, Jacqueline leaned forward with her arms folded on her desk. "You have my attention now, Mr. Bishop."

Sailor didn't make the mistake of believing the deal was anywhere near done. "It's all about perception," he said. "With the Crafty Corners sites, the crafts themselves are the landscaping." Each store was fronted by a whole bunch of jumbo-sized craft items that drew the eye. "Fast Organic needs the same type of tailored approach. Everything must give the impression of health and green and a commitment to the earth."

He brought out a sketch. "Here's my first concept," he said. "Partially grassed-in parking spots, including two with charging stations, the entire area edged in living green walls. A water feature here, depending on the budget." He indicated the spot on the sketch. "A small external seating area so that customers downing your thirty-dollar tofu burgers will feel as if they've also bought access to a refreshing piece of paradise in the middle of the city."

"Show me more," Jacqueline said, and it was an order.

Giving her a quiet smile, Sailor leaned back in his chair. "Not until we come to an agreement," he said, putting a touch of steel in his own tone. "I'm not about to show you everything I've got without getting something in return."

Jacqueline Rain was a ruthless businesswoman whom Sailor admired but knew not to underestimate.

Piercing green eyes narrowed. "Or I could throw you out right now and pick up the phone to hire a much bigger company. I'm sure they'd come up with fantastic ideas based on the general concept."

Sailor shrugged. "True, but are you sure you want to go with a settled enterprise when you can hire me and spin it in the media as all part of Fast Organic's commitment to small businesses—like the mom-and-pop organic suppliers you intend to use? Also, a bigger company will probably charge you three times as much."

Another raised eyebrow. "While you're willing to do it for pennies?"

"Not so low." Sailor had his own financial realities, and he knew exactly how far he could push things. "But I *am* willing to do it for a lot less than an established company, because if I get this project, my work will be front and center at all the Fast Organic stores." The openings would unquestionably be covered widely in the business and foodie media. "That's worth taking a hit on the profit margin."

A smile curved Jacqueline's lips. "I like you," she said, tapping a manicured and polished finger on the oak. "Store one opens in two months. You get that up and running in time and do a good job of it, then we talk about the other two."

Sailor didn't grab at the offer. "Three stores or no deal," he said. "I'm going to be doing this for very little margin. I need at least three to make enough of a profit that I can pay my workers." He didn't *have* any workers aside from his brothers right now—and they worked for free—but Jacqueline didn't need to know that.

"I need to see a breakdown." Jacqueline's tone made it clear that was nonnegotiable.

Slipping out a piece of paper from his file, Sailor pushed it across.

Jacqueline scanned it, said, "You can really do it on this budget?"

"I can do an even better job if you give me a higher plant budget," he said honestly. "It depends how high-end you want to go. What I've quoted is nice but not expensive. You want a more exclusive feel, really hit your target market, you'll need a bigger budget." He ran through a few specifics to give her an idea.

Jacqueline made a couple of notations on his quote before handing it back to him.

He saw that though she'd extended his supply budget, she'd cut his profit margin in half. Shaking his head, he said, "Look, I need this job, but it's pointless if it's going to put me out of business." He held her gaze.

She held his gaze in turn, judging him, assessing him....

Her smile was sharp, unexpected... and it reminded him all over again of his runaway redhead. Taking back the quote sheet while he struggled to corral his thoughts, she returned his original profit margin. "All right," she said, "three stores."

Sailor didn't allow himself to celebrate. "We should sign a contract."

Jacqueline laughed even as she pressed the intercom on her desk. "I really do like you," she said, before instructing Annalisa to organize a contract from a contractor template they had on file. "Enter these changes. Also, I need finance up here in ten."

While she went over the specifics—which he planned to inspect with a fine-tooth comb—Sailor scanned the office to get a better bead on the woman with whom he was dealing.

The wall to her back and left held the most personal items.

Framed awards that the business had won, a few photos with notable people, including the current prime minister. However, what caught his eye and sent his heart thumping was a small grouping of images set toward the center. In particular, the image of a woman with skin of moonlight and hair of a red so vibrant, he knew only one woman who possessed it.

"Your family?" he said to Jacqueline when she finished talking to her assistant. He took care to keep his voice even, though the light of battle was sparking in his gut.

Following his gaze, Jacqueline nodded. "Yes. Now, let's hammer out certain details."

By the time Sailor left the office forty-five minutes later, he had a signed contract in hand and Jacqueline had already ordered her finance department to pay his invoices as they came in. Though, of course Fast Organic would be keeping a close eye on his spending.

"We'll be assigning you a point person," Jacqueline had told him. "They'll have the authority to make future calls on the finance front." A pause. "You're a new contractor for us, so you'll be under extra scrutiny."

"Understood."

Flushed with success as he left Jacqueline's office, Sailor was already mentally rearranging his schedule to carve out time to begin the project today. But, underneath that, he was thinking about fur-lined handcuffs.

His lips curved, satisfaction unfurling in his gut.

His spitfire thought she'd kissed him, seduced him, then made a clean getaway, but now he knew how to track her down. Talking of which... He took out his phone and ran a simple search using the terms "Jacqueline Rain" and "daughter."

His redhead's face appeared beside her mother's at what looked like an evening function. The caption read: Jacqueline Rain with her eldest daughter Ísalind.

Ísalind.

His smile deepened. Putting away his phone as he headed for the stairs, he considered his next move when it came to a certain runaway redhead. Of course, she was also the boss's daughter, and he really shouldn't be thinking about messing with her.

That was when fate laughed.

13

SHARP KITTEN HEELS AND FUR-LINED HANDCUFFS

*I*SA COULDN'T BELIEVE WHAT HER mother had done.

So angry that she could burst, she barely managed to say hello to James and Lana. She knew them, of course; she knew everyone who worked for Crafty Corners, the business having one of the best retention rates in the industry. Because she did—and because they had nothing to do with Jacqueline's latest chess move—she made an effort to be polite even though she wanted to kick the desk.

Today was the icing on top of the hideous cake that had been her Saturday night. A night she'd run through her mind over and over again as she stared at Sailor's number. She'd almost pushed it a thousand times, almost called him just so she could yell at him for having awful taste in friends.

How was she supposed to let down her guard around a man who *liked* Cody?

A man who'd seen what Cody had done to her and still called him a friend.

That infuriated her the most.

But at this instant, it wasn't Sailor who was the focus of her temper.

"She's got someone with her." James physically got in her way, having clearly read her mood and figured out where she was headed.

He wasn't a big man, and Ísa was pretty sure she could take him, but she reminded herself that James wasn't responsible for this, that it was Jacqueline who deserved to be at the other end of Ísa's volcanic rage.

"Not one of us," James added with a mischievous cast to his expression. "Possible contractor, Ginny thinks. Gorgeous as hell, killer blue eyes."

Ísa hated gorgeous men right now. Especially ones with blue eyes.

Fisting her hand by her side, the cotton of her floral summer dress brushing against her knuckles, she said, "I'll go up and wait" through teeth it took her conscious effort not to grit. "It won't take me long to say what I have to say."

Running up the steps before James could find a way to delay her any further to give her temper a chance to cool—Ísa did *not* want a cool head right now—she was mentally eviscerating her mother when she took a step up and almost crashed into a big man in a dark gray suit, his shirt a vivid blue.

"I'm so sorry," she began… and then the hot, masculine scent of him punched into her system and her eyes met his.

Blue, so very blue. "Hello, little rabbit."

Her heart stuttered, her entire body motionless. So convinced was she that she was hallucinating that she reached out and poked him in the chest. "You're real," she said, her brain struggling to shift gears.

Eyes glinting dangerously, he grabbed hold of her wrist, the grip steely. "Just as real as I was when you were wrapped around me, all slippery wet and naked." He smelled like soap and aftershave today, but below that was a raw earthiness that was just *him*.

Her lips parted, her skin flushed, and—

An elevator dinged in the distance.

Ísa's brain came to a screeching halt, the gear set firmly on FURY. "What," she said in a tone as frigid as she could make it despite the erotic heat low in her belly, "are you doing here?" The only mercy was that this part of the staircase was hidden from view by the curve of the wall. Two steps in either direction and they'd be back in public view.

"Had a meeting with your mother," said the six-foot-plus symbol of Ísa's terrible instincts. "Landscaping contract." A tug on her wrist. "But we have something else to discuss, Ms. I'll Call You When I Get Home." He actually had the nerve to sound as if *she* was the one in the wrong.

Ísa gave in. She kicked him right in the shin with the pointy tip of her kitten-heeled shoe.

Wincing, he glared at her. "I bought handcuffs especially for you. Obviously I need to get leg cuffs too." He'd backed her up against the wall before she realized what he was doing.

Too furious to worry about someone coming up or down the stairs, she narrowed her eyes. "How's Cody?"

His expression turned to granite. "What Cody did that night," he said, proving he remembered the entire ugly incident, "was an asshole thing to do, but then that's who he is. Someone needs to teach him a lesson."

"Right"—Ísa barely resisted the urge to kick his other shin—"as if you two aren't creepy best buds."

"Spitfire, I was a sixteen-year-old kid who managed to get into a college party." He pressed his weight into her body, as if reading her violent thoughts on her face. "Cody was just some guy I knew from around."

Wait, what? Sixteen?

"How old are you?" she asked through a bone-dry throat.

A wicked grin. "Younger than you. You be my cougar, I'll be your boy toy."

She was going to strangle him, honest to God. Now he was playing with her, as if everything was hunky dory. "Are you seriously asking me to believe you two aren't buddies now? I saw a photo of you at a rugby game."

A blank look. "We play for different clubs. I was probably saying thanks for the game. Doesn't mean I can stand the guy. My parents brought me up to be a good sportsman."

Ísa wasn't ready to let go of her fury. "Right," she said in a tone that called him a liar. "That's why you didn't mention that night when we first met."

Thunderclouds across his face. "I didn't make the connection then," he said, his voice ominous. "And as for that…" He gripped his chin, rubbed in mock thoughtfulness. "I do believe I was *innocently* going about my work when a certain redhead decided to use me to scratch an itch. She didn't seem interested in introductions or talking."

He refused to let her break the demanding eye contact.

"You weren't innocently working," Ísa said desperately because he'd just smashed her defenses to pieces. "You were doing a striptease!"

Pressing his forehead to hers, Sailor ran the pad of his thumb over the sensitive skin of her inner wrist. "Are you saying I set you up by taking off my shirt? That you were rendered helpless by my manly physique? If so..." A slow smile. "I'll take it."

He smelled far too good, and she was losing the thread of why she'd been so furious with him. "You really don't stay in touch with Cody?" she found herself saying.

"He's not my kind." Open disgust in his words. "Can't avoid the guy totally though since he plays rugby in the same social league as me."

It was no surprise that this strong, physical man would play a game that involved bruising tackles and hard runs.

A strong, physical man who was twenty-freaking-three!

Ísa wasn't into robbing the cradle. Or following her father's example into multiple marriages with increasingly youthful lovers. "I have to go. If you could please get out of my way, I need to speak to Jacqueline before her next appointment arrives."

He didn't move so much as an inch, his body a heated wall of muscle that taunted her. "That's it? You just use me and discard me?"

"You weren't exactly complaining." Neither was he acting his age—no one five years younger than Ísa should be this self-assured.

"I was expecting flowers or maybe a goodbye kiss," was the unrepentant response.

Deciding he'd deserved that kick even if he wasn't guilty of being a slimeball by association, Ísa shoved at his chest. "I'll buy you pink carnations from the gas station. Now let me go, you rugby-playing lunkhead. I need to catch Jacqueline."

Chuckling, he finally lifted away, his fingers unclasping her wrist after one last, teasing brush. "You need better insults, spitfire. Don't worry, I have a whole catalog for you to study from."

"I won't be seeing you again," Ísa said firmly over Devil Ísa's loud protests. "I don't cradle-snatch."

"I haven't been a baby for a while." No playfulness this time, just that intense self-possession she'd already noted.

Her hand closed on the stair railing. "I have to go." She matched action to words.

"Hey," he called up in a quiet voice meant for her alone. "Don't forget my name. It's Sailor. Just in case you need to know it for the next time I take off my shirt and you feel the urge to accost me." A smile that told her they weren't done yet. "See you soon, beautiful."

Ísa had to pause at the very top of the stairs and consciously remember the reason she'd come to the office. Fury poured through her anew the instant she did. Holding on to that fury because she simply didn't have the emotional capacity to process Sailor right now, she stormed over to confront the Dragon.

It only made her angrier when she was brought to a premature halt by the security door beyond which lay the inner sanctum, the stupid keycard lost somewhere inside her satchel.

Where was the damn—

Fingers closing over the cool, hard plastic, she pulled it out and flashed it across the reader.

Ginny and Annalisa were talking at Annalisa's desk.

Taking one look at her, Annalisa said, "I can get you ten minutes." A glance at her fellow assistant. "Ginny? Doable for you?"

The other woman nodded. "Don't worry. I'll get the

next appointment a fancy coffee and keep him entertained by making him glue together a random crafty thing."

"Thanks, Ginny, Annalisa." Striding into her mother's office without knocking, Ísa closed the door behind herself.

Neither Ginny nor Annalisa would breathe a word of anything they overheard, but this was family business and the two assistants didn't need to get caught in the crossfire between a dragon and the daughter she expected to be her ruthless reflection.

Jacqueline looked up, a stunning woman dressed in a long-sleeved shirt of dark green that flowed like liquid over her body. While Ísa couldn't see her lower half, it was a good bet that she wore a fitted pencil skirt in black, high heels of the same shade on her feet.

"Ah, Ísa." A gleam in her eye. "I wondered when you'd come in, the vanquishing Valkyrie."

"I *knew* it!" Ísa could feel steam escaping from her ears. "You planned this!" It was the motivation behind Jacqueline's manipulative actions that Ísa couldn't figure out— because while Jacqueline was no maternal tigress, she'd also never been cruel. "How could you do this to Harlow?"

"You know why." Jacqueline tapped the gleaming gold and black of her Montblanc fountain pen on the edge of her desk as she leaned back in her executive chair. "I don't want to give the boy any false ideas."

"The *boy* is your stepson." He also happened to think Jacqueline was the most wonderful human being on the planet.

Otherwise-brilliant Harlow had a giant blind spot on the subject of Jacqueline Rain.

The situation was exacerbated by the fact Harlow's

biological parents had both remarried: for the third time when it came to his father, and for the second time when it came to his mother. Each had created a brand new family with their spouse, complete with adorable children under five years of age. Harlow had been left in the middle, forgotten and left to fend for himself when it came to the kind of emotional support a parent was meant to provide.

"Look," Jacqueline responded in a crisp tone, "Harlow is a highly intelligent young man, I agree. I also happen to like him more than I do many other people in this world, which is why I continue to stay in touch with him regardless of my divorce from his father. However, he doesn't have my or Stefán's killer instinct. You, on the other hand, have both."

A pleased smile on her face. "Your father and I might not have worked as a couple, but we did our best work in creating you. You'll build a bigger empire than either one of us."

Ísa threw up her hands. "I don't have the killer instinct! Of either variety!" She also had zero interest in building empires.

But this wasn't about her needs or wants.

Pressing her hands on the aged wood of the desk, she stared down at Jacqueline. "You know Harlow is determined to go into the business world—it's all he talks about when he talks of his future."

Ísa's teenaged stepbrother might've only officially been part of Jacqueline's family for two years, but those two years had had a huge impact on his psyche. "He also admires you beyond any other adult in his life." The force of Harlow's worship was a shining glow. "He wants to *be* you."

"Harlow's only seventeen." Putting down her pen,

Jacqueline rose to walk around and brace her hip against the side of her desk, causing Ísa to push off the desk and put several feet between them.

She didn't trust herself not to strangle her mother right now.

"And, quite frankly," Jacqueline continued, "I can't see it—the boy is great at making robots and writing code, but running a business requires an entirely different skill set."

"He can learn." Ísa waved the flat of her hand to cut off Jacqueline's reply.

Her mother's eyes narrowed... before a smile curved her lips. "You see? The killer instinct."

Ísa's hands itched to wrap themselves around Jacqueline's swanlike neck. "One thing you can't deny," she said instead of giving in to her homicidal instincts, "Harlow won the internship fair and square."

The summer internship at Crafty Corners was hotly contested among high school students—her stepbrother had submitted his application under a pseudonym and done a phone interview so as to avoid any accusations of favoritism. "*You* chose him as the winning candidate." Only to reverse her decision once she discovered his real identity.

The one bright spot in all this was that no notifications had been made. Jacqueline hadn't yet broken Harlow's hopeful heart.

"I see I'll have to talk to Ginny again," her mother responded a little too casually.

"Why?" Instincts spiking to code-red status, Ísa folded her arms. "You told her to trust me like she'd trust you."

Jacqueline's smile became that of a dragon, full of teeth. "Take on the vice president position and you can do whatever you want with the internship program. Until then, I make the calls, and I have no intention of granting Harlow the position."

Check and mate.

14

CRIMINAL ACTS... AND A WELL-DESERVED PUNCH TO A SMUG FACE

Í SA REALIZED SHE'D BEEN MASTERFULLY played.

This had been Jacqueline's plan all along. But if there was one thing Jacqueline Rain had done well as a parent, it was to raise a daughter who was no pushover. "Trying to mold me into a cutthroat businesswoman will just leave you with the migraine to end all migraines," she pointed out without budging from her spot. "I don't have the head or the desire for it."

"You have the head," Jacqueline countered. "I made sure of that. As for the desire, we both know teaching was your rebellion against my lack of maternal instincts."

Ísa rolled her eyes. "Hate to break it to you, Mother, but the world doesn't revolve around you."

"Whether it does or not," Jacqueline said easily, "you only have two options at this point. Take the VP position and appoint Harlow as the intern, or don't."

"You're truly stooping to blackmail using your own stepson?"

That dragonish smile returned. "It's not blackmail, my

dear. After all, I'll be paying you a rather large sum of money for your services."

Ísa was surprised to realize she could still be taken aback by Jacqueline's cold-blooded nature. "And you think I'm like you? You think I'd do this to a child of mine?" Ísa would love her child with fierce devotion—she'd have to be careful not to love too much, that was her problem.

Ísa always loved too deeply, too openly once she let someone into her heart.

"You're very much like me, Ísalind," Jacqueline said, her smile turning amused. "You might as well admit it. However, since you also inherited my stubbornness and won't admit anything that might give me a psychological advantage, I'm going to show you." She straightened. "I want you to see what you're capable of, what you're throwing away in your childish rebellion."

Ísa tried to think like a dragon—or like a man with demon-blue eyes and far too much confidence. "Aren't you worried I'll sabotage you from the inside?"

"What I've built, this company, it's a family legacy." Unperturbed, Jacqueline crossed the carpet to Ísa. "You'd never do anything to harm that."

Unfortunately, her mother was right. Ísa had too much family loyalty running through her blood to destroy the company out of spite. Especially not when it was Harlow's dream and might well one day help Catie achieve hers. "There are more senior people in the company."

"All of whom know this is a family operation—most of them helped train you through your teenage years. They're all aware the VP position has always been yours."

That, too, was unfortunately true. Ísa had been groomed to be her mother's successor since childhood.

"So, do we have a deal?" Jacqueline held out her hand. "I'll give the boy a shot. In return, you take on the VP's job and do it to the best of your ability."

"Only for the summer."

Jacqueline shook her head. "No."

"That's my offer, take it or leave it." Harlow would've proven himself by the end of that period, of that Ísa was certain—and what Catie needed, Jacqueline would never stint in providing. That was the thing with Jacqueline—she could, at times, have blood full of ice, but she'd also rewritten the rulebook for the entire company after Catie came out of the hospital.

Many corporations talked the talk, but very few put their money where their mouth was. Crafty Corners, in contrast, did not ever operate out of—or hold external events in—any building that wasn't fully accessible to all. That single change had wide-ranging implications, one of which was that employees weren't cut off from the internal promotion track by default because they couldn't physically make it to important briefings or networking opportunities.

Staff also had access to company vehicles modified for use by people with disabilities, with a number specifically adapted for particular individuals who weren't able to utilize the pool vehicles. It wasn't unusual to find brail text next to printed text in places like the elevators, and all staff, from front line to senior executives, were expected to learn and understand sign language.

That was only the tip of the iceberg.

Jacqueline had a standing order that issues of access were to be referred straight to her for immediate remediation.

All of that was public knowledge. But what only a

handful of people knew was that Jacqueline sponsored a program that helped children and teenagers get back on the educational or training track after they'd lost months, possibly years, in a fight for their very lives.

Maybe all that was why Ísa couldn't just cut the bond between them. Because, despite appearances to the contrary, there was a speck of humanity inside the Dragon —a deeply, *deeply* hidden speck. Now that same dragon's eyes glinted with unhidden pride, as if Ísa had made her day with her mutinous lack of cooperation.

"Fine. Your VP contract will be for the summer only."

It was obvious Jacqueline thought Ísa would be well entrenched in the corporate world by then, with no desire to leave. Which told Ísa exactly how well Jacqueline knew her. Because Ísa would rather take up chewing nails as a fun downtime hobby.

"I've already committed to teaching night classes at the school. I won't pull out of that. I gave my word."

"If you'll recall, I'm the one who taught you to keep your word." Still clearly in a good mood after her bout of familial blackmail, Jacqueline put her hands on her hips. "How many hours will that take out of your schedule?" When Ísa told her, she said, "Done. I'll have Annalisa bring in the contract."

Ísa was entirely unsurprised to discover the contract had already been drawn up. Jacqueline had been sure she'd win. She always won. Except when she didn't care about the outcome. Then she just pulled out of the fight. As Catie's father had discovered when he'd made noises about a custody battle.

Jacqueline had taken the opportunity to sign over full custody to Clive.

It was forty minutes later, after Ísa had read and signed

the contract, insisting on a number of changes along the way—all of which made Jacqueline beam like a proud lioness—that she couldn't stand it any longer.

"Who was the man I met as I came in?" she asked in a voice as casual as casual could be while her heart thumped and her thighs pressed tightly together.

"Noticed his blue eyes did you?" Jacqueline asked, her own gaze on the contract as she checked that Ísa had signed everywhere she was required to sign.

Obviously, the Dragon didn't trust her progeny with the killer instinct not to wriggle out of the agreement unless it was ironclad.

"You have good taste," Jacqueline continued. "Have fun, but don't let him distract you from the job. And for God's sake, don't start believing you're in love with a nice piece of ass like I did with Clive and make the mistake of marrying him. Sleep with him and get him out of your system."

"*Mother*." That was pushing it even for Jacqueline.

Not appearing the least abashed, her mother put down the contract at last. "Sailor Bishop's a new contractor—landscaping. Some excellent ideas, so if you do sleep with him, try not to dump him until after he's completed the job. I once made that mistake with another contractor—he kept breaking down in tears on the job and couldn't even give me a concise site report."

Ísa wondered if Nayna had ever had a conversation like this with her mother. "Maybe we should talk about my duties as VP," she said, the topic of Sailor Bishop fraught with far too much danger.

"I was getting to that. I want you to handle the Fast Organic project from here on out." Jacqueline began to bring up the files.

And Ísa decided there was a silver lining to being blackmailed into being a VP: given the workload, she'd have no time to surrender to the temptation to see Sailor Bishop again and finish what they'd started.

SAILOR COULDN'T STOP THINKING ABOUT his redhead... and that single flash of hurt he'd glimpsed in her expression before she went all mad Fury on him. What Cody had done, the cruelly and planned humiliation of it, had really, badly hurt her. Enough that the shadows lingered to this day.

He stabbed his shovel harder into the earth, his shoulder muscles tight. "Asshole."

Sailor truly didn't consider the other man a friend of any kind. The idea of being associated with a guy who'd done what Cody had was abhorrent to him. Sailor's mother and father would tan his hide if he *ever* disrespected a woman that way—hell, Sailor would tan his own useless hide.

But Cody, it appeared, had gotten away with it.

Sailor had never heard a word about anyone confronting the other man on the subject. He'd considered doing so himself, but he'd been on his own confused path back then, and getting arrested for assault had simply not been on the agenda. Not even for a beautiful redhead whose tears haunted him.

Only now she wasn't a mysterious redhead.

She was Ísa, his glorious, fiery spitfire with skin of moonlight and a heart that carried scars still from that night. Scars that had almost put a halt to their relationship before it began.

So, even though he had a hundred things on his plate,

he picked up his phone and managed to find someone who had Cody's number. The other man was understandably startled at hearing from Sailor but agreed amazingly quickly to meet up with him for a drink after work.

Sailor was waiting in dirt-streaked khaki shorts and a light brown Bishop Landscaping T-shirt, dirt-caked work boots on his feet, when Cody drove into the small parking lot behind the bar where they'd agreed to meet. The other man parked his shiny white Audi in the spot next to Sailor's battered truck, Cody's car the newest model on the market.

Sailor knew that because his brother Jake was a gearhead. Jake was mostly into grunty muscle cars, but he kept up with all kinds of car news and had a habit of sprinkling car facts into the conversation. He'd also left a couple of his magazines behind at Sailor's place the last time he'd hung out there.

So Sailor knew the car Cody was driving was worth in the vicinity of a hundred thousand.

He'd have been impressed if he didn't know the Audi was courtesy of Suzanne's parents' money. Sailor had no interest in Cody's life, but one of his teammates knew the family socially and had let things drop over the years. Apparently Cody *did* work—as a financial consultant, whatever that was—but it was in Suzanne's family's business. As far as Sailor was aware, the other man had never held a position totally independent of his girlfriend's family company.

Getting out of the vehicle, the suit-and-tie-wearing male with a modelesque jawline and impeccably cut hair of rich brown shot him a smile. "Hey, Sailor. It was great to hear from you." There was something too enthusiastic about the greeting, directed as it was to a man Cody had only ever run across when their teams played one another.

"I have to tell you," Cody continued before Sailor could respond, "I haven't had a chance to catch up with any of the boys for a while. My fiancée, Suzanne—oh, yeah, we just got engaged—likes me at home."

Sailor wondered exactly how long a leash Suzanne permitted Cody. From the way Cody was tugging at his tie, it looked like the other man was contemplating an escape. Sailor didn't think he'd get very far before he remembered the fancy car and the fancy house and the fancy yacht. "I'd say it's good to see you Cody, but it isn't."

Face falling, Cody appeared to only then notice the otherwise empty parking lot. "Hey, is the bar not even open?" A hint of trepidation.

"No. It opens in an hour." Which was why Sailor had asked to meet now.

Cody took a step back. "Look, Sailor"—he lifted up his hands, palms out—"whatever you've heard, I didn't do it. I haven't even thought about you in months, not since that last game."

That last game where Cody's team had been beaten to a pulp by Sailor's. And where Sailor might've taken a little too much pleasure in tackling Cody facedown into the muddy earth.

He always had the most fun at the games that involved Cody. He hadn't consciously realized why until this instant. No one could arrest you for assault on the rugby field. Not when body-slamming contact was part of the game and bruises expected.

"Back in college," he said, "do you remember Ísa?"

A sudden blink... followed by a tide of creeping red.

"Yeah." Cody dropped his head to stare at the oil-stained concrete of the parking lot. "She was sweet. She never ragged on me like Suzanne does."

"So why were you such a fucking asshole to her?"

A long silence before Cody sighed. "Suzanne told me if I said those things, she'd go out with me."

"Are you kidding me?" Sailor's hands fisted. "You're blaming your fiancée?"

"I was just going to break up with Ísa when Suzanne... when she told me she wanted me, but Suzanne has this thing against Ísa."

Because Ísa was blindingly beautiful in both body and spirit. Something Suzanne's jealous little mind couldn't handle. "And you went along with this plan to hurt Ísa, hurt the girl you were supposed to love? What the fuck kind of man are you?"

Cody looked up with a befuddled frown. "I didn't know she was your sister."

That was when Sailor decided there really was no point to the conversation. Instead, he said, "This is for Ísa."

And then he punched Cody.

15

ÍSA THE BARRACUDA

THE MAN HAD A GLASS jaw. He crumpled to the asphalt with a whimper.

Sitting up afterward, his suit jacket torn at the elbow and his hair no longer so flawlessly combed, Cody cradled his jaw as blood poured from his nose. "What the fuck?" Pinching his nostrils shut, he tilted back his head. "You punched me." The words came out whiningly nasal.

Sailor flexed, then fisted his hands. "Tell me you didn't deserve that."

Going pale when he lowered his head and saw Sailor's hands, Cody gulped. "Jesus. Yeah, yeah I did." Weirdly, the words actually sounded genuine.

Sailor watched as the other man sat up on the concrete with his back against his fancy car and dug around in his jacket. Finding a wadded-up tissue, he tore it up and began to plug his nose.

"I think I made the wrong choice that night, Sailor." A pitiful moan, the torn tissue sticking out from his nose like a fungal growth. "I've been thinking about Ísa for months. Ever since I saw that photo of her on Trevor's page. She was at some theater event with her mother that Trevor's cousin put on."

Sailor had no idea who Trevor was and he didn't care. "You're too late," he said. "I don't think she'd give you a chance even if you turned up with a truckload of chocolates and diamonds." The idea of Cody going anywhere near Ísa ever again had him seeing red.

Breathing past the urge to plant another one in Cody's face—it'd be unsporting against such a pathetic opponent—he said, "And what about your wedding? Bit too late for regrets, don't you think?"

Cody nodded, face set in glum lines and his white nose growths now faintly pinkish. "Suzanne's got everything planned. I just have to turn up on the day." A shuddering sigh, his hand rising to cradle his jaw once more. "Do you know something? Her family doesn't even have as much money as Ísa's."

Sailor looked at his scraped knuckles and seriously considered smashing Cody's nose in, unsporting or not. He managed to control himself only because he realized he'd probably already done a very stupid thing for a man trying to get a new business off the ground, one that required bank loans and the trust of CEOs like Jacqueline Rain.

And yet he couldn't make himself be sorry.

"If you're planning to press charges," he said, "here's my phone so you can call the cops." Cody's phone had fallen out of his pocket when he crashed to the ground; the screen was so cracked it looked like someone had taken a hammer to it.

"I don't want people to know the real reason why you punched me." Cody lifted pleading eyes to Sailor. "Don't tell anyone, okay? I'll make up some story to explain the face and jaw."

"Fine." Sailor turned and got back in his truck before he shoved the fungal growths even further up Cody's nose, his anger at the other man unabated.

Finally getting to his feet, Cody called out, "Hey, so is she your sister or not?"

Sailor thought of Ísa's lips under his, her thighs so sweetly tight around his body, the scent of her drugging his senses, and said, "No Ísa isn't my sister... but she is mine." He screeched out of the parking lot before Cody could reply.

Sailor had to get to a job, finish the work he'd promised to do.

Again, his eyes fell on the scraped knuckles with which he held the steering wheel. Nope, not sorry. No one had a right to do what Cody had done to Ísa.

ÍSA MADE IT THROUGH HER first day in the vice presidential office without murdering Jacqueline. She'd never admit it to her mother, but the company had a nice feel to it, the employees cheerful and genuinely happy to be there. As for the work, it was difficult, but to Ísa's intense horror, she understood it all. She couldn't even fake stupid questions—she was a terrible liar. In desperation, she tried working slowly, so as to annoy Jacqueline, but found that her brain refused to cooperate.

It was like her mother had brainwashed her while she was still in the womb.

Frustrated with herself for being so good at a job she hated, she deliberately took every single break to which she was legally entitled, using that time to work on the poetry that was her outlet and the saver of her sanity. The breaks slowed things down a little. But not anywhere near enough.

When Jacqueline came to see her after lunch, she had a beaming smile on her face. "I knew you'd be perfect for this position," she said. "Look how well you fit in."

Ísa banged her head against the desk after the door closed behind Jacqueline.

She had to figure out a way to sabotage this without breaking her word, or her mother would be blackmailing her into eternity. But how could she let down Catie and Harlow? Harlow would probably survive—his heart would be broken, pulverized more like it, but he was a smart kid. He'd be all emotionally messed up, but he'd be able to support himself and he'd eventually set up a business to rival Jacqueline's.

But Catie... Catie needed her mother in ways she'd never articulate. And if Jacqueline cut Ísa off in punishment, Ísa would lose her ability to make sure Jacqueline paid at least some attention to her thirteen-year-old youngest child. Clive certainly wouldn't be able to manage that—he hadn't even been able to make mother-child moments happen while he and Jacqueline had been married.

It was a teenaged Ísa who'd negotiated time for Catie in her mother's schedule.

In return, she'd agreed to learn the ropes of the company without complaining.

"Knock, knock."

Glancing up at her open door, she saw Ginny with a huge latte balanced on the tray she'd clipped to the arms of her wheelchair so it'd be stable. "It's like you read my mind," she told the other woman as Ginny wheeled herself in and put the latte on Ísa's desk. "You've been fantastic today."

"It's far more interesting working for you than being Jacqueline's junior assistant," the brunette confessed. "I haven't had to make a single stupid craft thing all day."

"Don't get too used to it," Ísa warned after stretching out her back, then taking a restorative sip of the coffee. "I have no desire to be trapped in Crafty Corners hell."

Ginny's face fell. "Oh, come on Ísa," she wheedled. "You're *really* good at this—I did some work for the last person your mother put temporarily in this position, and you're like a rocket compared to his hand-powered car. You have the instinct."

That was the last thing Ísa wanted to hear.

"Oh," Ginny said, "I almost forgot. A small package arrived for you." She reached into a bag she had on the back of her wheelchair and pulled it out.

"Thanks, Gin." Putting the unassuming brown box aside as she returned to the work she'd been doing, Ísa forgot all about the package until seven that night. Ginny had already clocked out, and Ísa was packing up to go too when her eye fell on the box.

Guessing it was either a corporate gift from a client or a sample from a hopeful craft inventor, she made quick work of opening it. "Ouch!"

She instinctively brought her finger to her mouth. But there was no blood, not even a real dent in her skin. Opening the flaps of the box with more care this time, she frowned at what she saw within. Not quite certain what it was about, she found a craft knife and began to cut open the box so she could remove the object without further stabs.

Box surgically dissected, she pulled out the packing

peanuts to free the perfectly potted cactus within. Dark green with wicked spines, it was potted in a pretty terra-cotta pot... on which someone had written in white ink: *Pointy spiky things don't scare me.*

Beside it was a tiny sketched image of a kitten-heeled shoe.

Ísa pressed her lips tightly together to keep from smiling.

Putting the cactus aside to take home, she looked in the remains of the box for any other sign of who'd sent it, found nothing. The external packaging didn't provide much of an answer either. There was no return address. But Ísa didn't really need any further evidence. Who else but a gardener would fight with plants?

Her lips tugged up at the corners despite herself.

She carried the cactus carefully down to her car, then into her apartment building. Slogging up the stairs instead of taking the elevator, she tried to think of a fitting rejoinder.

"No, Ísa," she ordered herself. "No playing this game. He's too young, and you have a plan." To find a man who was ready to settle down and create the kind of family foundation she'd always lacked.

A firm place on which Ísa could stand and where she could shelter Catie and Harlow. And a strong pair of arms on which she could depend, a man as rooted as an oak, with a heart in which Ísa wasn't an afterthought but a priority.

She could almost taste it, she wanted that dream so much.

A twenty-three-year-old with demon-blue eyes was not going to be on the same page as her. He'd just begun to stretch his wings, sow his wild oats. Even Devil Ísa knew that. Though it didn't stop her from whispering sinful suggestions in Ísa's ear about how she should follow Jacqueline's advice and have a whole lot of fun with him.

Naked fun.

Handcuffs and leg cuffs included.

Ísa's toes curled… before she was smothered by a blanket of self-recrimination. Look at her, thinking about using a man for her own degenerate purposes. A man who was younger than her and… well, okay, he wasn't exactly innocent, but that wasn't the point! She was acting just how you'd expect the offspring of Jacqueline Rain and Stefán Óskarsson to act.

Like a barracuda.

Maybe this was who she was—a ruthless corporate machine created by two other ruthless corporate machines —and it was time to stop fighting destiny. If genes made the woman, Ísa's genes were written in business black.

Putting her bag on the counter on that indigestible thought, not even the adorable little cactus lifting her mood, she was thinking about running away to join the circus when she got a call from Nayna.

"Can I come over?" her best friend asked. "I don't feel like going home for dinner. The folks are all excited about the next meet and greet they're trying to set up."

"You know you never have to ask," Ísa said. "I just got in myself. I was going to grill some chicken and make bad-for-the-hips buttery mashed potatoes."

"I'll pick up a mixed-bean salad from our favorite place." Nayna's tone was brighter already. "See you in half an hour."

Feeling better now that she knew her friend and confidante was on the way, Ísa got out of her work clothes and into a pair of shorts and a spaghetti-string tank top that she only ever wore at home—she didn't want to risk blinding blameless strangers with her whiteness. Nayna, however, had seen her in a bathing suit during their mutually hated phys-ed classes in school.

After pulling her hair up into a jaunty ponytail, she got the chicken pieces into the oven, set the potatoes to boil, then took a quick minute to check her phone. She smiled at seeing that she had a couple of messages from a friend she caught up with maybe three or four times a year.

She and Michelle, aka Micki, had been in many of the same classes at university and though their lives had gone in different directions, with Michelle already married and a mother of one, they still had enough to talk about that those coffee dates were fun for both of them. Expecting that Michelle wanted to set up a meet, Ísa clicked open the message. But her friend had something far more juicy to share this time: *Oh my God, Ísa, did you see this picture of Cody? I thought you'd enjoy it!*

Attached was an image of Cody with what looked like a broken jaw, the bruising ugly and his eyes scrunched as if in pain. His nose didn't look too great either, and he definitely had the beginnings of a black eye.

Her own eyes wide, Ísa scanned down to see that Michelle had also screenshotted the message posted along with the photo. Suzanne had apparently been the one who'd posted the image. And she was fuming.

Look at what some loser did to my amazing fiancé! Cody was only trying to help a woman who was about to get her bag snatched! He's my hero even though he refuses to go to the police because he doesn't want to waste their time. And that woman he got hurt helping ran off too, the bitch! That's what you get for trying to help people. And now Cody's jaw is broken and our wedding is going to be ruined!!

Ísa blinked and read the message again. Cody? Valiantly fighting to help a mugging victim? Ísa's bullshit meter swung over to blazing red.

She quickly typed a reply: *Micki, is this for real?*

Michelle must've been online because she answered almost immediately. *Absolutely,* she said. *I lurk on Suzanne's friends list just so I can gossip about her. I have no shame. Not after she turned frenemy when we were sixteen and stole my boyfriend. She thinks I forgave her—ha-ha! Micki never forgives or forgets!*

Anyway, I heard from another mutual friend that Cody really does look like he went two rounds with a professional boxer and came out the loser. Jaw's not broken, sadly. Not like the drama queen says. But that ass is still going to be bruised for the wedding, which means Suzunne's wedding photos will forever make her grimace, and that makes my evil heart cackle.

Ísa messaged back with a row of cackling faces of her own.

Then she put down the phone and thought of the playful man with steely confidence who'd scowled and said someone needed to teach Cody a lesson. Surely, surely… Her heart thumped. No, it couldn't be. She was just a teacher who'd molested him in a parking lot and then gotten naked with him in a secluded little water spot.

There was no reason for Sailor Bishop to have punched out Cody on her behalf. Cody had probably fallen on his face and made up that heroic story to explain the bruises so Suzanne wouldn't blame him for her ruined wedding photos.

Ísa's hand clenched around her phone.

She had Sailor's number.

16

THE WAR OF THE CACTI (WITH A CAMEO FROM A SWAMP CREATURE)

A KNOCK ON HER DOOR, Nayna no doubt having used Ísa's security code to come up.

Figuring that was a sign from the gods, Ísa put down her phone and went to open the door, dying to fill her friend in on Cody's unfortunate facial situation. Then she took in Nayna's own expression.

"Hey," she said, enfolding her friend in a huge hug. "What's the matter?"

Nayna made a face as they drew apart. "Sometimes," she muttered, "I get tired of being the dutiful daughter." She shut the door behind herself. "Let me help you finish prepping dinner, and then I'll tell you the story of my sad, sad life."

It didn't take them long to get everything together.

Taking their plates, they sat on the sofa in front of the television; it was currently playing their favorite trashy reality show.

Nayna began to speak halfway through the episode. "It's Madhuri," she said, referring to her older sister.

"Has she done something rebellious again?" Ísa

asked, well aware of the big scandal in Nayna's family history—the eldest Sharma daughter had eloped with a boy from her college when she'd been a bare nineteen years of age. Nayna herself had only been fourteen at the time.

Shaking her head, Nayna mumbled her next words through a huge mouthful of mashed potatoes. "She's mostly the reason why my parents have been so strict with me, but this morning she was sitting in the kitchen, chatting away to our parents while I helped my mom make breakfast."

"Your sister's been welcome back in the family for a few years." Ísa ate a big scoop of the bean salad, made an "mmm" sound that had Nayna nodding.

"I don't care what strange herbs and spices they put in that salad," her best friend said, "they'll pry my bean salad out of my cold, dead hands."

Swallowing her current bite of sweet, salty, beany goodness, Ísa said, "Anyway, I thought you loved having her around." The family estrangement had lasted six long years, during which Nayna had desperately missed her big sister. Her parents had refused to talk to their eldest daughter even after Madhuri's relationship broke up four years after the elopement.

"I do." Nayna's face fell. "But today I *truly* realized just how much my father loves her." Wet in her eyes, her voice thick. "She was always his favorite—the one who could make him laugh, coax him to give us extra sweets, or let us stay up to watch TV. She was the sister with the spirit, the child full of color and joy and wildness. That's part of the reason I've always loved her too."

Personally, Ísa had always thought Madhuri an attention-seeking flibbertigibbet, but she figured everyone had blinders about something. Nayna's happened to be about her sister.

Nayna tore off a piece of chicken with her teeth even as a tear rolled down her face. "Today I saw that, despite everything, she's still his favorite. I don't mind that, I really don't. It's just... I can't even get him to give me a 'well done' hug."

Another gnawing bite of the chicken as she sobbed. "I'm trying so hard to be the perfect daughter, Ísa, and it just struck me today that none of it matters." She gesticulated wildly with her drumstick. "I will *never* be well-behaved enough, never ever follow the rules well enough, never see my father's eyes light up with pride. I'm fucking killing myself toeing the line, and it doesn't fucking matter!"

In all their years together, Ísa had only heard Nayna swear maybe five times. So she didn't hug her best friend —she could tell the other woman was as furiously angry as she was sad. Instead, she said, "I know you don't like to talk about it, but part of the reason you went the whole arranged-marriage route was to make your parents happy. Are you rethinking that?"

Nayna put down the drumstick. "This isn't just about my father. There's also my grandmother. I want her to be happy—she never got to have the big wedding for her granddaughter that she dreamed about while we were growing up. I want to give her that."

Ísa scowled. "Your grandma loves you unconditionally, you egg." Ísa had been hugged by those same soft arms, her impression of Nayna's grandmother a fusion of textures and scent—the softness of the white sari that was her daily wear, the hint of incense that clung to her because of her early-morning prayers, the fancy perfume she loved and that Nayna gave her for her birthday every year.

"She's had a lot of pain in her life," Nayna countered. "A lot of loss. I want to give her this one bright, shining moment."

"You really think she'll be happy when she realizes how unhappy you are?"

Nayna stared at her empty plate. "I should've bought ice cream when I got the salad."

"Please," Ísa muttered. "Like I'd ever run out of ice cream. But read this in the meantime." After pulling up Michelle's messages, she handed her phone to Nayna. "It'll make you feel better."

Nayna was laughing in open glee by the time Ísa returned with the two-liter tub of rocky road ice cream and two spoons. "If you ever find the man who did this to Cody's face—and to Suzanne's precious wedding," Nayna said, her eyes shining, "you need to offer him a blow job at least. It'd only be polite."

Ísa's face went hot red between one second and the next.

Of course Nayna caught it. "You know who it was!" she accused. "Tell me!"

"I'm not sure." Ísa thrust the container of ice cream into Nayna's lap.

Not the least distracted by the cold, Nayna waggled her eyebrows. "Anyone to whom you'd be happy to offer a lusty sexual favor?"

When Ísa's breath turned shallow, her face even hotter, Nayna's smile cracked her face. "It was *him*, wasn't it? The hot gardener? The one you went skinny-dipping with at the party? I knew he couldn't be an asshole, not with the

135

way he looks at you! And oh my God! He avenged your honor!"

"I'll tell you when I know." Ísa pointed her spoon at her grinning best friend. "And I thought you were depressed."

"Hearing about Slimeball Schumer's comeuppance has had a reviving effect." Having opened the container, she put it between them and dug in.

One spoonful later, she said, "Ísa, seriously—if Mr. Sexy Blue Eyes punched out Cody for you, he might be a keeper."

Ísa stabbed her own spoon into the ice cream. "He's twenty-three." And definitely, absolutely not anything like the kind of man for whom Ísa was searching. Even if he haunted her in her dreams. Even if she kept seeing that image of him on the stairs, a maturity to him that belied his age. Even if she kept hearing him whisper "spitfire" in her ear while promising to lock her up using handcuffs.

AFTER FINALLY GETTING HOME AT eight that evening, Sailor dug out a frozen meal. He showered while it was cooking in the microwave, then pulled on a pair of low-hanging shorts and, taking the meal to the kitchen table—where he did most of his theoretical work—sat down to fine-tune the plans for Fast Organic.

Jacqueline's assistant had sent him a message to say that a representative from the company would meet him tomorrow at three at the first Fast Organic site to go over the details. She hadn't sent him a name, noting that she'd send through final details tomorrow, once this new project was integrated into everyone's schedules. Given Jacqueline's driven nature, the rep had to be someone equally intelligent and competent; they'd no doubt have countless questions.

Sailor wanted to have all the answers ready.

After he finished this, he'd have to get to work on his taxes. The problem with being a one-man shop was that he had to do everything. Which didn't leave a lot of time for extracurricular activities. He played rugby during the season, ran for exercise during the off-season, but that was about it. Today, however, he decided that he needed to add "flirting with a cute redhead" to his schedule.

When he was around her, he felt young in a way he hadn't felt since he was fifteen and had set himself the goal that drove him every single day. She made him realize that he'd put part of himself into deep freeze a long time ago— but there was no ice around her and never had been. His redhead had hit him straight in the gut from the first night he'd laid eyes on her.

A man would have to be very stupid to walk away from that.

Sailor wasn't stupid.

He was also very, very determined.

The cactus was just stage one of his plan to lure his redhead into his lair.

ÍSA RAN INTO HER LEAST favorite person in the entire world the next morning after she parked her car in the Crafty Corners parking lot. She hadn't slept well, tormented by dreams of a man with devil-blue eyes who teased her body without ever offering relief. What she needed was a tall black coffee. What she got was a tall, blackhearted swamp creature.

"Hello, Trevor," she said with a tight smile and tried to walk past him.

"Hey." He put his hands on her upper arms. "Is that any way to talk to your stepbrother?"

Not about to put up with unwanted contact, Ísa deliberately stepped back. If he touched her again, she'd break out the painful little-finger twist she'd learned in a self-defense class. "I don't think it works that way when parents marry after their children are adults." It wasn't the first time she'd made the point.

Trevor laughed, his perfect white teeth gleaming in his perfect square-jawed face with its perfect salon-tousled blond hair. He was like a living, talking, walking magazine model. It was creepy. "Are you going in to see Jacqueline?" he asked. "I was hoping to have a word with her."

"I don't know if she's in yet," was all Ísa said. She had no desire to know what Trevor wanted to discuss with Jacqueline, though she could guess. Trevor had been angling for a senior position at Crafty Corners ever since his father Oliver had the good fortune to marry Jacqueline.

While Oliver Jones was a somewhat vague professor who, oddly enough, seemed to "get" Jacqueline in a way none of her previous husbands had, Trevor Jones was very much a smooth operator out to line his pockets. He'd quickly figured out that getting into Jacqueline's good books was in his best interest.

Unfortunately, good-looking, charming men were Jacqueline's weak point.

Except in business, of course. Nothing distracted Jacqueline in business. Not even "a nice piece of ass."

Trevor had, so far, managed to walk the fine line between being a charming man whose company Jacqueline enjoyed and a calculating operator who wanted to wheedle his way into her business empire. Ísa wondered how long that would last. Jacqueline might have a weak spot for charming men, but she also had a razor-sharp intellect—sooner, rather than later, she'd figure out that Trevor was muscling in for a piece of the family pie.

That might've intrigued Jacqueline had Trevor been up to her standards, but Trevor wasn't even on Jacqueline's radar as someone she'd employ. While he was apparently a competent lawyer, he wasn't a shark who could rip the competition to shreds without ever losing his smile. Jacqueline's entire legal team was made up of sharks—which occasionally made for interesting office politics, but when it counted, the sharks worked together as a team.

They'd chew Trevor up and spit him out without so much as pausing in their work.

"I hear Jacqueline's made you acting vice president." Trevor's smile was so dazzling that she half expected to see a glint off one pearly white. "Congratulations."

Ísa settled the strap of her satchel and gave him the same tight smile as earlier, hoping he'd get the message. "It's only for the summer," she said. "I'm sure she'll find someone permanent during that time."

"Oh, don't be modest, Ísalind." Trevor's smile rang hollow. "We all know you're a genius. You've got your mother's instincts."

Now what the hell was he up to? "Um, thanks," she muttered. "I'd better go in. There's a lot to do." She had an evening class to teach tonight, the reason why she'd arrived at Crafty Corners so early. She wasn't about to do extra hours for Jacqueline, but neither did she plan to shirk on her part of the blackmail bargain.

Trevor fell into step beside her. "I don't want to keep

you. I know how important this is to Jacqueline. She looks to you as her successor you know."

That was hardly a state secret.

"I want you to know," Trevor added in a tone that dripped sincerity, "that if you ever need a hand, I'm here. Being thrown into the vice presidential position at only twenty-eight has got to create an immense amount of stress on you. I've got the legal know-how to give you backup anytime you need."

It was a good thing no one from Crafty Corners' in-house team of sharks was present to hear Trevor's offer—she wouldn't have given him high odds of survival in that situation. "Thanks," she said, deciding to take his words at face value. It was possible he was genuinely trying to be helpful and nice. Maybe she shouldn't think of him as a blackhearted villain just because he checked all the boxes.

Probably she should feel bad about mentally naming him Trevor the Creeper. But just like ivy crept over a wall until it smothered it, Trevor was on a campaign to creep all over Jacqueline and Crafty Corners.

He touched Ísa on her lower back.

She elbowed him hard enough in the gut that he sputtered out an "oof" of breath. "You shouldn't startle women," she said calmly instead of apologizing, because she was Jacqueline Rain's daughter and her mother had taught Ísa never to apologize to men who were attempting to force their way into her space.

Every so often, when meetings or conferences or networking events didn't interfere, Jacqueline had been one hell of a mom.

Still a little breathless, Trevor held up his hands. "Sorry, my fault," he said with a dental-commercial-worthy smile. "I was just going to suggest we should have dinner together. Our parents are married, and yet I feel I don't know you at all. How about it, stepsister?" He made the last word sound vaguely incestuous.

Ew.

"I'm sure we'll get to know each other over the summer," she said rather than answering his invitation. "Mother's been talking about having more family dinners." Actually, it was Ísa who'd been talking about family dinners—but she hadn't been thinking of Trevor at the time. She wanted her mother to pay attention to her other two children.

Catie, the child to whom she'd given birth.

Harlow, the son whom she hadn't birthed but into whose life she'd blasted at a critical point.

When Trevor opened his mouth again, Ísa beat him to the punch. "I've got to head up and make a start on work. Have a great day, and I hope you manage to catch up with Jacqueline." She deliberately made sure the door locked behind her after she entered.

With it being so early, there was no one else around to let him in.

And oh, oops, she'd developed temporary hearing loss and couldn't hear him knocking.

Devil Ísa grinned.

After reaching her office, she got immediately to work. It was about an hour and fifteen minutes later that she got up and went to see if Ginny had arrived; she needed the other woman to find some records for her.

Ginny's computer was up and running, but Ísa couldn't spot her.

Detouring to the staff room, Ísa grabbed a mug of coffee before wandering back into her office. A little potted plant sat in the center of her desk. She blinked, glanced over her shoulder—and saw Ginny coming back from the photocopier.

"Did you see where that potted plant came from?" she asked her assistant, her heart thumping triple time.

"*Apparently* it was dropped off at reception by that hunky blue-eyed contractor. Looks like he wants to make nice with the boss." Mischief in her expression, she added, "James said he was wearing khaki work shorts and a sand-colored T-shirt. There was also mention of a thigh tattoo." She pretended to melt into her chair. "I wish I'd seen him. Such a dishy sight to start off the day."

Cheeks threatening to blaze, Ísa made some vague statement before shutting herself in her office. And surrendering to memories of the first time she'd seen adult Sailor—he'd been wearing his work shorts then too, a gorgeous, sweaty man who looked good enough to lick.

Ísa shivered as she made her way to her desk. The potted plant was another miniature cactus, this one tiny round balls with a thin "fur" of spikes. Tiny yellow flowers erupted from the tips. It was adorable.

But what she was really interested in was the message.

17

OPERATION CATCH THE REDHEAD
—STAGE ONE

PUTTING DOWN HER MUG, ÍSA plucked out the note tucked into the soil. It proved to be a small envelope. The envelope was homemade... Very badly homemade.

It was like he'd never been near a Crafty Corners store in his life.

Lips curving, she tore open the well-glued and duct-taped miniature envelope to withdraw a piece of notepaper that had been folded multiple times. Inside, she found a message written in neat writing with generous loops. It said: *I have spike-resistant gloves. Just FYI.*

Ísa couldn't help her smile.

Even though Sailor Bishop was a big, sexy distraction from her goals, a charming man who was threatening to derail all her carefully laid plans.

And why exactly was she even thinking about this?

She had work to do, blackmail to pay, playful men with blue eyes to forget.

SAILOR WASN'T SURPRISED NOT TO hear from his redhead. From Miss Ísalind Rain. A name as unique and exotic and pretty as her. Well, Ísalind could be stubborn all she liked. Sailor could out-stubborn a goat.

And he was still in stage one.

"You're not getting away this time," he murmured as he hefted a bag of soil... and thought about lifting Ísa up to his mouth for a kiss so deep it was sex. She was gloriously, lusciously naked in his fantasy—the end goal of Operation Catch the Redhead.

He was adding fine details to the fantasy when his phone chimed with an incoming message. It turned out to be from Jacqueline's assistant—she was confirming the meeting he had later today with one of Jacqueline's people. It was, he saw, to be their VP.

The name beside the title made him blink... and then begin to cheerfully whistle. His day had just gotten monumentally better.

ÍSA MANAGED TO FORGET ABOUT the cactus for the next few hours; okay, she was lying through her teeth—she never forgot it, but she managed to ignore it for long enough to get the work done. It was two hours after lunch when her cell phone chimed with a rock 'n' roll ringtone from the eighties.

"Catiebug," Ísa said with a smile. "What are you up to today?"

"We ran out of money," her thirteen-year-old sister muttered. "Dad got hold of my bank passbook. It's like he's one of those money-sniffing dogs they have at the airport."

That, Ísa thought, was giving those hardworking dogs a bad name. "He cleaned you out?"

"Yeah. The electricity company just called to say they'll be cutting us off if we don't pay the bill in the next week."

Ísa wanted to drive down to Hamilton and punch Clive in the face. How could he do that to his own daughter? And how could Jacqueline allow it to happen? She should've fought for custody of Catie—Clive was a lovely father at times and a clearly incompetent idiot the rest of it. But Jacqueline's choice was hardly surprising; she hadn't even fought for custody of Ísa, her first born with the "killer" instincts.

"It's all right, Catie," Ísa said through her fury. "How much do you need to pay off the current bills?" She wrote down the number on a piece of notepaper.

It wasn't too bad.

The real damage was to Catie's account. "Did he take the money I gave you to use for movies, manicures, and mayhem over the summer?" No teenage girl should have to be stuck at home during her summer vacation; Ísa had made sure Catie understood she could and should spend the gift money for fun.

"Yes," Catie admitted. "I don't know why the bank let him have it. You're meant to be the only person other than me who can sign for the money."

"I'll talk to the bank myself." Ísa had already specifically discussed the financial setup with the bank, but Clive *was* Catie's legal guardian. He had the papers to prove it, and he took full advantage of those papers. "For now I'm going to transfer the money you need, fun money included, into Martha's account." The former nurse was Catie's live-in helper and utterly trustworthy. "Take the cash she gives you and hide it in your underwear drawer."

Even Clive wouldn't stoop to searching his teenage daughter's underwear drawer.

"I know you don't have that much money, Ísa," Catie began.

"I'm a millionaire," Ísa pointed out dryly, her fingers playing with the tops of the fuzzy round cactus Sailor had brought her. "It's fine, Catiebug. I'll take the money from the dividend account." Ísa never touched the income from her Crafty Corners shares when it came to herself. It was a matter of principle—she wasn't going to use Jacqueline's money when she didn't want to work in Jacqueline's company; however she had no qualms about accessing it for Catie.

Catie began to cry down the line, the break sudden, as if she'd been holding the tears within until something snapped. "I'm so sorry, Ísa. I let you down."

Heart twisting at hearing her usually sparky little sister be so down, Ísa spoke in a firm tone. "You have *nothing* to apologize for. And if it makes you feel better, we all have our moments of weakness—look at me, I'm currently sitting in the vice president's office waiting for the Dragon to come in and breathe fire at my face."

Wet laughter. "So, are you enjoying being a highflier?"

"Like you wouldn't believe." Her dry tone made her sister laugh again, and this time it was less wet and more Catie.

"You stay strong, okay?" Ísa said. "And you go to the physical therapy sessions for your balance. If anything else happens, don't try to hide it from me. I'll always have your back." As she'd dreamed of someone having hers when she'd been Catie's age.

Catie blew a breath down the line. "That was me blowing you a kiss, Issie. You're my favorite person in all the world. Don't tell Harlow though—he gets kind of jealous sometimes I think. And squish him for me. He's so excited about this internship."

Smiling, Ísa put down the phone after saying bye to Catie. Only to look up and find her brother hovering in the doorway. "Harlow!" She got up at once and went around to hug her tall and lanky brother. "How's your first day going?"

"Awesome!" His excited eyes were dark and sharply slanted behind his wire-rimmed spectacles, his black hair slick straight and cut with ruthless neatness. Catie always moaned about how Harlow got the razor-blade cheek-bones when he didn't even care about them and she got soft, rounded features that weren't yet adult.

"So," Ísa said to the sibling she'd first met when she was twenty-three and Harlow was twelve, "what do they have you doing?"

"Mailroom." A roll of his eyes. "Apparently, it's where all the interns start. So here's your mail—Ginny said I could do a personal delivery this time."

Accepting it with a laugh, Ísa kissed him on the cheek —though he looked around to make sure no one was watching before he'd bent down so she could reach. Then she waved him off to continue his rounds and went through the business mail. Nothing much.

A notation popped up on her phone calendar as she was scanning an invitation to an open house at another company: *Meeting at Fast Organic #1*. It was for a meeting set thirty minutes into the future, giving her just enough time to get to the location.

Grabbing her satchel, she put her laptop and a notepad into it before walking out. "Ginny, do you know what this meeting at Fast Organic is about?"

"Oh, I forgot to tell you. It's with someone your mother hired to do… I think it was interior decorating? Annalisa handled it to help me out." Ginny bit down on her lower lip. "I'm so sorry, I was so flustered when Jacqueline promoted me to assistant to the vice president, and then she was throwing all this information at me—"

"That's fine," Ísa said, knowing exactly how overwhelming Jacqueline could be. "I've been through all the files—I can handle this." No doubt her mother had hired an individual who was in tune with the needs of the restaurant. If not, Ísa had a very good grasp of the intended look and could nudge the designer in the correct direction. "What else is on my calendar today?"

Ginny took a quick look. "I've got a note here that you teach night classes on Tuesdays, so I've made sure not to schedule anything after three thirty for you."

"Excellent." Ísa glanced at her watch. "I won't return to the office after the meeting—but if anything comes up, you have my number."

"Okay, boss," Ginny said brightly. "You make a really great vice president!" the brunette called out a minute later as Ísa headed down the corridor.

Ísa just waved behind her. It didn't matter if she was good at it; she didn't love it in the least. Not like she loved the poetry of William Butler Yeats and Percy Bysshe Shelley and Elizabeth Barrett Browning as well as the works of innovative modern poets like Nikita Gill. Not like she loved sharing the joy of those works with young minds. For her, the VP position was just a job. A job she'd been blackmailed into taking.

"Only for the summer." Leaving the colorful environs of Crafty Corners on that quiet reminder to herself, she got into her car.

She was mentally reviewing the concept plans for the Fast Organic stores when she turned into the parking lot of the first location. Her eyes widened, her mouth going dry as her heart pulsated with a hard beat.

"Oh, Ginny." She groaned as she brought the car to a stop next to Sailor's truck. "It wasn't interior decorating but *exterior* decorating."

And there he was, crouching in one corner of the parking lot as he measured something. His thighs were strong and thick and really impossible to avoid staring at, given how he was crouching down. She could also see part of the tattoo composed of intricate shapes and lines on his left thigh, and it made her want to run her fingers over it... Maybe her lips too, if she were being honest.

No, Ísa, she told herself sternly. *There are many, many reasons why he is very, very wrong for you.*

Even if she was willing to be stupid and forget all those other reasons, Sailor Bishop struck her as a charmer—and Ísa had seen firsthand what happened to women who fell for charmers. It never ended well for the woman.

Not even Jacqueline had managed to hold on to her favorite charmer—Ísa's father.

There was a reason Jacqueline was now in a happy marriage with a professor twelve years her senior who couldn't charm to save his life. He and Jacqueline had a quiet joy between them that Ísa coveted.

Meanwhile, Stefán kept on charming women and racking up the young brides.

There was a lesson there in glaring neon.

But..., the devil in her whispered, not for the first time, *while you're waiting to find your forever, how about some naughty times in the back of Sailor Bishop's truck?*

Telling Devil Ísa to shut up and that the debate was

over, Ísa got out and crossed the parking lot to Sailor, her satchel banging against her hip. He looked up with a smile at her approach.

Blue heat in those eyes, open male admiration.

"So," she said, "you're going to be our landscaper, are you?" She folded her arms and tried desperately to think of something nasty to say that would make him stop trying to charm her—because Ísa wasn't so sure about her own self-control where this man was concerned. "What a big surprise."

Dark clouds swept across his expression. "I don't need to sleep with anyone to get work contracts, spitfire." A slow grin. "Though I am flattered that you think I can use my body to climb my way to the top."

Cheeks threatening to go hot, Ísa said, "Let's get this over with. What's your plan?" Jacqueline had given her the basic outline during the file handover, but that was it.

"All the plans are in the truck," he said, nudging his head that way as he rose to his feet. "Did you get the gift I left for you with the front desk?"

Ísa was about to answer when her eyes fell to his knuckles. They were red and scraped. As if he'd punched someone in the jaw. "You hit Cody," she said, the words coming out a stunned whisper.

Even though she'd suspected, she hadn't really believed it.

A shrug of those big shoulders. "Yeah, I did."

"Why?"

"Because it needed to be done." His hand cupping her jaw, the pad of his thumb brushing across her lips—and his eyes steely in a way that kept startling her. "I should've done it that night, but I never went back into the warehouse after I ran out behind you."

As if that was enough. As if men went around punching other men all the time for the simple reason that they'd once badly hurt a woman.

He stepped closer, the heat of his body a rough caress and his smile like sunlight on her skin. "You planning to kiss my knuckles better?"

That scary, beautiful charm again.

Like melted chocolate and sin and all things just a little bit bad.

18

TEMPTATION & DISTRACTION

HIS REDHEAD GLARED AT HIM.

Sailor knew he shouldn't be messing with the vice president of the company for which he was doing the biggest job of his career so far, but he couldn't help himself.

"Is this what you call professional behavior?" Her tone was so icy that he almost bought it for a second—but then he caught the flush at the very tips of her ears.

Fascinated, he nearly gave in to the urge to lean down and nip at the nearest tip to see if she was sensitive there. He hadn't done that while she was naked in his arms in the water. In fact, he hadn't done a lot of things he wanted to do with and to this redhead with her blushes and her smart mouth and her way of looking at him as if she'd like to eat him up—after ripping off his clothes and running her hands all over him.

Sailor was quite willing to be her sacrifice.

Even if she was a curvy distraction.

Because this distraction didn't only make his blood burn, she made the day brighter just by being in it. Every time he was lucky enough to be with her, he was just... happier. That was worth fighting for. Worth any prickles. Worth the bruised knuckles. Worth the super-early-morning starts just so he could carve out time in his day to play with her.

"My apologies, Ms. Rain," he said. "I'll keep it strictly professional from now on."

A distinctly suspicious glint in her eye.

Hiding his grin as he grabbed his stuff from the truck, he spread out the detailed plan on the hood. Anchoring the top of the plan with his cell phone and the tape measure, he put his hand on the third edge and Ísa put her hand on the final one.

"This is what I see," he began.

"Wait," Ísa said before he could continue. "You're talking about digging up the existing parking lot. Jacqueline didn't mention that."

"It's the basis for everything else." Sailor handed her a copy of the quote he'd done for Jacqueline. "There's no way to get the look the senior Ms. Rain wants for Fast Organic without—"

"I'm the one in charge of this account now," Ísa said. "You have to sell me your idea." She shot him a narrow-eyed glance. "And I don't have a weakness for pretty and charming men."

This time when Sailor scowled, it was for real. "Don't you think that's a little sexist?"

"Excuse me?"

"Ignoring all my skills and bringing me down to being just a pretty man?" Part of him was delighted she saw him that way, but the hard-nosed businessman within was pissed—and irritated. He didn't want Ísa thinking of him as anything but smart, a worthy opponent.

"Now you know what women feel like in the workplace," was her tart response. A moment later, she added, "Sorry. I shouldn't have said what I did, especially after I asked you to be professional."

"So you don't think I'm pretty and charming?"

An even narrower-eyed glance. "Let's talk about your plan." It was an order.

Startled at this unyielding side of her—and turned on as well—Sailor began to go through the finer points of what he intended to do. "It's all about working to create a certain atmosphere from the moment a customer drives in."

Excitement was a crashing wave inside his body as he laid out his vision. "We're talking green and healthy, and with this kitchen garden that I'm suggesting"—he tapped it on the map—"your customers will actually be able to see where a little of their food is coming from. Obviously, it's going to be mostly for show because you won't be able to grow enough, but you'll be growing some at least."

Sailor continued when Ísa didn't interrupt. "People feel good about buying sustainable products, especially people in your targeted customer base. There's also the lack of a carbon footprint in taking lettuce from the garden to the kitchen and then to the plate. You can use that in your advertising and customer outreach. I'm betting the garden will also get a lot of play on social media."

Ísa looked intrigued. "Can we extend that?" she asked. "Fast Organic is going to be fast food, but we won't be doing huge volumes. Our prices are at the premium end, which means we need to sell at a lower volume to make a profit. The plan is to grow a small but dedicated client base."

Sailor saw where she was going with this. "You want

the kitchen garden big enough that you can actually supply most of the needs of the restaurant?"

Ísa nodded. "Even if it's only certain items per season," she said. "For example, if we could say that all the tomatoes in the salad this month come from the Fast Organic gardens."

Sailor nodded slowly, his blood heating at having a client who was willing to work with him. That it was this woman who made him crave things he'd long pushed to the side, that was just the icing on the cake. "I'll have to rework the plans, but yeah, we could make that happen."

He took a pencil from his pocket and began to sketch in a few changes. "You'd then need to have a long-term gardener on contract who could make sure the garden stayed healthy. As it so happens, I know a gardener with excellent rates." Yes, he preferred to do landscaping, but he wasn't too proud to take maintenance jobs—it was all cash flow for his bigger dream.

Ísa gave him a look that was pure Rain. "Let's do this first and see how good you are, Mr. Bishop."

Sailor wanted to kiss her and kiss her and kiss her. Telling himself to focus, that playtime was later, he said, "If we put in a larger kitchen garden, we're going to have to lose the little seating area here."

"Not necessarily." Ísa stared at his plan. "What if we make it so people are welcome to do things in the garden during their lunch break? They can sit there. They can weed if they're in the mood."

"Like a community garden?" Sailor drew in a breath, and with it came her scent. "Might work with staff keeping an eye on things. The larger issue is what happens when the restaurant is closed."

He frowned at the map while Ísa's scent tangled

around him like invisible chains. "I only have sustainable fencing created of hedges in this plan, and I still think that's the look you should be going for, but if you're talking about a true kitchen garden, then we have to build in some way to protect the garden at night so folks don't sneak off with your produce."

He tapped his pencil on the plan before beginning to draw in a system of strong trellises that would let in light and look beautiful while still acting as protective walls. "One side can open to let people in during the day," he murmured. "We can train climbers over the rest. Something edible. Beans maybe. Or… will you be using edible flowers in your dishes?"

Ísa was so close now that he could feel her hip brushing against his thigh. "No, I don't think so. But we should be able to work with that. I'll talk to the chef who's finalizing the menu. We can move quickly because Fast Organic will be doing a number of limited-run products across the seasons."

Sailor continued to alter the plan. Snuggled up next to him in a way she probably didn't realize and he wasn't stupid enough to point out, Ísa kept on asking questions, her face alight with interest. He realized that though she'd called him a pretty man, she was dead serious about him and his work.

He also realized she had a brain as dangerous as Jacqueline's.

His third realization was that he badly, badly wanted to stroke his hand down her back and over the curve of her rear. He'd probably squeeze, because an ass that beautiful deserved nothing else. Then he'd bend down and kiss his way up her spine and to those ears with their fascinating blushing tips.

That was when, out of nowhere, he realized a fourth thing that he'd simply forgotten to factor into his whole pursuit of his redhead: Ísa was rich.

Way out of his league rich.

Even if he got his business off the ground as he wanted and was hoping to achieve, he wouldn't make any real money until at least two or three years into the future. And that money wouldn't ever compare to Crafty Corners unless he managed to achieve the biggest dream in his heart.

His fingers tightened around the pencil.

Hard as it was to bear the thought, his spitfire would most probably only ever see him as an amusement. Women as wealthy and as smart and as sexy as Ísa tended to stick within their social and economic class when it came to serious relationships.

Mood suddenly dark even though he had no room in his life for a relationship and the removal of a distraction should've made him happy, he began to roll up his plan. "I'll need to rework the financial end of things in light of these changes. But," he continued, "I don't think it should make that much of a difference as we'll be taking out the seating area to extend the garden."

Not looking at her because, right now, his desires weren't the least bit civilized or professional—there might be biting involved—he wrenched his mind back to business. "How much leeway do I have to move ahead, given the changes? I have a line on some plants I can get for a lower than usual rate, but I have to act fast."

"Go ahead and get the plants," Ísa said. "But send me the updated quote tonight so I can keep the bean counters happy."

Stepping back from the truck on that very vice presidential statement, she gave him a searching look that was… softer, gentler, made his hunger to kiss her even more voracious. "Is everything okay?"

Sailor nodded. If he did this right, his work might well be featured in magazines and other publications across the country. Ísa's full kitchen garden concept was an incredible one, especially when it related to fast food—it would take his work into truly groundbreaking territory.

He *had* to be professional. Even when he was shaking off a blow he'd never seen coming. The years between them, her stubbornness, even the fact she was now vice president of Crafty Corners, he'd been ready to deal with all that—but the amount of money at Ísa's disposal? It was at such a level that it simply took her out of his orbit.

And still Sailor wanted to tumble her into the back seat of his truck.

Even if Ísalind Rain, daughter of Jacqueline Rain, heir to a fortune in the tens of millions, would break his heart in the end.

ÍSA WAS STILL CHEWING OVER the mood shift at the end of her meeting with Sailor when she drove into the school parking lot for her evening class. However, try as she might, she couldn't figure out what had happened. One moment he'd been flirting with her with his eyes, his body a hard line against hers, and the next he'd grown oddly distant and formal.

A knock on her car window. She jerked. "Oh, Diana." Getting out, she said, "Sorry, woolgathering."

"No problem" was the cheerful response from the thirty-something woman with ebullient black curls around a rounded face. "I thought we could go in together. I have to tell someone about the *amazing* violin concert I went to last night."

Smiling, Ísa hitched the strap of her satchel over her shoulder and walked in with the gregarious music teacher. She had to get her head back in the game, and that game was the teaching that she loved whether it was adults or children.

The good thing about adults was their sheer dedication. No teenage groans here.

In fact, they were so enthusiastic and had so much to discuss that her class ran into overtime. It meant she was the last teacher to leave, but with it being summer and the entire country running on daylight savings time, the world was still bathed in light. Several of her students were also yet lingering just outside the main doors. From what she overheard, they were involved in a heated discussion about the true meaning of a Coleridge poem.

Ísa wanted to grin and tell them they'd never truly figure it out. Coleridge had had a love affair with opium, and the drug had undoubtedly influenced his works. But he'd created incredible, haunting imagery that Ísa loved to sink into. Hearing her students' passion about his work gave her deep pleasure—this was what she loved doing: sharing the joy of the written word with other minds.

It was only after she'd locked up that she spotted a familiar truck parked on the other side of the lot. She didn't know what made her do it. After saying goodbye to her students, she walked in the direction of the truck. And there he was in the distance, shirtless and sweaty and an erotic dream come to vivid, masculine life.

Groaning, Ísa told herself to stop it. He was *not for her*. But her feet kept on moving until she was standing on the far edge of the section of the grounds where he was doing his work. He hadn't seen her. She could still walk away. But instead, she put her feet on the grass and crossed the remaining distance to him.

Far too late, she realized he wasn't alone. A lanky teenager worked alongside him, his attention on digging his spade into the earth; the boy had been hidden because he was working behind a number of tall flax plants. The teen's features were strongly reminiscent of Sailor's, though his skin was a warm shade of brown in comparison to Sailor's more golden tan.

The teenager was laughing and saying something to Sailor when Sailor looked up and saw Ísa. His lips curved, and those blue eyes flickered with heat before he seemed to consciously stifle the response. A response that had gone a long way toward eliminating the uneasy sensation that had dogged Ísa since their meeting.

Smile fading, Sailor came over. "Hello, Miss Rain," he said, wiping the back of his forearm across his forehead, his sweaty chest streaked with dirt and his eyes narrowed against the sunlight. "Strange place for a VP to hang out."

"I work here too. And it's Ísa," she said firmly, even as her skin began to prickle with awareness and her lungs seemed to be having trouble drawing in oxygen. "Stop teasing me. You know full well I didn't mean for you to start calling me Miss Rain."

The demon blue glinted. "Whatever you say, Ísa. You're the boss."

He was, Ísa decided, being deliberately provocative. Whatever had caused the change in his behavior earlier, it was still in effect. "Something is definitely wrong—and I'm not leaving until you tell me what." Folding her arms, she set her feet.

"You shouldn't play with the hearts of simple gardeners, spitfire."

"I'm quite sure you're not a simple anything." The playfulness was on the surface. Below that was a highly intelligent man whose passion and drive spoke to Ísa in ways she didn't want to hear.

Because no woman would ever be a priority for a man that driven. Ísa would never be a priority. "And," she said on the heels of that depressing thought, "when was the last time your heart was involved with a woman?"

Chuckling, he turned to wave the teenage boy over. "Jake, this is Ísa Rain. Ísa, this is my brother, Jake."

Ísa held out a hand. "Hi, Jake."

The teenager shook it with a small smile. "Hi," he said before looking up at his brother. "Shall I dig up the rest, Sail?"

Sailor nodded, and Jake went back to his task. "Had to draft in some slave labor." Sailor's voice held an edge. "It's all I can afford right now."

Ísa realized he probably wanted to get back to work. "Sorry, I'm keeping you."

But Sailor didn't take the chance to step away. "You're the prettiest distraction a man could have."

Distraction.

Ísa had heard that word many times over her lifetime. Both her parents had often told her to stop being a distraction before they bent their heads to much more important tasks. "When I was young, I once deliberately broke an expensive vase," she found herself telling Sailor, the words just rising out of her throat. "It was when my parents were still married. I wanted to see what they'd do."

"My parent's would've grounded me, then docked part of my pocket money to teach me not to throw a tantrum with other people's things," Sailor said with a grin that told her he was speaking from experience. "I'm guessing yours did something similar."

"No." Though Ísa had wished so hard for exactly that type of a reaction, exactly that type of *involvement*. "The maid swept away the shards and I was told to go play in my room." Where she wouldn't be a distraction. "I was never punished." Neither parent had had the time to deal with such an insignificant matter. "Lucky, right?"

Sailor's eyebrows drew together, his lips parting, but a familiar ringtone shattered the air before he could speak.

19

CHEESECAKE AND A NAKED GARDENER
(IN VERY CLOSE PROXIMITY)

"THAT'S MY YOUNGER SISTER," ÍSA said, relieved. She didn't know why she'd done that, given Sailor a key into one of her deepest vulnerabilities... as if he'd hear her, as if he'd understand her. "I better answer it."

Sailor was still scowling when she raised the phone to her ear and began to walk back to her car. "Catie? Is everything all right? You got the money?"

"Yes, I paid all the bills," her little sister said. "But Dad hasn't been home since he got into my account."

Ísa didn't immediately panic. "Is Martha with you?"

"You know Mrs. M. would never abandon me," was the outwardly upbeat response that struggled to hide Catie's worry. "I just... Can you see if you can find out where Dad is? So I know he's okay?"

Ísa rubbed at her heart, hurting for her little sister. Catie kept on loving Clive even though he let her down over and over again. Ísa often thought that what Clive was doing to Catie was worse than what Jacqueline and Stefán had done to Ísa. At least being ignored came with a sense of certainty that eliminated hope. Clive, by contrast, showed Catie just enough care to keep her hopeful that, next time, he'd act more like her father and less like an overindulged child.

"Of course I can," Ísa said in response to her sister's halting request. "I'll call you back tonight."

"Thanks, Issie."

Hanging up, Ísa got into her car and began to go through her list of Clive's friends—she'd collected their names and numbers over the years for exactly such a situation. It took her a half hour to track him to a casino in Sydney, Australia.

Leaving the country without telling his daughter?

That was a new low even for Clive.

When she got him on the phone, he was full of apologies that she knew were meaningless. Clive was from her mother's "pretty arm candy" phase.

"Martha's so dependable," he said, all warm bonhomie. "I have total faith in her. I'd never have left my little girl otherwise."

"Call her," Ísa ordered, channeling the Dragon, her tone blasting Clive with fire. "If you don't, I swear I'll report you for child endangerment. Imagine what that'll do to your credit line." Because that was the only thing about which Clive appeared to care.

"Sure, sure, sure. No need to get tough, Ísa. I'll call her right now."

"I'm going to check with her in five minutes to make sure."

She was sitting in the driver's seat waiting for those minutes to pass when there was a knock on her window. Jumping for the second time that day, she glanced up to see Sailor on the other side, his forehead scrunched in lines that could've been either concern or anger.

Ísa didn't have the mental or emotional capacity to deal with the man right then. He reached too deep into her without even trying, was dangerous to her dreams. But, given that he was also as stubborn as a goat and still staring at her, his jaw getting increasingly more set, she rolled down the window and said, "I had to deal with a family thing," before he could ask her why she was still sitting in the parking lot as the world went dark around them.

"Is it done?" Sailor asked. "I won't leave you here alone."

Something tight uncurled inside her, and she didn't know what it was. Ísa wasn't used to someone looking after her. The thought was ludicrous. She'd been looking after everyone since before she could drive. But Sailor was giving the distinct impression that he wasn't about to budge until she did.

Right then she didn't feel like just a distraction. An annoyance maybe… but an annoyance important enough to make him alter his own plans. "Who made you the Ísa police?" The cool words just fell out of her mouth.

As the vase had once been thrown from her hands.

He made a distinct growling sound. "My truck's not budging until you drive out of here, spitfire, so stop trying to scare me off."

Ísa scowled back at him even though the fluttering, mushy thing inside her was getting worse. He was really going to stay. Even though he was clearly tired after a long day of hard, physical work. "I'm nearly done." Her phone rang in her hand even as she spoke.

It was Catie on the other end, ecstatic that her father

had gotten in touch. "Thank you, Issie," she said on a delighted laugh. "I knew you'd do it."

Happy for her sister but worried about how many times she'd have to do this before Catie was old enough to move out and have an independent life free of a father who was, quite frankly, a charming parasite, she said the words her sister needed to hear, then hung up.

"All done," she told Sailor, the vulnerable mushiness inside her terrifyingly close to the surface. "You can go home with a clear conscience."

And still he didn't leave.

Reaching out, he rubbed gently at her forehead as if rubbing away a frown. "Have you eaten, spitfire?"

Ísa tried to bring his actions down to the physical, to the erotic tension that simmered between them, and failed. There'd been too much tenderness in his question, in his touch. "I was going to pick up takeout on the drive home," she said, terrified in a way she'd never before been terrified.

If he kept acting this way, how was she supposed to keep from falling for him? For this twenty-three-year-old man with huge dreams and an ambition to match? A man who wouldn't be ready to settle down for probably a decade yet, when a stable home was all that Ísa had ever wanted to build.

She couldn't wait ten years. It would destroy her.

And she could never be with a man for whom his business was his priority.

She should start her engine and drive as far from him as possible.

Brushing his knuckles over her cheek, the affectionate action freezing her in place as surely as if he'd placed those handcuffs of his on her wrists, Sailor glanced at his truck. "I've got to drop Jake home. But after that I was planning to go to my place and throw a fish steak on the grill, then work on the updated quote."

Ísa looked up, met his eyes.

It was a mistake.

Because his smile was a light in the blue as he said, "I could make that two fish steaks and you could help me with the quote." Another brush of his knuckles. "It'll go much faster if my demanding boss is right there to tell me what expenses she won't authorize."

Ísa knew she shouldn't. This was shaping up to be a horrible, horrible mistake. But no man had ever smiled at her that way, as if having Ísa with him was the best thing he could imagine. As if she was his version of rocky road ice cream and chocolate cake combined. She knew it was an illusion, that Sailor Bishop was probably just very good at charming women, but she said, "That sounds nice."

Maybe a woman had to make that horrible mistake before she finally learned her lesson.

"Here's my address." Sailor tapped it into her phone. "Meet you there in forty minutes?"

When Ísa nodded, he rose, patting the top of her car. "Drive safe, spitfire. We'll follow you out."

That strange feeling in her stomach again at the idea of Sailor watching over her.

Ísa didn't know what to do about it, how to process it.

So she just drove out, waving at Sailor when they split in different directions at the road. Since there was no point going home, she decided to head to a large grocery store that she knew was open till ten. Sailor was fixing dinner, so the least she could do was pick up dessert.

Once inside the brightly lit store, the aisles wide and mostly empty at this time of the evening, she found herself just standing by the row of freezers. Lost. Uncertain. She was never more glad to hear her phone jingle with a cheerful Bollywood song.

"Nayna, I'm so glad you called!"

An older man with a mass of stiff gray hair gave her a censorious look from the ice cream section. As if the grocery store turned into a library at night.

Ignoring him, Ísa walked over to the cheesecake section with the phone to her ear. "Why do you sound like you're hyperventilating?"

"My parents have set up another date for me—he's coming by tonight!" Nayna wailed. "I've been rethinking the whole arranged-marriage situation, but I haven't had a chance to talk to my parents. And I just got home and now I can't get out of this meeting without making them lose face and I'm hiding in the bathroom!"

"You did say today?" It was already past eight thirty.

"In ten minutes! He works long hours too." Nayna sounded like she was breathing into a paper bag now. "My dad called me at work and told me to be home by eight thirty for a surprise. This isn't a surprise! It's a nightmare!"

Ísa forgot about the cheesecake and turned to pace to the other end of the refrigerated-goods aisle. "All right, don't panic." She thought quickly. "Just do the same thing you did with the other five. Tell your folks you have nothing in common with him and can't see a marriage working out."

"The other five were asses." More paper-bag breathing. "My family didn't like them either. What if this guy isn't an ass and my parents and grandmother love him?" Nayna's tone was becoming increasingly more agitated. "What if I'm trapped in a marriage I don't want?"

"Look," Ísa said to her smart best friend who was

usually the most practical and calm person in the room. "This is your life. Your family can't force you to the altar."

"I love them, Ísa." A soft confession. "No matter what, I love them. I can't be like Madhuri and risk being cut off."

Ísa understood the complex ties of family and love, understood that sometimes it was impossible not to be bound even when you knew the tie was unhealthy. "How about if…" Ísa snapped her fingers. "Say that during your private talk, you discovered that he's a little dim in the brain department."

Ísa felt bad for plotting against some poor, hardworking man, but Nayna came first. "Knowing your folks, he's likely to have a degree or two, so maybe also hint that perhaps all isn't kosher there. Or that you got the impression he barely scraped by."

"Oh God, you're a genius, Ísa!" The sound of the paper bag being scrunched up. "My parents are already planning for grandchildren with doctorates—a less-than-intelligent son-in-law will *not* do."

Having returned to the cheesecake section, Ísa said, "You better go get ready."

"That won't take me long. I'm not exactly going to go all out." Nayna's tone brightened. "In fact, I think I'll wear that pale pink outfit that makes me look like a brown wraith. What are you doing?"

"Trying to choose between boysenberry cheesecake and passion fruit cheesecake."

"Are you eating cheesecake without me?" A glare in the words.

"I'm making a horrible mistake, that's what I'm doing," Ísa admitted. "I'm having dinner with Sailor at his place."

"Do it, Ísa." Nayna's voice was suddenly quiet, potent.

"I've played it safe my whole life, and now I feel like I'm going to shatter if I don't spread my wings. Take a chance. Make that mistake. Even if it hurts... At least you'll have lived instead of being driven by fear."

And that was the heart of it: *fear*.

Of rejection.

Of hurt.

Of not being enough to hold his attention.

NOT LONG AFTERWARD, RIGHT ON the dot of when she'd promised to meet Sailor, and Ísa still couldn't believe she was about to do this.

Sailor was just getting out of his truck when she brought her car to a stop on the street outside his apartment. He'd parked on the street too. It looked like his apartment was one of those converted townhouses that didn't have a garage. Most people who lived in this area likely didn't care since they worked in the city and didn't bother to keep a vehicle, but with Sailor...

"Aren't you worried about your truck?" she asked after stepping out of her own car. "You've got equipment in the back."

He indicated a standalone, old-fashioned garage with a peaked roof that she'd assumed belonged to the neighboring property. "I rent that as well," he said. "But it's too old to have an electronic door, so I have to go and push it up before I move my truck inside."

As she watched, he jogged over to unlock the garage. "Sorry for the wait," he said after coming back to the truck. "This will only take a minute."

"I don't mind," Ísa said.

Shooting her a smile that made the butterflies in her

stomach take flight all over again despite the fear knotted around her spine, he backed his truck expertly into the garage, then got out and locked up.

He was beside her seconds later, his big body making her want to curl into him.

"Let me grab that." He took the grocery bag she'd been holding. In his other hand, he held a bag filled with what looked like lettuce and possibly cucumbers. "From my mother's garden," he said after catching her glance. "She'd kill me dead if I dared buy salad stuff." Moving both bags to one hand, he took her the three steps to the front door, unlocked it with a key code.

"The place is separated into four apartments," he told her after following her inside, his hand touching her on her lower back for a moment that made her breath catch. "Honestly, the apartments are a little small, but because they're so small, the four of us pay a good rental for this part of town."

Taking her hand in a warm and callused grip that felt dangerously possessive, he tugged her up the stairs. "Downstairs, both men work for an airline company and are on rotating shifts, so some months I see them, others they're ghosts. Upstairs, it's me and a city type whose hours hardly overlap with mine since I start with the light and end with it while he starts and finishes later."

"All men?" Ísa said. "Was that on purpose?" An immature part of her did a little booty dance because the idea of Sailor sleeping in close quarters with another woman just rubbed her wrong.

Yes, she was in big, BIG trouble.

"No." Sailor unlocked his own door using a key. "Just turned out that way. Welcome to my humble abode."

Ísa walked in on curious feet. When she saw him

kicking off his boots by the door, she toed off her kitten heels as well. Seeing what she'd done, Sailor grinned. "Cute toes, spitfire. But don't worry about the shoes. I just take off my boots because they tend to get filthy over the course of the day."

"It's not a problem." Ísa was itching to explore every inch of his private space. "I like feeling the carpet under my feet." That carpet led into a small living area, beyond which was an equally small balcony. To the left was a kitchenette that looked out into the living area over a breakfast counter, while to the right was a corridor with three doors that opened off it.

Ísa assumed those led to Sailor's bedroom and the facilities and maybe a closet.

Devil Ísa whispered for her to invite herself to explore. Clothing optional.

She was glad for the cool air coming from outside when, after putting the groceries on the counter, Sailor opened the balcony doors.

"It's not much," he said. "Certainly not what you're probably used to. But it works okay for me."

And Ísa's brain clicked.

20

HEALTH NOTE: SLEEPING IN THE NUDE
HAS MANY BENEFITS

"I'M NOT ACTUALLY RICH, YOU know," Ísa said bluntly.

Where Cody had pursued her to get at Jacqueline's wealth, it seemed Sailor was discomfited by the same. "It's my parents' money, not mine." She held his gaze. "The only reason I have a fancy apartment that I can't afford on my own is because I need room so my siblings can come stay." Not quite the truth, but close enough.

Because both Harlow and Catie would've happily crashed on a couch or on a mattress on the floor. As a child, Catie had spent more than one night cuddled up to her big sister. She'd been so small, a wee thing, but she'd often taken over the whole bed while Ísa clung to the side. But Catie was thirteen now, and her life had changed fundamentally. There were things she needed to not be self-conscious, to be her sparky self.

Ísa and Jacqueline had worked together to ensure the apartment had all those things.

"Do you understand?" she said to the blue-eyed man

in front of her. "It's important to me that I make my own way in the world. Teachers don't earn that much." Especially teachers who'd taken an entire year off in the middle of a rising career.

Ísa had zero regrets about her choice.

"Yeah, spitfire, I get it." Sailor chucked her under the chin as if she were five years old. Her scowl just made him grin. "I need to have a shower—I'm filthy. Do you want to grab a seat and watch TV while I wash off the day?"

Ísa's mind immediately bombarded her with images of Sailor half-naked and gleaming wet, soapsuds dripping down his chest... and lower. Closing her hands into fists by her side, she said, "Why don't I get to work on a salad?"

"I didn't bring you here to work." It was his turn to scowl, the five-o'clock shadow on his jaw just adding to his dark sexiness. "I brought you here because you looked like you could do with a little TLC."

A strange feeling invaded Ísa's bones. "I won't exert myself," she promised, flustered into breaking the eye contact. "I'll leave the hard-core cooking to you."

"I have a feeling you're laughing at me," Sailor grumbled, "but since you're cute, I'll let you get away with it." A tug on a strand of her hair. "The kitchen's tiny—I'm sure you'll find everything you need."

Ísa couldn't help but watch him move as he headed down the short corridor to the right. It was unfair how beautiful he was from the back as well. The man worked with his body all day and it showed, but it wasn't just the physical that attracted her. Not now that she'd learned of his passion and drive, seen the rough affection with which he treated his brother, glimpsed a hint of what it would be like to be the woman Sailor considered his own.

When, of course, he was ready for a relationship.

Which wouldn't be anytime soon.

I'm married to my business. She's also my very demanding mistress. Doesn't tolerate other women for long periods.

Grabbing the lettuce leaves on that harsh mental reminder, she began to wash them out; the crisp green leaves had small specks of dirt on them from being newly taken from the garden. She wondered if it was Sailor's mother who'd given him his love for the earth. And she told herself not to care.

Because none of this would last. Sooner, rather than later, Sailor Bishop would make a choice, and that choice wouldn't be Ísa. Sailor had big dreams, a huge passion for his work. Even though Ísa knew that passion would only hurt her in the end, she couldn't help admiring him for it. To be so driven and determined at twenty-three, it said a great deal about the man he'd become in the years ahead.

Take a chance. Make that mistake. Even if it hurts... At least you'll have lived instead of being driven by fear.

Ísa shuddered under the memory of Nayna's words.

A door opening and then closing down the hall. The sound of the shower came on a couple of seconds later. Despite her troubled thoughts, Ísa found herself imagining Sailor naked and wet all over again, his muscles moving as he lifted his face to the spray and pushed back his hair, washing off the sweat and hard work of a long day out under the summer sun.

Groaning, she tried to wipe the images from her brain. But said brain refused to cooperate, the images too beautiful and luscious to discard. So she listened to the shower and she tortured herself and she tried not to think about anything but this moment in time. The future would still be there tomorrow.

So would Sailor's dreams.

And Ísa's.

Both heading in different directions.

SAILOR SHOWERED QUICKLY, EAGER TO get back to Ísa and see if he could find out what was bugging her. She'd looked so sad sitting there in the car, the sparkle gone from her face and worry carving heavy lines into her forehead. The desire to just close his arms around her and hold her tight was so potent that he figured he'd have to sneak in a hug at some point.

Drying off, he pulled on the clothes he'd brought with him into the bathroom. Normally he just walked naked from the shower to his bedroom. As long as he'd closed the bedroom blinds before he left for his shower, he wasn't in any danger of permanently scarring his neighbors.

For a second, he thought about playing with Ísa by hitching a towel around his hips and walking out—she did seem to like the look of him, and he was man enough to enjoy the way her eyes ate him up, but he had a feeling that today wasn't the right time. So he pulled on a faded and worn pair of jeans along with an equally soft and faded white T-shirt.

Running a hand through his hair to settle it, he stepped out and padded barefoot to the kitchen. A salad sat neatly covered up in a bowl on the counter. Since there weren't many places Ísa could be—the bonus of a one-bedroom apartment—he quickly located her on the balcony.

Going out to stand behind her in the tiny space, the night quiet around them, he fought the urge to nuzzle her as he pointed south. "If you squint really hard and cross your eyes at the same time, you can almost see the dark of water out in the distance." He wrapped his arms loosely around her, sneaking in that hug while she was distracted.

Ísa laughed. "What about that mountain in the way?"

"Details, details." Drawing in a long breath of her, he decided to mess with the boss even though he shouldn't.

He tightened his arms just enough that she noticed, then dropped his head and kissed the curve of her neck. Her shiver delighted him. So he stole another kiss and another. Until his redhead melted back into him. "You have skin I could kiss all day," he purred against her throat before forcing himself to rise to his full height.

Oh, he had every intention of seducing Ísa.

First, however, he'd look after her, give her that TLC she needed. Which included a good meal. "Let's get this food cooking—I don't want you hungry," he murmured. "I'll eat up the rest of you later." Another shiver.

He smiled just a little smugly before releasing her to turn on the grill he kept on the balcony. Once he had that going, he went inside the house and quickly wrapped up a couple of sweet potatoes in tinfoil. Those he chucked onto the hottest part of the grill, where the flames licked through, to roast while he prepared the fish.

Ísa followed him inside, watching as he seasoned the fish.

"My brother's recipe," he told her. "The brother you met today. He loves muscle cars and cooking, wants to be a chef with a Mustang if he doesn't make the top rugby squads." Having a fallback passion could only be a good thing in the high stakes world of sports. "Our youngest brother, Danny, still thinks cooking is for girls."

Propping her elbows on the counter, her face cupped in her hands—and her skin a little flushed from their play on the balcony, she said, "The rest of you don't?"

"Ha! My mother made damn sure we never grew up with that particular belief—even Danny only mumbles about cooking being for girls when she's out of earshot." His kid brother would grow out of that soon enough; at fourteen and the baby of the family, he was currently on the border between child and youth.

"We're not great cooks, Gabe and I, but we can feed ourselves. Though," he admitted, "Mom feeds me too when she thinks I haven't been taking care of myself. She'd do it for Gabe as well except the team nutritionists take care of the players' diets." Not that it stopped his older brother and closest friend from turning up for Sunday dinner.

Ísa dropped her hands to the counter, her expression soft, vulnerable. "I can't imagine that, you know." Again that lingering sadness in her.

Sailor decided to hell with it. Leaning forward, he kissed her nose before he went back to dusting on a bit of some herb Jake had left him with strict instructions not to go overboard with it. "What can't you imagine?" he asked the redhead who was staring at him as if he were an alien... but an alien she liked. Sailor could work with that. "Me and my brothers cooking?"

"No." A shake of her head, her hair a burst of sunset. "A mom who cooks for you even though you've moved out of the family home. Does she make you frozen meals?" She said the last as if they were talking about some magical discovery, all wide-eyed wonder.

Sailor was fascinated by her fascination. "It's a little embarrassing to admit, but yes. She knows I'm working all hours to get my business off the ground, so every so often, she makes extra of whatever she's cooking and sets a few portions aside for me that I can reheat." Seeing Ísa's continued interest, he figured he might as well admit the whole of it. "And my dad has been known to drop off fresh groceries so I won't live on canned goods."

Sailor knew he was lucky with his tightly bonded family, had always known he was lucky, but it was only now, as he looked into Ísa's wistful face, that he understood exactly how lucky. "I'm guessing Jacqueline wasn't much of a cook," he said, with another kiss on the nose. "Your dad?"

This time she smiled, as if warming up to the nose-kissing alien in front of her.

"My dad's basically the charming male version of Jacqueline." Dry words. "When I was a toddler, they both spent so many hours at the office that I apparently started to call my nanny Mommy and the cook Daddy. Jacqueline and Stefán had to switch to short-term contractors to keep me from getting confused."

Ísa rolled her eyes as she said that, as if it was just an amusing little anecdote, but Sailor saw nothing funny in a child so disregarded by her mother and father that she'd tried to find family in her parents' employees. Who the fuck did that to their baby? And then to take those familiar figures away just so Jacqueline and Stefán could still feel like parents?

Unforgiveable.

Sailor clenched his jaw. Hoping she'd at least had grandparents who'd given her love and spoiled her rotten, he was about to ask about her extended family when her phone rang.

The ringtone was the theme music from *Star Trek*.

"It's Harlow," Ísa said with open affection. "My brother."

Sailor tried not to listen in on the conversation, but

there wasn't much he could do to make his apartment bigger. So even though Ísa had stepped out onto the balcony, he still heard pretty much every word.

Her first words were cheerful. "Hey, Harlow."

Silence for a minute or two before Ísa spoke again. "You got the job fair and square." A firm tone. "I spoke to Ginny—she told me that HR had no idea who you were until it was time to actually offer you the position and you confessed your identity."

Another period of silence followed by "Of course I'm sure. Have I ever lied to you?" She listened again. "No," she said in response to Harlow's reply. "Mother wouldn't have taken it from you. You know she admires initiative."

Sailor happened to be looking over at her right then, and so he saw the fingers she'd crossed behind her back.

By the time she finally hung up and came back inside, he was finished with the fish prep. "Problem?"

Pressing her lips together, she put her hands on her hips. "Harlow won an internship at Crafty Corners after applying under a pseudonym so there'd be no cries of favoritism. But an unsuccessful applicant from his school posted something nasty online about it." Her eyes sparked with temper.

Impressed at the steps her brother had taken to make the process fair, Sailor said, "So why are you crossing your fingers behind your back?"

Ísa's skin flushed a delicate pink. Folding her arms, she said, "You weren't supposed to have seen that."

He wanted to take little bites out of her. "Come on, fess up."

"It's family business."

Sailor put together what he'd heard of the phone call

with what he knew of Ísa's family. "Jacqueline being a hardass?"

A scowl from his redhead. "Stop using your telepathic powers on me."

Feeling young in a way he rarely did, he grinned. "How old's your brother?"

"Seventeen." Ísa regarded his grin with suspicion. "Technically we're stepsiblings. Jacqueline married his father when Harlow was twelve."

Sailor hadn't paid too much attention to the tidbits about Jacqueline's personal life in the research he'd done. He'd been far more interested in her business strategies. Some of that information *had*, however, stuck, so he knew the marriage Ísa was talking about couldn't have lasted long. Yet she'd embraced Harlow as her brother.

That said a lot about his curvy spitfire.

Her phone rang again just as she'd parted her mouth to speak, the ringtone a generic one. Ísa glanced at the screen. "It's Oliver, my mother's current husband."

Lifting the phone to her ear on that mystified state ment, she answered in front of Sailor. "Oliver, hello." Then, "What?" in pure astonishment. "You know I don't have that kind of influence on her." She listened for a while. "Oh, I'm sorry. Look, I'll try, okay? Can't promise anything though."

Hanging up, she blew out a breath. "I have to make a call. Is there any point in my going to the balcony?"

"Nope. You want to go in my bedroom? The sheets are still messy from this morning," he said in deliberate provo-cation. "Hot dreams about a hot redhead."

Color on her cheekbones, but she held her ground. "Probably matches my bed. I took off my pj's in the middle of the night, I got so hot. Nude sleeping apparently has a lot of health benefits."

"Oh, I know, spitfire," Sailor drawled. "I don't own pj's."

Her pupils dilated, her breath catching.

And Sailor's body began to push for hard, dirty, physical TLC.

21

KNIGHT IN GARDENING ARMOR

S AILOR GRIPPED THE EDGE OF the counter and tried to count to a hundred to get his erection under control while, across from him, his wicked little playmate made her call. Her voice, he was pleased to note, was breathy, the pulse in her throat moving too fast.

"Mom," she was saying, "Oliver cooked you an anniversary dinner, even timed it for your usual late finish. You know this is a big deal for him. Go home." A long pause before she said, "Shall I order the divorce cake now? Chocolate or red velvet?"

When she hung up a few seconds later without further words, Sailor figured Jacqueline had decided to go have dinner with her husband. "Does that kind of thing happen often?" he asked as he walked out to the grill to put on the fish.

"That's a new one." Ísa leaned in the doorway of the balcony, and it felt intimately comfortable—as if they'd been doing this forever.

As if he knew her bone deep.

Yeah, Sailor wasn't stupid. This, what they had, it was something special. He'd do whatever it took to convince his redhead to stick with him. Even if it meant using his manly wiles and body to confuse her every time she thought of a good reason why they weren't suited.

"Poor Oliver," she said with a shake of her head. "It's like a marriage between a befuddled puppy and a barracuda."

Her phone rang for the third time before Sailor could reply.

Worry swept over Ísa's features like a tidal wave. "My sister's a texter except when there's a problem." She lifted the phone to her ear. "Catiebug?" Her body straightened. "Catie, honey what's the matter? Is it—" A pause. "Yes, I'll do it now."

Shoving a hand through her hair after hanging up, she paced back to the counter as she made another call. Then it was back to Catie. "Your father's fine, sweetheart. He must have his phone on silent. The hotel concierge confirmed for me that Clive is on the gaming floor."

A minute later, she walked out to take a seat on the single chair he had on the other side of his postage-stamp-sized space. "Sorry about that," she said, her arm hooked over the back of the chair. "Catie heard about a Kiwi man of her dad's age getting mugged at the hotel where he's staying and panicked."

Yet instead of calling Jacqueline, the other girl had called Ísa. And Ísa had just handled it, was now sitting chatting with him as if the past fifteen minutes hadn't been extraordinary, as if she hadn't just put out three emotional fires without blinking.

Sailor was both proud of his redhead and irritated by the other adults in her life who clearly weren't pulling their weight. From what he'd witnessed so far, it was starting to look like she was the main support for her siblings. "He's your dad too?"

"No, Jacqueline and Stefán were long divorced by then," Ísa clarified. "Catie's father is a smooth-talking idiot named Clive. He deliberately turns off his phone when he just can't be bothered. I swear to God, if I could microchip him, I would."

"Remind me never to get on your bad side." Sailor braced his hands on the arms of her outdoor chair. "You're cute but ferocious."

"Grr."

Shoulders shaking as her eyes danced on that mock growl, he snuck in a kiss before going into the apartment. When he returned, it was with a girly cocktail in hand, the color a lush pink. He'd even managed to find a tiny toothpick umbrella to stick in it.

"Here," he said. "Nothing fancy. Just a frozen cocktail mix that I keep for when my mom visits."

HE KEPT ON DOING THAT. Kept on doing things that made her happy.

Accepting the drink with a feeling of falling deeper into a dangerous hole, Ísa took a cautious sip. Cold and sweet and tart, the flavors exploded on her tongue. She'd have told him it was delicious regardless, she was so undone by the way he kept giving her the TLC he'd promised, but now she didn't have to.

"I love raspberry daiquiris," she said and was rewarded with a pleased grin from where he stood by the grill, carefully flipping the fish steak.

He looked so good standing there against the backdrop

of the night, dressed in comfortable clothes. And she felt so good sitting here, the two of them just relaxing after a long day at work. It was a flash-fire moment, her dreams colliding with her reality.

Be in this moment, she whispered to herself. *Don't fear the heartbreak to come.*

"I can tell it's not very alcoholic," she said when her throat threatened to close up. "That's good, because I'm a bit of a cheap drunk."

A deep chuckle. "Now I want to see you being all drunk and adorable."

"The night has just begun." Feeling silly and young, Ísa pretended to open up the cocktail umbrella and use it as a parasol.

Sailor grinned, and they talked about this and that as the food finished cooking.

She discovered that his elder brother was Gabriel Bishop, a gray-eyed force of nature who was the most worshipped rugby player in the country. Both his younger brothers were also aiming for a professional rugby career.

"I'm the black sheep," Sailor said with an unrepentant grin. "I just play for fun. There has been talk of disowning me."

Compelled by this new glimpse into what was clearly a very close-knit family, Ísa asked more questions as they sat down to dinner. He asked some in turn. She couldn't remember time ever moving so fast, but they'd finished dinner before she knew it.

"I'll get dessert," Sailor said.

But rather than the cheesecake she'd picked up, he put a perfectly decorated miniature cake in front of her, the frosting dusted with sparkles. "There's a café-slash-cake shop real close to my parents' house. I saw this in the window and thought of you."

Ísa couldn't take it anymore.

Fisting her hand in his T-shirt, she hauled him down to her mouth.

He tasted like red-hot sin and temptation designed to lure a woman into the worst mistake of her life. Ísa didn't care. Sliding her hand around to the back of his neck, she gloried in the strength of him as he angled his head, and, thrusting one hand into her hair, licked his tongue against hers.

Her nipples furled into tight points, each brush against the lace of her bra making her want to rip off her clothes to free the excruciatingly sensitive flesh. So he could touch them with those big, capable hands. So she could press them to the hard wall of his chest.

When he broke the kiss to crouch in front of her chair, she bit down on her swollen lower lip. His eyes zeroed in on the act, his chest heaving as badly as hers. "We need some ground rules."

Ísa blinked. "What?"

"I'm not your employee, but I am working for your company." He pressed his finger to her lips when she would've parted them to speak. "The first rule is, when it comes to the physical stuff between the two of us, it's only Sailor and Ísa. Not a contractor and the VP."

Ísa was too far in to back away now. "Done." That was when Devil Ísa took over her mouth. "Where are the handcuffs?"

A sucked-in breath, a dangerous smile.

Rising to his feet, Sailor held out his hand. "Come into my lair, my innocent redheaded spitfire. I promise to only bite a little."

Breasts aching and skin electric, Ísa was about to go all in when her fantasies of being at Sailor's mercy died a sudden death under the burst of a ringtone she'd already heard once earlier that night.

"This isn't good." She scrambled to grab her phone from her satchel. "Catie is scarily competent for all that she has to deal with. If she's calling me again..." Phone in hand, she lifted it to her ear. "Catie?"

The voice on the other end made her blood run cold. "Martha? Why are you on Catie's phone?" The former nurse's answer had her trembling. "Where was she taken?" Mentally noting the location, she said, "I'm on my way."

Hanging up, she looked at Sailor, her heart a huge piece of concrete in her chest. "I have to go. My sister's had an accident."

Eyes grim, Sailor put his hands on her upper arms. "How bad?"

"Martha—her live-in helper—says she's fine, but I need to see for myself." Breaking away, she grabbed her satchel. "Catie *hates* being in the hospital." She wasn't the only one; the mere smell of antiseptic was enough to send Ísa right back into a nightmare.

Looking up at Sailor, she forced herself to meet his eyes. "I know this wasn't how you probably wanted the evening to go. I'm really sorry." All the reasons she'd listed for why they were so wrong for each other and she'd forgotten one thing: the ties of family.

What twenty-three-year-old male would want to be with a woman who was basically the parent-on-call for two teenagers? Ísa would *never* regret giving Catie and Harlow the solid foundation she'd searched for her entire life, but she was horrified to find herself on the verge of tears at the idea that this was it with Sailor. That she'd never see him again, never kiss him, never make that horrible mistake.

He scowled at her. "Don't think you're getting out of the handcuffs, spitfire. That's just been delayed."

God, he was *wonderful*. "I'll call you. I promise. Not like with the cookie date."

But Sailor shook his head. "No need, because I'm going to be with you. Let me grab my keys. I'll drive you to the hospital—I know my truck looks a little beat up, but it's a smoothly oiled working machine."

Ísa could think of nothing better than to do this with him, but it wasn't possible. "No, you don't understand. Catie lives in Hamilton."

Sailor tapped his finger on the table. "It's doable," he said. "With the new roads and the lack of traffic at this time of day, we should be able to get there in an hour and forty-five minutes."

"I might have to stay overnight. You have work here."

"You're my boss," he pointed out with another one of those affectionate nose kisses that kept on sweeping her feet out from under her. "It's not like you're going to put me on notice."

When she went to speak again, he just shook his head. "I'll never forgive myself if you have an accident, Ísa. You're too anxious to drive."

Since her hands were trembling, Ísa couldn't do anything but nod. "Thank you."

"No need. I'm just adding it to your time-in-fur-lined-handcuffs tab."

Grabbing his wallet and keys on that wicked statement, Sailor shoved his feet into an old pair of sneakers. They were on their way to Hamilton five minutes later.

"SO," SAILOR SAID ONCE THEY were away, "what kind of an accident was it?" He didn't immediately assume vehicular. With three brothers, he'd seen all kinds of accidents, from falling off ladders, to falling off skateboards, to being smashed in a rugby tackle. "I once lost a tooth after Gabriel threw a small pumpkin at my face."

A startled movement from Ísa, his words apparently slicing through her tense concern. "Were you two fighting?" It was a highly disapproving question.

"Nah, we were playing 'dodge the pumpkin.' All fun and games until Sailor loses a tooth and we both end up grounded."

"How old were you?"

"Old enough to know better." The two of them had laughed so hard while playing that most of their throws had gone wild. "Gabe caught the pumpkin in his gut at one point. We didn't realize he had a cracked rib until after the tooth."

"Good grief. And your poor parents had to deal with *four* of you?"

"Two at a time, really," Sailor said in defense of his brothers. "Gabe and I had grown out of the idiocy by the time Danny and Jake grew into it. Mostly."

He caught the twitch of Ísa's lips in his quick glance. But it wasn't until ten minutes later as they were streaming along the motorway, rock playing softly on the radio, that she spoke.

"Catie fell," she said at last. "And yes, I know I'm overreacting. I can see myself doing it, but I can't stop it." A shuddering exhale. "When Catie was born," she continued, "I was *so* happy. I thought she was the most wonderful little being ever created. I loved her at once, wanted to protect her from any pain—but I couldn't. Catie was born with a heart problem. Not a big thing. Fixable."

"But?"

Ísa pressed a hand over her chest, Sailor seeing the movement with his peripheral vision. "She got an infection after the surgery, has this scar on her chest from where her suture site threatened to go septic. But she pulled through, came out healthy on the other side."

"Tough kid," Sailor said.

"Yes, she is." Fierce pride. "Despite all the pain, all the needles, she was such a happy baby. She used to smile and giggle every time she saw me."

Ísa was smiling herself, Sailor could hear it.

"We'd cuddle for hours," she added, "and when she had too many wires coming out of her to be moved, I'd sit there and play with her little fingers and toes, and she'd giggle at me in this contagious way that would set me off."

As Sailor heard the ease with which Ísa spoke about Catie's hospital stay during infancy, he realized that period in their lives wasn't the cause of her panic. "What aren't you telling me, spitfire?"

He heard Ísa swallow. "You'd think after all her problems as a baby, she'd have had more than her quota of bad luck. But two years ago, just after she turned eleven, Catie was at the lights waiting for the crossing signal when a delivery truck slid on the road and spun sideways... right across the spot where Catie was standing."

"Hell." Sailor's gut twisted. "How bad?"

"Bad, but not the worst," Ísa said. "No brain damage or sensory loss, and the doctors managed to save most of her limbs."

Most.

Sailor clenched his jaw, furious at fate on behalf of a thirteen-year-old girl he'd never met. "Which couldn't they save?"

"Both her lower legs. She was a runner before, had dreams of going to the Olympics. Fastest girl in her school, already being considered for training squads. You'd never in a million years guess she'd had a heart issue as a baby."

For an athletic child to become a double amputee... Fuck, for any child to wake up without limbs. "How did she handle it?"

"Better than I did." Ísa's laugh was shaky. "After the first shock wore off, she said, 'Can you do my homework while I grow some new legs, Issie? I don't want to be that kid who says she didn't hand in her homework because her legs got chopped off.'" A shake of Ísa's head. "That's her father's sense of humor."

"And her sister's grit." Catie must have learned not to give up from someone, and from what Sailor had seen so far, he didn't think it had been Jacqueline who'd taught her that resilience. Because to teach a child something, you had to be present and part of her life.

"Catie's still set on heading to the Olympics," Ísa said with a smile. "She was determined to get out of bed and learn to use prosthetics as fast as possible. And I'll say one thing for Clive—he's an unreliable flake most of the time, but he didn't budge from her side at the hospital."

"Your mother?"

"Jacqueline doesn't deal well with sickness," Ísa said softly. "But by the time Catie left the hospital, Jacqueline had renovated Clive's house so that it had everything Catie needed, including a gym where she could work on her rehabilitation—with the aid of a private physiothera-pist. My mother can be a complicated woman."

One who clearly relied on Ísa to pick up her emotional slack, Sailor thought with a frown. And if Ísa was the one who took care of giving Catie and Harlow the affection and love they needed to thrive, who the fuck had taken care of Ísa when she'd been their age?

22

OH DEAR. ONLY ONE SPARE BEDROOM

Í SA, UNAWARE OF HIS SILENT fury on behalf of the girl she'd once been, was still speaking. "Catie had everything down pat—you should've seen her go on those prosthetics."

"Let me guess," Sailor said, thinking about why an athletic girl comfortable with prosthetics would suddenly fall hard enough to end up in hospital, "growth spurt?"

"Yep. I swear, she's taller every time I turn around!" Ísa threw up her hands. "But the constant changes are messing with her head. Each time Catie gets used to a prosthetic, it has to be adapted or changed out."

"It's tough for an athlete when their body doesn't cooperate." Sailor had grown up in a family of athletes, seen that frustration firsthand.

"EXACTLY." ÍSA FELT A TENSION she hadn't realized she was feeling, just fall away. Often, well-meaning people downplayed Catie's dreams of being a champion runner, telling her it'd be better if she focused on creating an independent life for herself by studying for a position "she could handle."

Quite aside from the fact that Catie was talented enough to create an independent life for herself *with* her running, the idea of anyone trying to limit her sister infuriated Ísa. As if, unlike the rest of the world, Catie didn't get to have big dreams to strive toward.

"It's like containing the wind. You should see her in motion, Sailor."

"Did she fall today because of an unfamiliar set of prosthetics, or did she just fall?"

Ísa was startled by his perception until she realized this was a man whose brother was one of the top sportsmen in the country—he understood that, sometimes, performance didn't have anything to do with the body. "I think she probably wasn't paying attention because she was worrying about her father."

She took a moment to think about it. "I'm going to have to strangle Clive. That's all there is to it."

"Is that why she's not living with you? Because she worries about her father?"

"That, and she loves the moron." Ísa shoved a hand through her hair. "When I made noises about moving down to Hamilton, maybe getting a job in one of the local schools, Catie said a flat-out no. She thinks if I'm there, she'll rely on me too much—and that I'd be too overprotective."

An amused glance from Sailor. "You think?"

"Oh, shut up." She pushed lightly at his arm, oddly comfortable with this man she'd only known for a short time—and far calmer than she'd been at the start of this drive. "She's only *thirteen*, but she's got this fierce need for independence."

"Your sister sounds like a tough little cookie." Sailor's deep voice wrapping around her. "A chip off the old block." His tone made it clear he wasn't talking about Jacqueline.

The words felt like a hug.

SAILOR HAD PLANNED TO STAY outside the hospital room while Ísa went in to see her sister, but the auburn-haired teenager in the bed within was having none of it.

"Ísa," she said, arching her neck to see more of Sailor, "who is *that*? Hey, mister!"

Unable to stop his smile, Sailor walked in. "Hey, yourself."

"This is Sailor." The tips of Ísa's ears turned pink. "My... friend."

"It's good to meet you, Catie." Sailor positioned himself beside Ísa's curvy form. "I didn't think your sister should be driving down here alone—she was pretty worried about you."

Catie rolled her eyes. "Martha told you that you didn't have to come." Even as she spoke, her hand remained tightly curled around Ísa's. "It was just a stupid fall. I was walking up and down the drive to stretch my muscles and looking at my phone instead of my feet, and well... splat." She made a face, her poor nose all scratched up and her upper lip busted. "Docs don't think I did any real damage. Just some bruising that means I'll have to go easy during my next training session."

"You make sure you do that." Ísa pressed a kiss to Catie's forehead on those firm words. "As for me coming down here—that was nonnegotiable. I'm always going to worry about you, Catiebug."

Catie leaned so quickly into her sister's body, into her touch, that Sailor realized just how desperately the teenager had needed Ísa to be here tonight, holding her. Jacqueline might've birthed Catie, and Clive might call himself her father, but Ísa was her rock. Sailor's redhead knew how to love her people.

Sailor's heart clenched, a raw craving in his gut.

Turning her dark brown eyes toward Sailor without pulling away from Ísa, Catie said, "So, you two are friends?" A waggle of her eyebrows, dimples peeking out in both cheeks. "What *kind* of friends?"

"*Catie.*"

Sailor grinned and folded his arms. "The kind of friends who can road-trip together without fighting over the music, Brown Eyes," he said to a delighted smile from Catie. "So, any idea when we can spring you from this joint?"

A plump older woman bustled in from the corridor right then. Her hair was dark and her features a mix of what Sailor would bet was Chinese and Samoan. She reminded him of one of his younger cousins on his dad's side, his middle aunt having married an engineer from Shanghai after meeting him during a language-exchange program.

"Oh, Ísa, you're here," she said, her face breaking out into a smile. "I just went to grab a muffin for our girl. The café was closed, so I drove over to the nearest convenience store."

"Thanks so much for looking after her, Martha," Ísa said, enfolding the older woman in a tight hug. "And for calling me. Do you know if the doctors are ready for her to go home?"

"Oh yes." Martha handed Catie a brown paper bag.

"Another half hour's observation and they'll sign off on her release."

"That's fantastic." Ísa stroked back her sister's unbound hair.

Catie tucked herself up against Ísa once more while stuffing her face with what appeared to be an enormous orange chocolate chip muffin. Seeing Sailor's interested glance, she held out the bag. "Want some?"

Sailor shrugged and tore off a piece. "Thanks." No sane member of the Bishop-Esera clan ever brought only one muffin—the ensuing riot would end in bloodshed.

When Catie smiled at him this time, it was a little devious. "Are you going to stay the night?" she asked with utmost innocence. "It's just that we only have one spare bedroom."

"I'm guessing you have a sofa," Sailor responded with deadpan solemnity.

Catie pulled away her muffin with a scowl so reminiscent of Ísa that Sailor knew he'd have to be very careful not to be charmed. "This is *not* like how it goes in the romance movies."

"Eat your muffin, Catiebug." Ísa tapped her sister on the nose in what seemed to be an affectionate holdover from Catie's childhood. "We'll go get your discharge papers sorted."

Sailor stayed with Catie while Ísa and Martha stepped out. The kid decided to share more of her cake-sized muffin with him while bombarding him with questions. During the interrogation, she managed to figure out that he was working for Fast Organic and that Ísa was technically his boss.

"No way." A long whistle. "How does that work? I mean, having your girlfriend be your boss?"

"She's not my girlfriend." Sailor found he didn't enjoy speaking that sentence. "Though if she was, I'm man enough to handle it. Only wimps fear strong women."

Catie held up a hand for a high five. After he'd returned it, she said, "Thanks for driving my sister. She worries a lot about me."

"And that's not good?"

A shrug that was very teenage in nature. "I mean, it's not her job, is it? I feel like I'm always calling her when it's my dad I should be calling." Her lips turned down at the corners. "Martha couldn't even get hold of him after my fall."

Not so much as a mention of Jacqueline.

And while dear dad didn't appear much better than Catie's absentee mother, the man *was* Catie's father. Some things were set in stone, and trying to change one of those immutable facts was a sure way to get a cracked skull and a bleeding soul.

Sailor knew that all too well himself.

"Your sister told me you're an athlete," he said, shifting the topic before he said something he probably shouldn't. "I've got a few in my family."

For the first time, Catie's response was a touch wary. "Yeah?"

"Rugby."

Her eyes narrowed... then widened. "Holy freaking crapazoids! No wonder you look familiar!" A poke to his abdomen. "Your brother's the Bishop. Admit it."

Sailor grinned. "Yep. Fan?"

"Are you kidding me? He's the *best*! Did you see how he took down that opposition player last week? Just mowed him down. Boom, Bishop slam!"

Always ready to talk rugby, Sailor discussed the game

with Catie before nodding at the prosthetics he could see sitting against a chair on the other side of the bed. "Those your walking legs?" The metal parts were sleekly robotic with no flesh-colored exterior.

"Yeah. I had really awesome skins on my last ones— dragons and stuff blowing up, but then I grew again. No point making these look amazing when I'm still growing. Argh!" She fell back dramatically against her pillow. "It's such a *major* pain to get new prosthetics fitted. It takes forever to get everything just right."

Even though she was lying down, Sailor could tell that Catie was already over Ísa's height, would probably nudge five seven or eight on her prosthetics. He chuckled. "My youngest brother has the opposite problem. He's fourteen and still waiting for his growth spurt." Catie would tower over Danny.

"Ouch." Catie winced. "That must be sucky."

"Danny's pretty chill about it." He took another look at the prosthetics, which appeared articulated for fluid move- ment. "When you run, do you use blades? I've always wanted to see what they look like in real life."

Catie's face lit up. "I have a set of basic running legs. My mother said she'll pay for the specialized sprinting blades I want as soon as I've stopped growing. They're insanely expensive." Bouncing in her hospital bed, Catie added, "I'm going crazy waiting for them, but she's right —it'd be dumb to waste the money when I'm beanpoling. And I'd be sooooo mad if I got a pair fitted just right, only to grow and have things go out of whack."

The two of them were talking the specifics of running blades when Ísa and Martha walked back into the room. Sailor, still sore about having been forced to deny that Ísa was his girlfriend, reached over to tweak a lock of her hair.

As Catie giggled, Ísa stood on tiptoe and brushed her mouth softly over his.

His gut clenched, his heart melting right into her hands.

THEY REACHED HOME AFTER ONE that morning. Martha's phone beeped with an incoming message just as they were about to walk into the house Catie shared with her father and the caregiver.

"It's my daughter wanting to talk," Martha said. "I texted her to say I was up."

"Tina's got a new baby who keeps her up," Catie volunteered. "But Martha only babysits sometimes because she thinks Tina should take responsibility for her own baby. Martha's not a nanny, and she raised her daughter on her own, didn't she?" The last words were spoken in a near-perfect mimicry of Martha's voice.

Martha pressed a noisy kiss to Catie's cheek. "Cheeky girl."

"Lies. Look at me—I'm shining my halo."

Grinning at the obvious affection between the two, Sailor left Martha to her call—the other woman decided to stay outside in the balmy summer night while the rest of them went in.

Catie's home had plenty of open space and lots of glass to let in light, but—as Catie had pointed out so helpfully back at the hospital—it had only a single spare bedroom. And the couch looked to be some sort of medieval torture device.

"Oh dear," Ísa said, looking at it, then looking at Sailor. "I'll take the couch."

Sailor, his hands on his hips, just shook his head. "No way, spitfire. Even you wouldn't fit on that."

They both looked at the torturously architectural thing with curved wooden arms; not only did it look hellaciously uncomfortable, it was barely wide enough to accommodate two *seated* adults. Forget about even a small person who wanted to stretch out.

"Catie!" Ísa called out. "What's with the couch?"

Catie, whom Ísa had already ensconced in her bedroom, tucking her in with kisses and hugs, called back, "Dad sold it! He said it wasn't up to his standards of style!"

Folding her arms, Ísa tapped her foot on the carpet. "I bought that couch," she muttered. "In fact, I furnished most of this house. I couldn't trust Clive with the money. Speaking of which, where the hell did he get the money for this thing? Anything this uncomfortable must've been expensive."

Another glance at Catie's bedroom, Ísa's volume soft when she said, "It was probably gambling winnings. Every so often, Clive hits it big, and that gives him just enough encouragement to keep going."

Sailor ran his hand down her back. The idea of leaving his child and going off to gamble was alien to him—he never even left his kid brothers alone when he was in charge of them—but he knew there were men like that. He and Gabe had spent their whole lives fighting to prove themselves a different breed, more akin to the man who'd raised them than the man who'd sired them.

While Gabe had long ago conquered his demons, Sailor's still howled.

"Come on," he said, "let's go check out the spare bedroom."

Ísa knew which room was Martha's, so they skipped that. Next to it was Clive's, the door open.

Ísa took one look inside and backed off with her hands raised in front of her. "I'd feel weird sleeping in there. He *is* technically my stepfather. Ex-stepfather."

"That would be weird," Sailor agreed. "And I don't feel right sleeping in the bed of some random dude. Especially one who puts black satin sheets on his bed." He scratched his jaw. "I bet they're slippery."

"I don't want to think about it."

Together, they opened the door of the third and final bedroom. It proved to be neat and tidy, with what looked like a king-sized bed made up with white cotton sheets. "It's big enough to share," Sailor said.

Ísa looked up at him through her lashes. The tips of her ears began to go pink.

His entire body humming in reaction, Sailor leaned down to whisper against one adorable ear. "We can carry on from our session in the water." He ran his hand down the lush curve of her rear. "To jog your memory, it involves a deliciously nude redhead in my arms."

23

SIZZLE AND ORGASM

"A RELATIONSHIP BETWEEN US WOULD never work," Ísa blurted out, terrified of how fast she was falling for this gorgeous, driven man. The way he'd been with Catie, it was *exactly* how she'd imagined the man of her dreams would be with her baby sister. Comfortable, affectionate, amazing.

Catie was already half in love with him.

Just like Ísa.

"Why not?" he asked with a black scowl. "Are you still hung up on the age thing?"

"You're *twenty-three*. I'm ready to settle down, have a child, build a life with someone."

Tipping up her chin, he pressed his nose to hers. "Yeah? And who's this perfect man you're going to dump me for?" It was a growl of sound.

Ísa scowled back at him. "I haven't met him yet."

"So you're dumping me for an imaginary man?"

"You're deliberately misunderstanding." She glared. "How am I supposed to find him when I'm with you?"

A shrug. "I don't care. I'm not going to cooperate in your dump-Sailor-for-an-imaginary-man scheme."

"You're infuriating." Fisting her hands in his hair, she kissed him, releasing all her fear, all her need, all her worry.

His hands powerful and warm at her hips, he pulled her up against the hard length of his body and met her tongue lash for lash.

Heart pounding when it was over, she broke the kiss—and he said, "Want to hear my suggestion?"

"No." She folded her arms and drew her eyebrows together.

"Too bad." A kiss on the nose again, the affectionate act smashing her walls to tiny fragments. "I say we don't run, we don't hide. We *try*." No laughter in his expression now, only a passionate tenderness. "I'm no poet, Ísa. I can't give you fancy words. But I know what we have is special. It's worth a fight."

Ísa had never backed down from a fight in her life. But this fight could well leave her bloodied and broken at the end. But her heart, her traitorous heart, it wouldn't let her walk away. Because what she felt for Sailor, it was a shooting star and an incandescent candle flame. "What," she whispered, her voice hoarse, "were you saying about a deliciously nude redhead?"

A slow, sinful smile. "Sexiest woman I've ever met. Heartbreaker curves and skin like moonlight."

And that was how Ísa found herself getting ready for bed in the bathroom attached to the guest bedroom, with Sailor doing the same in the bedroom itself. Devil Ísa had hissed at her to strip in front of him, but she had her limits.

She'd told Sailor they'd work up to nudity.

After kissing her until her toes curled, he'd said, "I'll enjoy unwrapping my redhead."

Her thighs clenched as she pulled on the large T-shirt she'd borrowed from her grinning sister, the soft fabric covering her panties and hitting her mid-thigh.

And she was dressed.

Ready to be unwrapped.

Stepping out of the bathroom, she caught Sailor in the process of throwing his jeans onto a chair that already held his T-shirt, his only covering white boxer briefs. That body... it made her want to whimper. He was all ridges and valleys and smooth golden skin and a tight butt that she wanted to bite. After she'd licked her way around his tattoos.

God, what was happening to her? Ísa Rain didn't have thoughts like that.

Except, it seemed, when it came to Sailor Bishop.

Turning around to face her, Sailor whistled. "Spitfire, you make that innocent T-shirt look indecent."

Ísa might've been unsure how to take those words if Sailor's body hadn't been making it blatantly clear exactly what he thought of hers, the ridge of his erection pressing demandingly against the front of his briefs.

She sucked in a hungry breath.

And he began to stalk her.

Ísa couldn't help it. She stumbled backward and backward... until her back hit the wall.

Coming to a stop in front of her, Sailor placed his hands palm-down on either side of her head, blocking her in against the wall in a private prison. His smile was wolfish, hungry. "No way for you to cut and run this time around."

The warning made every tiny hair on her body rise to quivering attention, her nipples tight points.

"Too bad I didn't remember the handcuffs." A nipping kiss of her lower lip. "We'll save them for next time."

Her breath coming in shallow rasps, Ísa gripped futilely at the wall. Her skin was overheated. Her heart racing. And she wanted nothing more than to tumble him to the bed and tear off his briefs with her teeth. But if her mother's life had taught Ísa one thing, it was to be aware of the consequences of her choices.

Wetting her throat, she managed to say, "Did you bring protection?"

Sailor froze. A second later, he groaned and dropped his head. "I hate myself right now," he said. "My cock hates me even more." Another pause. "Your ex-step—"

"*No.*" Ísa shuddered. "We are not going looking in his bedside drawer. That's—" She shuddered again. "Just no."

"Right. Which means…"

Ísa wanted to cry. "I hate us both," she muttered, clawing at the wall in her frustration.

Sailor looked up, a gleam in his eye. "When," he said, "was the last time you made out like a teenager?"

Not even when I was a teenager. She'd been too conscious of her weight and pale skin. "Is that what you're suggesting?" Her core felt silkily damp, and they'd barely begun.

"My briefs stay on." His body heat pulsed against her, a near tactile caress that taunted her to lift her hands, indulge herself in him. "Everything of yours can come off."

Brain cells finally firing, Ísa put her hands on her hips. "That doesn't seem fair."

"Who said I planned to play fair?" A deep rumble of

sound as he pressed close enough that the engorged tips of her breasts were crushed against his chest. "What I *am* planning is to make you come so hard that you keep on wanting more of the same." His mouth closed over hers, his hands shifting to grip her wrists and pin her hands above her head.

Ísa shivered, fingers curling into her palms.

Sailor's scent swept over her, deeply masculine and with an undertone of earth, as if the soil he so loved had seeped into his very cells. When he transferred both her wrists into one of his big hands, using his other hand to stroke her thigh as he began to kiss his way down her neck, it was all she could do to suck in air.

Then he said, "Breathe," and she realized she hadn't been doing it at all.

Her lungs expanded on a rush of oxygen that was almost painful, and a second later, she was sucking in another breath and sucking him in with it, the raw beauty and rough, earthy scent of Sailor a drug. "Let go of my hands." She was desperate to touch him.

"No." His voice was a deep rumble against her throat.

"No?" Ísa struggled to think. "That's not how this works."

"I threw away the rule book," said the unrepentant man who was currently sliding his fingers under the edge of her panties.

Chest heaving, Ísa scowled. "I get to touch you too."

He kissed her, nipping at her lower lip as if punishing her for her reprimand. Only this punishment made her blood turn to honey, especially when he moved his hand to her breast and squeezed. She'd taken off her bra because she couldn't stand the thought of sleeping in it but now realized she'd made a tactical mistake.

Her moan was throaty, sounded more like a porn star

than sensible Ísa Rain. Thank God their room wasn't right next to Martha's.

Sailor's smile turned very, very wicked. "Oh, I see." Another squeeze.

Moaning again, she scrambled to find the words. "Stop... ah... distracting me." Her breasts seemed to grow beneath the intense delight of his attention. "We were... ah... having a discussion."

Chuckling, the infuriating man kissed her again. And this time, as he stroked his tongue against hers, he ran his thumb over her nipple in the same languid rhythm until it was hard and pebbled and so exquisitely sensitive that she felt as if she'd die.

"*Sailor.*" It came out a command.

"Want something, spitfire?" he whispered against her mouth.

"Touch me."

Sailor squeezed her breast before dipping his head to kiss her neck once more. "I am touching you." His other hand tightened around her wrists.

"You know what I mean."

"I'm no mind reader," he said with a teasing glint in his eye. "And right now I'm very interested in this beautiful throat." He nipped sharply at it.

Ísa kicked him.

Unfortunately, since she was in bare feet and he was pressed up so tight against her, she made exactly zero impact. "You're a horrible man."

"You like me, admit it." A sucking kiss over her pulse. "Talk dirty to me, Ísa. I'll give you whatever you demand."

"Touch me... on my bare skin." She met his gaze when he looked up this time, the fire in the blue scalding.

Ísa had never been so wanted. "I love the feel of your hands on me," she said on a rush of erotic confidence. "Love how you have calluses that make your touch *just* rough enough."

"Oh, I like the things you say." With that gritty purr of a statement, he ran his hand over the top of her T-shirt and lower until he hit the very bottom edge. His knuckles brushed against her thighs for an electric second before he slipped his hand under the fabric and spread his fingers over the sensitive skin. "See," he said. "Asking for things gets you rewarded."

Ísa's skin shimmered with sensation, her pulse a skittering rush.

Leaning in, he kissed her again. Soft, teasing little kisses that played with her mouth, made her arch toward him. When he ran his thumb across the flesh of her thighs, the very tip of his thumb brushed against the elastic edge of her panties.

Ísa couldn't help her whimper.

"Shh." A smiling command. "We don't want Catie or Martha to hear."

Looking at Sailor, falling into that smile, Ísa shook her head. "I don't think I can be quiet if you keep doing things like that." She had to be honest, had to get him to stop before she screamed down the house.

But she didn't say stop.

And he didn't stop.

"Then," he said, "I'll just have to spend a lot of time kissing that sweet mouth of yours while I do terrible, dirty, delicious things to you." With that erotic promise, he moved his hand oh so slow over the soft and silky fabric of her panties and to her hip.

Utterly breathless, Ísa tried to gulp in some air. It

seemed to do nothing, as if her breathing had altered permanently to short gasps that left her light-headed.

Her stomach tensed when Sailor paused at the center of her panties. But he shifted his hand up instead of down. Wanting to moan at the loss, Ísa bit down on her lower lip to still the sound.

Sailor caught the motion, shook his head. "Don't you bite your lip, Ísa," he ordered. "We don't want any cuts in your pretty flesh."

"Let go of my hands, you demon, and I'll bite you instead." She didn't know where the words came from, but they made Sailor grin and press his chest more heavily against the tips of her breasts.

It was sweet pleasure and even sweeter pain.

He slid his palm onto the small of her back at the same time and, before she knew it, tucked his hand under her panties to cup her rear.

"You can bite me later, spitfire," he said while she drowned under the taut edge of an opulent pleasure that gave and gave. "Tonight's my playtime. Your punishment for having run off on me." A dark look. "Not once. Not twice. *Three* times."

"I'll torment you as badly," Ísa warned, though deep within, she was astonished and wonderfully delighted at the realization that he'd never given up. She was important enough to him that he'd kept on trying to catch her.

"I'll have no mercy," she added in a rough whisper.

"You'll have to get man-sized handcuffs to keep me in place." A hot, wet kiss, his hand squeezing and massaging her pliable flesh. "No way I'm keeping my hands off this luscious body otherwise."

Ísa had read more than her share of romantic novels, including stories so racy they'd made her go hot red and fan herself, but she'd never been drawn to bondage fantasies until her blue-eyed demon had started talking about handcuffs. Now the idea of having Sailor at her mercy, of having all the time in the world to learn his body, to lick those ridiculous soda-commercial-worthy abs, to stroke her hands over the heat and silk of him, to sensually torment... Yes, Ísa was on board.

"I'll make sure they're good, strong handcuffs," she said. "And I won't forget the rope to tie down your ankles."

He dipped his hand lower, the blunt tips of his fingers rubbing outrageously against a part of her body so sensitive that she arched against the wall. "That's my redhead," he said, the pride in his voice intermingled with a sexuality that was rough and ready and very real. His erection pressed demandingly against her stomach, his touch delighting her body, his mouth initiating a kiss so deep it felt like a prelude to sex.

Her bones turned fluid, the place between her thighs so sticky that, for a heartbeat, she wondered what she'd wear under her clothes tomorrow. Because her panties were going to be wrecked. Then Sailor moved his hand out from her panties and cupped her breast again, this time bare palm to bare flesh.

She jerked, might've let out a little scream except that he had his mouth on hers and his tongue was laving hers as his hand molded her breast with blatantly possessive pleasure before his thumb returned to its torture of her nipple.

Ísa pressed up against him in a silent demand. Smiling into the kiss, he kept on provoking and torturing her with wicked attention to detail. First one breast, then the other, then back down to stroke the inner skin of her thighs without ever coming close to the spot where she most wanted his touch.

Tearing away her mouth from his, she said, "Touch me again."

His eyes glinted, a red flush high on his cheeks. "Where?" he asked, his own breathing not exactly steady.

It did something to her to see her effect on him. Her effect on this big, beautiful man, a man many a woman would want to bed. But he wanted only Ísa. And the devil in her wanted to give him what he wanted in return—that dirty talk he'd asked for and that got him so hot.

Feeling young and wild and playful, she said, "Sailor, darling, will you touch me on my pussy?"

He was the one who shuddered this time. "Since you asked so sweetly, spitfire," he said with another little kiss, "I'll have to oblige."

As Ísa tried desperately to hold herself together, he nudged aside the gusset of her panties and then his finger —so damn thick—was sliding over and into her as the work-roughened pad of his thumb pressed against her clit.

Ísa had no hope or desire to resist. She came apart on a single stroke.

But instead of stopping when he felt her body clench convulsively around him, Sailor kept on stroking in and out of her with lazy focus. He circled her poor, over-sensitized clit until her breathing calmed, then began rubbing and playing again even as he slid another finger into her and pumped in and out.

Harder. Faster. Deeper.

Ísa had heard of women who came more than once during a sexual encounter, but she'd never *really* believed it could happen. She discovered the truth on a crash of pleasure, Sailor pushing her over a second time until she was limp and satisfied and his.

Kissing his way to her ear, he whispered, "One more time, spitfire."

Ísa had nothing more to give him, but she couldn't find the words, and when he began to kiss her and touch her and stroke her, and her body began to clench, she decided that Sailor Bishop wasn't a demon. He was a sorcerer, and he knew exactly what magic to do to take a woman on a breath-stealing ride she'd never forget.

24

DAWN LIGHT IN THE SHADOWS

SAILOR DECIDED HE'D DONE AN A+ job of torturing himself.

Removing his hand from Ísa's panties when she went boneless against him after her third orgasm—yes, he *was* proud of himself—he scooped her up into his arms and took her to the bed. While placing her on top of the sheets, he "accidentally" managed to strip off her T-shirt.

Oops.

Discarding the T-shirt, he stood beside the bed with his hands on his hips and just looked down at her sated body.

She was flushed a soft pink, all curves and temptation.

Her eyes, heavy lidded, ran up his body—and snagged to a hard stop on his rampant erection. Sailor wasn't expecting anything, but he *was* hopeful—he was a man after all, and Ísa fired him up in a way he'd never before experienced.

His redhead hadn't realized it yet, but if she crooked a finger, he'd obey the summons without hesitation.

She sat up on the bed and looked at him with sleepy-eyed interest, and her head was at exactly the right height to do bad things to him. That, however, was probably not in the cards tonight.

"Oh, fuck!"

Ísa had raised her hand, run a finger down the outline of his cock.

Gritting his teeth, he exhaled through them and stepped out of reach. "I think," he said on a wave of frustration, "I might have a noise problem too." He couldn't *believe* he was turning down her offer; he'd obviously lost his mind—his brain cells were all in his cock at this point. "Can I take an IOU?"

Ísa's smile was an invitation. "That doesn't look comfortable," she said, moving onto her hands and knees and prowling to the very edge of the bed. "How will you sleep?"

Holding himself back took every ounce of his control. "I'll only have a noise problem with you," he said through clenched teeth. "I can take care of the problem myself without alerting everyone in the house."

But when he would've moved into the bathroom, Ísa said, "Stay" in a husky voice that made his already ragged control close to useless.

When he looked at her, he saw that her gaze was locked on his cock.

"Show me," she said. "Show me how to touch you."

Sailor was about to lose it, but he'd be an idiot of monumental proportions if he didn't take this opportunity. The idea of Ísa watching him...

Stripping off his briefs, he chucked them aside, toward his other clothes.

Ísa gave a little gasp and reached out a hand, but Sailor shook his head, staying out of reach.

"No touching," he said. "Your sister doesn't need that kind of a sex education."

"Just a little taste," his redhead negotiated. "Bite down on your arm to muffle any sound."

Sailor's brain cells surrendered.

Closing the distance between them, he lifted one forearm to his mouth while putting the hand of his other arm gently on the back of Ísa's head. She didn't seem to mind, and—

A roar of sound rising in his gut as the sumptuous heat of her mouth closed over the engorged tip of his cock.

Sailor broke contact a bare second later. "No." His breath came out in harsh bursts. "I am going to be way too noisy for even a gag to work."

When Ísa's eyes gleamed, he knew he'd given her another idea.

His cock jumped.

Taking it in hand, the tip shiny wet from her kiss, he decided to put himself out of his misery before his balls turned electric blue and fell off. "Sometimes," he told her, "I like it slow." He showed her exactly how slow. "I think about a certain gorgeous redhead, her pretty white thighs clamped around my head while I lick her, and I stroke just like this."

His words, the fantasies, were doing nothing for his control, but it was Ísa's reaction that interested him. She was flushed, her breathing uneven, her nipples dark pink and pouting.

"But," he continued, "today I don't have the patience for slow. Today I want it hard, fast, so fucking good." He moved his hand in time with his words until he lost the rhythm and, throwing back his head, allowed his body to buck into his hand.

He hadn't come in his hand in a while; it was usually easier to do this in the shower, but when he opened his eyes and saw Ísa watching him with an expression that said she wanted to devour him, he had zero regrets.

Blowing her a kiss with his free hand, causing a startled light to come into her eyes, he walked into the bathroom, cleaned up. He was surprised to see Ísa—T-shirt back on—walking in as he stepped out.

He ran the back of his hand over her cheek. "Everything okay, spitfire?"

Her eyes skimmed down his body, his very naked body, and the tips of her ears went pink. This time Sailor didn't fight the temptation. Leaning in, he nipped gently at one.

She jumped, her hand coming to lie against his chest. "What was that?"

"Just a thing I wanted to do." And something he'd be doing more often, because it was so damn adorable. "You need the bathroom?"

Her ears went even more pink if that was possible. "Yes," she said before entering the bathroom and shutting the door firmly behind herself.

Sailor frowned... right before he got it.

He was grinning when she came back out. "Naked under that T-shirt?" he asked, unable to resist teasing his cute redhead.

She glared at him. "Had to wash out my panties. Thanks to you."

He took a bow. "You're welcome." He'd pulled his own briefs back on since he had nothing else in which to sleep and he didn't trust his naked cock around Ísa. He'd go commando tomorrow.

However, the idea of Ísa being sweetly bare under that T-shirt, it was a damn fine one.

He pulled back the covers. "Get in," he said. "I promise to only molest you a tiny bit."

"Just remember the noise issue," Ísa replied with spitfire spunk and slipped in.

Smiling, he got in after flicking off the light. He made sure to snuggle her close to him so that she was tucked against his chest, his thigh pushed up between hers. He'd had a long day. Lots of satisfying manual labor, topped off by a powerful sexual release that had flooded his body with endorphins and turned his limbs lazy.

So despite his threat to tease and play with his redhead, it only took him a couple of minutes to fall into a dark, dreamless sleep.

ÍSA FELT SAILOR DROP OFF; no wonder, his muscles had to be exhausted after the day he'd put in—the days he'd been putting in one after the other. She knew the kind of grueling work it took to start a business, then take it to the next level. She'd seen both her parents do it.

It scared her to see Sailor walk the same unforgiving path.

Because the one thing, the *one thing* she'd always told herself, was that she was to never ever fall in love with a man who had a business to run. She had no intention of repeating her lonely childhood as an adult.

The idea of eating dinner with relative strangers, or alone as she had as a young teen who'd outgrown nannies, was her own personal vision of hell. She'd survived those early teen years mostly because of Nayna's family, who'd semiadopted her. It was why she understood the complex dynamics of her best friend's family, understood the intense, abiding love entwined with the strict rules that threatened to crush Nayna's spirit.

After Catie's birth, Ísa had made sure the tiny girl who was her sister never felt lonely as she had, even though Jacqueline had been her usual absentee self once Catie was out of the hospital, while Clive was a brilliant, adoring father one day and off racing cars in Los Angeles or some other harebrained thing the next. Catie had been three, Ísa eighteen when Jacqueline and Clive divorced. Only Ísa had remained a constant in her sister's life.

She'd always be there for Catie. Just as she would be for Harlow.

But her siblings couldn't fill the hole in Ísa formed during her own childhood. They were children. What Ísa needed desperately was a deeply adult thing—for the man she loved to not constantly push her aside for more important matters. She needed him to *see* her on the most primal level.

She needed him not to forget her.

This isn't love, she thought, comforting herself. *You're just confused because of the orgasms.*

Ísa had to believe that; it was the only way she could risk continuing this relationship. Because sooner or later, Sailor Bishop would come to a crossroads and have to make a choice: go all in on his business dreams or live a life with a little more balance, a life that included time to love a woman, time to build a family.

Having seen his drive and ambition, Ísa had no illusions about the choice he'd make.

I'm married to my business. She's also my very demanding mistress. Doesn't tolerate other women for long periods.

When that time came, Ísa had to be ready to walk

away. She couldn't risk being tied to him by love while her soul shriveled with loneliness. Throat thick, she whispered, "Please don't break my heart, Sailor" while knowing that to be an inevitability.

THEY HAD AN EARLY BREAKFAST the next morning. Despite the late night, Sailor had woken at five, as was his habit. Usually he made time to go out for a run. You'd think with such a physical job, he'd have given up the running, but he liked that early-morning stretch. Today, however, he had nothing to run in even if he'd wanted to leave the bed.

Ísa woke when he stirred, and he nuzzled a kiss into her neck. She'd been an easy sleeping companion, no wiggling around from Miss Ísa Rain; she'd stayed nicely tucked up against him all night long.

"You're very cuddly," he told her with another kiss.

The tips of her ears went pink again. "I've always had big hips."

Sailor wanted to scratch his head. What the hell had he said about hips?

Deciding to leave that one alone, he snuggled her soft curviness even closer. "So," he said, "what should we do today?"

Ísa turned so that she was on her back. "Let's see how Catie is this morning." Concern darkened her eyes. "I know she was very gung ho about us leaving this morning when we spoke to her last night, but she might feel differently if she wakes stiff and sore."

Sailor nodded. He couldn't imagine his younger brothers being without support should they be hurt and scared.

"If she does want me to stay," Ísa said, "then I want you to go back to Auckland."

Frowning, he said, "I won't be going anywhere as long as you need help." The idea of abandoning his redhead didn't sit right with him.

A wary vulnerability in her expression before she pressed her fingers against his lips. "Thank you," she said with a smile so deep that he felt as if he'd watched dawn break right here in this tumbled bed, "but I know you need to get back to work. You're on a very tight deadline for Fast Organic. Plus there's nothing here I can't handle."

He nipped at her fingers, annoyed with her for making sense. "How will you get back home?"

"I can easily hire a car." Pausing, she snapped her fingers. "No, I'll borrow Clive's car. It's just sitting in the garage anyway. And he always flies back into Auckland; he can pick it up."

"Yeah," Sailor grumbled. "I suppose that works."

Cupping his face, Ísa kissed him with wild affection. "Thank you for caring."

He rolled his eyes. "That's like thanking me for breathing." She was his; of course he'd care for her and those who were important to her. "Since we're both up, how about we go rustle up some breakfast?"

His stomach growled on cue.

Ísa laughed. "Early bird?"

Deciding she was much, much better than an alarm, Sailor stroked the warm curve of her thigh as he spoke. "Always have been. I used to help my mom prepare lunch for Gabe and me when we were at school. After Jake and Danny came along, I used to help her with theirs too." It had been a special time between him and his mom before the rest of the household was awake.

Sailor still did the same the odd night he stayed over at his parents' after watching a late game on their big-screen TV.

Waking, he would stumble down into the kitchen to find his mother brewing him a cup of coffee, she was so certain he'd show. These days he usually made her sit down and took over the task of cooking their traditional postgame breakfast.

Alison Esera had worked more than enough for one lifetime.

Jake and Danny, they hadn't seen the hard times that Sailor and Gabe had, and so sometimes they gave Alison a little more back talk than their older brothers. Not much, and it was never disrespectful—they hadn't been brought up that way, not with Joseph for a father and Gabe and Sailor for older brothers—but it was a type of childhood rebellion their mother had never seen in her older sons.

It made her happy to know her younger sons were growing up in the light—but she still worried about the damage done to Sailor and Gabriel during the early part of their lives. Sometimes he'd catch her watching him with gray eyes awash in concern and love and hope, and he'd enfold her in his arms, safe against the scars of the past.

Ísa's fingers across his jaw, her gaze searching. "Where did you go?" she asked softly, having turned to face him while he'd been lost in thought.

Used to keeping his secrets from the women who shared his bed, Sailor went to shake his head and change the direction of the conversation... and realized two things.

One, Ísa was far more than a bedmate. She was his redhead.

And Sailor was a stubborn, possessive bastard under the surface.

Also, two, he wanted her to know who he was, wanted her to understand that he was far older than his chronological age. "I was thinking about early mornings helping my mom cook," he admitted. "They're some of my favorite childhood memories."

Face lighting up, Ísa said, "How old were you when you started?" So much hunger in her, so much sheer *need*.

25

BAD FRIENDS AND GREASY HAIR

HER PARENTS, HE THOUGHT FURIOUSLY, had abandoned her without ever actually discarding her. "I can't remember," he said on a rough wave of protectiveness, tugging her even closer to his body so he could cuddle her more. "Mom likes to say I never learned to sleep past five in the morning."

"It sounds like a happy childhood."

"It was." He'd been too young to understand as much as Gabriel, had known only that he was safe and warm and loved.

Ísa's expression changed. "Then why are your eyes so sad?"

He ran his fingers through the glory of Ísa's hair. "Things changed when I was five." Sailor never talked about this, didn't like to remember how desperately that five-year-old boy had hoped, but he could do no less when Ísa had trusted him with her own family. "The man who fathered Gabriel and me walked out on us. Just left one day and didn't come back. After cleaning out all the accounts."

Ísa's anger was a magnificent thing. "How could he do that to his own children?"

"Because he's an asshole." And a man in whose footsteps Sailor would *never* follow, not even if he had a gun pointed to his head. "It was always grand plans and no follow-through with Brian." Sailor remembered enough to understand that. "That's why the only man I acknowledge as my father is Joseph."

Sailor felt his lips curve. "He and my mom met a year after the asshole walked out, and to hear my dad tell it, she treated him like a piece of stinking dead fish at first. Every time he asked her out, she'd say no, she was too busy, she had to clean the toilet." Sailor's shoulders shook. "So one day he turned up with a toilet brush and said he'd clean her damn toilet for her every week if that was what it took."

Ísa giggled with him. "It must've been hard for her to trust another man. Especially with having two young children."

"Yeah, but Dad... He knows how to love, and he does it without flinching." Breathing in the warmth of Ísa's scent, he told her the rest. "It took Mom months to trust him enough to even introduce me and Gabe, but when she did, he repaid her trust a thousand times over. He's the man I want to be."

"You love him very much." Ísa's hand stroking his shoulder and arm.

"He put so much love into me, into Gabe, that we had no choice." Never had they not felt as much his sons as Jake and Danny. "The tattoos on my body? They're traditional Samoan designs, given to me piece by piece as a gift after I turned eighteen."

No gift had meant more in his life. "Dad drew each and

every line, and his youngest brother inked them. Only reason I'm a Bishop instead of an Esera is because Brian refused permission for a legal adoption when they tracked him down to ask." A pathetic attempt at holding on to the family he'd thrown away. "Gabe and I were gutted, but Dad sat us down and told us nothing would change the fact that we were his boys."

Tears shimmered in Ísa's eyes. "I think I'm in love with your dad."

Kissing her... letting her hold him, cuddle him, Sailor said, "Don't try anything funny though. My mother's a little possessive." He dropped a kiss on the tip of her nose... and his stomach growled again. "That's enough deep emotional stuff." He felt as if he'd run sandpaper over his soul. "I need food."

Ísa kissed his lips, then his cheeks, then his nose.

He was grinning by the time she got to his ears.

Finally separating several minutes later, they took turns in the shower before dressing in their wrinkled clothes from the previous day. As tidy as they could be, they crept out into the kitchen. It was now five forty-five, and the birds were tweeting up a storm outside the windows.

Tiptoeing around, they checked out the fridge and pantry.

"Want blueberry pancakes?" Sailor whispered to Ísa. "I saw fresh blueberries in the fridge."

Bright eyes. "Do you know how to make them?"

"I'm an expert," he bragged. "There's bacon too. Why don't you fry some while I whip up the batter?"

They had the pancakes going and the bacon sizzling when the light came on in Catie's room. The teenager stumbled out a minute later, her hair sticking up like a baby's and her prosthetics nowhere to be seen.

"Is that bacon?" she whispered, as if she'd smelled ambrosia from heaven.

"Bacon and pancakes." Ísa pointed a spatula at the teenager, her volume low in deference to the sleeping Martha. "You know your doctors don't like you doing the knee-walking."

"I know, I know." Catie turned back around, hustling as fast as possible. "Give me time to put on my legs, then I'm coming out to eat *all* the food."

"Why not the wheelchair we used last night?" Sailor asked after the teen disappeared back into her room. "Wouldn't that be faster since she's obviously hungry?"

"Catie hates using the wheelchair. Obstinate runs in the Rain line." It was an affectionate statement. "She got very good at walking on her knees for a while, until her physio-therapist drummed it into her head that she might cause flexion contractures." Ísa bent her knee to demonstrate. "It's where the muscles kind of lock and the knee won't straighten out fully."

"Got it. Bad for a runner."

Ísa nodded. "She only forgets now and then, not enough to harm her." A quick grin. "But she ordered us all to tell her off when she does."

Catie returned as Ísa was pouring her a glass of orange juice. The teen had washed her face and brushed her hair back into a ponytail but remained in her pink pajamas dotted with tiny blue stars, the pants short and the top long sleeved with buttons down the front.

Thumping her fists lightly on the counter after scrambling up onto a stool, she whispered, "Where's my food, minions?"

A mini-spitfire, Sailor thought, taking in those dancing eyes. "Here you are, Your Majesty."

Already stuffing her face, Catie nodded at the fridge, mumbling something that had Ísa opening the fridge and searching within. "Got it." She put a pressurized can of whipped cream next to the syrup she'd already found, and Catie went to town with it, smothering her pancakes in the white goop.

Sailor was more of a purist while Ísa stuck with syrup.

"You guys are going back today, right?" Catie said some time later, her plate bearing evidence of a pancake massacre.

"There's no rush." Ísa took a sip of her coffee. "I can stay as long as you want."

"The Dragon will eat you."

"Apparently I'm indigestible. She keeps spitting me back out."

"It's okay," Catie said with a laugh she muffled behind one hand. "I really am fine. I was just being a baby last night, that's all."

Ísa ran her hand down Catie's back. "Hey, as far as I'm concerned, you are a baby. I remember changing your diaper five minutes ago."

"Ugh, total embarrassment!" Despite the outraged statement, Catie leaned over to kiss Ísa on the cheek, the two sisters sitting side by side on the breakfast stools with Sailor next to Ísa.

"Thanks for coming, Issie."

"Always, Catiebug."

The love between the two was a banner, their relationship clearly as tight as Sailor's with his brothers. A point of commonality he'd highlight to Ísa at the first opportunity. He had a feeling she wasn't yet convinced about the wisdom of this relationship, that if he wasn't careful, his skittish redhead might yet run.

Hell if he'd let that happen.

Catie ate another pancake before saying, "I think you should go. I'm feeling okay now, and I'll be busy with the training I have coming up." A gulp of orange juice. "Plus I think Harlow really needs you. He was messaging me last night—he's freaked out about the job. More than he shows."

Ísa's brow furrowed. "He's only just started. What's freaking him out?"

"He heard a rumor that the other interns all had sit-downs with Jacqueline every day. He's worried that Jacqueline doesn't like something he's done and he's already been sidelined."

Ísa rubbed her face. "None of that is true. Why is he acting crazy?"

"It's the Dragon—you know how he wants to be her mini-me. Any sign of trouble and he turns into emo-Harlow." Catie shook her head at Sailor. "Normally he's smart, sane Harlow, but the Dragon scrambles his brain cells."

"What about his parents?" Sailor asked, intensely curious about the dynamics of Ísa's family.

"Losers from Loserville," Catie said before Ísa could answer. "They both got married again and are totally doing the happy new families thing like Harlow's not even there." A curl of her lip. "Good thing he has me and Issie and his nutso crush on the Dragon, or he'd probably get bad friends, turn to drugs, and have greasy hair."

Yes, definitely a mini-spitfire. One who knew how to love as fiercely as the woman who haunted Sailor's dreams. Even when he slept, he dreamed of his Ísalind. Nope, no way was Sailor letting her go. Not this time.

THE DRIVE BACK TO AUCKLAND was surprisingly easy once Ísa managed to leave Catie. She'd waited until Martha was up and able to confirm that Catie had a busy schedule that wouldn't be impacted by her minor injuries.

Catie had given her a crushing hug before she left. "I love you, Issie."

The sleepless nights, the sheer terror, that made it all worth it.

A brush of knuckles against her cheek. "You still worrying about Catie?"

Not fighting the urge to rub up against those knuckles before Sailor had to return his hand to the steering wheel, Ísa said, "No. I know her independence is important to her." More important than most girls her age. "She can be militant about it sometimes, but it didn't feel like that today."

"Kid's crazy about you."

Ísa looked at Sailor's profile and thought, *Yes, like I'm crazy about you*. But she couldn't say those terrifying words. "At least she hasn't turned to drugs, taken up with bad friends, and started going in for greasy hair."

Sailor's chuckle was a warm caress, the glance he shot her just as caressing.

Scared and happy and breathless, Ísa settled back to enjoy the early-morning drive, shoving thoughts of the future out of her mind. Those thoughts, those fears, would still be waiting in the shadows when she was ready to face them again. Ísa wasn't willing to give in to them and ruin this gorgeous morning.

The direction of her thoughts had her frowning and realizing that Nayna hadn't messaged her the previous night. Her best friend always gave Ísa the lowdown on her marriage dates, and given her panic over this latest one, Ísa would've reached out herself if she hadn't been so stressed out over Catie. Either something had gone wrong, or Nayna hadn't been able to find privacy to make the call until it was too late.

Ísa made a mental note to touch base with her friend once she was back in Auckland.

It was a half hour of comfortable silence later that Sailor nodded at a sign for an upcoming rest stop that had one of those little full-service cafés. "You want to fill up on coffee?" he asked. "It's been at least an hour since our last one."

Ísa laughed, wanting desperately to kiss him. "I didn't know you were a coffee hound."

SAILOR DECIDED HE COULD VERY easily come to live for that laugh. First, however, he'd have to convince her that he planned to cherish her as she deserved. It was dead clear to him that his redhead was used to giving and giving.

Sailor planned to care for her in turn, so she'd smile, so she'd laugh, so she'd play with him. But he knew it wouldn't be easy. Not with the demons that howled at him to achieve his ambitions, be something better than the man who'd sired him had ever been. Those demons threatened to possess him body and soul.

No, he vowed. *That bastard doesn't get to steal Ísa from me.*

"Coffee is nectar from the gods," he said on the heels of

that mental promise. "I try to keep it to two cups a day, but sometimes I crack under the pressure of its siren call."

Ísa laughed again. "In that case, we'd better pull in."

Jumping out at the coffee stop before he could, she said, "You're driving, so I'll be the assistant. What kind of coffee do you want?"

"Plain black." Sailor took in the delight in those pretty gray-green eyes and barely resisted the urge to tug her back into the vehicle and into his lap. "I like coffee that puts hair on my chest—though I prefer yours hairless, just in case you were getting ideas."

She blew him a kiss before turning to walk to the café, the scarlet of her hair brilliant in the morning light and the smile she threw him over her shoulder a sucker punch to the gut.

Ísa Rain was perilously close to owning his heart.

Now all he had to do was figure out how to convince her that he could be trusted with hers.

26

A LITTLE INDUSTRIAL ESPIONAGE TO SPICE THINGS UP

AUCKLAND'S URBAN SPRAWL APPEARED FAR too soon, the highway splitting off into many more lanes, the traffic intense, the bridges that arched over the roads steel constructions that shone in the sunlight.

Usually Ísa loved her city, but today she wished it was a little farther away.

At least she and Sailor had managed to finalize the financial changes to the Fast Organic project during the drive. It was important to her that Sailor not be hamstrung in what he could achieve because of her own family crisis.

Sailor took her to his place so she could pick up her car; she'd called Jacqueline from the truck and updated her on what was happening. As usual when it came to her youngest daughter, the Dragon hadn't said much, but Ísa knew Jacqueline wouldn't breathe fire at Ísa about being late.

"Hey." Sailor's hands on her hips, his body pinning her to the side of the truck. "Were you going to run off without a kiss?"

Last night was already beginning to feel like a dream, a sensual, astonishing dream. But when Ísa rose on tiptoe and touched her mouth to his, the dream became red-hot reality. Fisting one hand in her hair, Sailor cupped her face with his other as he kissed her, and Ísa felt both utterly cherished... and totally devoured.

Her fingers curled into his chest, her breasts aching. "What kind of kiss was that?" she said severely when they broke for a breath. "I'm meant to be in a state to go to work."

A wicked grin, the hard wall of his chest crushing her against the warm metal of the truck. "Just so you don't forget me." He took another kiss, sucking on her lower lip before releasing her. "I don't want you to think of me as just a one-night stand."

Though his tone was light, she caught the seriousness in his eyes and realized suddenly that she held the power to hurt him. "I don't do one-night stands," she said, because the idea of hurting this man who treated her as if she was a beautiful, perfect, precious creature was simply not something she could do.

Sailor Bishop would soon break her heart into a million pieces, but he wouldn't hurt her in the interim. And she couldn't hurt him.

"I'll call you."

A heavy scowl on his features. "Oh, you mean how you were going to call me about our cookie-bar date?"

She poked at his chest. "That was *one* time!"

Snorting, he kissed her again, the hard warmth of him so delicious that she could stay in his arms forever. "I'll be waiting to hear from you," he said, his tone dark. "And in case you lose my number, I know where you work." He began to twirl an invisible mustache like some B-movie villain.

Ísa laughed, pushed at his chest, once again feeling younger than she had in forever. "Shoo, you demon." She got into her car. "I'll see you tonight."

"Bring cookies," he ordered.

AFTER DRIVING HOME, SHE DID a rapid change into a full-skirted dress in a vivid yellow that picked up the golden threads in her hair, that hair twisted up into a neat bun, before sliding her feet into black kitten heels with a thin ankle strap. A simple turquoise necklace finished off the outfit.

She felt as sunshiny as her dress as she caught the elevator down.

Once in her car, she activated the hands-free phone system. It was one Harlow had found on sale a couple of years back; her brother had even hooked it up for her.

Calling Nayna as she drove out of the parking lot, she said, "Can you talk?"

"Let me shut my office door." Nayna was back on the line a few seconds later. "I know, I know. I should've called you, but I was—still am—kind of weirded out."

Ísa frowned at her best friend's discombobulated tone. "Why?" she asked. "Was the guy that awful?" She couldn't imagine Mr. and Mrs. Sharma choosing someone truly unsuitable for their girl.

"He wasn't an accountant," Nayna said. "He wasn't a doctor. Or a lawyer. Not an engineer. Not an IT guy. Not a CEO or COO or any fricking O!"

Diverted from her own problems, Ísa only just stopped

herself from driving straight to Nayna's office so they could dish in person. "Unemployed?" she asked, stunned.

"No." The single word came out a moan. "It was *him*."

"Who?" Ísa asked before her eyes widened. "*Nooooo.* Not the hunky guy from the party? What was his name? Raj?"

"Yes. Raj. The man I told to shut up because I didn't want his brain." Nayna sounded like she was smashing her head against the top of her desk.

"Hey, hold on! What's he doing going out to meet prospective wives while he's picking up women at parties?" Ísa was outraged on her best friend's behalf.

"Er, Ísa, there were two of us tangoing at that party," Nayna pointed out. "But he's not a slime. He convinced my parents to give us a couple of minutes alone at the start. When I walked in, he had his back to me and said that he was sorry. His parents had set up this meet last minute, before he could tell them he was pulling out of the whole arranged-marriage thing because..."

Ísa was on the edge of her seat. "Because?"

"He never finished telling me why! He turned around as he was speaking and saw me standing there and, well, the nightmare of awkwardness began."

"Oh God."

"He scowled at me the entire time."

Ísa winced. "Did he say anything?"

"Oh yes, Mr. Tall, Dark, and *Quiet* had plenty to say once our parents joined us. He asked me if I enjoyed going to parties."

"What did you say?"

"I didn't have to say anything. My parents jumped in, laughing and saying he didn't have to worry about my being a party girl." Nayna ground her teeth together. "Meanwhile, Raj sits back and says, 'Oh' in a certain *tone*."

"Tell me you got back at him."

"Are you kidding? I smiled like the perfect Indian princess, asked him one sugar or two and put in seven. You should've seen his face when he had to choke it down or risk insulting my entire family." Total evil satisfaction in her tone.

Grinning and delighted for her friend, Ísa said, "You know there's one good side to this—you've found a man you're madly attracted to *and* your family approves of him."

Nayna's return words were a growl. "I *can't* be attracted to a guy my parents introduced me to—that goes against all my principles now that I've decided to break free."

"I actually understand that nonsensical statement." Ísa stopped at a traffic light. "But principles aside, do you think it might work?"

"I don't know," Nayna muttered. "All we have between us is that stupid scene at the party where I basically told him to keep his mouth shut, I was only interested in his body." More head slamming. "And honestly, that was probably a one-night type of attraction on his part. I don't know what my parents were thinking matching us—he's the kind of man who could walk into a bar and have his pick of the women there."

Ísa didn't tell Nayna she was beautiful. Her friend had grown up with an astonishingly stunning sister who was always the center of attention; Nayna had certain hang-ups even a best friend couldn't erase. "So have you responded? Or have they responded?"

"He texted me this morning," Nayna confessed. "Said

we should go out for lunch and have a proper talk. That there was no point trying to make a decision about the rest of our lives when we just had a few minutes together." A pause. "He also added that, of course, that was only if I was interested in his brain now."

Ísa winced again, but she was actually starting to like Raj. He was the first one of Nayna's suitors who'd taken the initiative and was actually attempting to get to know the woman behind Nayna's lovely face. "Are you going to go?"

"My parents would find it shocking," Nayna said, "but since I'm being a rebel now, what do I care? I want to know what the hell Raj thinks he's doing coming to my house for an arranged-marriage meeting when he's *so* clearly not the kind of guy who would be happy in an arranged anything!"

"Um, Nayna," Ísa murmured, "you went along with your family too."

"That doesn't count." Nayna huffed, completely illogical for such a logical woman. "I guess I'll find out what he's up to at lunch today."

"Call me as soon as it's over."

"I will. Anyway, enough about me. Did you get up to anything interesting last night? Maybe with the hot gardener?"

Ísa told her about Catie, reassured her best friend that Catie was all right. Then she spilled the rest. "I'm terrified," she admitted afterward. "So scared that I'll never be anything but a peripheral part of his existence."

"Don't judge him just yet," Nayna said quietly. "He stepped into the breach this time, didn't he? Maybe you can make it work."

Yes, he had. Magnificently. But— "It's not the moment

that counts, it's the long-term commitment to being there, day after day." She swallowed down the knot of worry as she approached the parking lot for Crafty Corners. "Getting back to you, give this Raj guy a chance too, okay?"

"We'll see," Nayna said in a noncommittal tone before they hung up.

Ísa was walking to her office when she saw Ginny doing a wheelie, her wheelchair tipped up off the front as she spun it around. Ísa's lips kicked up. "Since when is that acceptable corporate behavior?"

Her assistant grinned. "Since I just joined my local wheelchair basketball league."

"Didn't you tell me you don't understand the appeal of putting a ball in a net?"

"When the league is coed with some superhot players for me to ogle, it's all details, details." Waving insouciantly, Ginny said, "Jacqueline wanted to see you as soon as you got in." She came closer, dropped her voice to add, "Thought you'd want to know that she's changed Harlow's internship program. It's way tougher than the usual."

"Thanks, Gin." Ísa dropped off her satchel before going over to Jacqueline's office.

She found her mother in the middle of a phone call. Seeing her, Jacqueline held up a finger to indicate that she would only be a minute. Ísa shut the door behind herself and walked over to look at a large concept plan that was sitting on an easel to one side of Jacqueline's office.

It was a design for a mega Crafty Corners store in the central part of the city.

Jacqueline still wasn't sure about the economics of the possible expansion, so it was all very conceptual right now. If and when her mother did decide to move ahead, she'd have worked out every financial angle in advance.

"So Catie's fine?"

Turning at Jacqueline's statement, Ísa nodded. "Clive's been dodging my calls, but I left messages. He'll call Catie this morning if he knows what's good for him."

"Fortunately," Jacqueline replied, leaning back in her chair, "Catie is far more practical and clearheaded than you were at her age. She might hope for more from Clive, but she understands the reality of his personality." Raised eyebrows. "You, on the other hand, always expected your father to change and become the kind of father you needed."

"Head in the clouds," Ísa said, echoing something Jacqueline had said to her more than once.

"Too sensitive." Jacqueline picked up her fountain pen, tapped it against the side of her desk. "I wish you hadn't been born that way—and God knows where it came from —but it's who you are. It's what makes you so good with the people who work for us—they follow me because they respect me. But they'll follow you because they just like you."

"I chose to go into teaching for a reason, Mother," Ísa said for the umpteenth time. "I chose to make my living with poetry and novels and the written word for a reason."

Jacqueline held her gaze. "We have an agreement. For the summer you're mine."

"Yes," Ísa said, "about that. What's this I hear about Harlow being put through a different internship program than usual?"

Setting down her pen, Jacqueline smiled that barracuda smile. "You say the boy has the balls for this kind of work

—I'm giving him the chance to prove it. He's going to be brought up through the entire business, and I'll be getting reports from all the people he works under."

While Ísa was glad her mother was giving Harlow a chance, it was an unfairly difficult one. "He's still only seventeen," she said. "You can't judge him against standards set by grown adults."

"You passed those standards," Jacqueline said flatly. "When you were sixteen."

Damn her teenage self, so eager for her mother's approval.

Now she couldn't say anything against Jacqueline's plans for Harlow because the instant she did, she'd be confirming her mother's doubts about her brother's abilities. On the flip side, should Harlow pass the tests, he'd well and truly win Jacqueline's approval and support. And that was all Harlow wanted.

"Why did you need to see me?" she asked, trusting Harlow and his skills.

Jacqueline's mouth tightened. Waving Ísa over, she pointed to something on the computer screen to the right of her desk. "Look at this."

The headline was impossible to miss: *New Crafty Corners megastore in progress.*

"I didn't think the news was out." Ísa skimmed through the article. "I wasn't aware you'd made a final decision."

"I haven't." Jacqueline's tone was frigid.

Sucking in a breath, Ísa glanced at Jacqueline's icily controlled face. "Someone leaked this information?"

A crisp nod from her mother. "Since I'm not sold on the idea anyway, it won't do too much damage. I've been thinking we should locate it in a less busy area with plenty of parking and spin off a birthday-party package. There are a lot of parents like me and your father who have more important things to do than plan birthdays."

Ísa glanced at her mother's profile and saw that Jacqueline was, once again, frowning at the newspaper article onscreen. Powerfully intelligent as Jacqueline was, she didn't seem to realize how deeply her words had once cut the child Ísa had been.

She'd spent every single one of her childhood birthdays without her parents. She'd never had a party while her parents were married, as neither Jacqueline nor Stefán had thought to instruct the staff to organize it.

Ísa had made damn sure Jacqueline showed her face at the parties Ísa had thrown for Catie. The last time Jacqueline said she couldn't make it, when Catie was four, Ísa had relocated the party to Crafty Corners HQ and invited every single one of Catie's preschool friends.

She'd also hired child entertainers who came with their own live band.

Jacqueline had learned her lesson very quickly.

"So," she said with an inward grin at the memory of the look on Jacqueline's face when confronted by twenty-seven excited tiny tots with fingers sticky from cookies and cake, "you're not worried about this specific leak, you're worried about who it is that's doing the leaking?"

"I knew you'd understand," Jacqueline said with a cool smile. "This leak won't damage the business, but further disclosures might. I want you to track down the identity of the leaker."

Ísa already had a lot on her plate but she didn't demur, well aware Jacqueline was asking her because she knew Ísa would never betray the family. "How long have you had this mock-up out here on the easel?"

Glancing at it, Jacqueline frowned. "At least two

weeks. You know I like to have visual aids when I'm thinking on a project."

"I'm going to talk to Annalisa, find out who's been in your office during that time." That shouldn't be a tough task. Jacqueline's office was accessible only by keycard, with any guests escorted in. Even the maintenance and cleaning staff came in during the morning, after Annalisa was already at her desk to supervise.

"The landscaping contract," Jacqueline said without warning. "Sailor Bishop. He's the only new contact I've had in here during the time since the concept's been up on the easel."

Ísa bristled. "No," she said. "He's got no reason to mess up his relationship with us." More, he was a man with a strong code of honesty and honor—but she knew better than to base her argument on that.

Emotion never won with Jacqueline.

Tamping down her instinctive anger on his behalf, Ísa responded with cold, hard logic. "Whatever the reporter paid for this piece of information," she pointed out, "it'll have been peanuts in comparison to what Sailor will earn out of the Fast Organic stores in publicity alone."

Jacqueline gave her a piercing look. "I fell for pretty eyes once," she said. "Clive was very good at telling me what I wanted to hear."

27

FUR-LINED HANDCUFFS AND AN
EXECUTIVE DESK (OH MY)

FOLDING HER ARMS, ÍSA HELD firm; she might have doubts about what she was doing with Sailor on a personal basis, but she had zero doubts about his integrity. "Do you know anybody at the paper you could call?"

"It's that asshole Jay Mason at the helm," Jacqueline responded. "He hates me because I wouldn't sleep with him." A snort. "As if Jacqueline Rain needs to sleep with a third-rate editor to get good press."

Nope, no options there then.

"Leave this problem with me," Ísa said. "And Mother"—Ísa paused until Jacqueline looked up—"don't do anything against Sailor Bishop in the interim."

"This is my company."

"It is. But if you want me to take the reins on projects and issues, then you take your hands off them. I will not have my decisions second-guessed and micromanaged."

Jacqueline's lips curved. "Too sensitive, but also brilliant. You really are a chip off the old block. Have at it, Ísa. Succeed or fail, it's on your shoulders." Her next words were quiet. "Did you know your father used to read poetry?"

Ísa froze with her hand on the doorknob.

Glancing over her shoulder, she said, "What?" She'd *never* seen her father with a book of poetry in hand. But then, she'd seen little of her father while growing up and even less after he'd handed her over to Jacqueline when Ísa was thirteen. Not because Jacqueline particularly wanted custody, but because Stefán's own mother had passed away, leaving no one who could look after Ísa.

Old grief made Ísa's heart ache as she stood there, waiting for her mother's response. *Amma* Kaja had thrown Ísa her first ever birthday party when Ísa was nine. She'd invited all the children in the remote but painfully beautiful Icelandic village where she lived and where Stefán had dumped Ísa after Jacqueline signed over custody—which Stefán had demanded in a fit of divorce-induced madness.

Ísa still missed her *amma*. It was why she'd never made any effort to rid herself of the accent that touched her words to this day. It was her way of honoring the gentle woman who'd given life to the language Ísa had first learned from tutors—because Stefán had been adamant his New Zealand-born child speak the language of his birth.

"When we first met," Jacqueline continued, "Stefán wanted to be a poet." A shake of her head. "Can you imagine? He came to his senses soon enough—after he found out how much poets earn. But even then, he used to write me poetry…" Jacqueline's gaze turned distant. "For a while anyway. Then life and business took over. And there was no more time for poetry."

Jacqueline's next look was sharp. "It never lasts, Ísa. The passion, the smiles from the pretty eyes, the endless time to love." Her words were crisp and pragmatic rather than harsh. "Don't make the same mistakes I did—choose a man like Oliver, a man who is comfortable and kind and who'll love you into old age. Passion is not a good indicator of success in a relationship."

ÍSA REFUSED TO BE HAUNTED by Jacqueline's words. Her mother might be right, but Ísa was already well aware she was making a dangerous mistake with Sailor. She might as well dive all the way into the fire if she was going to emerge crisped on the other side anyway. Which was why she picked up the phone and called him.

"Hello, spitfire." The deep tones of his voice were a caress. "Late dinner okay for you? I'm hoping to work till last light."

"Jacqueline just handed me another project, so I'll be here late too." She rubbed the back of her neck. "Come by my office after you're done. I'll order in."

It was only after hanging up that she realized it was already happening. Work, stealing away their time for each other. But Ísa wasn't going to just give up and accept it as inevitable. She was going to fight.

The only question was if Sailor would fight with her.

That question haunted her when she let him through the locked front door of the HQ. Still in his work clothes, streaks of dirt on the khaki of his shorts, he made her heart beat faster just with his mere presence.

Yes, she had it bad for Sailor Bishop.

Frowning at seeing the dim lighting downstairs, he said, "You the only one in here?"

"It's perfectly safe. My car's right outside." She nodded at his right arm. "Why are you carrying a picnic blanket?"

Bending his head, he kissed her breathless before saying, "For our indoor picnic, of course."

Her silly heart, it gave a huge sigh. "Come on, the food's already here."

He ran his hand over the curve of her hip and ass and playfully distracted her the whole way up. Ísa was giggling like a schoolgirl by the time they entered her office. Sailor grinned at seeing the cactus she kept on her desk, the second one he'd sent her. But he was absolutely delighted by the soft, warm cookies she'd paid extra to have delivered.

"You know how to romance a man," he said with a nuzzle to her neck after inhaling an entire cookie. "Sorry I'm so dirty." He dropped the picnic blanket to the floor. "Couldn't wait to see you."

Ísa buried her face in his neck, drew in the earthy scent of him, and tried not to listen to the panicky voice inside her that said time was running out too fast. "I'm not complaining."

Hands on her hips, he hitched her up onto her desk. "Sit here, Miss Trouble." With that stern statement, he moved aside the visitor chair, then flicked out the tartan blanket, the colors blue and black. "I forgot this in back of my truck after our last family barbeque."

He was back between her legs before she could answer. "Hungry?" It was a sensually loaded statement, his hands pushing up the sunny yellow of her dress to bare her thighs.

Lower body clenching, Ísa said, "Yes." It came out husky, her eyes locked on his mouth.

But he didn't kiss her this time, his attention on other matters.

Dipping his head, he hooked his fingers on either side

of her panties and slid them down her thighs and off. Ísa's toes curled at the scandalousness of being panty-less on her desk with a deliciously sexy man between her thighs.

When he tucked the panties into his pocket with a wicked smile and said, "I'm keeping these hostage," she melted.

Feeling more than a little wicked herself, she reached for his belt, undid it with quick hands. He oh-so-cooperatively took off his T-shirt for her. Ísa leaned in to lick at his chest while she undid the top button on his shorts. He was salt and heat and Sailor, and he scrambled her brain cells.

His bigger, warmer hands colliding with hers as she stroked him through the fabric. A nip of her lower lip. "Foreplay?" He reached into the back pocket of his shorts.

"Let's save that for a bed." Tonight, Ísa just wanted him inside her. "Did you—?" She gasped as he pushed her hands behind her and together.

Handcuffs snicked into place a second later. Something soft and lush caressed her wrists. Pink, she'd glimpsed pink. "I ordered a strong pair for you," she warned.

"Bring it on, spitfire." His smile slow, he pulled out the thick length of his erection.

It was suddenly hard to breathe. "*Sailor.*" She sank her teeth into her lower lip. "Tell me you have protection."

He was already pulling a thin foil packet from his wallet. "I don't make the same mistake twice."

Skin shimmering with heat, Ísa watched him get naked.

Dear Lord. The man was like a sculpture of raw masculinity. All ridges and valleys and skin kissed by the sun. The odd scar here and there. Those phenomenally gorgeous tattoos that spoke of his history and family.

Honed muscles that flexed with every movement.

And he was all hers. "I want to spend an entire day in bed with you." It came out throaty, like she was a sex kitten on steroids. "With my hands and my mouth all over your ridiculously beautiful body."

"That could be arranged." Shooting her a grin that said he was in favor of the idea, he sheathed himself with quick hands.

Then he was back between her thighs and—after an erotically rough stroke with his fingers to check her readiness—pulling her forward to slowly sink the thick heat of himself inside her. She moaned, the inability to touch him, to do anything to control him, causing her muscles to flutter in warning of the primal pleasure to come.

And Sailor began to talk. "You are so perfect, Ísa, so hot and tight around my cock." A flush across his cheekbones, his eyes glittering. "I fucking love your body." His hand palming her breast through her dress, squeezing. "So damn sexy."

Utterly helpless, Ísa watched him luxuriate in her body, his muscles bunching and unclenching as he claimed her in rolling thrusts that hit nerves inside her she hadn't known existed. When he kissed her, she arched into the contact. "Sailor."

"That's it, spitfire." His mouth on her throat, one of his hands gripping her wrists just above the handcuffs while the other closed over her thigh. "Talk to me."

"You're scrambling my bra— *Oh*."

Rising at her shuddering moan, he gripped her jaw with one hand and took another ravenous kiss before drawing back and speeding up his thrusts without breaking eye contact. "You want me to grind deep, Ísa?" His demonstration had her inner thighs quivering. "Or do you want it faster?"

The untamed eroticism of him took her to the edge. "Anything you want," she said, her chest rising and falling in a ragged rhythm. "Slow, deep, fast, I don't care. Just keep going. I love how thick and hard you feel inside me."

"You are going to kill me," he said with a groan before pressing the pad of his thumb against the taut bud of her clitoris.

Ísa's body spasmed in an intense pulse that would've had her falling to her back if Sailor hadn't hauled her against him.

"Next time," he gasped in her ear as he pumped into her with relentless force, "we have to remember to move the cactus."

Ísa's shoulders shook even as her body clamped ever tighter around him. She'd never thought she'd laugh during an orgasm, but she did and it was glorious. Especially when she lifted her head and saw that Sailor was grinning.

Limbs lazy in the aftermath of the orgasm, Ísa decided to even the playing field. Leaning forward, she scraped her teeth down the flat nub of his nipple.

His groan of completion was harsh, his fingers digging into her thigh.

28

LOVEFESTS, FACE SLAPPING, AND STRAWBERRY CHOCOLATES

T HE REST OF THE WEEK passed by at the speed of light for Sailor as he dove into the Fast Organic project in earnest. He barely took a break and Ísa didn't have time to come by the site, but they met in the dark hours of night, loved each other into exhaustion. Yet no matter how fiercely he stroked her, claimed her, he knew she didn't yet trust him. Not the way he needed her to trust him.

It was as if she were mist he was trying to capture.

Well, if she was, he thought with a scowl as he shoved a spade into the earth, he'd build a better mist trap. He *was not* going to give up on the best thing in his life.

Come Friday and he'd managed to pull enough hours through the week that the weekend was his—and he intended to spend that time coaxing his skittish redhead into his arms for more than a night at a time. Sailor wanted Ísa to be his, the need a bone-deep one. Some things a man knew. And Sailor knew Ísa was meant to be his.

He also knew he was fighting a lifetime of pain inflicted on her by the very people who were meant to love her. If Sailor could strangle her parents, he would. Since he couldn't, he'd just have to love her so well that she'd risk her heart. Risk trusting a man who had demons that would drive him for years yet.

Sailor knew he wasn't a dream man. He was scarred inside in ways that didn't show, was haunted by a childhood that had been softened by what had come after, but nothing could erase the anguish of the five-year-old child he'd once been. Nothing could wipe away the primal determination threaded through his psyche.

He was no perfect Prince Charming.

But he was a man who would love Ísa forever if she just gave him the chance.

Because she was it for him. For now and always.

After cleaning up that night, he drove to the Crafty Corners HQ, his intention to talk Ísa into that long-delayed cookie-bar date. Her car was still in the lot. He'd parked his truck and was about to get out when he spotted her leaving by the front door. His entire body smiled.

Jumping out, he called her name as he jogged toward her.

Her head jerked up, but that sometimes sweet, sometimes sinful, always dangerous smile of hers was nowhere in evidence. "Do you like strawberry chocolates?" she asked when he reached her, a mulish expression on her face.

"Not really my thing, but my mom's into fruit chocolates." Sailor took in the lines of strain around her lush mouth, the tension in her shoulders. "I used to buy her a box as a teen when I was in trouble." He still got them for his mom, but now it was just to make her happy.

"Here." Ísa shoved a flat box at his chest. "Please, take it. I hope your mom enjoys them."

Sailor closed his hand around the box, took a quick glance at the black label with gold-foil writing. "Why would a box of fancy chocolates make you mad?" He scowled. "Is some guy stalking you? Aside from me, I mean."

Her lips twitched just enough to ease the fist that had closed around his heart. He didn't like it when she was sad. "I hate strawberries," she muttered. "Always have. Fresh ones, the flavor, everything."

"Ah." Since they'd reached her blue compact, he put the box on the roof so he could focus on her. "Someone should've known that and they didn't?" he guessed, because no corporate gift would incite this kind of fury.

"Yes." She unlocked her car using the remote. "Though honestly, I don't know why I'm surprised. My father still thinks I love going to his weddings when I'd rather chew nails."

"Hold up. Weddings? Plural?"

"Number eight is coming up later this year." A frown. "No wait, it's number nine. I keep forgetting the one-month lovefest that ended in a face-slapping breakup in the middle of a charity ball attended by royalty."

Feeling like a country bumpkin he was so shocked, Sailor nonetheless jerked a thumb back at the box on the roof of the car. His curiosity about Ísa's father could wait; Ísa came first. "Were the chocolates for a special occasion?"

"My birthday," she said, grumpily opening her car door and thrusting her satchel inside. "I don't know what possessed him to send me a gift. He usually just throws shares at me. Probably his new fiancée's influence. He always listens to them at the start."

Sailor only heard part of that. "It's your birthday?" he asked, stunned. Despite the nights they'd spent together, she hadn't so much as hinted at it. "Happy birthday, redhead-who-drives-me-crazy."

"Thank you." Appearing oddly embarrassed, she said, "It's not a big deal."

Sailor wasn't the most intuitive guy—he preferred the practical—but he had an instant of crystal clear understanding right then. What were the chances that two people as self-absorbed as Ísa's parents had thrown their baby girl a birthday party or made any kind of a fuss over her?

The likely answer made him want to strangle them all over again.

"It's a big deal to me." Deciding he'd damn well make a fuss, he put his hands on her hips. "It's the first birthday we've had together." Stealing a kiss, keeping it sweet and romantic until she softened against him, he said, "How was the rest of your day?"

She fiddled with the top button of his shirt. "I snuck out for brunch with Nayna, and Harlow and Catie and I are going out for a belated birthday dinner in the new year." Her smile lit up her eyes. "Do you know what those two got me for a present? One of those dancing hula dolls that you put on your desk. It's incredibly tacky, and I know it'll drive Jacqueline crazy."

"Let me guess, you put it right at the front of your desk?"

Laughing, Ísa nodded. "I can't wait to see her face the first time she spots it."

No mention of Jacqueline in connection with any kind of a birthday wish, but then, that was hardly surprising. "How about we have a party for two tonight?" Sailor wanted to cuddle her in his lap and kiss her silly. "We can go to the cookie bar and have a birthday cookie cake."

Bristling like the cacti he kept sending her—he was now up to four—she poked him in the chest. "You're exhausted. You're going home, having dinner, and getting to bed. I'm going to do the same."

"We could go to bed together."

"We don't sleep when we're together."

No, they didn't, both of them desperate to drink each other in.

Scowling, Sailor considered his options. But he already knew his Ísa far too well to think he could budge her—when it came to the people who mattered to her, Ísa was a stone wall. "Tomorrow then," he said, becoming a stone wall himself. "We're going to have a birthday celebration."

A wary scowl. "Why?"

"Because I said so." He kissed her on the nose.

Eyebrows drawing together even more heavily over her eyes, she said, "What are you planning?"

29

WATCH OUT FOR THE DEADLY FACE-EATING FISH

ISA WOKE, STILL NOT KNOWING what Sailor was planning. He'd teased her unmercifully last night, told her to wear a swimsuit and something over the top to protect herself from the sun, but wouldn't tell her which beach he intended for them to visit.

Not that it mattered.

Isa was already beyond charmed at the thought that he was throwing her a private birthday celebration. He could have no idea how much that meant to her. She was waiting for him in the lobby of her apartment building when he drove his truck into the parking lot. Having missed waking up to his kiss, she immediately headed out with her beach-ready tote bag.

He threw open the passenger door from the inside, all gorgeous male appreciation of her—though she was wearing a tankini over which she'd pulled on a pair of shorts and a floaty white garment that covered her arms.

Her legs were a matching flash-fire white.

But where she saw a wraith, he saw a woman who made his eyes glint with sexual heat. "I love your skin," he murmured as she got in, placing one big hand on her thigh and stroking as he leaned in for a kiss.

How was Ísa supposed to resist him when he said things like that? And when he touched her as if she were some precious Rubens painting, his own breath turning uneven by the time the kiss ended.

"Hold that thought," he ordered before putting the truck in gear and pulling out.

It took Ísa a few minutes to find her brain cells again. "What's in that odd-looking duffel bag on the back seat?" It was tubular in shape and seemed to be made of waterproof fabric.

"My beach gear, plus I made us a picnic."

Grinning at his open pride, she said, "Which beach are we going to hang out at?"

His chuckle sent all her instincts prickling. "A very nice one."

Ísa narrowed her eyes. "Sailor, we *are* going to go lie on a beach and read books and drink champagne right?"

"Sure. After."

"After what?"

"You'll see."

No matter what Ísa threatened, he wouldn't tell her his plans. And then, a half hour later, they were obvious. He parked his truck in a spot not far from Mission Bay. But the actual bay closest to where they'd stopped—Okahu—was the hub of a kayak-rental business.

"Tell me we're not going kayaking," she said, making no effort to hide her horror.

He grabbed her hand and lifted it to his lips. "Trust me, spitfire. I'll keep you safe."

"That's not the point, Sailor. I can't row those stupid things!" The last time she'd tried had been during a high school camp, having been forced into the "fun" activity by a teacher who hadn't understood Ísa's lack of coordination. "I'll drown and the fish will eat my face."

"I've got you covered."

"Oh, are you going to magically row my spindly death boat?"

Laughing, he just tugged her down to the rental place, where they showed him to the double kayak he'd already apparently booked.

"You could've told me," she said to the demon by her side.

He chucked her under the chin with a playfulness that made her stomach go all fluttery. "Why?" he said. "It was so much fun having you send me death rays with your eyes."

"You haven't seen my death ray eyes yet," Ísa muttered while putting on the lifejacket he gave her. She was glad to see him donning one too. Sailor was strong and athletic, but she'd feel better if they were both protected even though they'd just be paddling about in the relatively sheltered waters of the bay.

Then she saw him placing the tubular duffel into a hatch in back of the kayak after removing a few items. That done, he picked up her tote, handed over her floppy hat, added the bottles of water he'd pulled out from his bag, and put the entire tote into another bag that looked waterproof—before placing it in a hatch at the front of the kayak that the person sitting up front could easily access. He neatly sealed up both hatches.

Ísa swallowed. "Sailor, how far are we going?" There wasn't anything out there except the islands of the Hauraki Gulf.

Oh God.

"Please don't say Rangitoto." The dormant volcano was a dramatic triangular shape on the horizon—and it was really, really, *really* far away.

"Okay." He shot her a grin. "We're going to Motutapu. It's just behind Rangitoto."

"I know where it is." Even farther away. "In case you missed it, ferries cross that water. Yachts zip across it. No one's going to notice a toothpick-thin kayak. Those face-eating fish are going to get a good meal out of the two of us."

Her dark prediction only made Sailor's grin widen. "Trust me on this, birthday girl. I can take us the whole way, and I know how to dodge or ride the wake from the larger craft." A grip on her chin, a quick kiss. "Come on, where's my wild, skinny-dipping Ísa?"

"She's scared of face-eating fish," Ísa muttered but stuffed her hat on her head. "Will this stay on?" Even slathered in sunscreen, her face would be fried bacon if she went out on the water without a hat. The sunscreen should protect her legs, but she could always throw her towel across them if the skin began to go pink.

Sailor checked the hatches were secure. "Wind's calm, so yeah." Sliding his hand up her calf and higher, he rose to his feet. "Let's go celebrate your birthday in style."

Wanting to do her bit now that she'd agreed to this insanity, Ísa helped him lift the kayak. Once it was on the sand, just nudging the water, Sailor made her get into the front seat. "I can control it better from the back," he told her. "And with our gear pretty balanced, the heavier person should be at the back."

Ísa's lips parted in an instinctive demurral... when she realized he *was* heavier. All that muscle on a six-two frame made him deliciously heavy when he was on top in bed.

Two days ago, he'd talked her into being on top. And then he'd talked dirty to her until she'd ridden him like he was a thoroughbred.

"Fuck me, Ísa. Just like that, baby."

"You're so good at this, sweetheart."

"You have the body of a centerfold."

Cheeks flushing at the memory of his harsh, sexy words before his back bowed in a shuddering orgasm, she took her seat.

Sailor put her paddle across the front and told her to hold on to the middle.

"Got it," Ísa said just as a small wave crashed over the bow and washed away the erotic echoes from their night together.

Ísa tried desperately to reassure herself that this plan wasn't destined for disaster.

If the kayak flipped, she and Sailor just had to float until someone got to them. And if a fish or three nibbled on her toes, well, apparently that was considered a pedicure in some places. She'd seen it online. So she'd get a free fish-nibble pedicure. Nothing to worry about.

We're going to die. At least my last will and testament is up to date.

Sailor pushed the kayak forward, deeper into the water, then somehow managed to jump in without causing it to rock wildly before starting to paddle... and she realized she had absolutely no need to worry. He had total control of the kayak, his motions so fluid that she felt like she was on a smooth ride. She wished she could see him, see his biceps flexing, his golden skin gleaming under the sunlight.

They rode gracefully over an incoming wave.

"Shall I try?" she asked hesitantly, her hands tight on

the kayak paddle she still held across her front. "I'll probably mess up your rhythm."

"Don't worry so much, baby. This is about having fun," he said, the affection in the words making her blink her eyes hard against a hot, wet burn. "But wait until I have us past the waves so it'll be easier."

That didn't take him long.

Once they were in calmer waters, he stopped and taught her how to angle her paddle so it cut through the water rather than fighting it. It took her several tries, but she finally got some semblance of a good stroke.

A smile broke out over her face. "This *is* fun." No one had ever been so patient with her when she was trying to learn to do something athletic.

"I don't like to say I told you so, but…"

She laughed at Sailor's smug tone and carried on. She did have to take frequent breaks as the trip was a three-hour one for someone as strong and experienced as Sailor. With him slowing down so she could paddle too, plus a water and snack break in the middle, it was well past the three-and-a-half-hour mark by the time they hit the choppier waters near the island.

CONTENT IN A WAY HE hadn't been in a long time, his demons unable to fight the happiness in his veins, Sailor watched Ísa dig in her paddle ahead of him. She was off-rhythm but determined and probably had a burned nose by now, though she'd slathered on more sunscreen midway through their journey.

If he'd been facing her, he'd have kissed her silly.

She'd probably have pushed him back with a stern warning about face-eating fish.

Grinning, he said, "Time for you to rest, spitfire. I need to take over now to get us past the more tricky sections."

"Okay," Ísa said and carefully put her paddle in front of her so it wouldn't be in his way.

Sailor dug in, powering them toward the beach at Motutapu where he intended for them to land. He saw a couple of yachts moored nearby, but there was no one else on the beach itself. It was a hard one to get to if you weren't coming by your own watercraft.

"Are you bionic?"

Ísa's question had him laughing. "Pure Kiwi male," he said, but his chest puffed up a little at her admiring tone. "You want to paddle some more? It's a straight shot to the beach now."

"Yes." A smile over her shoulder before she began.

He matched his rhythm to her gentle one, enjoying himself in a way he would've never expected at such a lazy pace. Usually when he kayaked, it was all about the burn in his muscles, his speed punishing in an effort to drown out the demons. "Stay in the kayak," he told Ísa when they got close to landing.

Jumping out into the water himself, he pushed the kayak onto the sand with her in it. She laughed in delight, and his heart, it flip-flopped in a way it had never done in his twenty-three years of life.

Yeah, she was it for him.

Didn't matter how many years he'd had on this earth.

He knew.

Extending a hand, he helped her out onto the soft sand. "*Now*," he said, "we relax."

First, however, they put their lifejackets in the kayak, then hauled the kayak up the beach to park it under the shade of a large pōhutukawa tree. Taking out Ísa's tote, he placed it on the sand. Next, he retrieved his duffel bag and pulled out a small waterproof sheet he'd brought along.

He placed the sandwiches he'd prepared onto the makeshift mat, bottles of orange juice beside them, then added apples and oranges plus fudge squares for dessert. "Jake," he said in explanation. "He's working part-time at a restaurant over the summer and keeps coming home with ideas he wants to try."

Ísa picked up a piece of the rich sweet and bit in. "Oh, this is divine." A throaty sound that made his cock want to rise to attention.

"Hey, eat your lunch before dessert," he growled at her. "But first..." He took out a lumpy cupcake with orange icing that looked even worse than it had in the early-morning light. "I tried to bake you a birthday cupcake. You don't have to eat it. But you can still blow out a candle."

Hands flying to her mouth, Ísa looked at him with wet eyes.

"Hey. It's not that bad," Sailor protested. "It kind of even looks cupcake-shaped if you squint really hard."

Laughing and crying at the same time, Ísa grabbed his face in her hands and kissed him all over. "You're wonderful, Sailor Bishop. And I'll eat your cake."

He felt like a well-petted cat. "No, seriously. I think I mixed up the salt with the sugar. And possibly the baking powder with the baking soda."

Her shoulders shook. "Light the candle," she ordered, all but bouncing on her knees.

Placing the cupcake between them, he poked a thin pink candle into the orange icing, then used a lighter to set it aflame, his other hand cupped around it to protect it from the faint sea breeze. "Make a wish, Ísalind."

Face aglow, Ísa squeezed her eyes shut for three long seconds. "Okay, I'm ready to blow out the candle."

"Not before the birthday song." He launched into it with gusto, Ísa listening with her hands fisted and crossed over her heart, as if he'd given her diamonds instead of a mutant cupcake.

After blowing out the candle in one puff once the song was over, she took a careful bite. He waited for her to spit it back out, but she actually swallowed, then took a second bite. "Try it," she said around the mouthful. "It's pretty good."

Sailor figured she was pulling his leg, but it was her birthday after all. He took a bite. And felt his eyes widen. "I'm a culinary genius." Actually, the cake was chewy and dense, but there was no salt instead of sugar, which, in his book made this a win.

But even better was seeing Ísa smile with open happiness.

Inside his heart, he cupped his hands, trying to hold the delicate mist of her. And those hands, they were calloused and marked with nicks and cuts from his work. Work that had consumed him since he was a fifteen-year-old haunted by the knowledge that within him lay the capacity for betrayal, for disloyalty, for cowardice.

30

SAILOR'S MIGHTY HORN

TEN MINUTES LATER AND SAILOR had banished his dark thoughts into the dungeon where he usually kept them. Today was for him and Ísa and happiness. Shadows not invited.

When Ísa took out her phone to glance at it, he managed to keep a straight face. Until twenty minutes afterward when she said, "Catie usually messages me a few times a day. I wonder if she's okay."

Busted.

"I told her I was kidnapping you," Sailor said. "She gave me her number when we went to Hamilton."

Sailor had given Catie his in turn and told her that if anything ever happened and she couldn't get ahold of Ísa, she wasn't to hesitate to call him. He didn't know if she would, but he'd wanted her to have the option. "She and Harlow will only message or call if it's an emergency."

Ísa's eyebrows drew together over her eyes. "Are you managing me, Sailor Bishop?"

"Yep," he said without any feelings of guilt whatsoever. "I know you're pretty much in loco parentis"—had probably been since Catie's birth—"but parents of teenagers occasionally leave them alone and trust them not to burn down the house." He pointed at himself. "My mother once left me responsible for Jake and Danny while she and Dad went to watch one of Gabe's out-of-town games."

"Did you set your brothers' hair on fire?" Ísa asked suspiciously.

Sailor gave her an indignant look. "Of course not. I only let them dye their hair peroxide blond. They asked, and I didn't see a problem with it—I just told them to use the garage sink so they wouldn't mess up my mom's nice new bathroom. See? *Responsible.*"

Lips pressed tightly together, Ísa was clearly struggling not to laugh. "You're making that up," she said at last.

"Scout's honor. I've got pictures to prove it." He'd show them to her when he took her to visit his family. "Catie and Harlow will be fine, spitfire. Neither one of them is an infant."

Her face fell. "Did they say something? Does Catie feel like I'm smothering her? I know I'm overprotective with her."

"All Catie said in reply to my request was 'Cool. I'll tell Harlow too.' Oh, and she sent a set of emojis." Taking out his phone, he showed her the response: Heart eyes, kissy faces, fireworks, a tree, big kissy lips, and a unicorn. "The only one I don't get is the unicorn. Does she think *I'm* a unicorn, or is that a sly teenage reference to my mighty horn?"

Ísa snorted out laughing.

Pushing at his chest, she tried to speak but was giggling too hard to create words.

Delighted with her, Sailor pounced and stole a kiss, two. "Admit it, you like my mighty horn."

"You make Devil Ísa take over my brain" was the response.

Sailor grinned. "Good. Now, let's make out and scandalize anyone on those yachts who might be watching."

ÍSA HAD A QUICK SHOWER after she got home in order to wash off the sunscreen and the salt from their swims. Sailor had driven to his own place after dropping her off in order to do the same. It would've been much easier if he had some clothes at her place, but Ísa couldn't bring herself to make that invitation. If she kept a few walls between them, she told herself, the pain wouldn't be so bad when it ended.

And knew she was lying.

After drying her hair, then dressing in a simple blue scoop-necked tee and soft gray velour pants that would've horrified Jacqueline's fashion sense but that felt soft and good around her body, she pulled her hair into a ponytail.

Her phone rang with a Bollywood dance number seconds later. "Nayna! How was the day?" She knew her friend was taking part in—in Nayna's words—"a big, fat, OTT Indian wedding" this weekend.

It was scheduled to carry on into the following week since a lot of people were now on Christmas vacation. Ísa knew Nayna had the next three weeks off, her accounting firm having closed for the holidays.

"It's not even the actual ceremony yet," her best friend replied, "and already ten thousand aunties have squeezed my cheeks and told me I was a pretty girl and why wasn't I married?" Nayna muttered. "Youth won't last forever,

Nayna *beta*. Tut, tut. Then they turn around and compliment me for being a strong career woman."

"Have you heard from Raj?" Nayna had been suspiciously quiet on that topic over the past few days.

"Yes. But we're not talking about him today." The words came out a near-growl.

"*Nayna.*"

Her best friend cracked like an egg. "I kissed him, okay! I didn't meant to, but it's like I see his mouth and my lips become magnetized in his direction."

Biting back a grin, Ísa said, "I've had that problem. I understand."

"Oh, shut up," Nayna said with the ease of old friendship before there was a rustling sound down the line. "Thank God. I thought I'd never finish putting on this sari," she muttered. "Give me a minute to put on the bling —you know too much is never enough for an Indian wedding." Gentle metallic tinkling sounds as Nayna put on her bangles. "How was the belated birthday celebration with the hot gardener?"

A deep warmth uncurling in her stomach, Ísa said, "Wonderful. *He's* wonderful."

Her own words rang around in her skull after she hung up from her conversation with Nayna. Sailor *was* wonderful, and he'd been there for her whenever she needed him. Maybe it was time she let go of her fear and went all in.

Cold hands snatched at her gut, chilling the warmth.

She knew Sailor was nothing like her father, but she couldn't help remembering how Stefán was at the start of his relationships—so accommodating, so generous with his attention. All the women who'd married him thought that was who he was. They didn't see the workaholic with his eye constantly on the financial markets until he'd put the ring on their finger and no longer had to expend any effort to capture them.

To be ruthlessly fair, Sailor had never done anything to hide his goals from Ísa.

If she went all in with him, she had to do so with the full knowledge that work would eventually eat up more and more of his time. It was inevitable. There'd be no more picnics, no more kayaking, no more time in his life for his "spitfire" except on his own terms.

Ísa couldn't live that way.

But neither could she let Sailor go. Not before she'd lived every possible moment with him. Not before she'd fought as hard as she could for the dream she wanted to build with him—a family, a life together in the light rather than frantic couplings in the dark to make up for endless days apart.

Buzz.

Jerking at the sound of the door buzzer, she got up to let Sailor in, determined to do everything in her power to bind him to her. Until he wouldn't ever forget her. Not even if he had a million other things on his plate.

SAILOR HAD WANTED TO TAKE a bite out of Ísa all night, his possessiveness riding a hard edge. Because even though he was in her home and even though she'd been sassing him all evening, he had the gut feeling that something was off.

Frustration gnawed at him.

His need to claim her, brand her, was more than a little primitive.

And he didn't care.

When she said, "Do you want dessert?" he pressed his

mouth to hers, drank her in, curving his hands over her rear at the same time with blunt possessiveness.

"Yes," he murmured when they came up for air. "I want dessert. Where's the bedroom?"

A glint came into her eye. "Did you bring your truck?"

His cock turned to granite, his breath punching out of his chest. "Devil Ísa in charge?"

"Maybe."

"I have my truck. The school?"

"God no" was the horrified answer. "You find us a nice, quiet spot."

"I know just the place." Sailor's blood pounded with need, but if Ísa wanted a fantasy, he'd give her that fantasy.

He'd give his redhead everything she needed.

All she had to do was say the word.

ÍSA STARED AT HIM WHEN he brought his truck to a stop in front of his town house. Getting out without saying a word, he pushed open the garage, then drove the truck in before pulling down the garage door from the inside. There was a little light hanging from the ceiling that he turned on, but it didn't do much to illuminate things.

"So?" he said to the woman he wouldn't share with anyone, not even a glimpse.

Sliding out of the passenger-side door, she opened the door to the back seat and climbed in.

Sweet mercy.

He ran his hand over the lush curves of her as she got back into the truck, the ache in his groin a deep pleasure-pain. She made a breathy little sound before sitting herself down on the cracked leather of the seat. Holding his gaze, she dropped her hands to the bottom of her T-shirt and tore it over the top of her head.

Creamy skin.

The plump invitation of her breasts under mint-green lace.

Sailor was inside the truck with his hand on her breast before she finished dropping the T-shirt to the floor, his mouth on hers once again. Making that deliciously husky sound in her throat, she dug her nails into his back. His cock throbbed.

And he wanted more of her. *All* of her.

Dropping his hand from her breast to her thigh, he tugged down her pants.

When they caught on her tennis shoes, he tore them off and soon had one sleek leg wrapped around his waist, Ísa backed up against the other door. He felt like a great big cat about to lick up his favorite meal. "Your skin is so deliciously smooth." Like cream and sugar and all things nice.

Ísa shivered, her lips on his throat.

Groaning, Sailor put his hand back on her breast. "Your bra's pretty." Soft and feminine. "But I want it off." Sailor wasted no time in making that happen. He was so hungry for her, so determined to brand her as his that he felt eighteen again and not like a struggling business owner barely hanging on by his fingernails.

The only downside was that teenage boys weren't known for their sexual stamina. And Ísa was his wettest dream. All opulent curves and gorgeous skin with nipples as pink as her lips. He had no hope in hell of resisting. Pausing only long enough to tear off his T-shirt so Ísa could touch him, he dropped his head and sucked one pouting tip into his mouth.

ÍSA'S BRAIN WASN'T MAKING MUCH sense right now. Her fingers clenched in the thick dark of Sailor's hair, the heat of his body surrounding her as he did things to her breasts that made her thighs squeeze around his hard body. The hand he put on her other breast was callused, his skin rough in contrast to the firm wetness of his mouth.

She shuddered, found herself clawing his back in an effort to tug him up for a kiss.

"Hellcat." A sinful grin as he released her aching, sensitive nipple to give her that kiss, deep and lush and erotically patient.

"Now," he said with a scrape of his teeth over her lower lip, "let me get back to work." With that, he dropped his head to her neglected breast while using his free hand to stroke her thigh.

When he began to pull down her panties, she knew this was it—the moment she either stopped him... or didn't. And they got busy in a garage on a suburban street.

Turned out she was still feeling reckless and insane.

And young.

So wickedly, wildly young.

Teenage-girl-in-the-back-seat-of-her-boyfriend's-truck young.

The mint-green lace of her panties was hanging around one of her ankles two seconds later. And he was stroking his hand up her leg and she shivered at the feel of his skin against her inner thigh. She would've screamed at his next touch, directly between her thighs, if he hadn't clamped his mouth over hers.

Gripping at her hair with his other hand, he held her in place for his kiss while his fingers stroked and flicked and made her come so hard she trembled from head to toe.

"Oh, that was good," he purred as if rewarding her.

She felt like telling him she'd already been rewarded. But her mouth wasn't working quite right and she didn't stop him when he hauled her across the seat so that she ended up in a half recline. He gave her no warning before he buried his face between her thighs.

Ísa's back bowed, her hands scrabbling for purchase on the faded and weathered leather of the seats as Sailor pushed her over with a relentless male focus. This time her scream was so deep it was soundless. She heard a wrapper tear, knew he was getting ready to enter her.

Her exhausted inner muscles clenched in greedy readiness.

Strong hands cupped her buttocks, squeezed. "You with me, beautiful?"

Ísa pushed up on her elbows, met the blue of his gaze, and smiled. "Yes, my studly boy toy."

Laughing in sinful delight, he bent to kiss her even as he thrust into her. The rest was steamy windows and dirty talk and a fantasy coming hotly true. And through it all ran a vein of terrifying joy. Because this felt *right*.

Dangerously, beautifully, heartbreakingly right.

31

THE COST OF DREAMS

THURSDAY WAS A HARSH RETURN to reality after five days beyond Sailor's wildest dreams. Following that intense, sexy, fucking amazing interlude in his garage, he and Ísa had driven back to her place, fallen into bed... and stayed there for most of Sunday. He'd stroked and petted and marked up her delicate skin, and she'd been as possessive with his body.

Sailor was good with that. More than good with it.

Then Monday they'd had a private Christmas Eve celebration in the afternoon, sharing small gifts they'd secretly bought for one another. He'd found a pair of pretty earrings for her that looked like bunches of flowers falling from her ears—from her shining eyes, it looked like he'd gotten it right.

She'd given him a belt with an aged buckle that he already knew he'd wear the hell out of.

Fighting their desire to shut out the world, they'd gone in different directions after that private celebration, both having promises to keep. Sailor's family was congregating at his paternal grandparents place ninety minutes out of

Auckland, and he'd promised to go down early and help his gramps and grandma set up. Ísa, meanwhile, had given her scattered family orders to show their faces at her apartment for a family dinner.

"Next Christmas," Sailor had promised as he kissed her goodbye, "we'll do it together. Combine the clans."

Gaze soft, Ísa had drawn him into another kiss instead of answering. And he'd known he hadn't yet caught the mist, hadn't yet convinced her to trust him with her heart. The thought haunted him even through the joy of the holidays, was still on his mind as he sat in his truck on his second day back at work.

He'd only taken Christmas Eve and Christmas Day off but hadn't managed to see Ísa yet, as she and Harlow had driven down to Hamilton with Catie on Christmas Day. The two had returned this morning and both were back at work too.

He'd have his redhead in his arms again tonight.

He was working on the next step in his plan to convince her to be his when his phone rang. His gut tensed at seeing his loan manager's name on the screen. Having just finished up the school project so he could focus fully on Fast Organic, he was still in his truck in the school parking lot.

"Jenni," he said, one hand braced on the steering wheel and his eyes looking through the windshield at the sun-golden school grounds. "I wasn't expecting a call until after the new year."

"I'm working between the public holidays, taking my break later, and I wanted to get back to you as fast as possible."

"Good news or bad?" He and the loan officer had a

friendly relationship—Sailor had already taken out and paid back a couple of smaller loans.

This one, however, would be a much bigger risk for the bank.

"Good and bad," Jenni replied in a tone as no-nonsense as her steel-gray bob. "The good is that the bank will give you the loan."

Sailor didn't start celebrating. "I'm waiting for the bad."

"You're going to need someone to cosign. You just don't have the assets to borrow against. Not at this amount."

Sailor's hand clenched on the steering wheel. "Thanks for trying anyway." He knew Jenni had gone to bat for him with the higher-ups.

"What?" Jenni's tone rose. "Sailor, this isn't a big deal. Your folks cosigned that first loan when you were eighteen."

Even then, it had been difficult for Sailor to accept any help. He'd done so only because he'd seen how much his parents wanted to be a part of his journey. But he wasn't eighteen anymore, and the need inside him to achieve this through his own hard work, it had become a second heart-beat that pounded day and night.

"Some things," he said to Jenni, "a man has to do on his own."

Jenni was made of stern stuff, didn't give up. "What about your brother?"

"Gabe would do it in a heartbeat," Sailor told her because it was true—and because he didn't want anyone thinking badly of his brother. "This is my call."

Gabriel had forged his own path, broken the chains of the past.

His brother's determination was legendary—Sailor had spent endless weekends running drills with Gabe, even more evenings going for runs with his brother, had watched game after game while Gabe analyzed plays.

Sailor felt the same way about his business. And Gabe had done for him what he'd done for Gabe. Over the years, his brother had dug countless gardens, helped unload trucks of seedlings, hauled bags of soil and fertilizer around, kept Sailor company on the drive out to the nursery he rented some distance away.

But money was a different matter.

Sailor wasn't going to ask his brother to subsidize his dream in any shape or form. That would destroy the dream. Sailor needed to do this without expecting the people he loved to pay for what he wanted. That was the whole fucking point. To not be a taker. A user.

To give back to the people who loved him.

"You sure, Sailor?" Jenni asked.

"Yeah. How big a loan can I get on my own?"

It proved to be a far smaller amount, but it was better than nothing.

After setting up a meeting with Jenni to go over the paperwork, he just sat in his truck for long minutes, staring out at the late-afternoon sunshine. The brightness seemed to mock the shadows threatening to swallow his dream.

Without the money, he couldn't implement the next step of his plan. And if he didn't implement it within the next year, then it was inevitable that someone else would step in and fill the gap in the market. This would only work if Sailor stayed ahead of the competition.

For that, he needed cold, hard cash.

"No," he said with a scowl. "It's just a hurdle. You've jumped hurdles before."

Ten minutes of doing the mental math and he realized he *could* make enough money to launch exactly when he'd always planned to launch. But he'd have to work from dawn to dusk, seven days a week. Holidays included.

Sailor tapped his finger on the wheel. Working hard wasn't an issue. Neither was finding enough work to fill those hours. Yes, big corporate jobs made it easier, but multiple residential jobs would do as well—and he had enough experience at this to know where to advertise to find clients.

As for his family, his brothers didn't mind hanging out with him on the job, so he'd see them often. He could shoehorn in time to watch a few of Jake's and Danny's games, while Gabe would understand Sailor's obsession with his dream. And he still had to eat, so he could drop by for dinner now and then to keep his folks happy.

What *was* at issue was his redhead.

Ísa deserved to be cherished and treated like a priority in his life. By working as many hours as he needed to work, Sailor would inevitably be shoving her to the sidelines when he hadn't yet earned the right to ask for her patience, when he hadn't yet shown her that she could trust him to only do this for a year. Not only that, he'd be expecting her to fit her life around his.

His jaw clenched. If he did that, he was no fucking better than her parents.

And he risked losing her.

But if he didn't do what he needed to do, he risked losing his self-respect, risked becoming the kind of man he'd always despised. A man who gave up when the going got hard. A man who just fucking quit.

32

THE FAMILY CHRISTMAS FIASCO & A
LOVE MUFFIN

*I*SA WORKED TILL EIGHT THAT night without a break, not just handling the usual duties of a VP but also going over the information she'd collected about the people who'd been in and out of Jacqueline's office. She had to admit she had a favorite suspect, but she knew it was based on nothing but her personal bias against slimy swamp creatures. Just because she disliked Trevor didn't mean her stepbrother—*yeah, no, that description was never going to fly with her*—was a louse who'd leak information to the media. Not when he wanted to be in Jacqueline's good books.

On the flip side, Ísa couldn't ignore that he'd been in and out of the company—and Jacqueline's office—far more often than explicable for a man who had absolutely nothing to do with the business. Unless you factored in his campaign to convince Jacqueline to give him an executive position at Crafty Corners.

Which could put Trevor the Creeper in the clear.

"Argh!" Ísa threw down her pen and gave up—for

tonight at least—and decided she needed to get some food into her. Normally she'd have hit Nayna up for a dinner date, but today she found herself thinking first of Sailor.

Her thighs pressed together, butterflies flittering in her stomach as a goofy smile lit up her face at the thought of seeing him again. She'd missed him over the past few days, had kept on wanting to whisper asides to him during the Christmas Eve dinner in her apartment.

Like when her father, having flown in for a couple of days, had put his arm around Elizabeth Anne Victoria and quite seriously declared they were soul mates.

At which point, Jacqueline had shaken her head and said—in Icelandic—"Stefán, you're a handsome man, but if you're not careful, you're going to turn into a caricature of a lecherous old man. Your 'soul mate' is an infant."

While the sweet but sadly vacuous Elizabeth Anne Victoria giggled and said how "amazing" it was that her "love muffin" spoke so many languages, Ísa's father had replied to Jacqueline, also in Icelandic. "She doesn't try to take over my corporations. I consider that a wonderful trait in a wife."

"That's because she doesn't know a balance sheet from a bedsheet."

Ísa had cut off that line of talk before it degenerated any further, but dinner had been interesting to say the least. Even being friends was a complicated matter for Jacqueline and Stefán. Poor Elizabeth Anne Victoria and poor Oliver, both of them with their own personal barracuda they had not a hope in hell of controlling.

Without Ísa, it would've been a bloodbath—after which Jacqueline and Stefán would've shared a toast and wondered what the fuss was about. As it was, Ísa had made sure no blood was spilled and even her combative parents had appeared to relax under the influence of good wine and food.

Catie and Harlow had had a grand old time talking with their eyes and fighting not to crack up while mouthing "love muffin" when Stefán wasn't looking, while Oliver had appeared sweetly befuddled until Jacqueline pressed a kiss to his cheek. Then he'd glowed— and Jacqueline had tugged him up into a slow dance in time to "Silent Night."

As for Trevor, he'd thankfully been nowhere in evidence, this being the year he spent the holidays with his mother's side of the family. Which Ísa had known when she'd made the dinner plans. She hadn't been born yesterday. And she did not intend to have Trevor creeping about in her apartment. Ever.

She couldn't wait to tell Sailor everything, laugh with him over her insane family, and hear about his Christmas in turn, her goofy smile getting wider by the second.

Telling herself to act like an adult, she texted Nayna to ask about the Raj situation. It turned out his family had been invited to the same big fat wedding as Nayna's family—and he'd had the nerve to come sit right next to Nayna, causing every eyebrow in the place to rise into the owner's hairline.

Single, unattached men did not sit next to single, unattached women unless there was "something going on."

And even though Nayna had kicked him under the table and hissed under her breath for him to go away, he'd kept on bringing her chai from the buffet, putting extra sweets onto her plate, and all around acting like a besotted suitor.

"Then he leaves an hour before everyone else and drops me in it." Nayna had fumed down the phone line yesterday afternoon. "My parents were beaming, the aunties were agog with questions, and I wanted to brain him. It was his revenge for my 'just want you for your body' moment, I'm sure of it."

Ísa had fought not to laugh—the more she heard about Raj, the more she liked him. Nayna needed a man who'd play with her, tease her, cause her shields to fall. As Sailor did with Ísa. Yes, it was dangerous and would hurt a hell of a lot when it ended, but that was a future Ísa was studiously ignoring.

Has he got back in touch? she messaged Nayna.

The evil fiend keeps sending me pictures of his abs and arms and all-around spectacular body. I'm weak. I save the photos.

Laughing, Ísa picked up the phone and called her friend. The resulting chat was hysterical and illuminating: Nayna, it seemed, was falling for Raj despite herself. Maybe as hard as Ísa had fallen for Sailor.

Even hungrier by the time she and Nayna finished their call, Ísa went and grabbed some Chinese takeout, then headed to the first Fast Organic site. Sailor had messaged her to say he'd be working there till full dark, and the summer light was only just beginning to fade by the time she arrived.

His truck was the only one in the lot. Or, she should say, his truck was the only one outside of what had once been the lot. It had been completely dug up, the concrete hauled away.

Ísa was astonished at the speed of it all.

Making her way gingerly through the work site, she noticed the warnings about health and safety and did her best to stay uninjured. The last thing she needed was for the company to be hit with a safety violation because she'd fallen on her face.

"Sailor," she called out, "where are you?"

"Ísa?" Sailor's face appeared from around the corner of the building.

Scowling when he saw her trying to make her way through the churned-up dirt where the parking lot had once been, he took off his gloves, then walked over in his heavy work boots. He'd lifted her up and was carrying her and the takeout beyond the danger zone before she'd realized what he intended to do.

Then he leaned in and kissed her in voracious welcome, one rough-skinned hand cupping her cheek. She felt deliciously devoured. It was as if he'd been waiting to kiss her all day, as if she was a drug and he was an addict.

Ísa decided she was quite happy to be Sailor's personal drug habit.

Only breaking the kiss when they were both breathless, he said, "You're a sight for sore eyes, spitfire." A long inhale. "And is that Chinese I smell?"

Toes still curled and cheeks flushed, Ísa pushed the takeout bag at his chest. "Men only want me for the food I bring."

"Oh, I have other priorities." He ran his hand down her back and to her rear, squeezing with open appreciation.

"Stop that," Devil Ísa ordered. "That's dessert."

He groaned. "You drive me fucking crazy, Ísalind. And I missed you bad."

"I missed you too," Ísa said, not about to play games with him.

He responded with one of those silly, sweet nose kisses that made her stomach drop, before he took her hand and walked her around the side of the building.

Her eyes widened. "Wow, how did you manage all this on your own?" The kitchen garden was marked out by a temporary border, the soil all in place.

"I could pretend to be Superman," he said, "or I could admit that I asked my brothers and Raj to pitch in. All four of them turned up today. My dad would have too, except that he and my mom drove back down to my grandparents place—my grandfather twisted his ankle last night."

Maybe that explained the tension Ísa had glimpsed in his gaze when he'd first come around the corner. "Is it a bad injury?"

"No. I think my folks just used it as an excuse to go spend some more time with them." An affectionate smile. "They're hoping to talk my grandparents into moving to Auckland, but I don't know if it'll happen—those two love the Waikato area."

Sitting her down on an upturned wooden box that looked to have once held some kind of gardening supplies, Sailor took a seat on a neighboring box. Hooking a third box with his foot and dragging it over, he laid the bag of takeout between them.

Wondering if it was just the stress of work that she'd read on his face, Ísa began to set out the food. "How was your Christmas?"

"Usual mayhem," he said with a grin. "Danny managed to get hold of a bottle of red wine while no one was looking and decided to see what the fuss was about." He laughed. "Let's just say he won't be going near alcohol again for a while. How was yours?"

When Ísa told him, he laughed so hard that he almost fell off his seat. "Am I your love muffin?" he asked with a grin.

Heart skipping a beat, Ísa replied in the same light

vein. "I prefer snookums." She began to open up the takeout to the sound of his renewed laughter, her own lips tugging up. Being with him just made her so painfully happy. "Are you close to your grandparents?"

"Yep. When I was a kid, I used to spend weeks at a time running wild on their farm back before they downsized." Accepting the box of fried rice she held out, he said, "You? Close to any grandparents?"

Grief stabbed Ísa's heart. "My paternal grandmother," she said softly. "I lived with her for five years in Iceland, starting at age eight. I loved her more than I'd ever before loved anyone." The best thing was that her grandmother had loved her back just as much. "She was warm and soft, and she rocked me if I had a nightmare."

Running the back of his hand over her cheek, his gaze dark, Sailor said, "She's gone?"

"A month after I turned thirteen." A month after a birthday picnic her grandmother had helped Ísa put together for her friends. "That's when my father brought me back to New Zealand and told Jacqueline it was her turn to take responsibility for me."

"That's a hard age to adapt to a country you last saw as a child."

Ísa made a face. "Especially when you have a 'funny' accent and weigh more than average." Shrugging off the old memories, she said, "I'm trying to give Catie and Harlow the kind of love *Amma* Kaja gave me."

"You're succeeding," Sailor said without even a heart-beat of hesitation.

Something warm and fuzzy burst to life inside Ísa's heart.

"Try this." Sailor held out a spring roll.

Leaning in, Ísa took a bite. He popped the other half into his own mouth. The small intimacy of the moment caught her breath. What would it be like to have this with him every night? These simple, sweet moments of connection as they grew together into the future?

33

THE GAUZY TRAGEDY GOWN

I T WAS DIFFICULT NOT TO clutch at the dream. Because despite how hard she intended to fight to make it work, the risk that it would all fall apart remained perilously high. It was a bad risk all around—no woman with a killer instinct and business-black blood would ever pour more resources into the campaign.

Unfortunately for her future self, Ísa was a romantic who was probably destined to produce her own personal Shakespearean tragedy, complete with a bloodied and broken heart and shattered dreams. Though she drew the line at wearing a flower crown and running through the streets in a diaphanous gown while rambling madly.

"A woman has to have certain standards," she murmured.

Sailor paused in the act of eating another spring roll. "I think they're pretty good," he defended. "Crunchy on the outside, delicious on the inside."

"What? Oh." Ísa's shoulders trembled, her smile cutting into her cheeks. "No, I just had an idea for a poem." She raised her hand to her mouth after the words escaped. "Forget you heard that."

Demon-blue eyes gleamed. "Not a chance, spitfire." Spring roll demolished, he tugged her fingers away from her mouth. "You write poetry?"

Blowing out a breath, Ísa nodded. "Finding *just* the right combination of words to get across a thought or an idea within the tiny, perfect form of poetry, it makes me happy." It was that simple. "I'm not hoping to be the next poet laureate or anything. It's a... passionate hobby."

"If you did become a famous poet," Sailor said to a laugh from Ísa, "would you give up the teaching?"

"No. I love teaching." It felt like a calling.

"Can I hear one of your poems?"

"I'll think about it." Ísa felt oddly shy about sharing her work with him, showing him those quirky little pieces of her soul. "You must be tired," she said to give herself time to think. "You've achieved an incredible amount in a short time."

"I've got probably half an hour of workable light left." He finished up the last of his food. "You done for the day?"

Ísa made a face. "No, I'm handling something for Jacqueline that's sucking up my time."

"Is it to do with that megastore idea that was in the business news the other day? Not your mother's usual style—revealing her plans before she's got everything in place."

Ísa should've known he'd figure out that something was off; Sailor Bishop was too smart for his own good. Going with her gut, she told him what was going on.

His eyes cooled when she began to talk about her

investigation into anyone who'd been in Jacqueline's office during the applicable period. "You think I did it?"

"Don't you start," she snapped, shoving her used chopsticks into their makeshift trash bag with unnecessary force. "I already spent far too long convincing my mother that it couldn't be you. You're not that dumb."

He let out a loud laugh, throwing back his head, a beautiful creature kissed by the late-evening light. Ísa's heart, it hurt.

"Who do you think it is?" he said afterward, his eyes sparkling.

"I've got nothing right now." She wanted to pull out her hair from the frustration of it. "But if someone does want to hurt Crafty Corners, they might try something here. A lot of people are watching to see if Fast Organic will fail or succeed."

"I'll keep an eye out." Sailor stared at the garden he'd laid out. "I didn't get a loan from the bank today," he said abruptly. "Or more specifically, I got half of what I need."

Ísa's stomach clenched; she understood instinctively that the setback was a bad one. She also understood what it meant for her fiercely ambitious and determined lover to trust her with this.

Closing her hand over his, she said, "Impact?"

"If I don't do anything to mitigate the loss, things will change too much for me to pull off what I've been planning for the past two years, ever since I identified a gap in the market."

He would've been *twenty-one* at the time. Already dreaming huge dreams and with the drive and willpower to make those dreams happen. Was it any wonder she was so hopelessly in love with him?

Oh God.

Why the hell had she done that, admitted the truth? How could she hide from it now?

"It sounds like you have a plan," she said past the lump in her throat.

Weaving his fingers through hers, Sailor held on fast. "I'll have to double my workload," he said, as if he wasn't talking about an insane time investment.

As if he wasn't breaking Ísa's heart.

She braced herself to hear that he'd have no time for a relationship. No time for her.

"I'll probably be a zombie," he said, lifting their clasped hands to press a kiss to her knuckles. "But if you'll let me, I'll be *your* zombie."

Ísa's lungs hurt, she was finding it so hard to breathe. "Oh?"

"We could make it work," he said, that same determined flame in the blue of his eyes that she'd seen when he talked about his business dreams. "Breakfast together at the crack of dawn"—a playful grin that asked her to smile with him—"then sophisticated dinner dates like this." He waved a hand. "Followed by mutual nakedness at night."

His passion was a wildfire that licked over her and asked her to believe even though she'd seen firsthand that no relationship could survive this kind of relentless stress. And no one as ambitious as Sailor would be satisfied with a single triumph.

There would always be more mountains to climb, more glories to achieve.

More important things than Ísa.

And *still* she wanted to believe. She loved him too much not to grasp at even the thinnest straw of hope. "What about the weekends?" Except for those magical five years with her grandmother, Ísa had spent countless hours alone as a child; the idea of repeating that existence was her personal nightmare.

Especially when it was Sailor she'd be missing.

"You could come with me," Sailor said, his hand still locked possessively around her own. "After your work with Jacqueline is finished, you could grade papers and write your poetry while I landscaped."

When Ísa parted her lips—to say what, she wasn't sure —he shook his head. "Try, Ísa. *Please.*"

It was the wrenching emotion in that last word that got to her.

Shaken by the naked power of it, she went against her every instinct and nodded. "When do you start your work schedule from hell?"

Hauling her into his lap, he thrust his hand into her hair, sent it tumbling around her shoulders. "I won't let you down, spitfire." A kiss that stole her will, threatened to steal all her own dreams, threatened to splinter her to pieces.

"I've already begun," he told her afterward as she lay curled in his lap. "But I'll have a break early in the new year—I made a promise to my dad months ago that I'd go on a family camping trip. Come with me?"

Shoving down her fear of being left behind in favor of bigger dreams, Ísa nodded. Because when Ísa Rain agreed to try something, she did so with her whole heart and soul. No regrets. No hesitation. "Yes," she said on a wave of determination as potent as Sailor's after stuffing her pain into a box and locking it shut. "I'll come."

Sailor kissed her knuckles again. And in his eyes, she saw a shadow that made her heart twist. He was hiding something else. "Sailor?" She scowled at him. "Talk to me." It was a demand.

"Not tonight, Ísa." Almost a plea. "Tonight let's just be us."

Not dropping her scowl, Ísa nonetheless ran her fingers through his hair. "You're on notice, Sailor Bishop. If you want me to be yours, then you be mine." She pressed her nose to his. "You talk to me."

A softening of his lips, a slight curve. "I'll talk at camp, boss lady," he said. "I promise."

Ísa would hold him to that promise. And she'd fight her hardest to hold on to the sexy, sweet, funny, powerful thing between them. Giving up was not in her vocabulary. Even when it might be good for her.

Just as well she didn't own a diaphanous white gown.

STANDARDS

A woman must have standards
Filmy white gowns might be all the rage
For madness or a nervous breakdown
But darling, black is far more dramatic
And lends gravitas to your insanity
~ *Isalind Rain*

HAPPY NEW YEAR

ONLY DAYS LATER, THE NEW year roared in on a blast of summer heat... and a kiss that ignited Ísa's blood to boiling point. Sailor had worked all day, but he was there for her at midnight, the two of them standing on the roof of her apartment building while, in the distance, fireworks erupted in splashes of light and color from Auckland's Sky Tower.

"Are you making a New Year's resolution?" she whispered after the kiss while the fireworks still bloomed and her romantic heart dreamed of kisses into forever.

Expression solemn, Sailor cupped her cheek. "To kiss my Ísalind as much as possible."

No, she stood no chance.

Rising on tiptoe, Ísa touched her lips to his as the balmy summer breeze twined around them, and all across the country, lovers kissed.

ÍSA AND NAYNA AND A BOTTLE OF TEQUILA

T WO DAYS LATER, WHEN ÍSA finally made it home—after nine that night—it was to find Nayna sitting in her car outside Ísa's apartment building.

Ísa had stayed late at the office to work on the Case of the Dastardly Leaker, as dubbed by Catie with a little help from Harlow. Both had decided "spy" was far too sophisticated a title. According to them, "Leaker" was way more low class. As to how they'd figured out the investigation was occurring, it wasn't exactly rocket science if you knew Jacqueline and how she'd react to such a breach.

"And who else would she ask to look into it but you?" Harlow had said guilelessly. "Family is everything to you, Ísa."

Her sweet, occasionally goofy brother had hit the painful nail right on the head.

Shrugging off the unintended blow, and her dream of standing on firm ground that would never shift—with a mate who always *saw* her—hidden protectively deep, she'd continued to work. She didn't have Jacqueline's labyrinthine contacts, but she had an English degree. It so happened that one of her classmates had ended up a journalist who worked for the newspaper that had printed the story.

When she'd called him up to ask about the newspaper's policies, he'd said, "We don't pay for information, doesn't matter what the story. That's what separates us from the tabloids."

That little piece of background had thrown a wrench in all her theories. She was still chewing over it when she pulled into the apartment block's parking lot and saw Nayna's car in a guest spot. Her friend was sitting inside.

Getting out of her own car, Ísa walked over to tap on the other woman's window.

Nayna visibly jumped. "Jeez," she said after scrambling out. "You gave me such a fright. I was away with the fairies."

"How long have you been waiting?"

"Not long, just five minutes. I was going to call, see if you were home, but I decided to sit and brood in my car first."

"Come brood with me instead," Ísa said, her mind filled with thoughts of a certain blue-eyed gardener who made her do crazy things like decide to try to make their relationship work even though it was surely doomed.

Once inside Ísa's apartment, both their purses down and shoes kicked off, Ísa made them a pot of tea.

"Mr. Blue Eyes coming over tonight?" Nayna asked.

"No, he promised to take his younger brothers to a late movie." Ísa loved Sailor all the more for being such a good big brother, for carving out that time even when he was pushing himself to the limit from dawn to well past dusk. It wasn't family commitments that had ever worried her—

family was Ísa's lifeblood. "Now sit," she said to Nayna. "Talk."

Settling into the sofa at Ísa's side, her friend said, "I need to get away" with a narrow-eyed expression on her face. "You know what I've realized? Raj is obstinate as hell in a quiet way. He's decided on me and he's not budging."

"And you're not sure yet?"

"I want to strip him naked and jump his bones like a sex maniac. Plus it turns out I like his brains." Nayna gulped her tea down like it was whiskey. "But there's all this other stuff in my head that's making it hard to think."

Slamming the teacup on the coffee table, she got up and began to pace, her breathing choppy. "Last night I got home to find my sister sitting at the kitchen table again, chatting away to my father. I love her, but at that instant I wanted to scream at her for ruining my life."

A harsh exhale. "And that was when I realized she hadn't done anything to me. This is my life, and I'm the one who's screwed it up." Slumping back on the sofa, she folded her arms, her expression set. "I'm taking some extra vacation time, getting the hell out of here so I can clear my head. I've already okayed it with my bosses."

"Where are you going?" No way was Ísa about to let Nayna run off without getting all the details so she could watch out for her friend.

"Here." Taking out her phone, Nayna forwarded the booking to Ísa.

"If Raj tracks me down and asks?"

"You know nothing."

"Got it."

Nayna did some more serious tea drinking. "So, you're going camping?"

"I hate you," Ísa said with a death glare. "I'm doing it for love."

Snorting and laughing at the same time, Nayna told her to make sure she took toilet paper.

After threatening to strangle her best friend, Ísa admitted the truth. "I'm terrified I'll come last with him, Nayna." The other woman had witnessed Ísa's lonely existence firsthand, seen the scars being formed. "I'm also scared that I'll talk myself into just another day, just another month, just another year, and when I look up, I'll be all alone in a big house."

"Bull. Shit." Nayna poked Ísa in the side. "You're not a child anymore. You're a kick-ass woman who takes no prisoners. You really think you'll let your Sailor pull that kind of crap?"

Your Sailor.

Ísa liked the sound of that. "I'm just as weak when it comes to Sailor as you are when it comes to Raj's abs."

Sighing, Nayna said, "I wish I'd shut my mouth at the party. He's so pretty, and he was going to let me touch him all over." A hard shake of her head. "But my dirty fantasies are not what we were talking about. Seriously, Ísa, you're way too tough—and too honest—to fool yourself into a nightmare."

As deeply in love as Ísa was with Sailor, she wasn't so certain.

Right then, the night beyond the windows blurred as a sudden burst of rain thundered down in a resounding crash.

And Nayna said, "Fuck the tea. Where's the tequila? I'll sleep over."

And that was how Ísa ended up with her first hangover

since college... and Nayna ended up drunk-dialing a certain man and telling him she wanted to lick his abs.

"TEQUILA IS THE DEVIL," NAYNA moaned down Ísa's private office line. "Oh, fuck, they're announcing my flight. And Raj just sent me another picture of his abs. He's added the tongue emoji."

Ísa couldn't help laughing, her stomach aching from the force of it. Thankfully, the over-the-counter painkillers she'd taken had finally kicked in. "How many does that make since you woke up?"

"Stop laughing," Nayna said grumpily. "Do you know how hard it is to think when my phone is full of half-naked pictures of him that I just want to ogle?" Her breathing picked up. "Last call for my gate. Talk to you later."

"Don't get into any more trouble," Ísa ordered.

"Forget trouble. Let's just hope I don't throw up."

After hanging up, Ísa logged into her computer and saw that company security had finally forwarded her the recordings she'd asked for. Crafty Corners didn't have internal security—that would just be creepy, the employees being watched all day. However, they did have security at all the main exits and entrances and in the elevators.

She still had a number of hours of footage to scan through when she had to stop and dive into the normal work of a vice president. When Jacqueline asked her to come to her office and report on the spy situation, Ísa replied that she was working on it and if Jacqueline didn't stop with the micromanaging, Ísa would dump the whole mess in her lap.

The Dragon backed off.

And Ginny brought her in a neatly boxed package that had been left for her at the front desk. This cactus was a round ball of fluff that had Ísa grinning like a goof.

You're a strange man, she messaged Sailor.

But I'm your strange man.

Ísa sucked in a deep breath, scared at just how much those words meant to her. But, determined to try, to have no regrets, she met him at the work site at seven thirty that night; she'd brought along a healthy "home cooked" meal. It was actually takeout from a family-style restaurant that tried for simple fare with little fat.

They did love their carbs, but she figured Sailor needed those carbs. Especially when she discovered he'd just grabbed a single sandwich for lunch. "Good grief, Sailor, muscles like that can't survive on a sandwich alone. And you know I'm just here for the muscles."

Grinning, he hauled her in for a kiss that was red-hot heat and possession, openly appreciative hands on her rear. Ísa tucked her own hands into the back pockets of his shorts and squeezed. He licked his tongue across hers in revenge. She slid off one of her kitten heels and ran her toes up his calf.

He broke the kiss with a groan. "You play dirty, spitfire." Another suckling kiss. "I like it."

"We should eat," Ísa managed to say. "I know we're standing next to a garden bed, but I hear those beds aren't very comfortable."

"Smart-ass." He petted that ass. "But yeah, you're right. Let's eat."

Afterward, Sailor's blue eyes captured hers. "Do you have to go back to the office?"

Ísa thought about it and realized she could plug in her

earbuds and review the security footage on her laptop. "No, I can work remotely."

He immediately brought over another empty wooden crate. "Ta-da! Your outdoor desk."

They didn't speak over the next hour and a half as the summer evening turned to dusk, but they were together, and every so often, he'd swing by and tip up her chin for a kiss. Ísa's toes curled a little more with each kiss, until by the time the light faded into night and Sailor had to pack it in for the day, she was so hungry for him that she would've attacked him in the back seat of his truck given half a choice.

As it was, she followed him home since it'd be easier for him to shower at his place. When he pressed her up against the closed front door and kissed her, all heat and sweat and dirt, she didn't care in the least. The earthy smell of him was a primal aphrodisiac that sank into her blood and turned it to molasses.

Squeezing her breast when she began to tug at his T-shirt, he pulled back enough to tear it off, then unzipped her dress and pushed it down to pool at her feet. "Fuck, spitfire. You're my favorite dessert." He bent to nip at her throat, his hands blatantly shaping her breasts.

She shivered, and he swore.

Her bra was on the floor a second later, quickly followed by her panties—though Sailor slipped her heels back on. "These make you just the right height." Spinning her around on those harshly uttered words, he said, "Brace your hands on the door" at the same time that he circled the pad of his finger around her entrance before pushing in for a teasing stroke. "Hands on the door, spitfire. Don't make me get the handcuffs."

A little shocked—and so aroused that she felt

combustible—Ísa did as he'd asked. He removed his hand from between her thighs with erotic slowness. She heard the metallic jangle of a belt, the soft crush of clothes being shoved aside, the crackle of a wrapper being torn.

Sailor ran his hand down her back and over her lower curves. "This skin," he murmured, his voice thick.

Then he was gripping her hip with one hand, his other coming around to hold her breast with firm possessiveness, and he was pushing into her and he felt so rigid and so long in this position that Ísa bit down hard on her lower lip at the sheer, raw pleasure of it. It only took her two strokes to come, the evening of watching Sailor working shirtless, his little kisses and touches, having aroused her to nymphomaniac status.

He didn't last much longer, thrusting deep into her body and sinking his fingers into the flesh of her hips as he grunted and came. Falling slightly forward onto her back in the aftermath, he pulled her hair back so he could nuzzle a kiss to her neck. "Now we're both dirty." He sounded highly pleased by that fact.

Ísa was turning into goo as a result of the affectionate contact. "How big is your shower?"

The answer was not very... and just big enough.

Ísa ended up pinned to the wall a second time around while Sailor stroked out of her slow and deep, with all the patience in the world. Her legs were jelly by the time they finally stumbled out of the steamy cubicle. Sailor threw her one of his T-shirts to wear while he pulled on an old pair of jeans that hugged his butt just right.

Sitting themselves at the kitchen table, they both got to work.

At some point they took that work and stretched out in bed and ended up falling asleep. Dawn the next morning and Ísa scowled at Sailor as she went to pull on her clothes from yesterday. "I can't believe I'm going to be doing the walk of shame. Pack a change of clothing. You're coming to my place tonight."

Not looking the least bit sorry, he drew her mouth down to his. And since he was warm and naked and in a playful mood, she soon found herself tumbled back into bed. It was fast and deliciously hard this time since Sailor had to get ready for work.

Ísa should've felt used, but how could she when he snuggled a kiss into her neck afterward and said, "See you at dinner?"

But deep inside, a part of her worried.

And even deeper inside, it hurt.

Because what Ísa needed was the one thing she couldn't ask from Sailor. To do so would destroy them both.

36

THE PHOTO CREEPSTER STRIKES AGAIN

ÍSA DIDN'T HAVE ANY TIME to look at the security footage before work; Harlow had managed to fall off his bicycle during a morning ride and injure his leg. After receiving a call from him just after she reached the office, she rushed to the hospital where she spent long minutes calming him down.

"Jacqueline won't fire you for being a couple of hours late," she said. "Even the Dragon understands physical injury. She fractured her ribs six months ago, remember?"

Ísa didn't waste her breath on asking him to take the day off.

Harlow was tough enough to work through the pain of the cuts and abrasions, and he wouldn't have agreed to any such demand anyway.

"I swear you're part dragon," she said after driving him in to work, with a stopover at home so he could change.

A delighted grin. "Thanks!"

"That wasn't a compliment."

Harlow laughed at her stern response, his eyes bright behind his spectacles.

As a result of the late start, she was still scrambling to catch up at eleven when her mother stalked in and threw a newspaper on her desk. It was open to the business section. Ísa's eyes went straight to the image of her walking out of a restaurant holding a large bag emblazoned with the restaurant's logo; the dinner she'd picked up for her and Sailor last night.

The headline was: *No Faith in the Fast Organic Product?*

"Fast Organic isn't live yet!" Ísa threw up her hands. "What am I supposed to eat? Air?"

"It's the asshole I won't sleep with," her mother said, icy fury contained in a custom skirt suit of deepest plum. "He's out to smear us, but you aren't exactly helping. Be a little discreet for goodness sake."

Ísa glared at her mother. "You realize this means some creep is following me around?"

"Or maybe it's someone who knew you were going to be picking up the takeout." Jacqueline raised an eyebrow.

"Don't go there, Mother." It was a hard rebuke, Ísa holding the green of Jacqueline's eyes. Ísa might be furious at herself for her inability to deny Sailor her heart, but she would not permit her mother to throw dirt on his name.

Her mother flung up her hands. "Get to the bottom of this, Ísa. This tiny-penised asshole's vendetta could sink our entire launch plan—we need to cut off his mole."

Calling in Ginny after Jacqueline left, Ísa said, "Wipe my schedule for the day. Push anything urgent to Mother." It was time Jacqueline got a taste of her own medicine. "I'm going to be focusing on another matter."

Ginny was wide-eyed but nodded. "What shall I do if she yells at me?"

"Tell her I'm working on the project she assigned priority." Ísa was going to dig out the truth no matter what it took.

SAILOR SCOWLED AT THE PHOTO of Ísa in the newspaper. "This is bullshit." He turned his phone screen toward Gabe, who'd turned up to help him for a couple of hours before he had to attend a team meeting.

His brother's scowl was just as dark. "Total BS," he agreed. "Anything you can do?"

"If someone's stalking her to get photos, then the black sedan I saw parked across the street yesterday might have something to do with it." It had been there when he and Ísa came around from the back of the site. "Keep an eye out for it."

Gabe nodded as he began to pound in a border piece Sailor had already finished. "Sail, can I ask you something?"

"Sure."

"Why are you so hell-bent on proving you're not like the piece of shit who fathered us?" It was a potent question.

Sailor clenched his teeth and continued to work on the next part of the border. His brother didn't push him, the two of them working quietly together until Sailor said, "It's not rational. I'm just a little bit fucked up in the head."

Gabe's steely eyes met his across the garden bed before his older brother blew out a breath. "Yeah, so am I." Gabe didn't speak again for a while. "Your Ísa know all this?"

"I'm easing her into the crazy slowly. Don't want to scare her away." Light words, but he was deadly serious.

Gabriel's lips kicked up, those incisive gray eyes intent. "You're nuts about her, aren't you?"

Sailor thought back to how damn good it had felt to wake up with her today; he could still feel the warm softness of her in his arms. "I'm fucking terrified that I'll lose her." He sat back on his haunches. "What woman is going to stick with me while I drive myself to the edge to finish what I've begun?" Especially a woman who'd already been let down so many times.

His brother didn't have any answers for him, and when Ísa called to say she couldn't make dinner because she had to drive Harlow home and make sure he'd be okay, Sailor felt another droplet of fear. It was already beginning, the distance. On the heels of the fear came harsh determination.

Fuck that.

Ísa had met her match in Sailor "Bullheaded" Bishop.

ÍSA HAD TAKEN HARLOW OUT to dinner; she'd known no other adult in his life would bother—and he'd needed to talk, to release all his excitement about this summer, and honestly, to just be with an adult who cared enough to be interested in his life.

"Some people shouldn't have kids," she muttered as she shoved through the door of her apartment. It horrified her to think what would've happened to sweet, smart, sensitive Harlow if Jacqueline hadn't married his father for a split second. Her poor brother would be stuck in the no-man's-land between his mother's and his father's new families.

Both seemed to have forgotten the seventeen-year-old son they already had.

Expression dark, Ísa kicked off her shoes, dumped her satchel on the kitchen counter, then collapsed onto the sofa. She was intellectually tired from the hunt to find the traitor, emotionally exhausted from worrying about Harlow, and angry at Sailor Bishop for enticing her with an impossible, beautiful dream.

Buzz.

Ísa groaned at the loud sound. One of her neighbors probably had a guest who'd pressed the wrong apartment number.

"Apartment 7A," she said after dragging herself to the intercom.

"Hello, Apartment 7A," replied a male voice that could seduce her into breaking all her rules. "You gonna let me in?"

An ache in her chest, she cleared him to come up and was waiting with the door open when he exited the elevator. She wanted to run down the hall to him, held back because showing him that much of herself was beyond frightening, but she'd made a promise. And Ísa Rain was no quitter.

She ran.

Dropping his duffel, Sailor grabbed her up into his arms and spun her around. "God, I missed you." Rough heat in his touch, his arms almost crushingly tight.

Ísa's bruised heart expanded. "Me too," she said, taking another risk, another chance.

Door shut and locked behind them a minute later, Sailor grabbed her hips and pulled her back against his chest. "First things first." His mouth on her neck, his erection pressing so urgently against her that she shivered.

His scent was all sweat and heat and man.

Turning in his arms, Ísa sought his mouth with raw desperation.

He kissed her, lashing his tongue across hers as he walked her backward into her living room and tumbled her onto the armless sofa she could convert into a bed. She landed with a soft "oomph," then watched as Sailor pulled off his boots.

"Shit, I got dirt on your carpet."

"Like I care right now."

He didn't laugh as he tore off his socks before rising to pull off his T-shirt. The man was built like a female fantasy; it was unfair what he could do to her with just his body. Knowing that body had been sculpted by stubborn hard work just made it all the hotter. "I want to touch and kiss and taste."

A motionless instant followed by a shake of his head… and an unsteady breath. "Nope."

When he shoved up her dress and tugged down her panties until they hung off one ankle, she was more than ready to have him inside her.

Where she could hold him. Where he'd be hers first, before the world took its bite.

But that wasn't Sailor's intent: kneeling without warning, he hauled her over the end of the sofa and put his mouth on the most sensitive place on her body, the flesh there delicate petals.

Ísa's brain exploded into tiny pieces of honeyed pleasure.

Pulling her legs over his shoulders, Sailor shoved his hands under her rear to hold her in place while he lapped her up; Ísa just gave in, riding the rippling waves until it felt as if she had no bones in her body and pleasure hazed her vision. By the time Sailor finally rose, stripped off the rest of his clothing and put on protection, she was liquid honey.

"Look at me, Ísalind."

Ísa opened her eyes at his guttural growl. It was erotic beyond compare to have him slide into her while their eyes remained locked in stark intimacy. And yet Ísa felt the biting edge of the loneliness that awaited. Somehow finding the strength to place her hands over his shoulders, she drew him closer. Eyes glittering, he lowered his body until his chest crushed her breasts... and then she watched as Sailor Bishop lost himself in her.

All the while trying not to feel the desperation in both their bodies as they fought to hold on to a dream that threatened to crumple under the weight of harsh reality.

37

WEASELS, RATS, AND OTHER ASSORTED RODENTS

*I*SA ROSE TO THE SOUNDS of someone moving around. "Sailor?" she mumbled.

"Hey, spitfire." Already dressed, his hair damp, he crouched down to kiss her. "I have to head out." A big hand cupping her face. "I'm driving to the nursery this evening. I'll get back too late to come over. Tomorrow?"

Ísa nodded and, despite his urgings that she stay in bed, got up to kiss him goodbye at the door. As she watched him walk away, his duffel in one hand, her heart squeezed. It only got worse when he waved at her from the elevator.

She was madly, passionately, terribly in love with Sailor Bishop.

And no matter how hard he tried, he could only give her short moments of his time.

"Story of my life," she whispered with a mocking smile aimed solely at herself. Because she was the one who'd put herself in this situation; she was the one who'd fallen for those demon-blue eyes; she was the one who'd traded in her dream to support his.

Ísa had to laugh or she'd curl up in a ball and cry until her eyes looked like they were made of spaghetti sauce.

Since she was awake anyway, she decided to put in some work on the last hours of security footage. That it was Saturday mattered little; she wouldn't stop until she'd hunted down the leaker. And if she needed to talk to Jacqueline, she knew exactly where to find her: Crafty Corners HQ.

Her mother considered Saturday a workday. Sunday too, though she was more subtle about that since even Oliver wasn't tolerant enough to accept a spouse who worked seven days a week, sixteen hours a day. So she worked on her gadgets at home. Oliver seemed happy enough with that.

Twenty-five minutes into the security footage, Ísa saw it. Frowning, she pulled up another file, cross-referenced. "Shit."

Her phone rang right then, Sailor's number flashing up. And her foolish heart went boom, boom. "Sailor? Is something the matter?"

"I scared off some guy who was taking pictures of the Fast Organic site when I arrived." He sounded a touch breathless. "I chased him, but the slimy weasel had a head start and his car was already running. He jumped in and took off."

"I don't suppose he's blond and looks like he should be in a toothpaste commercial?"

"I swear, his teeth glinted in the sunlight."

Well, that was the nail in the coffin. "I know who it was. I don't think my mother will be pleased."

THAT WAS AN UNDERSTATEMENT.

"Ísalind," Jacqueline said very precisely when Ísa showed her the evidence of Trevor's sneaking about, "never trust good-looking and charming men."

Ísa snorted. "I don't think Trevor is either." He was too smarmy for it. "What I do think is that he's the leak—this recording shows him getting into the elevator after your meeting with him, only to come right back up."

She tapped a piece of paper on Jacqueline's desk. "And this shows your keycard being used to scan back into your office area." For such a security-conscious woman, Jacqueline had a habit of leaving her keycard on her desk. "You've already confirmed that you and Annalisa were gone at that time."

Jacqueline looked pained. "I may have mentioned to Trevor that I was taking Annalisa out for a well-earned brunch."

"And you used Annalisa's card to get back in." It was on the list of swipe-ins. "I bet your card was back on your desk when you returned."

"I don't recall—but since I never missed it, it must've been."

"Trevor gets back in the elevator ten minutes later. Plenty of time for him to snoop around." The good news was that the concept plan would've been the only piece of juicy information to which he had access—the computers were password protected, and Jacqueline kept all her sensitive documents in a wall safe.

"Is there *any* way it wasn't Trevor?" Jacqueline asked hopefully. "He's poor, sweet Oliver's only son."

Ísa nodded in sympathy. Oliver really didn't deserve a disloyal toad for a son. "Suspicious as this all is," she said, "Trevor might somehow be able to explain it away. But he can't explain this." Ísa pushed across a photo of a car speeding away from the Fast Organic site; the location was identifiable because of the distinctive building on the other side.

Sailor had also managed to catch the license plate. "Taken about forty-five minutes ago by Sailor Bishop. Trevor was sneaking around snapping photos on his phone. He probably didn't expect Sailor to be there on a Saturday—or to start work so early."

"That fucking rat." Jacqueline's tone was ice as she tapped her pen on the desk. "If he took them less than an hour ago, they're probably still on his phone. Do you think he'd come in if you invited him in for coffee?"

"Nope. He knows I think he's a rodent." Ísa shrugged. "But you... I think you could sell it." Frowning, she leaned back in the visitor chair. "What I don't get though is why he'd jeopardize Crafty Corners in any way? Isn't he trying to get an executive position here?"

Jacqueline stared at her. "I never told you this," she finally said with a sigh, "because it was never an option, but the position Trevor has been angling for is yours. And" —Jacqueline winced—"I'm fairly sure I let it drop that I was planning to put you in charge of the concept megastore project."

"Ah. That explains it." Trevor had been attempting to undermine Ísa. "He must've thought you meant immediately."

"Yes. And Fast Organic is your baby too." Jacqueline's eyes narrowed before she smiled a cold smile. "It turns out I've lost faith in you, Ísa. In fact, I've lost so much faith I need to talk to Trevor and blow off steam. I might even need to invite him in to make it clear to you that you're on thin ice."

Ísa tried not to laugh—every so often, the Dragon

chose a deserving victim. "What's pushed you to this loss of faith? Surely not a single article?"

"No, apparently I've just heard of a security breach at the Fast Organic site. I can't believe my VP didn't take better care of such a prime site."

"Are you a little bit serious about the latter?"

"Of course I'm not." Jacqueline snorted. "No call to waste money on a security guard to monitor the site—there's no staff or any merchandise to protect and we have insurance." A shrug. "But I don't expect Trevor to know that. He thinks he has a great head for business, but what he is, is a good lawyer in his specific and narrow field."

"What do you plan to do to him?"

"Unfortunately, not what I'd like since Oliver does love him. But I'm going to make him sweat for a while by intimating I may share his behavior with his law firm—Trevor loves status above all else, and law firms frown at even a hint of illegality. The twerp deserves that punishment." Jacqueline's eyes glinted. "He'll also no longer be welcome at any of my properties unless it's a family event where Oliver is present. And at those he'll be a dutiful, loving son."

Ísa got up. "I'll leave you to it."

"This Sailor Bishop," Jacqueline said. "Are you sure, Ísalind?"

Ísa didn't have deep personal discussions with Jacqueline, but something in her mother's tone made her pause. "Why would you ask that?"

"I told you," Jacqueline said softly, "you always wanted your father to be different. To be a better man. But men don't change, Ísa. Don't forget that."

Ísa said nothing, but part of her wondered. Was that

what she was doing? Hoping for her gardener with demon-blue eyes to change?

"No," she said once she was back in her office, her eye on her row of cactus plants. "I see him. And I choose to be with him." Until the day he trampled so badly on her heart that even Ísa's stubborn will couldn't fix it.

WHEN SAILOR DROPPED BY HIS PARENTS' on his way to a job a couple of days later and told his mother he was bringing Ísa along on the family camping trip that coming weekend, she said, "*Oh? A friend, is she?*"

Sailor had been expecting the pointed question. He'd never invited a woman to join in any of the Bishop-Esera camping trips or barbeques; that time was about family, about connection, about love. None of his previous—and short-term—relationships had ever come close to that. But Ísa...

Ísa owned him body and soul.

"Mine," he said with unhidden satisfaction. "She's mine."

Pure delight in his mother's expression. "How did you two meet?"

"I was doing a job at the school where she teaches." It was hard to keep a straight face while giving that answer when he just wanted to grin at the memory of being jumped by his redhead.

Early that Friday afternoon as he drove into the parking lot of Ísa's apartment building, he was unsurprised to see not just Ísa but Catie out front. The teenager had messaged him to ask if she could come along, the request written in an offhand manner, but Sailor had seen right through it to her genuine desire and curiosity.

He'd not only invited her, he'd told her to bring along her brother. But it turned out Jacqueline was taking Harlow to an out-of-town social-slash-business event, so Sailor would have to wait to meet Ísa's kid brother.

"Two gorgeous ladies waiting for me," he said before bending Ísa over his arm to claim a ravenous kiss.

It had been two nights since he'd last seen her, their schedules out of whack. Sailor missed her like she was his heartbeat, and he'd made damn sure she wouldn't forget him or begin to second-guess her decision to stick with him.

"Did you get the flowers I sent?" he asked after coming up for air while keeping her in that dramatic pose.

Pushing at his shoulders, laughter in her eyes, she said, "I don't think increasingly spiky cacti count as flowers."

"Succulents," he murmured in her ear, too low for Catie to overhear. "Juicy, juicy succulents. Nearly as succulent as a redhead I know."

Ísa blushed, Sailor kissed her again, and Catie took a photo.

Finally rising to his full height, Ísa in his arms—where she belonged—he reached out to tug on one of Catie's twin braids. "Send me that photo so I can print it out and draw hearts around Ísa's face."

Though Ísa elbowed him for his teasing, she was laughing. So he stole another kiss, tasted her happiness. And felt things in him settle, become firm again. As if he'd been on quicksand and then, there it was, solid ground.

"Off to my lair we go," he said afterward, his exhaustion from the grueling week having disappeared as if it didn't exist.

Catie got into the back seat with a grin while Sailor lifted the luggage into the bed of the truck. "You can choose the radio station," he told Ísa after they were in the truck.

"Oooh," Catie announced from the back, "that's a sign of love, *twue* love."

Sailor saw Ísa's fingers freeze for a single millisecond on the buttons of the radio before she threw Catie a smiling look, then continued on as if everything was normal. But Sailor had caught that pause, and he felt it like a punch to the jaw. Did Ísa not know exactly how much she meant to him? Had he fucked up that badly?

Running his knuckles over her cheek, he clenched his gut and made a silent vow that he'd fix the fuckup before the weekend was over. A single moment of privacy with Ísa and he'd lay his heart at her feet. And hope she wouldn't kick it.

"Hey, Issie," Catie said from the back, "did the Dragon breathe fire on you for taking off early?"

Sailor had meant to ask Ísa the same thing. "Yeah, spitfire, did Jacqueline give you any flak?"

Ísa shook her head just as her phone rang. "I swear, if you two have summoned her by speaking her name," she muttered while digging into her handbag, "I'll put a hex on you." Having located her phone, she looked at the screen. "You're safe. It's my father."

"Hi, Dad," she said in English before switching to what he guessed must be Icelandic.

After she hung up, she checked something on her phone. "Dad's fiancée just sent me her 'visual concept' for the bridesmaids dresses. Because—according to Dad—she'll be 'devastated, honey, just devastated' if I'm not part of the bridal party."

Catie, whom Sailor had thought was listening to music on her phone, said, "Uh-oh. How bad?"

"Purple. Make-your-eyes-bleed purple."

Even Sailor knew to wince at that. "It's the thought that counts?" he suggested.

Ísa shot him a speaking look… before bursting out into giggles, laughing too hard to say anything. Catie fell victim to the same moments later.

And that set the tone for the rest of the drive. Having grown up with three brothers, Sailor hadn't realized how different it would be to make the drive with two females who were sisters. They laughed, argued over music, teased Sailor, and filled the car with cheerful noise.

When Ísa went looking in his glovebox for a charging cable and found his marked-up copy of *Poems by Elizabeth Barrett Browning*, she shot him a smile so luminous it stole his breath. "I didn't know you were into poetry."

"My brothers caught me reading that book," Sailor muttered, his voice husky from the impact of Ísa. "I hope you know what I've suffered for you."

She blew him a kiss.

And Sailor decided he'd take any ragging his brothers cared to throw his way. Ísa's delight was worth everything.

38

NEVER TRUST A CUTE REDHEAD

THE CAMPGROUND WAS BUSY THIS time of year, but Sailor knew exactly where to find his family. The Bishop-Esera crew always booked the same spot.

"No vehicles on the grass," he told Ísa and Catie after bringing the truck to a halt in the paved parking lot. "We'll have to schlep our stuff to the tents."

Catie flung open the door and sniffed suspiciously. "It smells green and salty." Despite her disdain, the teen put away her earbuds and phone, then came around to help Ísa and Sailor carry their gear.

Sailor wasn't sure what she could handle since she'd already be navigating uneven ground. Instead of asking Ísa, he asked Catie directly.

The teenager put her hands on her hips and checked out the grassy area they'd be crossing. "Better give me something that won't break if I drop it."

He handed her his small duffel.

She could sling it over her shoulder, and since he mostly just wore shorts and tees out here, it wasn't too heavy. To Ísa he handed the lightweight backpack that held her clothing, then piled her arms with bedding. He put on Catie's heavier pack. "You want your crutches, Cat?" She'd left them in the back of the truck. "Probably safer to take them and just leave them in your tent if it turns out you're stable enough without the help."

Catie made a face but didn't argue.

Lastly, Sailor grabbed the cooler he'd packed with all the snacks and drinks, then hefted a large outdoor umbrella.

The two females flanked him as he walked into the campground—there was definitely something to be said for being accompanied by a cute redhead and her smart-aleck miniature sidekick.

"It's more spread out than I expected," Ísa commented. "The sites aren't right next to one another."

"It's more expensive than usual, that's why. My parents insist on paying—they say it's their version of a summer house." The last time he and Gabe had tried to chip in, the money had been quietly deposited back into their accounts.

Leaves rustled in the wind, the campground surrounded by rich native forest. Ponga ferns grew out plush and silvery-green from treelike trunks, while pōhutukawa trees bloomed a stunning scarlet along the waterline. Those trees also provided shade in that part of the campground, dappling the area in a leafy pattern that meant it was possible to sit outside without being fried to a crisp.

"Hmm," Catie said in a sage tone. "That's actually supersmart. Your mom and dad don't have the hassle and expense of insurance and upkeep but still get to come hang out at the beach."

Startled at the deeply mature statement, Sailor glanced at Ísa. She shook her head subtly and mouthed, *Clive.*

Right. A kid with a father like Catie's had probably had to become money-smart at a young age. "You make sure you tell my dad that," he said to Catie with a wink. "You'll be his new favorite person."

A dimpled smile. "We're getting closer to the beach."

"See that large dark green tent right before the sand? That's my folks. It has a separate living room, so if it rains or whatever, we can hang out in there."

"Are those your brothers putting up the blue tent?"

Sailor nodded at Catie's question. "Jake and Danny get to have their own tent—then they can hooligan around all they want, listen to their music, stay up late." It wasn't like the boys could get into any trouble this far out from civilization. The worst they might do was sneak a cigarette with friends in the campground, but Sailor and Gabriel had both done that and survived.

"We'll put you two there." He pointed to a spot to the left and slightly in front of the main family tent. "Gabe and I will share one between you and the boys." It'd create a small square with the entrances all facing the center, where his father would set up the mobile barbeque and where they'd kick back in the evening.

"Sailor!" Danny came running over, skidding to a stop when he saw that his brother wasn't alone. His eyes went to Ísa, then to Catie. And though Catie was dressed in three-quarter-length capris that exposed her articulated metal legs, that wasn't what caught Danny's attention.

"You're wearing makeup." It was a disdainful statement.

Catie curled her lip at Sailor's youngest brother, who, despite being a year older than Catie, was much shorter and looked far more like a child. "And you have dirt on your face, hunter-gatherer caveboy."

Scowling, Danny folded his arms. "At least I don't come to *camp* with goop on my face." He fluttered his lashes and pretended to put on mascara.

"Danny." Amused by the two of them, Sailor nonetheless cut off the insult-fest before it degenerated any further. "Where are Mom and Dad?"

"They got all smoochy"—rolled eyes—"and went for a walk on the beach. You're early."

Sailor nodded—they'd hit almost no traffic on the way down. He indicated the bedding Ísa was carrying. "Take that into Mom and Dad's tent."

While Danny did that, Jake waved at Sailor from where he was pounding in a tent peg. Sailor called out a hello to his brother before he had Ísa and Catie put their things in the center of the site. After doing the same himself, he grabbed one of the tent packages it was Gabe's job to bring. He hadn't seen his brother's SUV in the parking area; he had a feeling Gabe had made a run into the small local township to buy something they needed before the shops all shut.

"Come on," he said to his girls. "Let's put this up."

They were ridiculously bad at the task—but they laughed throughout, making random and terrible suggestions as to how to speed up the process, which had him cracking up. Catie fell once, her smile fading for a second before Sailor hauled her up and told her to stop trying to get out of putting up the tent. She stuck out her tongue at him, but the light was back in her eyes.

But it was the naked emotion on Ísa's face that got him. Running his hand down her back while Catie was distracted, he nuzzled a kiss to her temple.

She said, "Thank you for taking care of my baby sister."

"If she's yours, she's mine," Sailor said, because that was the absolute truth.

Ísa's gaze shimmered.

"Hey, eyeshadow girl, what happened to your legs?" Danny's curious question had them both looking up.

"A crocodile ate them."

Sailor bit back a grin while beside him, Ísa fought not to laugh.

Danny, meanwhile, was having none of it. Narrowing his eyes, he said, "Yeah? What *kind* of crocodile?"

"*Leggus eatus crocodilus.*"

Ísa snorted a laugh. "*Catie.*"

Gabe walked into the campsite just as Danny seemed to be building up to a scowling response. Sailor's elder brother was a broad-shouldered and muscled man, six foot five inches in height. Not many people wanted to get in his way on the rugby field. But women liked his size, black hair, and gray eyes just fine.

Unfortunately for those women, Gabe's focus was on his stellar rugby career.

But Sailor's brother always found time for family.

Currently his arms were full of shopping bags that Jake and Danny quickly grabbed and ran off to store. "Potato chips," Gabriel said to Sailor. "Mom forgot to put that on your list, and the boys were about to have a meltdown at the idea of camping without their favorite salty snacks."

"Ísa, Cat," Sailor said, "this is my brother Gabriel."

"Hi." Catie waved from where she was pushing in a tent peg with the kind of concentration most people reserved for surgical operations, her admiration of Gabe's rugby skills well hidden under a layer of teenage nonchalance. "Did you bring chocolate too?"

"Sorry, Cat." Gabe looked at the badly constructed tent with an amused glint in his eye. "I will next time."

Going over to the cooler, Sailor rummaged around in it before he found the large family-size bar he'd added to his shopping list after recalling the chocolate he'd seen in Catie's kitchen. "Hide it," he said after passing her the bar. "Or Jake and Danny will see it, and then it's all over." His brothers didn't have much of a sweet tooth, but they were teenage boys—they ate anything and everything in sight.

Beaming, Catie quickly put the chocolate bar into her backpack. "Thanks, Sailor."

"It's lovely to meet you," Ísa said to Gabriel at the same time.

"Right back at you." Those steely eyes took in the way Sailor was hovering close to Ísa's side. His lips curved. "You sure Sail here isn't a bit puny for you?"

"Hands off." Sailor pointed a finger at his troublemaking brother. "I may not be able to take you down in a fair fight, but I can spike your beer with laxatives."

"Try it and feel Mom's wrath," Gabriel said darkly before nodding at the tent. "You want some help?"

"Nah. Why don't you get ours up?" Sailor bumped fists with his brother while Ísa and Catie gave them strange looks. "I'll make sure the girls' won't collapse on them."

"Hey," Ísa protested. "It's not that bad. We got that central pole thingy up, didn't we?"

Sailor didn't resist the temptation to kiss her. "You're so cute."

Eyebrows drawing into a dark vee, she said, "You and

Gabriel—is that normal brother behavior? Insults and warnings, then being best buds?"

Sailor shrugged. "Yep."

"Boys are weird," Catie pronounced.

Ísa nodded in agreement. "But, sadly, I appear to like this one a whole lot." She was the one who stole a kiss this time.

And Sailor's heart, it melted.

"Hey, enough mushy stuff." Catie scowled at them. "Gabe's gonna beat us with putting up his tent."

Driven by the spirit of competition, they finished up at the same time—just as Alison and Joseph walked up from the beach.

His mother made a beeline for them. "This is wonderful," she said to Ísa after a round of tight hugs. "I'm usually surrounded by so much testosterone I begin to worry I'm going to sprout chest hair and start belching."

Catie giggled while Ísa's smile was shy but real. "I should admit that we're not the most experienced campers," she told his mother.

Alison waved a hand. "I wasn't either until I met my husband." Turning just as Joseph reached them, she introduced Sailor's father to Ísa and Catie.

Both Sailor's redhead and her sidekick fit into the Bishop-Esera family like keys turning in a lock. Though Catie's version of fitting in seemed to be to make fun of Danny. His youngest brother, in turn, made a production of pretending to paint his nails or put on mascara anytime Catie so much as looked in his direction.

As for Ísa, Sailor could literally see her falling in love with his parents.

Hope burst in his heart. It'd work.

But even as he thought that, his gut told him he was

being a bullshitter of the highest order. Yes, it might work. He'd planned it all out, hadn't he? And he'd gotten Ísa's agreement. It'd involve a serious lack of sleep and a serious lack of spare time, but he and Ísa would soldier through.

At what cost, dumbass?

The question came from the part of him that was all about harsh truths. And the truth it showed him was a staggering one that cut his legs out from under him.

OF COURSE THERE HAD TO be a rugby game post-dinner. Ísa tried to sit it out, but Sailor dragged her onto the field. "No shirkers, that's the rule," the blue-eyed demon said firmly. "Cat! You too!"

Her sister, who'd been sitting by the tent pretending to play on her phone while Ísa knew her heart was breaking, looked up. Mouth dropping open, she said, "I don't have legs, in case you haven't noticed!"

"I noticed that you're an athlete who's very stable on those prosthetics now," Sailor said with total equanimity. "Don't tell me you can't play a friendly family game."

Growling low in her throat, Catie got up and limped onto the field.

"Oh, honey, you're limping." Alison's worried tone. "Did you fall?"

Looking abashed, Catie said, "Oh wow, looks like my leg is all better." She took position when a scowling Sailor pointed.

Across from her, Danny snickered. "Busted."

"Shut up, caveboy."

Putting two fingers to his mouth, Sailor whistled.

"Ladies and gents, let's get this show on the road. Gabe, you want to call teams?"

Nodding, Sailor's ruggedly handsome older brother stepped forward to quickly divide them into two teams.

Gabriel, Alison, Ísa, Catie.

Sailor, Joseph, Danny, Jake.

"Hey!" Sailor protested. "You can't have all the women. Here, we'll give Danny back." He pushed his younger brother across with rough humor.

"Whatever," Danny said good-naturedly. "I didn't want to be on the losing team anyway."

"Catie." Sailor called her over.

Ísa's sister switched sides with a grin, smirking at Danny along the way.

He smirked back and began to stretch. "For my victory dance," he told Catie.

Sailor grinned at Ísa, his earlier intensity erased by a familiar playfulness. "Sorry, Ísalind, but you're on the opposition and it's war."

Ísa pretended to shove up her nonexistent long sleeves. "Bring it on."

Beside her, Gabriel shot her a grin so similar to Sailor's that she couldn't help but like him. "That's the spirit," he said to her. "Now, team, it's time for a huddle so we can talk strategy."

That huddle lasted three minutes, Sailor talking to his own team on the other side just as secretively. The rules were simple—no tackling, only touches on the hips, pass backward, never forward, and run like hell toward the try line if you managed to get your hands on the oval-shaped ball.

Ísa raised her hand. "I'm not very fast."

"I am," Danny piped up. "I'll run up behind you if you get the ball. You can pass it to me."

"Good plan." Gabriel ruffled his brother's hair, then looked sternly at his mother. "No stopping to kiss any boo-boos."

Alison Esera scowled at her eldest son. "You have children, then you talk to me about kissing my boys' hurts."

Danny groaned. "*Mom*, it's totally embarrassing when you do that. Especially with a *girl* around."

"I'll kiss her boo-boos too," Alison said, unbending. "Are we playing or what?"

The motley crew got into position, Sailor and Gabe flipping a coin to decide who got the ball first. It ended up with Sailor's team, and they began with a bang—until Danny managed to make Catie turn it over on a touch.

Catie glared at him.

Danny smiled smugly—and spun the ball back at Ísa. She actually "eeped"—which made Jake crack up on the other side—but somehow didn't drop it. Not quite sure what to do with it, she froze for a second until Gabriel said, "Run, Ísa!"

She ran.

Sailor pounded after her... only to be crashed out of the way by Gabriel's flying body. She heard Alison yell, "No tackling!" but the men were wrestling too fiercely to pay attention. And Ísa realized she only had to get past Catie to make the try line.

She lowered her head and ran.

Her sister came at her, just as determined. Ísa went to circle around her; Catie changed direction. They crashed in a tumble of limbs.

Ísa was horrified. "Catie!"

Her sister grabbed the ball, got up, and ran.

"Hey!" Ísa's mouth fell open.

Danny raced after Catie, but he was too late. Her sister put down the ball on the try line with a triumphant air before launching into a victory dance of her own.

And Sailor came over to scoop Ísa up into his arms. "Never trust a cute redhead."

39

A CONFESSION IN THE MOONLIGHT
(ALSO, BABOONS)

Í SA COULDN'T GET TO SLEEP.

Even though the gloriously peaceful silence was broken only by the crashing waves.

Picking up her phone, she texted Nayna. *How's the whole 'running away to the jungle' thing going?*

She wasn't really expecting a response given the late hour, but Nayna must've been up. *A freaking jungle would've been noisier than this. They have baboons in the jungle, right? And baboons are noisy. It's so QUIET here I keep expecting to hear ghostly wails and rattling chains.*

Ísa bit her lower lip to keep from laughing. *I am currently suffering from the curse of peace and quiet and nature as well.* Obviously, city girls didn't do well when plucked out of their environment. *Do you think the ghost will come with a dashing duke to rescue you?*

I'm more into the stubbled-jaw, blue-collar man these days, Nayna admitted. *Do you know what I'm watching right now? A rerun of a home-renovation show full of construction types. I hate myself.*

Why don't you invite Raj to join you? Ísa suggested wickedly. *Have a little fun away from prying eyes.*

Nayna's response took five minutes to come. And it had Ísa jerking upright on the large air mattress Sailor had inflated for her and Catie.

I did it. I called him. He sounded all sleep-growly and he was pissed that I'd gone AWOL, but he said he'd come. I just hope he wasn't lying—if he tells my parents where I am, that's it, I'm done.

Grinning and doing a little dance for her friend, Ísa said, *Take my advice and do every dirty thing you've ever dreamed.*

You, my friend, are not helping my attempts to calm down, Nayna accused. *Anyway, I'm going to leave the TV on for noise and try to catch some sleep. He was booking an early-morning flight down when we hung up.*

Ísa, too, attempted to go to sleep—to no avail.

Maybe she should try Catie's trick; her sister had fallen asleep with her earbuds snugged to her ears. Her prosthetics sat neatly to the side of the tent. She'd admitted to Ísa that her stumps hurt a little as a result of navigating the unfamiliar terrain, but she'd been smiling as she removed the silicone liners that protected her flesh from the prosthetic sockets.

"Sailor's family is awesome," she'd said, her smile a far sweeter one than she permitted the outside world to see. "I sent Harlow pictures of like the game and stuff, and he was bummed to be missing out even though he's all googley heart eyes over the Dragon. He totally wants to come next time."

Ísa's heart ached. Her baby sister was falling as hard for the Bishop-Esera clan as Ísa. Catie had joined in every activity so far, including a walk on the beach to collect shells. Sailor had just hauled her up each time she stumbled, as had Gabe, and they'd done it the same way they'd hauled up Danny when he attempted a backflip and landed flat on his back.

Catie had stopped feeling self-conscious at some point, and by the end of the walk, she'd even gigglingly climbed onto Gabriel's back as Ísa got up onto Sailor's, the two brothers having challenged each other to a race.

Ísa still wasn't sure who'd won. There'd been laughing accusations of cheating because Catie had removed her prosthetics beforehand. According to Danny, it made her lighter and therefore disqualified her and Gabriel. Catie, in turn, had pointed out that Ísa could hold on tighter with her legs whereas Gabriel had to use energy supporting Catie, so "Suck that, caveboy."

When Danny said he didn't fight girls, Catie had threatened to beat him with a prosthetic. At which point the entire camp had collapsed into hysterics—the two combatants included. Ísa had never seen her sister so comfortable with anyone so quickly. Catie had even shared her chocolate with both Jake and mortal enemy Danny.

If it all fell apart, it wasn't only Ísa's heart that would break. But it wasn't going to fall apart, she thought furiously. She and Sailor had a plan.

And that plan relied on Ísa taking a back seat to Sailor's ambition.

Cheeks hot with a burn that had nothing to do with embarrassment, Ísa sat up, arms linked around her knees. She'd been trying not to face that truth so bluntly, had put all her energy into figuring out how her and Sailor's relationship could survive this. She'd been tough, fierce Ísa.

A fighter.

While her heart was cracking. Because all she'd ever wanted was for someone to put her first. To fight for her.

Pressing the back of her hand to her mouth, her eyes burning, she decided to take a walk in the cold night air. There was no point in giving in to self-pity. She'd made a decision and she'd see it through. Because no matter all her admonitions and plans to the contrary, Sailor Bishop owned her heart.

The idea of walking away from him, even to protect herself... it *hurt*.

Before sneaking out of the tent, she picked up the flashlight he'd given her. But it wasn't as dark outside as she'd expected, the moon huge in the sky, which was a glittering carpet free of light pollution. Deciding she'd be fine without the flashlight, she slid it back into the tent where Catie would be able to find it, then began to pad barefoot over the grass toward the beach.

Bare feet aside, she was wearing flannel pajama pants paired with an old navy-colored T-shirt, her hair braided back, so she was decent, if not fashionable.

It was only seconds later that she realized the beach wasn't empty.

A man sat on the sand, staring out at the water.

Ísa would recognize that profile, those shoulders, anywhere. And though she felt far too vulnerable to face Sailor's blue eyes, she hated the sight of him so alone. It was no real decision to continue on in his direction. He glanced around right then, as if he'd sensed her.

"Couldn't sleep?" he said when she was almost to him, his expression lighting up with a wild welcome that made all the pain worth it.

As long as Sailor kept looking at her that way, as if she were his personal Christmas, Ísa might just forgive him anything. It made her feel naked to admit that to herself, to realize how defenseless she was against this man.

Gut tight, she came down beside him on the sand. "Too much peace for this city girl."

He put his arm, warm and strong, around her shoulders. "Cuddle closer." It was a playful order. "I like my armful of redhead."

Snuggling into him because she could deny him nothing, Ísa looked out at the moon-kissed water. "It is beautiful though."

"Want to know a secret?"

"Always."

"I was sitting here plotting how to reach into your tent and wake you without also waking Catie. For future reference, would you have screamed if someone tugged at your toes?"

Her shoulders shook. "I'd probably have kicked too."

"Hmm, I need a new plan." Tilting up her head, he kissed her so slow and deep and romantic that Ísa wasn't the least surprised when she found herself on her back on the sand, the stars glittering behind Sailor's head.

She brushed her fingers over his unshaven jaw. "You weren't just sitting here plotting how to wake me. Something's bothering you. What is it?"

"My demanding spitfire."

Her glower had him grinning before he rose up and possessively manhandled her until she was kneeling between his raised knees, face-to-face with him. Ísa couldn't help but drink in the attention. After this weekend, he'd have only brief minutes for her, and then she'd need the memories to carry her through.

"Is it the loan situation?" she asked, running both hands through his hair.

Hands linked at her back, he shook his head. "There are two things. The first is that I need to find the words to explain to my parents and my brother why I need to go it alone on the business front." Raw emotion in his voice that he made no effort to hide. "I'm hurting them and I don't want to—but I can't accept their help."

"Why?" It was time she understood what it was that drove Sailor so relentlessly.

"My biological father was a serious asshole," he said flatly.

"You said he walked out on your family."

"Went out to the corner shop and just never came back." His lips twisted to the side. "We thought he'd return eventually—he'd pulled his disappearing acts before. But that time Brian decided to forget he had a family."

EVEN AFTER ALL THESE YEARS, the betrayal was a kick to the gut. "I waited the longest," Sailor admitted on a harsh breath. "I couldn't believe he'd just leave us like that. I used to spend all my free time at the front window, watching for him. At least until we were evicted."

Ísa's gentle stroking, her hands weaving through his hair, it took the pain and turned it into a tenderness that was a fist around his heart. He had things to say to his Ísalind, but he'd show her all his scars first, reveal all his secrets.

And hope she'd forgive him.

"When my fucking *father* cleaned us out, he even took the money from mine and Gabe's accounts." Sailor's hands fisted behind Ísa's back. "That was money our mother had put in literally five dollars at a time so we wouldn't miss out at school, so we'd have the money for supplies and extracurricular activities." Sailor could barely bring himself to say the next words. "I loved that bastard so much."

"You were a child." Ferocious words, hands fisting in his hair to force him to hold her fiery gaze. "And he was your father. Of course you trusted him."

Spreading his hands over her T-shirt, he pressed his forehead to her own and told her the worst of it. "I look like him." He'd been fifteen when he'd stared into a mirror and seen the truth. "Mom never did anything dramatic like throw out all pictures of him. She's always said that he's our father and she wasn't going to deprive us of our history."

"I want to steal your mother," Ísa said seriously. "She's the kind of mom I want to be one day."

Sailor caught the hesitation before the last words, wanted to punch himself. No, Ísa should be the one to punch him. He'd even give her a boxing glove so she could pound his stupid face without hurting herself.

"Hey," she said when he went quiet, "don't think you're done yet. Keep on talking."

God, he was crazy about her. "After Dad came into our life, I never really felt the need to look at photos of Brian. Dad was the one who was there for us, the one who did my homework with me, the one who held my hand when we crossed the road." Joseph Esera had shown Sailor what it meant to be a real father, what it meant to show up and do the job with love and a quiet strength that told Sailor it was okay to lean on him when he needed it.

"But," he continued, "then we did this family-history class in high school, and I decided to open up that can of worms." As far as life decisions went, it hadn't been one of his best. "I found a picture of Brian from when he and Mom first got married. It was like looking at an older reflection of myself."

Sailor could still remember his dawning sense of rage. "Gabriel has the black hair, but he's got our mother's eyes. As for my brother's build, I don't know where that came from." A grin born of old memories. "I used to say he took all the good food in the womb, leaving me the scraps."

Ísa wrinkled up her nose. "You're not exactly small." Her hands on his shoulders, massaging with a proprietary touch that gave him hope. "What are you? Six two?"

"Good guess." Only next to Gabe's six five did he look in any way short. "I guess from your point of view, shorty, I'm a giant."

Ísa poked him in the arm. "I'm a respectable five six, I'll have you know." The words were followed by a scowl. "So you look like him. It doesn't mean you're in any way who he was."

"It's not just that," Sailor said. "I remember a lot of things from my childhood before he left. More than usual when you consider I was only five when he took off." He'd never told anyone else the depth of his memories, not even Gabe.

"Not surprising." She kissed him, tender and affectionate, his Ísa looking after him as she looked after all her people. "That was a dramatic time in your life."

Sailor decided that if it turned out he had to fight dirty to keep her, he'd fight dirty. Even if it meant admitting to his most pitiful emotions and stripping himself bare. "Sometimes I feel like I'm picking up the memories brick by brick and looking at them. And what I see is that I have so many pieces of him in me." He began to play with a lock of Ísa's hair. "I almost didn't become a gardener."

Ísa's eyebrows drawing together over her eyes. "But you love it so much."

"He didn't work much—Gabe remembers more, tells me Brian was always more interested in get-rich-quick schemes, the next big score," Sailor said, wondering if Gabriel truly had conquered his own demons when it came to their father; he was Brian's oldest son, after all, and they'd had a different relationship than Sailor had had with Brian.

His brother was so tough and so together that it was hard to think of him as a child, especially when he'd always been Sailor's rock. "I remember holding tight to Gabe's hand the day we were evicted. I was so scared, but I saw that Gabe wasn't crying, so I didn't either."

Ísa's lips curved. "I can just see you, two tough little men. That must've helped your mom so much when she was fighting to fix things."

Sailor hadn't felt so tough back then, but Ísa's words showed him a new way to look at the terrible memories so they weren't about abandonment but about love and strength and being family.

Yeah, he wasn't about to let go of his redhead. Not ever.

"The odd times when Brian did work," he continued, returning to what he'd started to say, "it was often for landscaping companies. He gave me a child-sized spade a couple of months before he left. Mom likes gardening too, but I've always associated it with him." With the man who'd left his family behind. That choice, Sailor might've one day forgiven, but to clean out the accounts so that his wife and children didn't even have enough money for food? Who did that?

And how did a man get past such a vile genetic legacy?

"But one day," Sailor said, curling Ísa's hair around his finger, "I decided the dream was *mine*. He'd stolen so much from us—I wouldn't let him steal this too." He looked into the soft, moon-washed gray-green of Ísa's eyes. "Do you see?"

Expression gentle and her heart unhidden, Ísa said, "You need to do this yourself, because your father took and took. It's not rational and maybe it's not even sensible, but it's important to you."

He shuddered because he was a fucking lucky man; she got it. Got him.

"Your parents and brothers love you," she said decisively. "Involve them in nonfinancial ways and I think they'll be happy. Talk to them about choices you need to make for the business, ask for feedback. And keep on accepting the frozen dinners and grocery deliveries."

There she went, being Ísa again. Looking out for everyone but herself.

Well, fuck that. If she wouldn't do it for herself, he'd do it for her.

"You know how I said there were two things?"

She nodded.

Taking a deep breath, Sailor decided to lay himself at her feet. "I was imagining the future and thinking of how if everything went according to plan, I'd have a very successful business with a high turnover."

He made sure his hands were locked behind Ísa's back —just in case she decided to leave him in her dust a fourth time. "And since I'd be rich, I'd be able to buy houses and other nice things for my family."

Ísa frowned. "I don't think your family expects that."

"They don't exactly need my largesse either," Sailor

muttered. "But in my future fantasy, I'm buying everyone fancy cars and houses. Go with it."

Ísa's lips twitched. "Okay, big spender. What else is fantasy Sailor doing?"

"He's building a ginormous mansion. Swimming pool, tennis court, the works."

"Is he hiring a buff personal masseuse named Sven?"

"Hell no." He glared at her. "The masseuse is a fifty-year-old former bodybuilder named Helga. Now, can I carry on?"

Pretending to zip up her lips and throw away the key, Ísa made a "go on" motion.

"Future Sailor is also creating a huge walk-in closet for you and filling it with designer shoes and clothes. He's giving you everything your heart desires."

A flicker of darkness in Ísa's gaze, but she didn't interrupt... though her hands went still on his shoulders.

"And there's a tricked-out nursery too," he added. "Plus a private playground for our rug rats."

Throat moving, Ísa said, "How many?" It was a husky question.

"Seven, I think."

"Very funny, mister."

"I'm not done." Sailor was the one who swallowed this time. "And in this fantasy house, future Sailor walks in late for dinner again because of a board meeting, and he has a gorgeous, sexy, brilliant wife and adorable children. But his redhead doesn't look at him the same anymore. And it doesn't matter how many shoes he buys her or how many necklaces he gives her, she's never again going to look at him the way she did before he stomped on her heart."

40

DREAMS AND DEVOTION

Í SA'S LOWER LIP BEGAN TO quiver, but she didn't speak.

"I'm so sorry, baby." Sailor cupped her face, made sure she saw the sheer terror he felt at the thought of losing her. "I've been so tied to this idea of becoming a grand success that I forgot what it was all about in the first place—*being* there for the people I love. Sticking through the good and the bad. *Never* abandoning them."

Silent tears rolled down Ísa's face.

"But that great plan of mine?" he said, determined not to give himself any easy outs. "It'd have meant abandoning *everyone*. How can I be there for anyone when all I do is work? When I shove aside all other commitments? When the people I love hesitate to ask for my time because I'm too tired and too busy?"

Using his thumbs, he rubbed away her tears. More splashed onto the backs of his hands, her hurt as hot as acid. "Spitfire, please," he begged, breaking. "I'll let you punch me as many times as you want if you stop crying. With a big red glove. And you can post photos online."

Ísa pressed her lips together, blinked rapidly several times. And pretended to punch him with one fist, the touch a butterfly kiss.

Catching her hand, he pressed his lips to it. "That's more like my Ísa." He wrapped his arms around her again. And then he told her the most important thing. "I realized that I could become a multimillionaire, but it would mean nothing if my redhead didn't look at me the way she does now, if she expected to have to take care of everything alone like she's always done—because her man was a selfish bastard who was never there."

Ísa rubbed her nose against his. "You're being very hard on future Sailor," she whispered, her voice gone throaty.

"That dumbass deserves it," Sailor growled. "He was going to put his desire to be a big man above his amazing, smart, loving redhead." Thrusting his fingers into her hair, he stole a kiss. It tasted of salt, and that just infuriated him again. "I love you, Ísalind Rain. You are the most important part of my dream. Please tell me I haven't fucked up beyond redemption?"

ÍSA COULD BARELY SPEAK. "IF I say you have?" she finally whispered with a smile.

"I'll tell you how my cat died yesterday so you'll feel sorry for me." A downturned, pathetic face. "Poor Fluffy. I had him for twenty-three years. I walked him every day."

Laughing wetly, she said, "I think a cat that geriatric has earned his rest."

"*Ísa.*" And there it was, his emotions laid bare. No defenses. No walls. The love, the *devotion* in him, it gutted her.

Never, not in her wildest dreams, had she dared to imagine that she'd be *that* important to someone. As if she was air and without her, he couldn't breathe.

"I love you too," she whispered. "And I forgive future Sailor for being a dumbass." Linking her arms around his neck, she spoke through the storm inside her. "In fact, I think future Sailor is going to be an incredible man I'll adore more with each and every day."

"Yeah?" His lips kicked up in that familiar smile, but there was a question in his eyes, a quiet hunger. "What's he going to do?"

Ísa knew what he was asking her, what he needed her to tell him. "He's going to be a man who works hard but who has time for the people he loves. And he definitely has time to get up to wicked things with a certain redhead."

"I like this guy's priorities already."

"He's also the kind of father who takes a turn doing the school run because he enjoys spending time with his child." It was scary doing this, laying out her dreams, but Sailor had given her everything.

Ísa would be brave enough to give him the same back. "He has time to play with his baby, and to kiss his wife, and even if he forgets things now and then, or if he gets a little busy for a while, it's all right because his wife and child and all the members of his family know they're loved beyond measure." Perfection had never been what Ísa wanted. "Because when it matters, he's there. He *sees* the people who love him."

Demon-blue eyes solemn, Sailor said, "I can do that." It was a vow. "I can be that guy."

"You already are," Ísa whispered. "You're my dream, Sailor."

But Sailor shook his head. "You ain't seen nothing yet, spitfire. I'm going to court the hell out of you." After a meditative pause, he added, "Nakedness during said courting is optional but highly encouraged."

He was wonderful. And he was hers.

Ísa felt like a kid in a candy store.

Tumbling him onto the sand, that muscled body hard and warm under her own, she said, "Tell me the truth."

"About what?" His hands shaped her rear. "How much I love fondling you?"

"Shh." She looked up with a pounding heart. "What if one of your parents comes out?" she asked, Devil Ísa suddenly turning into a scandalized prude who wouldn't dream of doing anything naughty.

"I've caught them making out twice this summer alone." Winking, Sailor tucked his hands inside her pajama pants. "We keep telling them to get a room."

Not about to be distracted, Ísa pinned him with her gaze. "You've been working on your business plan for years." It had been his driving ambition, the shining star on the horizon. "You really want to make it come true, don't you?"

"Not at the cost of us" was the firm response, his hands equally firm where they massaged her weak, weak flesh.

Slipping off him, she lay on her back on the sand. Which left him free to come up over her. "I like this position too," he said as he bent to kiss her neck.

"Sailor, this is serious."

He looked up at her tone, his expression solemn. "I'm okay with the trade-off, spitfire. I get you. The rest is immaterial."

But Ísa knew about dreams and about how much it hurt to give them up. Sailor had made hers come true with a wild passion she'd remember to her last breath. She wasn't about to do any less for him. For her blue-eyed demon who looked at her as if she was his Christmas.

"Tell me your plan," she said. "I won't stop asking, so just give in and spill."

Bracing himself on his forearm beside her, his free hand on her abdomen, Sailor narrowed his eyes. "I should've brought the handcuffs."

"If you play nice," Ísa said, "when we get back home, I'll show you the ones I bought for you."

His eyes glinted. Then he began to speak.

His plan was beautiful and detailed, and Ísa's business brain flared at the simple brilliance of it. It was like Crafty Corners, a basic idea taken to the next level. But where Jacqueline's breakthrough had been in crafts, Sailor's focus was on plants. Specifically, on small gardening stores that didn't just sell plants and other garden items but that became a community hub through a finely tuned program of events, classes, and hiring local.

The entire concept was based on building bonds and adapting to the needs of a specific area. No cookie-cutter shops. Each one would be unique, its personality formed by the local environment and community. As such, it would also feature the work of local artisans who created handcrafted items that could be used or placed in gardens, such as one-of-a-kind mosaics—thus drawing in another sector of the community.

The boutique, child-friendly cafés within would be the icing on the cake.

"Damn it," Ísa muttered. "We have to figure out how to pull it off."

"What?" Sailor blinked.

"It's too good a plan to abandon." She tapped her

lower lip. "Money is the problem. Especially since you want to do it on your own." Ísa didn't make the mistake of offering him financial help—that would break Sailor's heart.

It was *so* important to him that he didn't take, that he gave.

She saw his scars now, understood how deep they went. "Did you ask anyone else for the loan?"

Looking wary, he said, "No," and she realized he thought she was talking about family.

"An angel investor," she said with a poke to his chest. "That's what you need. Someone who'll forward you the money on the strength of your idea and your track record so far. Someone who takes risks on start-ups in the hope of a big payoff." She frowned. "I know you want to go it alone—"

"No, I have nothing against an investor," Sailor said. "It's a commercial decision for them, and they'd be getting a return. It's just, with family…"

Ísa could see him struggling to find the words to explain. "I understand, Sailor. It's a different ballgame when it's a bank or an investor for whom this type of thing is their business—any risk is weighed and calculated, no emotions involved. They won't invest in you out of love, and they expect you to return far more than they're giving."

Sailor nodded. "That's exactly it." His kiss was tender, his hand stroking the curve of her waist. "But with an angel investor—I thought that kind of thing was only for tech start-ups?"

"Are you kidding? My mother has a fund set aside for investment opportunities at the ground level." She winced. "And oh God, Jacqueline will kill me because I didn't nudge you in her direction, but we must all sacrifice for love." If Sailor didn't want family investment, then so be it.

"I know that world," she continued. "I can do the basic research for you, find out which investors are reliable and trustworthy." Ísa would turn barracuda for this, make damn sure no one unscrupulous got their claws into Sailor's dream. "You'd have to do the hard sell yourself, but since you convinced Jacqueline over the phone, I have total faith in your ability to talk your way into an agreement."

Catching his stunned expression, she winced. "Um, that is, if you want my help."

He kissed her, all heat and smile. "You're amazing, spitfire. I'm so glad I wasn't a dumbass." When she laughed, he peppered her face with kisses. "But Ísa," he said in a more serious tone, "if this doesn't work, never think I'll have regrets. Not for a single fucking second."

Nothing but resolve in his expression.

Nothing but a love that said he *saw* her and adored her.

"I won't," she managed to get out. "But... we're going to do it." Because she loved him back just as madly.

"Has anyone ever told you that you're stubborn?"

"It's a gift."

EPILOGUE

(It Involves Monsters, Terror, a Dragon, and Twue Love)

ÍSA TRIED TO REMEMBER TO do that "huff, huff, huff" breathing she'd been taught. "It's happening," she said almost to herself, putting down the volume of Elizabeth Barrett Browning sonnets she'd been reading. "Harlow, Jake."

The two boys, who were hanging out in her and Sailor's lounge playing video games, didn't take their eyes from the screen on which they were vanquishing monsters and hunting treasure.

"Yeah?" one mumbled.

"Hospital."

The single word had them jumping up like jackrabbits, game forgotten and abandoned. On the screen, a monster ate Harlow's head while another bore down on Jake with predatory intent. The boys, however, had other priorities.

One went to the cupboard to snag the bag she'd packed

and put in there, while the other grabbed his keys. Both were qualified to drive, but it was more experienced Harlow who was assigned as driver. Because this entire smoothly oiled operation was as a result of Sailor's unrelenting care—and slight terror.

Ísa called her husband as she got into the front passenger seat. "Snookums," she said in a private joke that still made her smile, "I'm on my way to the hospital."

A sucked-in breath. "Meet you there."

Hanging up with another smile, she began to do her breathing again, her mind filling with thoughts of what it had taken to get here, to this moment when she was about to give birth to her and Sailor's baby, adding a tiny new person to their already huge extended family. It hadn't been easy. It had taken determination and grit and a firm belief in both their dreams.

Also included had been the vanquishing of a dragon.

Jacqueline had *not* been pleased when Ísa handed in her notice at the end of the previous summer. She'd been gearing up for more blackmail when Ísa told her to make a choice—a relationship with her eldest child and any children Ísa might have, or a cold, empty existence devoid of any family contact.

Unspoken had been the fact that if Ísa cut her off, Jacqueline would have to maintain the bonds with Catie and Harlow on her own. And Jacqueline frankly sucked at being maternal. It was Ísa who was the glue, Ísa who made sure Jacqueline wasn't lost and out in the cold.

"As for Harlow," Ísa had pointed out, "he'll be fine." The summer had been good for her brother—he'd come out of the internship with a new confidence that had girls suddenly giving him a second look. He was still in awe of

Jacqueline, but at least now he knew he could hack it in a business workplace.

"If you think I'm letting that boy go after all the work I put into him this summer," Jacqueline had snarled, "your head's been addled by love hormones." A gimlet-eyed glance. "When did you learn to be so ruthless?"

"I have your genes," Ísa had said with a dry smile. "I try to keep the ruthless under control, but every so often it just bursts out."

A twitch of her mother's lips. "You know you have me over a barrel." There was a strange vulnerability to her in that moment. "I have no desire to grow old surrounded by money and no children but Trevor." Her lips curled up. "He sent me flowers the other day. As if Jacqueline Rain's forgiveness can be charmed."

Caught by that vulnerability, Ísa had done something she rarely did—she'd hugged her mother, the scent of Jacqueline's perfume swirling around them. When she drew back, she'd held her mother's eyes. "Keep the dragon breath under control and we'll be fine. Also, you need to schedule a visit to Catie this weekend and take her out for a mother-daughter lunch."

Jacqueline's eyes had glinted, but she'd made the appointment in her diary. Then she'd sighed. "Poetry, Ísa, really? You're truly going to waste that incredible, ruthless mind on poetry?"

"Nope. I'm going to use it to educate thousands of young minds through the years—and hopefully, one day, send my own words out into the world." Ísa felt nothing but peace with the choices she'd made. "I'm also going to use it to love my family and create a legacy of love."

Expression softening in a way Ísa had rarely seen, Jacqueline had touched her fingers to Ísa's cheek. "Does that Sailor Bishop know what he's got? Does he understand the gift of you?"

Yes, Ísa thought now, he did.

Two weeks ago, he'd brought her home a surprise, a refurbished antique writing desk that Ísa adored and petted and sighed over every time she sat down to work on her poetry. Sailor had found the beat-up and badly treated desk online, then brought it back to a gorgeous condition himself.

He'd stashed it in Gabriel's garage and worked on it during the times when Ísa was in Hamilton to see Catie. Sailor usually came along, but every so often, she and Catie would have a girls' weekend and he'd stay back to hang out with Gabe, his older brother's life having been turned upside down as a result of a career-ending on-field injury.

"Gabe's always been impossibly strong," Sailor had said to her a month after it happened. "That grit's still there, under the grief. He just needs a little support to find it again."

Ísa agreed with Sailor; she had a feeling Gabe would surprise them all with his next step in life. What she also saw was that the brothers shared an innate strength—they simply showed it in different ways. The man she loved with all her heart and soul grinned and just kept on going step by step, while Gabriel was more intense.

As for those girls' weekends she had with Catie, Jacqueline was starting to turn up and join in once out of every three times. Mostly because Ísa would call her assistant and make sure Jacqueline's schedule was blocked out for the weekend. But at least the Dragon was making an effort. And it was slowly paying off; Catie had gone as far as to invite Jacqueline to a school event—to which Ísa had driven Jacqueline when her mother made noises about canceling in favor of a strategy meeting.

Dragons didn't change their scales without some help.

Harlow wasn't only thriving, he'd become best friends with Jake despite the year that separated them and the fact that Jake was as sporty as Harlow wasn't. Ísa's brother was also, for the first time in his life, part of a group of boys and men who hung out together doing "manly-man stuff" as Catie had put it.

He'd gone white-water rafting with the Bishop-Esera males, tutored Danny in chemistry, and analyzed entire rugby games for Jake using statistical methods. Inspired by Jake's dreams of playing for international clubs, he'd also been talking to Ísa about working abroad after he qualified.

Her brother was like a butterfly coming out of his cocoon.

Catie, meanwhile, had finally stopped growing—after reaching five feet nine. Which annoyed poor Danny no end. Sailor's baby brother was still the shortest kid in his class, but Ísa had started to spot the signs of a growth spurt. Given the family genes, she had a feeling he'd one day be able to loom over Catie.

To which point Catie had the perfect comeback: "I'll just get taller prosthetics."

Laughing inwardly at the memory of Danny and Catie's last bickering session, Ísa stroked her hand over her belly, her thoughts on the man who'd turned her dreams into reality. Tough or not, she and Sailor had done it together every step of the way, sharing their dreams with one another and in so doing, making those dreams even better.

"How about Calypso?" Jake said from the back.

That happened to be the name of Jake's girlfriend—his first real one. The two had been in puppy love for the past six months. It was adorable.

"I like Sofia," Harlow said, pushing up his glasses at the same time. "Or you could name her after Jacqueline." A pause. "You know she was hinting for that last weekend."

"We'll see," Ísa said, not giving away the fact she and Sailor had already decided on a name for their daughter.

It had taken lots of whispered late-night conversations and laughing disagreements before they'd agreed, but they'd been using the name for the past month when they talked to their baby girl, and it fit.

"Oh, geez, they're doing work on the road." Harlow swallowed and glanced at Ísa's belly. "I really love you, Issie, but I totally don't want to deliver your baby."

Amused at the petrified look on his face, Ísa patted her brother's unshaven cheek. Somehow he'd started growing into a man while she hadn't been looking. "You're safe. We should get there in plenty of time."

But as the traffic dragged on, Ísa started to worry that she'd been overconfident. Because her contractions were coming closer and closer together. Biting the inside of her cheek, she managed to keep that from the boys.

When Jake said, "Do we have to change diapers?" she said, "It's one of the duties of an uncle."

"Oh, man." Both boys groaned.

Someone's phone rang. "It's Catie," Jake said from the back. "I messaged her."

Ísa hadn't, aware her sister was attending a training camp this weekend. But she was happy to hear her voice. "Hey, Catiebug. How was training?"

"Who cares! You're having a baby. I'm gonna catch the

bus to Auckland! I already told Coach and he was a grump, but he said okay!"

Ísa laughed, knowing she wouldn't be able to talk Catie out of that decision; her kid sister had inherited a full share of Jacqueline's relentless will. "I'll see you when you get here." It was only midmorning—Catie would have plenty of time to make it safely to Auckland. "Message Sailor along the way, just in case I'm otherwise occupied."

"Eee! I can't wait!"

Ísa wished her baby would wait. A little longer, she begged mentally. "Come on, baby," she whispered under cover of the boys' conversation. "Wait for Daddy."

Their baby listened—*just*.

Sailor was waiting at the hospital entrance, Jake having called to tell him of the delay and which entrance they'd be heading to. Seeing her face, he didn't ask questions, just kissed her once before scooping her up into his arms and rushing inside. Ten minutes later, Ísa squeezed his hand tight as their wriggling, squirming, pink-faced daughter made her way into the world.

Taking her indignant little body from the midwife, Sailor snuggled her. "Hello, Emmaline."

A kiss before he placed her against Ísa's skin. Ísa had read up about skin-to-skin bonding, and she'd been very clear with her birth team that, unless it was a medical emergency, she and Sailor would not be separated from their baby for the first hours of her life. She wanted Emmaline to know beyond any doubt that she was loved, was wanted, would never be shoved aside and left to fend for herself.

Emmaline would *never* feel the loneliness that was a marker of Ísa's childhood.

"Hello, sweet baby." Tears rolled down her cheeks as

she snuggled their angry little baby to the skin of her chest.

Sailor leaned down to kiss her, this blue-eyed man who'd helped make all her dreams come true.

"How was the meeting?" she asked some time later, after she and Emmaline were ensconced in a recovery room.

Sailor shrugged. "No idea. We started late and then Emmaline decided to arrive, so I left it in Nayna's hands."

Ísa knew her best friend—and the CFO of Bishop Gardening's first store—would do them proud in the negotiations, but she also knew how important this expansion opportunity was to Sailor. Despite that, he was seated beside the bed and was playing with Emmaline's tiny hand, utter fascination in his gaze.

"I love you, Sailor Bishop," she whispered.

He looked up after kissing one of Emmaline's teeny fingers. "I love you more, Ísalind with the moonlight skin and firelight hair."

Emmaline chose that moment to yawn, and it was so adorable they both lost long minutes to watching her—until they were interrupted by the boys tumbling in. Alison and Joseph arrived soon afterward, together with Gabe and Danny. Catie made it around the same time as Jacqueline.

Nayna rushed in the instant the negotiations were complete, Raj with her.

Everyone wanted to look at Emmaline, wanted to celebrate.

And it was all right. Ísa and Sailor had all the time in the world for the things that mattered.

Yet, love, mere love, is beautiful indeed…
~ *Elizabeth Barrett Browning (Sonnets from the Portuguese)*

∾

I hope you loved CHERISH HARD! If you'd like to read Gabriel's story, ROCK HARD is currently available everywhere. Two more Bishop-Esera brothers to go! To stay up to date with my releases and get exclusive access to deleted scenes and short stories, please join my newsletter at: www.nalinisingh.com. And if you feel like leaving a review, that would be awesome! - xoxo Nalini

ACKNOWLEDGMENTS

Thank you to Alison, Leena, and Rahaf for the feedback on early drafts of *Cherish Hard*.

My thanks also to the generous person who answered my questions about prosthetics and myriad other small matters that helped give depth to Catie's character. And a huge thank you to Nikita Gill for allowing me to quote part of her poem.

A great big shout out to Ashwini and Nephele, for all that you do.

All of these folks are awesome. Any errors are mine.

And to you, my reader, thank you for coming along with me on this adventure into love. :-)

ABOUT THE AUTHOR

New York Times and *USA Today* bestselling author of the Psy-Changeling, Guild Hunter, and Rock Kiss series, Nalini Singh usually writes about hot shapeshifters, dangerous angels, and sexy rock stars. With the Hard Play series, she decided to write about a sinfully gorgeous set of brothers who'll make your heart race… and put a smile on your face.

Nalini lives and works in beautiful New Zealand, and is passionate about writing. If you'd like to learn more about the Hard Play series or her other books, you can find excerpts, behind-the-scenes materials, and more information on her website: www.nalinisingh.com.